AR

RS™

VICTORY'S PRICE

VICTORY'S PRICE

An Alphabet Squadron Novel

ALEXANDER FREED

1 3 5 7 9 10 8 6 4 2

Del Rey
20 Vauxhall Bridge Road
London SW1V 2SA

Del Rey is part of the Penguin Random House group of companies whose addresses
can be found at global.penguinrandomhouse.com.

Penguin
Random House
UK

First published in Great Britain by Del Rey in 2021

www.penguin.co.uk

A CIP catalogue record for this book is available from the British Library.

ISBN 9781529101386
ISBN 9781529101393 (export)

Printed and bound in Great Britain by Clays Ltd, Elcograf S.p.A.

The authorised representative in the EEA is Penguin Random House Ireland,
Morrison Chambers, 32 Nassau Street, Dublin DO2 YH68.

Penguin Random House is committed to a sustainable future for
our business, our readers and our planet. This book is made from
Forest Stewardship Council® certified paper.

For Elias J. Marsh (one of them, anyway)

THE *STAR WARS* NOVELS TIMELINE

THE HIGH REPUBLIC

Light of the Jedi
The Rising Storm

Dooku: Jedi Lost
Master and Apprentice

I THE PHANTOM MENACE

II ATTACK OF THE CLONES

Thrawn Ascendancy: Chaos Rising
Thrawn Ascendancy: Greater Good
Dark Disciple: A Clone Wars Novel

III REVENGE OF THE SITH

Catalyst: A Rogue One Novel
Lords of the Sith
Tarkin

SOLO

Thrawn
A New Dawn: A Rebels Novel
Thrawn: Alliances
Thrawn: Treason

ROGUE ONE

IV A NEW HOPE

Battlefront II: Inferno Squad
Heir to the Jedi
Doctor Aphra
Battlefront: Twilight Company

V THE EMPIRE STRIKES BACK

VI RETURN OF THE JEDI

The Alphabet Squadron Trilogy
The Aftermath Trilogy
Last Shot

Bloodline
Phasma
Canto Bight

VII THE FORCE AWAKENS

VIII THE LAST JEDI

Resistance Reborn
Galaxy's Edge: Black Spire

IX THE RISE OF SKYWALKER

A long time ago in a galaxy far, far away. . . .

PART ONE

INDIGENOUS SONGS OF LOST CIVILIZATIONS

CHAPTER 1

NAVAL HYMNS OF THE OLD REPUBLIC

I

"This war is over," the admiral said. "We know it, and soon the Empire will, too."

General Hera Syndulla almost believed him, but reminded herself: *Only rebellions thrive on hope. Republics need sturdier foundations.*

The assembly room smelled of ozone and glittered like the interior of a sapphire, each facet a hologram flashing and wavering as transmission streams threaded the galaxy and manifested in the New Republic's military leadership. Eleven months prior—following the Battle of Endor, when the war had *first* been declared over—such a gathering would have been unthinkable. Now, thanks to the twin miracles of a newly reclaimed hyperspace comm network and the massive receiver systems of the ex–Star Destroyer *Deliverance*, the architects of the Rebellion's victory exchanged reports like conquerors dividing spoils.

"The core of the enemy force has retreated," Gial Ackbar went on, and flapped a holographic hand at an unseen assistant. A star map sprang up at the center of the amphitheater, and ghostly heads—along with the heads of the flesh-and-blood attendees near Hera—refocused their attention. "Coruscant remains under Imperial control, but the fleeing loyalist armadas have ceded the rest of their territory to us. That leaves the warlords and opportunists isolated; eliminating the last of them will take time, but few remain a serious threat. Our battle groups are even now removing the holdouts' fleet-building and transport capabilities."

Red blotches flashed onto the map, stains of Imperial presence on the galaxy. Blue arrows, each indicating an allied force, encircled the red. Hera recognized the larger occupied territories—the Anoat sector, the Faultheen sector, the Chrenthoan Abyss. Coruscant, where the Imperial regent controlled a single blockaded planet and trillions of lives, glowed softly in the map's center. A faint mark like a blood drop represented all that was left of the Imperial presence in the Nythlide Array, where the *Deliverance* had spent the past week smashing blockades.

It was, at a glance, a simple map with a clear message of New Republic supremacy. Yet fainter lines suggested a more complicated story: Trails from a dozen points led into a region where individual stars became a haze of fog in the poorly charted Western Reaches. What was left of the true Empire's military—what the admiral had called the loyalist forces—was secreted there, on the edge of the Unknown Regions.

Hera squared her shoulders and spoke in a voice that offered no challenge, no skepticism. Ackbar viewed the war in ways foreign to her, focusing on the ebb and flow of fleets like tides rather than the struggles of mortals on the ground. But she had come to recognize the artistry of his designs, even when she disputed their wisdom. "How close are we to finding the enemy's hidden base?" she asked.

The admiral smiled broadly and bowed his bulbous head. "We're launching probe droids as swiftly as Troithe and Metalorn can manufacture them. Chief of Intelligence Cracken will speak to other leads under investigation. Shall we begin with the division reports . . . ?"

The conference took on a familiar shape, and though Hera listened to what was said—filed away every word in the whirring part of her brain that cross-referenced tactical updates and coordinates for strategic significance—she found her attention less on the briefs and more on the emotional tenor of the room. Airen Cracken spoke of the Empire's efforts to remain hidden, cited rumors of a harsh world occupied by legions of stormtroopers, and there was a predator's excitement beneath the frost-bitten surface. General Ria appeared exhausted, but her mouth curled into a smile as she spoke of the campaign to drive the Imperial-Royalist coalition off Xagobah. Admiral Ho'ror'te's snuffling and grunting was harder to parse, but Hera thought she recognized a weary resolve as he spoke of the sacrifices of the *Unerring* and its escorts to destroy a conspiracy orchestrated by one of Palpatine's mad viziers.

Hera began shifting focus to her staff—felt discomfort behind her through a hint of human pheromones or movement in the air—when Ackbar called her name. "And your battle group, General? Nythlide is secure?"

"Under control, at least," she replied. "Two carriers under Major Jaun will stay to support the local militia. Now that the battle group has punched through the blockade, the *Deliverance* is returning to its primary objective."

"Back to the hunt?" Ho'ror'te growled, the bass entangled in static.

"Back to the hunt," Hera agreed. "We're continuing to work with New Republic Intelligence—" She cast a nod toward Cracken, neither expecting nor receiving acknowledgment. "—to locate the 204th Imperial Fighter Wing. Since that unit's departure from Cerberon, we've confirmed only a handful of sightings but remain confident we're on the right trail. Nythlide slowed us down. From here on out, though—"

"Your last report suggested the 204th—Shadow Wing—is working with the loyalists."

This interruption came in a voice Hera didn't recognize. A dark-haired man in civilian dress stood six meters to the right of Ackbar, alone on his holographic dais. Codes scrolled beneath his feet indicating his transmission's point of origin: Chandrila.

The temporary New Republic capital. Chancellor Mothma had been unable to attend the conference, but she was making her presence known.

"We believe they've made contact, yes," Hera said. "That's based on comm tracing—General Cracken can provide specifics."

"Then shouldn't the 204th be in hiding with the other loyalist units? Your pursuit is taking you far from the Western Reaches."

Hera swallowed her immediate dislike of the man's tone. It wasn't an unreasonable query. "We aren't certain *what* the 204th is doing in this part of the galaxy. However, I'm confident that whatever the particulars, Shadow Wing represents a real threat. Since the Battle of Endor they've been responsible for numerous military setbacks and lost lives, not the least of which were the genocide on Nacronis and the Cerberon uprising. The unit has proven its capacity, time and again, to inflict unexpected harm. We shouldn't doubt such harm is ongoing."

She was surprised by her own passion—nearly as surprised as Chancellor Mothma's aide, who had stiffened and retreated almost out of view of his holocam.

You're among friends, she reminded herself. *Maybe you should act like it?* She smiled with what she hoped was humility before continuing.

"That said, I am equally confident this operation will be over soon. Shadow Wing has nowhere to run, and despite some recent losses there's no one in the galaxy better equipped than Alphabet—than our Intelligence working group—to find and neutralize this foe."

Again she had the sense of discomfort from someone behind her. She suspected she knew the source, but she had one more point to make. "If by chance the Empire's fleet is located before we can find the 204th, the *Deliverance* retains the flexibility to disengage and support an engagement elsewhere. But I'm not worried about choosing one over the other. Shadow Wing can be defeated. The Empire as a whole can, too."

Mothma's aide nodded swiftly. The military leaders were less attentive, though Hera knew better than to feel slighted—each had come to the conference with their own concerns, and each had worked with the others long enough to have a measure of trust. If Hera told them the 204th was a threat, they would believe her; if she told them she would end that threat, they would believe that, too.

The conference moved to other reports from other regions of the galaxy and ended with inspirational words from Ackbar that Hera largely neglected to hear. Afterward the holograms vanished with a flash of light and a popping noise; when they were gone, Hera blinked away spots and heard the humming of the *Deliverance*'s reactor. The voices of her staff rose and she issued swift orders as they all moved toward the door.

She was proposing a comm array adjustment to Stornvein when a young man made as if to break away. Without interrupting herself, without turning her head, she placed a hand lightly on the man's shoulder and pushed her fingertips into the fabric of his flight suit. He stopped. She felt the tension in his muscles.

He was olive-skinned and wore his brown hair neat, contrasting with his unshaven cheeks and chin. His frame was slender and taut, like that of a jungle cat seemingly too thin for the size of its prey. When Hera finished dispensing commands and was left alone with the youth, she faced him fully and asked, "You're not going to make a liar out of me, are you?"

"General?" Wyl Lark said.

"Is your unit ready for the 204th?" She kept her tone matter-of-fact—Wyl would take her seriously regardless, so better not to unduly pressure him. "Are the squadrons up to the fight?"

She'd been monitoring Wyl since he'd taken command of the *Deliverance*'s starfighter wing. She'd spent an hour each week conferring with him—less time than she'd have liked, more than her aides approved of—and nearly as much time speaking to the individual squadron commanders about his leadership. She knew the status of the pilots and she knew that Wyl, despite his inexperience, was making fine choices regarding training and deployment.

She wanted to know what *he* knew, however. He frowned, and she waited for an answer.

"Yes," he said at last. "They are. We needed the time—reconfiguring the squadrons came with a cost—but they're working together now. The pilots who haven't faced Shadow Wing are doing their research. The ones who have . . . they want another shot, and they won't get more ready sitting in the hangar."

"Can they win?" Hera asked.

"In a fair fight?" Wyl smiled wanly, looking too tired for his age. "I think—maybe. But going at Shadow Wing head-to-head hasn't ever gone well before."

"I'll do everything I can to give us an edge," Hera said. "If it comes to it, though, we may have to strike in less-than-ideal circumstances." She saw resistance on Wyl's face and pushed on. "If Shadow Wing really is one of the only loyalist units operating outside Coruscant or the Western Reaches, that makes them one of few wild cards the Empire has left to play. That makes them—"

"—valuable."

You're learning, she thought, and felt a twinge of sadness. She tried to sound encouraging anyway. "Exactly. I don't want them still operating when it's time for the last battle."

They stepped together out of the assembly room and into the corridors of the *Deliverance.* Hera ignored a chill at the burnished black floor paneling, the pale lighting grids and geometric doorways. The crimson emergency indicators had been disabled, but the New Republic refit had proceeded too quickly to make the vessel feel like anything other than an Imperial Star Destroyer.

Somewhere in a distant star system, Hera mused, Commodore Agate was on the bridge of a newly built Nadiri Starhawk—the pride of the New Republic fleet, symbol of everything righteous, built from dismantled Star Destroyers into something more powerful yet. If things had gone differently—if the *Lodestar* hadn't been obliterated over Troithe and a replacement required immediately—Hera might have been aboard a Starhawk herself instead of a hastily overhauled death machine.

She didn't begrudge Agate her command. But it was hard to walk the *Deliverance* without bad memories.

Wyl matched her pace. "The last battle," he echoed. "You believe what the admiral was saying?"

"You have doubts?"

"I just remember what we heard after Endor. It's all been 'close to ending' for a year now." There was no bitterness in his voice. "I don't blame anyone for being wrong. But I trust your judgment more than most."

She'd been as guilty as anyone in believing the war would end after the Emperor's death. She'd known better, and still she'd believed. She'd longed for a return to her family, and she fought through that yearning now to answer Wyl as honestly as she could.

"I believe it," she said. "I keep telling myself it's optimism, but the facts add up. The Empire can't keep fighting."

Wyl smiled thinly. Hera wasn't sure if he wasn't satisfied with her answer or if something else troubled him. She didn't have a chance to inquire before he said: "We should hear from the others soon. Last word was 'sometime within six hours.'"

"Good. We'll talk as soon as anything comes in."

Wyl seemed to take the statement as a dismissal, and Hera let him go. *That* had been her chance to ask what was bothering him, and she suspected she'd berate herself later for missing it; but she had battle plans to concoct and drills to run and a chief engineer who needed replacing. There was far, far too much to do to bring about the Empire's end, and though Wyl's troubles were as real and vital as anyone's, *all* of her problems were urgent—Shadow Wing most of all.

Because in truth, she'd held back during the war conference. She didn't know what the 204th was doing, but the rumors escaping isolated systems were chilling—too horrifying, too unlikely, and too poorly sourced to discuss in the open.

Very soon—"within six hours," perhaps—Hera would know if her nightmares had become reality.

II

Nath Tensent bunched a beefy fist around wine-red cloth and yanked the curtain aside, only to find himself staring down the protruding nose of an H'nemthe. The reptilian humanoid emitted something between a hiss and a yelp, then slipped with surprising agility under the crook of Nath's arm, past Chass na Chadic, and into the crowd packing the shellmongers' tent of the Circus of Mortal Appetites.

"You making friends there?" Chass asked.

Nath didn't let go of the curtain as he glanced toward the Theelin woman. An oversized brown jacket buried her compact, muscular body, leaving her green crest of hair to sprout like a seedling. "It's what I do," he replied, and moved into the dark stairwell.

Chass grunted as she took the curtain and followed. Nath inhaled as he ascended, refamiliarizing himself with long-forgotten scents—Tionese cooking oils, whirlbat viscera, the waxy odor of Critokian silk. A memory of Piter, half-naked and spun into a cocoon, flashed through his mind.

The old crew had some fun *here back in the day,* he thought, and grinned as they pushed into another pavilion. The crowd was thinner and more subdued, lingering around the edges of a space full of yellow smoke. Low altars were piled with datachips and candles and rotting fruit, while the few merchants swapped cheap necklaces for credits. Nath barely paused to orient himself before heading for a gap in the curtains at the far side, but he slowed as he noticed Chass eyeing the hawkers and the altars.

"You didn't say this was a religious thing," she muttered.

Nath shrugged. "Way of dressing up the business. Oracle's got a style, but past that she's just another info broker."

Chass took a meandering route past an altar, then back to Nath's side. "It's all good. Let me know when I should start shooting."

"*If,*" Nath corrected, though he couldn't suppress a smile. "*If* you should start shooting."

"Whatever."

Nath laughed, but he watched Chass out of the corner of his eye as they pressed into the gap. Something was wrong with the girl—something new, different from the rat's nest of unconfessed self-loathing, bitter fury, and suicidal impulses she'd lived in when they'd first met. It had been wrong since Cerberon, and if he'd been closer to her he might've known whether it would be a problem. As things were—well, Chass was at the bottom of his list of troubled wingmates.

"Captain Tensent," a desiccated voice said as they emerged into a hollow. Circular screens hung on leather cords, framing the meter-high neck of the woman who sat in the room's center. Amber eyes stared out of a chalky head drifting from side to side, as if the weight of her skull might cause her neck to collapse at any moment. "How long has it been since your last confession? Three years? Four?"

"You're a few years short, though I can't say I blame you," Nath said. "Days go by fast, then they crawl. You get my message?"

"I did. You have more patrol routes, perhaps?"

Nath climbed over a low bench and lowered his bulk to the seat. He kept his expression game and tried not to show his surprise. "Haven't been with the Empire a long time," he said, and resisted the urge to add: *You must be the last one to hear. Not reassuring for an oracle.* "What do you say about some New Republic secrets instead?"

"Easier to find. Not worth as much. What do you have to offer?"

His instinct was to check Chass's reaction before moving on. He forced himself to meet the oracle's gaze and lowered his voice. "Troop movements through Hutt space. Could be handy for anyone doing business in those parts."

The oracle adjusted one of her hanging screens. "I think not," she said.

That's more like it. Still knows how to bargain.

He leaned forward. "Intelligence decryption codes for priority three transmissions. Good for a week—a lot a person could learn in that time."

"Better, but insufficient," the oracle said. The thin neck drifted backward and amber eyes rolled. Then the stalk snapped straight and eyes focused on Nath again. "You have connections within New Republic Intelligence?"

"Something like that," Nath said.

I am New Republic Intelligence.

Nasha Gravas, the late Caern Adan's protégée, had come to him after Cerberon and asked him to liaise between Intelligence and Syndulla's battle group. Nath had agreed, and now he had a medal, authority, and access to a treasure trove of classified intel. Turned out almost dying to save a planet of billions came with a few rewards.

"Well?" the oracle asked.

"Ten names," Nath said. "Undercover operatives of my choosing. No guarantee any of them will be useful, but that's the fun of it."

He watched the oracle as he listened to Chass's grunt. If she doubted he was authorized to make the trade, she was right. He was confident she wouldn't do anything about it.

The oracle's eyes closed and she swiped the back of her hand across the hanging screens. They clacked against one another, swinging from side to side and gaining unnatural velocity. It appeared inevitable that one would strike the oracle—but none ever did, and soon they lost momentum again. The oracle opened her eyes and waited for them to still completely before speaking.

"The Ink-Spotted Lord, Keeper of Secrets, will accept your sacrifice," she said.

"The Ink-Spotted Lord is generous, as always," Nath returned. The oracle handed him a datapad, and he entered a series of names and coordinates; after he was done, the oracle slid the pad into the folds of the enclosure's curtains. "Now," Nath said, "about the blessing we came for?"

"The Croynar sector," the oracle said.

Nath waited.

The oracle said nothing.

Chass cleared her throat. Nath raised a hand and said, "Narrow it down to one system for us?"

"Situations change rapidly. The sector will be enough for your needs," the oracle said.

"Now do we start shooting?" Chass asked.

Nath stood, feeling his knees creak, and waved Chass off. "If the Ink-Spotted Lord says the sector is enough, then the sector is enough. You've always dealt fair with me, Madame Oracle, haven't you?"

"I act in accordance with my master's wishes," the oracle said. "Be on your way, Captain Tensent, Hero of Troithe."

Guess you heard the news after all, he thought.

He wrapped an arm around Chass's shoulders, escorting her from the scene as firmly as he could without inviting a fight. "It's how business is done here," he murmured.

She shrugged away his arm and they returned to the stairs. "So why are *we* the ones out here, if we're just reading a script and taking whatever we get? Doesn't Intelligence have agents for this?"

"You'd hope so, but they're stretched thin. Besides, they trust me to find Shadow Wing."

Chass almost choked on a laugh. "They trust you, do they?"

"Close enough," he said, and led them through the labyrinth of tents and stairways and rope ladders. The Circus of Mortal Appetites was busy as Nath had ever seen it, and louder—no one feared Imperial patrols or snitches anymore, and the New Republic didn't engender the same concerns. He was nearly to the landing pads, strolling beneath the dim blue lamps of the Chamber of Lusty Holos, when he nearly crashed into a human broad as a wall and dressed in a coat resembling an inside-out bantha—all intestinal tubing and patches of fur.

"Captain Tensent," the coat's owner said. Beady eyes stared at Nath. "'Like a leaf adrift, he falls to ground; rots in autumn and 'neath winter rime; until decay becomes life anew, and he is home among the branches once more.'"

The face was distantly familiar. The poetry more so, but Nath struggled to attach a name to the half-remembered giant and settled for declaring, "Been a while, brother."

He saw the curl in the man's lip and the tremor in his hand as it hovered at his hip. *Might be spoiling for a fight,* Nath thought, *but he knows he's likely to lose. Or he's waiting for backup.* Neither notion pleased Nath.

"Hargus!" The name hit Nath and he grinned, recalling a dozen conversations from his days running protection rackets as a TIE pilot. Hargus had always paid promptly, kept his head down, and caused little trouble; but that had been long ago, and if *people* didn't change, *circumstances* certainly did. "Hargus, you've gotten old. You and the crew still working the butt-end of the Corellian Run?"

"With a few changes. Nice not to pay for the privilege." Hargus's eyes peered over Nath's shoulder. "Hear you're a big shot now. Big-time hero."

"Word really does get around. Lady at the docks gave us an entry discount."

Chass had shifted her stance, ready to run or to pounce. "Now?" she asked.

"Looks like," Nath agreed.

He couldn't locate Hargus's backup while focusing on Hargus himself. He hoped Chass understood her role as he brought his fist into the giant's chin, feeling his own knuckles bruise as his foe's head snapped back and Hargus's hand fell away from the blaster on his hip. The crowd jostled and yelled, and Nath hadn't reclaimed his balance by the time he felt Chass's palm between his shoulders, pushing him down and forward as she cried "Go!"

He heard the sizzle of blaster bolts overhead and felt heat. He went. Chass was on his heels, close enough that he caught a whiff of her sweat. "Three of them back there," she said. "Two meat, one droid. Nasty little hunter probe."

They plowed through another set of curtains. They could've split up to hide in the throng, but Nath figured they weren't more than a minute (three, tops) from the landing pad—better to run. Racing through the food pavilion, he shouldered aside a merchant laden with trays of fried beetles and spared a glance behind him; he glimpsed rough movement, crowds shuffling away, the glint of metal, but nothing his brain could render in detail. *At least they're not shooting anymore,* he thought. *Mob's giving us cover.*

He grabbed his comlink mid-stride. "Get ready for takeoff," he growled. "Coming in hot!" He didn't wait for a reply before swapping the link for the grip of his blaster.

Thirty seconds later they were outside the pavilions, clear of the crowds, and dashing over the slick marble bridge extending from the cliff face to the landing pad. A barrage of particle bolts chased them as

Nath prayed for traction. His eyes were on his boots, but he smiled as he felt a wash of heat from the pad ahead. When he looked up, the U-wing transport was a meter off the ground, its loading door open.

Chass was in first. She spun and hauled Nath after her, groaning with effort, while blaster bolts splashed against the doorframe and splattered sparks down Nath's neck. "Return fire!" he howled toward the cockpit.

The deck trembled and the door slid shut. The enemy barrage increased in intensity. The U-wing turned and tugged against the planet's gravity. Nath pushed past Chass and, in one motion, swung into the cockpit and dropped into the copilot's chair. Through the hazy viewport Nath could see Hargus and his associates at the far end of the bridge, one of them—a hairy brute bigger than Hargus—hoisting something onto his shoulder.

Is that a blasted rotary cannon?

If it was, it had enough firepower to shatter the U-wing's viewport and skewer Nath on the fragments.

He fumbled at the controls and turned to the woman seated beside him. She was dressed in a cloak and loose gray cloth that might have been sewn from stained sheets, and her face was a patchwork of chitinous plates—some a deep violet, others a lighter mauve marbled with white veins; some chipped and discolored, others polished and bright. Deep-set eyes peered out from that map of a splintered world, gazing into the bedlam ahead.

"There a reason we're not shooting back?" he asked.

"Not of the Empire," Kairos said in her guttural whisper.

Nath swore and charged the guns. "Not friendly, either." He adjusted the power and switched to manual targeting. From thirty meters away he could turn Hargus and his goons into ash.

And then what? They knew you were a New Republic hero. You want to stain that pretty reputation? You think your bosses will be happy with that diplomatic outreach?

He could handle the damage control.

Not to mention, Hargus has a legitimate grievance. He deserves to die for it?

It didn't sound like the Nath he knew.

He could hear Chass securing something in the main cabin. Hargus's rotary cannon was pointed at the U-wing. Nath swore, aimed the U-wing's weapons, and pulled the trigger.

The U-wing's cannons flashed and the marble bridge shattered, replaced by plumes of dust as shards fell into the abyss. He couldn't hear the reaction of Hargus and the goons, could barely make out their silhouettes at the span's far end, but their next volley missed the U-wing by ten meters. The ship rose and Nath returned his eyes to the console, checking the scanner—no approaching vessels, no energy pulses or missile locks.

You're going soft, he thought. No doubt Hargus was thinking the same. Maybe Chass, too.

"Next time," he said to Kairos, "you shoot back if someone's shooting at us."

The woman said nothing, adjusting the U-wing's power distribution as if she hadn't heard.

That didn't surprise Nath—she'd barely said a word since emerging from her healing slumber in Cerberon. He hadn't a clue what to make of her—whether she'd really changed from the masked predator she'd been or if putting a face and a voice to her actions simply gave the old killer a fresh look.

Sooner or later someone would have to ask her what the hell was going on. Someone who could wrest an answer from her.

"Quite a team we've got," he muttered, and grabbed the headset off the console. He had a message from the oracle for the *Deliverance,* and a long journey ahead to see what it might mean.

III

Hyperspace roiled around the A-wing interceptor, cosmic energies licking its viewport like sea-foam. Wyl Lark felt the vessel's engines pulse in time with his breath; his worn seat creak and flex with his every motion. Once, he'd found lightspeed travel wondrous and terrifying. Now it was almost meditative—a tranquil moment before a thunderclap.

How many more times would he travel this way? How many more jumps before he'd fulfilled his promises to Home and the New Republic?

An alarm chimed rapidly and he was rid of the thoughts, instinctively stroking the console before deactivating the signal. A countdown indicated his return to realspace in less than a minute. "All ships," he called, thumbing the comm, "prepare for arrival in Midgor."

There were only three star systems in the desolate Croynar sector with any possible strategic value—any known structures, extractable resources, or life-forms. That meant that if the intelligence Nath had transmitted to the *Deliverance* was correct, there was a one-in-three chance Wyl would find Shadow Wing waiting in the pale-green light of Midgor's sun. The star system had little to recommend it, but an old electromagnetic siphon could've been a target if Shadow Wing was desperate for technology or scrap metal.

Voices replied: "Hail Squadron ready." "Flare Squadron ready." "Wild Squadron ready."

More than thirty fighters ready to engage, but no Alphabet Squadron—not with Nath and the others still en route. The *Deliverance* itself was holding back in case of a trap. The mission was, as General Syndulla had put it, "heavy reconnaissance."

He drew a breath and spoke again. "Stay in contact, charge your weapons, but don't engage without instructions." He heard his own nervousness but didn't try to suppress it. It wasn't his duty to be fearless, only to inspire the best in the pilots. "If they're out there, they're just as on-edge as we are. They're very good fliers, but they're flesh and blood, not legends."

"Human blood, too," the trilling soprano of Essovin—Flare Leader—came through. "The thin stuff—no offense, Commander."

There was a scattering of awkward laughs, mostly from Flare. "None taken," Wyl said.

Flare Squadron's X-wing pilots hadn't met Shadow Wing yet—they were newcomers, summoned by General Syndulla to support the mission in place of Vanguard. Wyl couldn't blame Essovin for misjudging the emotional tenor of the moment. But Hail Squadron had lost many of its Y-wing bombers at Cerberon. Wild Squadron, too, had seen colleagues killed by Shadow Wing—formed from the remnants of Wyl's hodgepodge assault force of skimmers and cloud cars on Troithe, the squadron had been rebuilt from decimation and become a place for misfit pilots and misfit starfighters. Hail and Wild both viscerally understood Shadow Wing's threat—like Alphabet, they'd suffered slow attrition and swift, brutal massacres, and they needed more than cocky humor. They needed their traumas acknowledged.

"We've been training for this," he said. "They have no idea what we've become."

Wyl prayed he wasn't leading them all to their deaths. He felt a shameful relief that Nath and Chass and Kairos weren't present, as if their lives were more valuable than those of pilots he knew less intimately. (Even if he hadn't seen much of them lately; even if things with Nath had been difficult since Cerberon.)

The glow of hyperspace faded as the jolt of deceleration hit. Wyl's harness dug into his chest as stars fell into place and the jade light of Midgor winked from the darkness. His head swam and he looked to the console, trying to parse the readings as his instruments recalibrated themselves.

"Picking something up!" Wyl heard Vitale, curt and professional—the woman he'd flirted with, almost befriended, before he'd become her commanding officer on Troithe. "Three, maybe four ships."

"I hear you, Wild Two," he said. Wyl adjusted his sensors, felt the reassuring click of toggles through his gloves, and confirmed Vitale's assessment. His comm scanner flickered, suggesting encrypted Imperial chatter in the system.

"Wild and Hail, hold position," he said. "Flare, with me for a better look."

Affirmative responses came in. Wyl opened his throttle and swung his vessel toward the bright marks on his scanner. When his course was set, the universe seemed still and his roaring thrusters impotent—in the vastness of realspace, the only signs he was in motion were his console indicators and, far behind, the lights of the other starfighters.

It was almost a minute before he could pick out specks against the darkness. His sensors estimated the distant vessels' speed and mass. They were too large to be fighters but smaller than frigates—gunships, maybe, but Wyl couldn't guess at their specifications. He didn't have the encyclopedic knowledge Yrica Quell had possessed.

Quell.

Wyl had seen many friends die in the war. But the loss of Quell was different from the loss of Sonogari or Sata Neek.

"I need an ID," he said. "Anyone recognize them?"

"One in the back looks like an Imperial cargo hauler," Ghordansk replied. Ghordansk had an answer for everything, and half the time he was right. "Running hot, too—maybe a radiation leak."

Wyl altered his approach, angling to one side. The specks of the Imperial vessels were flickering around the edges, as if their shields were alive with energy or—

He checked his sensors again, noted the heat signatures.

"Keep your distance," he said. "I'm going for a flyby."

He sent a burst of power to his thrusters and adjusted the comm again as he accelerated toward the enemy formation. The garbled sounds of encrypted messages echoed in his cockpit. He squinted and leaned forward until the specks began to crystallize—boxy, black forms, clearly Imperial but lacking the predatory angles of a Star Destroyer. Flames and electrical arcs danced along their sides and spilled into vacuum.

"This is Starfighter commander Wyl Lark to the Imperial vessels. Please report your status."

It could have been a trap, he knew—bait left by Shadow Wing to lure in New Republic ships. The Imperial cargo vessels could have been rigged to detonate, or TIE fighters could have been hiding a short distance away.

An answer came, too distorted for him to understand.

"This is Wyl Lark. Say again?"

"This is Captain Oultovar Misk of the freighter *Diamond Tor*. We are in need of assistance and are prepared to surrender. Repeat: We surrender!"

Wyl had entered firing range. A flash of light caught his attention and he swiveled his head, fearing a cannon barrage and instead witnessing an eruption of fire and molten metal from the port side of a cargo vessel.

It wasn't a trap. He didn't *think* it was a trap.

It might be something worse.

"Captain Misk?" he said. "What happened to your convoy?"

The voice hesitated then replied, interrupted by bursts of static and mechanical whines: "We were in a battle. TIE fighters attacked us. Dismantled our escorts in minutes, then moved on."

"Why?" Wyl asked. "Why would they do that?"

"I don't know. We were—we were operating under the protection of the Yomo Council. One of the other factions must have taken exception, decided to come after—"

The voice stopped speaking. Wyl thought at first that transmission problems had shut it down, but then he heard heavy breathing and what could only be weeping.

"Imperial against Imperial," the voice said. "That's what the war is, now. Family killing family, oaths unraveling. How can it—are you going to *help us*?"

Wyl flinched as if struck. "Of course. Of course we'll help. Stay where you are, we've got more ships incoming."

He transmitted an all-clear to the *Deliverance* and ordered his squadrons into range to assist with evacuation and damage control. He tried to keep the fighters from exposing themselves without compromising the rescue. It *wasn't* a trap, not one set by the *Diamond Tor* and the other cargo ships, but that was no guarantee the danger had passed.

As Wyl worked, he thought of Captain Misk's words and what

Shadow Wing was capable of, and all the Imperial atrocities committed after the Battle of Endor. He'd witnessed none of them at the time,
but he'd read about Operation Cinder—the murder of worlds, like Nacronis, that had posed no threat to the Empire.

He wondered what horrors were in store for all of them now, when
the Empire was *truly* desperate.

CHAPTER 2

"SILT SEA THRENODY"
(NACRONIS BURIAL SONG)

I

The planet below the bulk freighter was a smudge of brown and green enlivened only by three rose-colored moons whose movement was visible unassisted if one watched closely enough, as a person might watch clouds known to be in motion but tranquil at a glance. The freighter's viewscreen accompanied this minor exhibition with a steady scroll of data down the margins, indicating the drift of debris off the freighter's port side and energy readings from the planet's surface that were almost certainly jury-rigged deflectors; but Soran kept his attention on the centermost moon. It gave him the appearance, he believed, of a man in deep concentration.

"This is Colonel Soran Keize of the 204th Imperial Fighter Wing and the carrier *Yadeez*. In response to the Yomo Council's treasonous actions—its defiance of Grand Admiral Sloane's order to direct assets to the D'Aelgoth sector, its refusal to acknowledge the Empire's rightful regent on Coruscant, and its alliance with the Shiortuun Syndicate, among others—we have been sent to bring retribution to your world."

The speech did not require deep concentration. But he owed his crew—and his victims—the appearance of gravity. He drew a long breath through his nostrils, smelled the stinging copper odor of old ore hauls, and went on.

"Over the next twenty-four hours, the planet Fedovoi End will be rendered uninhabitable. The Yomo Council will die with the territory it usurped. Governor Brashan, General Tuluh, and their criminal co-horts will be erased from history. This is not negotiable; surrender will *not* be accepted. Every traitor will be punished."

This is Operation Cinder, he thought, though he did not say the words aloud. He'd perfected the speech over the past weeks and found the elaboration unnecessary.

He shifted his gaze from the rose moon to scan the bridge crew. Cadet Coora—*Ensign Coora,* he had to remind himself, since he'd authorized her promotion—leaned too far over her tactical console, attempting to conceal her anxiety. Lieutenant Heirorius looked frequently to the bejowled Captain Nenvez as that man tapped his cane against the antique deck plating. Soran heard the soft breathing of his own aide behind him.

All as he expected. He returned his gaze to the screen.

"To the rest of the inhabitants of this world, I offer a choice. Once, you were Imperials—not in name alone, as now, but in heart and hierarchy. You can be so again, but only if you accept the demise of your disloyal superiors and the planet you now occupy. Reaffirm your allegiance to the true Empire. Abandon Fedovoi End. Join us in orbit, and you may assist the 204th in its mission—"

Its mission to purge every world tainted by Imperials who dared to escape the Emperor's shadow.

"—or if you are unqualified for such duties, you will be escorted to a rendezvous with the Imperial fleet. Either way, Fedovoi End must die. Refuse, and you die with it."

It was a valid choice, for some—for those who had ships to fly, who weren't held at blasterpoint by minions of the Yomo Council. Yet among those people *capable* of joining Shadow Wing, some would accept death as the alternative. They would be loyal to the Yomo Council for ideological or pragmatic reasons; they would wish to fight for their planet, bound to their home by ancestral ties; they would believe Soran's threats a bluff, or his forces beatable, or the remnants of the true Empire so desiccated as to be unworthy of their pledge.

There was enough pity left in Soran that he took no pleasure in their inevitable deaths, but he did not flinch from his task. He had given the 204th to the likes of Grand Admiral Sloane for a reason, and that reason hadn't involved any delusions that the Empire might avert its own gradual obliteration. Instead the 204th's troubles in Cerberon had reaffirmed his belief that Shadow Wing required *purpose* to survive—and had taught him the moral necessity of looking beyond his own unit and taking responsibility for all Imperial soldiers who crossed his path. Now, purging world after world, he saw his people cleave to the duty they'd been given. When they recruited newcomers into their fold, they celebrated; when they shot down TIE fighters and melted cities, they believed themselves patriots avenging themselves on traitors who'd cost them a swift victory after the Emperor's death.

The task he had been given by Admiral Sloane was not the task Soran would have chosen. Yet it sufficed. He needed the true Empire to keep his people alive.

At least until it doomed them all.

"Has there been any reply? Any signal from the planet?" he asked.

Heirorius spun from the comscan station. "No reply, Colonel. Reading energy spikes from the surface—I believe they're powering ion cannons."

Heirorius had joined Shadow Wing at Dybbron III, when that world had been engulfed by this second Operation Cinder. Soran could only assume the man was remembering what had happened there, though the twenty-year veteran was too professional to show it.

"Very well. Send the order to move in. The escorts will take position near the moons. Commander Broosh will lead the TIEs into the atmosphere."

The bridge, previously silent save for the hum of machinery and the chime of consoles, was filled with the susurrus of crew relaying orders and transmitting queries. The updates scrolling down the viewscreen altered in color and intensity as TIE squadrons set course and larger vessels readied covering fire. The *Yadeez*'s escorts included a pair of refitted and undercrewed *Raider*-class corvettes, a pirate gunship hauled out of the evidence yards of Dybbron, and a surveillance vessel stripped to the bone and rebuilt for combat. The TIE squadrons were Imperial standard only in comparison, with approved assemblies replaced by a technological patchwork and once-uniform squadrons of base-model TIEs freely mixing interceptors, bombers, strikers, and other esoteric designs looted from the 204th's victims.

No ship in Shadow Wing had the raw firepower to turn Fedovoi End lifeless. But improvisation had been the skill to learn ever since the Battle of Endor, and the first Operation Cinder had proved that every planet had its weakness.

"The TIEs are going straight to the capital?" his aide asked, behind and to the right of Soran.

"Simplest to eliminate the planetary defenses before turning to the real work," Soran answered.

"Simplest, maybe. What about the advantages of panic?"

Soran arched his brow and turned about. Lieutenant Yrica Quell stood with her arms folded across her chest, dressed in a loose shirt of dark fabric that did little to hide how gaunt she really was. When he'd first met the woman, she'd struck him as narrow but sturdy, like a steel beam; now the steel had been cut and burned away until it was a razor mesh.

"Explain," Soran said, with the curt command of an instructor to a student.

"They sent their heavy firepower at us already—they're no real threat except at short range. Hit the polar regions first and they'll piece together our plan but won't have the mobility to stop us. The longer we work, the more afraid they'll become. They'll be primed to make mistakes."

"They'll also have time to prepare," Soran said. "Suppose our assessment of their capabilities is off—when we finally do strike the capital, we could lose TIEs. We could lose pilots."

Quell blinked bloodshot eyes almost concealed behind strands of hair. "Or we could find the Yomo Council already deposed. The planet can't possibly be stable. Terrified civilians and loyalists might work together if we buy them time."

Soran weighed the argument. There was merit to it, along with risk. Quell was asking to introduce unknown elements into an equation nearly solved, and yet—

"Very well," Soran said. Over the past weeks, he had learned to appreciate Quell's instincts, if not always trust them.

He turned away too quickly to spot Quell's reaction, though he imagined her expression would stay flat as it had since she'd arrived aboard the *Yadeez*. He called new commands to Heirorius, and the voices on the bridge shifted subtly in timbre while the updates on the viewscreen continued scrolling. He waited a minute, then two, studying the battlefield for anything out of the ordinary—a secondary force hidden on one of the moons, a buried planetary defense network with superior range to the ion cannons—and saw nothing to concern him.

The first TIE bombers approached the northern ice cap. Soran adjusted the bridge comm and listened to Commander Broosh order bombs released above the target zone. Images transmitted from the TIEs showed ice shattering, flashing into steam in an instant. Larger ice sheets around the rim of the bomb crater collapsed into the hole, which in turn released a billowing fog—gases trapped underground for millennia, now freed.

Soran turned from the screen and gestured to Nenvez. "Summon me if I'm required," he said, and marched to the hatch leading from the bridge to the central corridor. He heard footsteps following him but did not look back.

Six meters into the narrow passage, out of hearing range of the bridge crew, Soran heard Quell's voice again. "You're not supervising?"

He kept walking. "I'm not."

"It's a combat operation."

"Until a counterattack begins, it's a geoengineering project."

There was an edge to her voice. "You're their commander—"

"And they have their orders. I have faith that they will execute them without my meticulous oversight—and I have other duties that require attention."

Genocide, Soran thought, was an onerous task without a Death Star to quicken it. The first Operation Cinder had involved weather control satellites and groundquakes and artificial tsunamis; Fedovoi End would find its atmosphere gradually poisoned as the TIEs opened up more and more gas pockets. The planet's military bases would naturally be protected against chemical attacks, but Shadow Wing could neutralize those bases via the traditional methods. The population was small enough that they were few in number.

He wondered whether the psychological toll of such an operation was greater than that placed on the Death Star gunners who eliminated billions with the throw of a lever. He quashed the thought before it got out of hand—it would lead to unpleasant and unsatisfying places while leaving him no choice but to continue.

He resumed walking. The footsteps did not follow. He flicked his hand. "Come if you like, Lieutenant. I could use your perspective."

"Of course," Quell said. She sounded chastened but professional as ever.

They maneuvered through the ship, squeezing down hatches and ducking beneath conduits and piping. The fragrance of old metal became masked by the aroma of boiled vegetables and mashed grains, then by sweat, and finally by oil as they passed the galley, crew billets, and engineering bay in turn. A Star Destroyer's oxygen systems were built to neutralize odor; the century-old bulk freighter was less luxurious. When Soran reached his cabin he punched in his access code three times before the locking mechanism pinged and the door slid back a whole two centimeters; he had to haul it open the rest of the way.

Inside, he took a single step to reach his desk chair and waved Quell to a seat on his bunk. He raised his terminal screen and scanned the feed.

"You wanted to talk?" Quell asked.

"Tell me again," he said, looking directly at her for the first time since the bridge, "about Traitor's Remorse."

"What about it?"

She attempted to conceal her wariness without success, doubtless concerned he was testing her. Maybe he was—after all, Yrica Quell was something of an enigma—though his conscious reasons involved no duplicity or subterfuge. "You said before that those like yourself—the Imperials who defected to the New Republic but who weren't selected to serve—were left in limbo, almost forgotten in the camp."

"That's right."

"That was months ago. What do you think has become of them?"

"Are they still there, you mean?" Quell waited; Soran nodded, and she went on: "Maybe not *there,* but probably still in limbo. I doubt the New Republic is taking many new defectors this long after Endor . . . in that case, they might've closed down Traitor's Remorse altogether. Transferred the dregs over to a permanent facility with whoever else they plan to put on trial and punish."

"Would they have tightened security after you escaped?"

"It's possible. I doubt they cared enough to expend the resources."

Soran nodded again, studying Quell and allowing his thoughts to wander. When she spoke about Traitor's Remorse she spoke with the detachment of an analyst, not the passion of someone who had experienced its indignities. That was no surprise—Quell would never admit to a loss of control, would fight to preserve her stoic dignity in the presence of a superior officer—but it left a veil between them he was unable to penetrate.

Soran was responsible for sending Quell to Traitor's Remorse in the first place. For telling her that the war was lost, that she would destroy herself if she remained with the 204th in the aftermath of the first Cinder, and ultimately insisting that she defect. Afterward, he himself had deserted the unit in a misguided effort to set an example, and while Quell had been confined and interrogated, awaiting sentencing while rebels recruited their pick of her colleagues, he had become the wanderer Devon.

In their time away from Shadow Wing, Devon and Quell had both learned that the New Republic was not a forgiving place. While Devon had returned to the 204th upon learning of the tragedy at Pandem Nai—a New Republic aggression that had killed Colonel Shakara Nuress and nearly destroyed a planet—Quell had been left rotting until she'd given up all hope of starting a new life under Chancellor Mothma's regime. She had escaped, she'd told Soran, and located Shadow Wing in Cerberon.

Since then? He'd vetted her story as well as he could, finding it plausible enough. There were gaps, to be sure, intentional omissions and obfuscations suggesting a more complicated truth. Yet he perceived a core of sincerity in her, and she remained his responsibility.

He'd offered her a place as his aide. She was a pilot at heart, but first there had been no TIE available for her to fly; then, when three damaged TIE strikers had been salvaged and added to the unit, she'd claimed that other pilots were in greater need of the vessels. She was clearly traumatized and avoiding combat. Soran didn't hold that against her, yet he didn't understand the extent of how she'd changed, or what his own changes meant for their relationship as mentor and student.

"They've begun the show trials," Soran said. He was unsure how long he'd been musing. Quell showed only polite interest. "Fara Yadeez is being paraded before a court and accused of gross violations of sentient rights—as if being the last governor of Cerberon requires she bear the burden of all her predecessors' sins." He lowered his gaze to his terminal again, skimmed a dozen lines of news copy and code. "I don't doubt there are Imperial soldiers who've done appalling things— but what are the odds that the rebels can judge the fates of their enemies fairly?"

"Is that a rhetorical question?" Quell asked.

"It's not. You've been closer to New Republic justice than I have."

She acknowledged this with a grimace. "I'm not sure what *fair* or *just* mean under the circumstances."

"Do you believe that the Empire was just?" Soran asked. He might have added: *That the destruction of Nacronis or Fedovoi End is just?* but it would only have injured Quell, not enlightened her.

"No," she said.

"Then you must believe that fairness, justice—whatever they are—represent more than the mere whims of whatever political power dominates."

"I suppose I must," she conceded. "I can't think of what."

"Then focus on the question: Can the rebels judge the fates of their enemies fairly?"

Quell's expression shifted from resignation to bitter amusement. It was the look of a woman who'd lost a game while admiring the artistry of her defeat. "No. I don't think they can."

"Yet they will judge us nonetheless, and as we attempt to elude their justice we will make of ourselves—" Soran raised a hand, about to gesture to the bulkheads and the stars beyond and the pointless atrocity taking place on the planet. Quell watched him with a keenness bordering on longing, but though he knew she was sick of bloodshed, oversaturated with death, he no longer knew her well enough to trust her with words that might be treasonous.

He was spared the choice by a sound from the corridor. The cabin's lock hummed and the door slid open its two centimeters. Quell stood from the bed and Soran gestured for her to remain as he rose and stepped to the doorway.

He saw nothing through the crack. There was no further sound. With a quick, forceful move, he pulled the door aside and revealed a figure in a red robe with a fractured plate of glass in place of a face. One arm dangled at its side, severed midway between elbow and shoulder. The figure was utterly still except for the robe's hem, which swirled lightly above the floor around absent feet.

As if revealed by lightning, a withered face flickered into view behind the faceplate before vanishing. "Defiance," a voice shrieked. "Defiance. Defiance."

The face had been the face of the dead Emperor Palpatine, but the voice had not.

"What does it want?" Quell asked.

"Nothing it can tell us," Soran said. "If the Emperor's Messenger still carries a message, it is locked within the thing's synthetic brain."

The machine remained in the doorway for another moment. Then, as if insulted, it turned and drifted down the corridor.

Soran felt his heart pumping and let out a hiss of breath. Once, he had believed himself rid of the Messenger—the herald of Operation Cinder, the embodiment of everything corrupt about the Empire as it had been, haunting Shadow Wing since the Battle of Endor. He had believed himself rid of it but it had come back. When he had succumbed to fury and cracked its faceplate it had done nothing.

Though it was small solace, he was grateful his people were too consumed by their mission to treat the machine as an icon of worship anymore. (He recalled the sight of Nord Kandende aboard the *Aerie* spilling blood before the Messenger in a perverse offering.) The trials of Cerberon had refocused the unit on survival, and since then the work of Cinder—the grueling, everyday work of serving the Empire, of reuniting with allies and taking part in the fleet's grand strategy— had distracted idle minds from superstition, at least for the time being. Isolation had brought confusion; hierarchy brought clarity.

How readily Shadow Wing had accepted the new Cinder, he thought—they were too grateful for direction to doubt the nature of their tasks for long.

"Go," Soran said to Quell.

"Sir?"

He stepped away from the open door and forced the barest hint of a smile to indicate that Quell wasn't at fault for his abrupt shift in tone. "You should rest. If Fedovoi End is as straightforward as it appears, then it's an opportunity to recuperate. There are other missions coming. They will be more challenging."

Quell watched him. He half expected her to ask: *What missions?* But she nodded at last and strode past him into the corridor. Soran shut the door behind her.

There was a great deal that deserved his attention: the updates, rumors, and decaying newsfeeds from across the galaxy on his screen; the massacre happening beyond the bulkheads of the *Yadeez;* the question of Quell and what to expect from her.

But all he could think about was the voice of the machine saying: *Defiance. Defiance. Defiance.*

CHAPTER 3

"THE KHUNTAVARYAN FALL"
(BALLAD, UNKNOWN PROVENANCE)

I

"This is Colonel Soran Keize of the 204th Imperial Fighter Wing and the carrier *Yadeez*. In response to the Yomo Council's treasonous actions—its defiance of Grand Admiral Sloane's order to direct assets to the D'Aelgoth sector, its refusal to acknowledge the Empire's rightful regent on Coruscant, and its alliance with the Shiortuun Syndicate, among others—we have been sent to bring retribution to your world."

The speaker's dark hair framed an angular, thin-lipped face, and his voice had the timbre of a coroner reciting an autopsy report. Hera Syndulla barely watched him. She'd seen the holorecording three times already, and what mattered was how the rest of the room reacted to its horrors.

Seated around the dark conference table were Wyl Lark, Kairos, Chass na Chadic, and Nath Tensent—the remaining members of what Caern Adan had called the "New Republic Intelligence working group on the 204th Imperial Fighter Wing." Each was silent, face lit by the holo's blue glow. Hera peered at them as if the intensity would allow her to penetrate their skulls—to understand why Wyl and Nath sat so far apart; why Chass na Chadic clenched her jaw so tight while staring blankly into space; why Kairos's outstretched hand twitched, as if she were a blind woman tracing the contours of Keize's face.

She didn't doubt they were disturbed, but she needed to know whether they were ready.

The recording pronounced its final threat and the holo flashed out of existence. The lights of the *Deliverance*'s conference room rose. The pilots shifted and straightened, and Hera broke the silence. "That recording is now three days old," she said. "It was repeating on a channel we accessed through that Imperial convoy we found—like someone left it as a warning. We haven't received word on the status of Fedovoi End, but we can only assume Shadow Wing has come and gone."

She went on, suppressing the outrage she felt and keeping her voice level. "At last count, Fedovoi End housed half a million troops and their families. It was primarily a military outpost, it's true—but we haven't seen slaughter of this sort since Operation Cinder."

Nath grunted, as if none of it surprised him. Kairos flattened both hands a centimeter above the tabletop.

"The Empire is eating its own," Chass said.

"Yes," Hera agreed. "The loyalists have gone to war with the breakaway factions—civilians caught in the cross fire be damned."

"Soran Keize," Wyl said. "We've heard that name before."

He wasn't grieving. He was focused. *Good,* she thought. *I know it's hard.*

"We have," Hera began, but Nath raised a finger and she prompted him with a nod.

"Intelligence sent over the files about an hour ago," Nath said. "Soran Keize, Colonel Shakara Nuress's second-in-command. Ace pilot, been in the game close to twenty years, trained most of the Shadow Wing lifers. Last we'd heard he was *Major* Keize, but . . ."

". . . but we also thought he was dead," Wyl finished.

Nath grunted again. "That's what Quell told us. Back at Pandem Nai he definitely *wasn't* around—taking out Nuress really did leave the unit headless. What we didn't know was that Adan had a lead suggesting Keize was alive and elsewhere."

Suggesting Yrica Quell lied about her mentor, the same way she lied about participating in Operation Cinder. The thought came to Hera with a pang of frustration and resentment, along with the weight of grief. Whatever Yrica Quell's failings—and they had been many—she had been Hera's charge, and Quell's involvement in the genocide of Nacronis had been revealed only hours before her death. Hera didn't know *what* she'd have done if she'd been on the scene—whether she'd have embraced the woman, imprisoned her for her crimes, or both.

And if that's what you're thinking, imagine how the others feel.

"Adan knew?" Kairos asked, barely loud enough to hear.

"He had people looking into Quell's background," Nath said, "and they stumbled on to Keize. Apparently, he left Shadow Wing after Nacronis, around the same time Quell did. They traced him to a mud heap of a world called Vernid, I think. He'd changed his name, took up work on a dig-rig . . . we never figured out what he was up to. When Intelligence caught up with him, he killed a pair of agents and disappeared."

Nath shifted his bulk, folding his arms across his chest. "We don't know when he rejoined Shadow Wing, but Nasha Gravas and her people have been sifting through evidence from Troithe. Street cam footage, bio traces, anything from when Shadow Wing was grounded. Put it all together and it's pretty clear Keize was in charge at least that far back."

Chass arched her brow. "So we can blame Keize for everything that happened? Blowing up the *Lodestar,* shooting my ship?"

"Seems like," Nath agreed.

"So we can also blame *Adan* for leaving us in the dark? About Keize? About Quell?" Chass's eyes glinted. "Or maybe we just blame Quell for not mentioning that her *mass-murdering boss* was still around?"

"Chass—" Hera began. Scolding the woman would only make tempers flare, but she didn't like the direction the briefing was headed.

Wyl cut in. "On Vernid, could he have deserted? Was Keize trying to go straight?"

Chass laughed. "He sure isn't *now*."

"Suppose it's possible," Nath said, "but I agree with Chass. Vernid was a while ago, and at the moment—" He waved a hand, as if to sum up the holo's message.

The conversation dissolved into chaos. Nath leaned back in his seat and speculated about Keize's connections to the main Imperial fleet. Chass sneered about Quell's secrets and those of New Republic Intelligence. Wyl asked how Keize's presence might change the 204th's tactics even as he surreptitiously pulled up data on Fedovoi End and its population centers.

"It's happening again," Kairos said, and no one seemed to hear but Hera. Nath and Chass kept talking.

"It's happening again," Kairos repeated, this time in a hoarse shout.

The others fell silent.

Hera nodded slowly. "They're killing worlds again. Yes."

This acknowledgment appeared to satisfy Kairos. She stared at the tabletop.

"How many?" Wyl asked. Now Hera saw he *was* giving in to grief, and she couldn't blame him. "Do we know? Is Fedovoi End the first?"

"We don't have confirmation, but Captain Misk—the convoy leader—suggested at least three planets have fallen." Hera rose to her feet. The meeting was hers again, though she wasn't sure she wanted it. "Dybbron Three, Kortatka, and now Fedovoi End. They've all gone silent, they fit similar profiles, and they're practically in a straight line for anyone traveling through this region."

"Do we know where they're going next?" Wyl asked.

Nath attempted to answer. This time Hera didn't allow it. "Not yet," she said. "The comm network is unstable this far outside the Core— makes it hard to pull updates from New Republic worlds, let alone Imperial ones—and we don't have enough recent intelligence. But we can assume Shadow Wing will continue their mission to wipe out any planet occupied by breakaway Imperial factions, and to that end—"

She drew a breath and released it. "—our mission is now to stop them. To save the lives of their intended victims."

She watched their expressions as they began to comprehend.

"All right," Wyl said, soft and resolved. "But what about Fedovoi End, and the others?"

"The ships we left in Nythlide were scheduled to rendezvous with us after operations there wrapped up. I'm rerouting them to look for survivors," Hera said. "That means the *Deliverance* is on its own for a while."

Hera saw Nath look to Chass, then Kairos. The Theelin was shaking her head as if swaying in a gentle breeze. Kairos was tracing invisible lines above the tabletop, describing what might have been star systems and hyperlanes. Nath finally shrugged and said, "This plan have Senate authorization?"

Wyl started to say something, but Nath wasn't finished. "We're talking about swooping in to defend Imperial strongholds. Risking our forces to protect an enemy."

"To hell with that," Chass muttered.

"There are civilians on those planets." Wyl's voice was calm but insistent. "Even if there weren't—"

Chass kept speaking under her breath. "Civilians who've stood with the Empire for the entire *year* they've been—"

Wyl spoke over her. "—we'd still have an obligation to—"

"I wasn't arguing," Nath said. "Asking a question, is all."

"Worlds bleed," Kairos whispered. "Stars bleed."

"Enough." Hera was still standing, and the snap of her voice demanded the others' attention. "This isn't a discussion. I command this unit, and we're not going to stand by while Shadow Wing commits new massacres *or* recruits fresh forces.

"The plan is this: We head straight past Fedovoi End, picking up the trail based on our best guess as to the next target and any fresh intel that comes in. You all need to start working toward that goal and be ready to fly."

No one argued, which was about as much as Hera could've hoped for. Five minutes later the conference was over and she was slumping down with her elbows on the table.

She'd avoided the worst outcome through bluster and force of will. No one pointed out that she hadn't answered Nath's query about Senate authorization, or asked what sort of intelligence she was expecting that would lead them to Shadow Wing.

As to the first: Hera believed in democracy, in the New Republic Senate, and in Chancellor Mon Mothma. But she also knew that expending New Republic lives to save unrepentant Imperials would cause controversy at the capital. She'd take the consequences as they came.

As to the second: New Republic Intelligence had brought them into this area of the galaxy thanks to lucky comm intercepts. Expecting continuing good fortune to stop Shadow Wing was a fool's game . . . but luck was the only weapon in her arsenal right now.

At least, she thought grimly, Soran Keize wouldn't be a problem if they couldn't catch the 204th at all.

II

Chass na Chadic left the conference room as soon as she was able, standing fast enough to induce vertigo once Syndulla had finished her speech. Outside, she shouldered her way past complaining engineers and flight officers and dataworkers, then stabbed the turbolift button at the corridor's end a dozen times over.

Screw the Star Destroyer. Screw Syndulla. Screw Colonel Keize and Shadow Wing and Yrica Quell and everyone who stands with monsters.

She was on a garbage mission working for garbage people on a warship built by an Empire that seemed more like the New Republic every day; an Empire they were, apparently, now fighting to protect.

One oppressor is the same as another, a voice said inside her mind. She thought at first it was her voice, but it wasn't. It smelled like attar and petrichor; like fungus blooming on a perfumed face. *But that's not what you're angry about.*

She was in the turbolift now, waiting for the car to activate. "I don't need something to be angry *about*," she mumbled. "It's what makes me so lovable."

The turbolift hummed. She pictured Colonel Keize's head on fire and found it less satisfying than she'd hoped. The voice in her mind said: *The Force wants the flourishing of life, tranquility, community—yet the ruling powers only fight, and lie to you, and eat one another alive. Where is your community, Maya Hallik?*

Her dizziness had passed. Her heart rate had decreased. She left the turbolift and walked into the hangar bay, where half-dismantled TIE racks hung like abstract sculptures in a corporate lobby and the ground crews scurried around New Republic starfighters. Sergeant Ragnell yelled something in Chass's direction—a warning, maybe?—and Chass sidestepped a loadlifter before reaching her destination.

The hangar wasn't private, but the cockpit of her B-wing was. She ascended the ladder, dropped into the frayed seat, and closed the canopy above her. The chatter of the ground crews and the hum of the *Deliverance*'s machinery was suddenly muted along with the perfumed voice in her head. Chass became attentive to the wheeze of her breath and the pop of her joints as she slumped. Shadows danced as curios swung from bolts in the canopy frame: a copper, ring-shaped medallion from the Church of the Force, stolen from one of her bunkmates; a plastoid star she'd found in a burnt-out apartment on Troithe while they'd awaited a new flagship; a handful of amulets from a faith healer at the Circus of Mortal Appetites.

After she'd calmed, Chass's right hand found the metal case tucked beneath her seat. She popped the lid, pressed calloused fingertips against sharp edges, and extracted an audio chip. She had to squint to read the label: LESSON 17.

Once, she'd had a music collection. She'd spent years snapping up recordings forgotten by time or banned by the Empire along with pop hits known to half the galaxy (because they were *good*, and even the idiots on Coruscant recognized a decent beat now and then). She'd owned six hours of earsplitting Zabrak conserlista and every song recorded by Yatch Corzum, Queen of Echo-Wave (except maybe "I Hate the Reefs [and You, Dearest Ex]," but that was probably an urban legend). The collection was lost now, likely drifting through the debris field of Cerberon, replaced by the lectures of the Children of the Empty Sun.

They were the parting gift of a cult that had held her (no, she'd *infiltrated* it as Maya Hallik, she'd *never* been a prisoner) while Wyl and Nath had built their own special squadron on Troithe. The gift of Let'ij, a power-snatching creep with a face hung with fungus who extolled peace and community while stockpiling weapons and gathering blackmail on her followers.

The cult was an abomination, but it had felt almost like home. If nothing else, it was far from Star Destroyers and galactic genocide.

Something rapped on the side of her ship. She dropped the chip and twisted to see what. Wyl Lark stood below her cockpit; his lips moved and she faintly heard him say, "Chass? Can you talk?"

"I can't hear you!" she yelled, and gestured to her ears before facing the console again.

She didn't expect it would stop him. It didn't, but it bought a few seconds of satisfaction before Wyl rapped on the hull again. With a grunt, she waved him up the ladder and retracted the canopy. "Yes, sir, Commander?" she asked. "Something I can do?"

"I'm not here as your commander," he said, smiling in his soft, insufferable way.

"In that case—"

She hit the toggle to close the canopy. Wyl grasped the transparent shell with one hand, unable to stop it as it began sliding into position. "Come on," he tried. "Five minutes?"

She sighed and hit a button, freezing the canopy halfway. Wyl needed to be put in his place from time to time—needed a reminder that they'd never been as close as he wanted to think—but he was decent, in his way.

She'd been surprised to find he was a decently effective squadron leader, too. Not *clever* the way Quell had been, not as efficient as Stanislok with Hound Squadron or as ruthless as the parade of Cavern Angel commanders, but people listened to him and he listened back, and somehow the whole wing of starfighters Syndulla had packed onto the *Deliverance* ended up working together better than they had any right to. The band he'd built deserved him (probably more than Alphabet did).

"Fine," she said. "What do you want? I'm—" She half snorted, half laughed as she finished the obvious lie. "—busy."

Wyl's eyes flickered to the trinkets swinging from the canopy frame. "Obviously, and I wouldn't want to get in the way. But you rushed out of there pretty fast, and I wanted to see how you're doing."

She echoed the words. "How I'm doing?"

Your community! Let'ij's voice said in her mind. She was cackling. Chass ignored her.

Wyl shrugged. "I don't know if you believe what you said—"

"I do."

"—about the civilians, the families of those Imperial troops. I know what *I* think, and I know I'm terrified of what's happening, but—" He sighed a little. "I'm not asking how you feel about what's going on. I'm asking how you're doing. Generally."

She narrowed her eyes. His fingers were curled over the rim of her cockpit. "Why wouldn't I be doing fine? *Generally?*"

"For one thing, you haven't punched anyone since Cerberon."

She laughed. She didn't mean to, but she laughed. "Thought you'd be better at a heart-to-heart," she said. "Ambushing me at my ship? At least get me drunk or something, yeah?"

"I'm pressed for time," he said, and sounded utterly sincere.

How generous, Let'ij said, though the real Let'ij had never been sarcastic. *I don't remember Gruyver hurrying through conversations with you, when you sat together for hours, or—who was the child who made you those little toys? She was* always *in a rush.*

Chass growled and threw her head against her seat. "I'm clean, right? I fly when I'm told to fly, I shoot who I'm told to shoot." She kept talking, more to keep Wyl and Let'ij from saying anything than because she had something meaningful to add. "You're doing great. *I'm* doing great. You're going to complain about that?"

"*Are* you doing great?" he asked.

She wanted to glower at him but she didn't have the strength to turn her head.

"Cerberon was hard for all of us," he said. "We're walking into something big, when none of us are really recovered—"

"Screw you," she muttered.

She hadn't talked about the Children of the Empty Sun with anyone. She'd *mentioned* them—it was simpler to admit a sliver of truth than concoct an elaborate lie—but she hadn't *talked* about them. Now she knew how the rest of the conversation would play out: Wyl would sniff something, and he'd push, and she'd feel guilty, and she'd have to tell him *something* more or else bash his skull in out of frustration.

Before she could decide whether to assault her superior officer, another voice cut in.

"Commander Lark?"

Chass followed Wyl's gaze to the hangar floor, where one of the *Deliverance*'s crew waited patiently with upturned eyes—a Cathar girl who couldn't have been more than eighteen, mane in knots around the fur of her face and missing three fingers on her left hand.

"Yes?" Wyl said.

"You asked for a long-range comm channel. It took time to align the signal relays, but we're ready to go."

"How long will it stay open?" he asked.

"Not long. We're lucky the beacons are syncing at all."

Wyl looked from the girl to Chass, who shrugged. "Go," Chass said. "Pretty sure we were done here."

Wyl parted his lips, hesitated, and said: "You can always find me." Then he was down the ladder and gone.

Bastard, Chass thought.

She wondered for an instant what was so very important about the call, then rejected the thought. Wyl could do his thing, and she would do hers. She scuffed her boot around the cockpit floor, searching for the datachip she'd dropped earlier, and felt a slight resistance against her toe.

She rolled the chip beneath her foot as if tormenting a bug. When it rested beneath her heel, she applied gentle force and felt the chip sink into the thin mat over the metal plating.

She gasped audibly, like a fool. She lifted her foot and snapped up the chip, turning it between her fingers like it was as precious and destructive as a death stick.

When the cockpit canopy was closed again, she plugged in the chip and listened to the chanting of cultists. One by one, every voice and every worry—all the thoughts of Wyl Lark and Shadow Wing and burning families and Colonel Keize (and Quell, don't forget Quell, never forget Quell and everything she did)—withered away and drifted out her ears. Even Let'ij's voice in her mind evaporated to make room for the Children of the Empty Sun.

III

Nath Tensent fancied himself a lazy man, but achieving true idleness took more effort than he cared for. Instead he settled for tolerable work and enough luxuries to take the edge off. When he'd served under the Empire he'd found joy in plunder and a thrill in exploiting weaknesses personal and systemic; in the Rebel Alliance he'd earned a fraction of the credits but he'd been smart enough to avoid a position of authority, thus enjoying periods of languor between missions.

He wondered now whether he'd miscalculated by accepting the job of Intelligence liaison. His day so far had been a string of conferences broken up by cursory reads of classified files; the highlight had been catching General Syndulla off guard regarding her operation's authorization. But where he should've seen to his squadron after the meeting, instead he'd spent the afternoon speculating wildly about Shadow Wing's next target with Nasha Gravas and her band of spies over garbled comm intercepts.

"Seems like a lot of misplaced effort," he said as he walked out of the maintenance bay, T5 rolling behind him. The drab-green astromech had blown a motivator almost a week before; it had taken that long to find replacement parts for the aging machine. "Shadow Wing's not doing us any harm, and we don't exactly have an unblemished track record against them."

T5 squealed with disapproval, and Nath laughed. "Real helpful. If you're tagging along, run diagnostics or something? Pretend to be useful."

He cataloged the tasks awaiting him as they entered the mess hall and got into line behind a trio of Hail Squadron pilots. General Syndulla would want a summary of everything he'd discussed with Intelligence, but that could wait until morning. The Y-wing needed its torpedo launchers recalibrated, but T5 would take care of that. Then there was Wyl—someone needed to talk to the boy after all that had happened at the meeting with Syndulla, though Nath wasn't sure he was right for the job . . .

Admit it, he thought. *You're afraid to talk to him.*

He'd protected Wyl on Troithe—averted the boy's suicidal attempt to strike a deal with Shadow Wing—and Wyl hadn't forgiven him. Not that Wyl was ever rude, but they'd barely spoken in weeks. Even though Nath had later put himself in the line of fire, nearly died to save that rusting blight of a world, the tension was still there.

Maybe it was for the best. Maybe Wyl would come around.

Boy still needs you, even if he doesn't realize it.

Somehow, while he'd been immersed in thought, he'd ended up in conversation with the Hail pilots. His mouth was flapping on autopilot, and they were laughing about some fool story Nath had told about searching for an ejected X-wing pilot only to tow a Hutt in an escape pod. "You seen Wyl Lark around, by any chance?" he asked when the laughter died down.

"Not since this morning. Think he's running Flare Squadron through the Shadow Wing drills," one of the pilots answered. "I know T'oknell said something about meeting with him."

So Nath wasn't resolving things with Wyl tonight. He tried not to feel relieved.

He settled at a table with a tray of gray meat braised in orange sauce. The meal smelled like wilted vegetables and tasted like cleaning fluid. T5 rolled awkwardly through the mess as more pilots and crew drifted in off their shifts, and a dozen gathered around Nath to hear more from the Hero of Troithe. He had the routine down, though it hadn't been how he'd wanted to spend dinner.

"You want to know what *I* think about Shadow Wing running around burning planets?" he offered when they prompted him. "Hell, I think they should've stayed in hiding. Now we're going to come down on them *hard* . . ."

They cheered and asked him for more, and he made them all feel like galactic saviors. He tried to wrap up until Genni Avremif—a good kid, a decent bomber pilot—asked, "You met the new ground crews yet?"

"The ones from Troithe?" Nath shook his head. The destruction of the *Lodestar* had left Syndulla short-staffed, and they'd hired as many locals as they could find for the *Deliverance*. "Just a few. Why?"

Avremif gestured to the entrance to the mess, where one of Ragnell's minions was arguing with a pair of waist-high Ssori mechanics while a slender, aristocratic woman with a shock of orange hair looked on. "Bet they'd love to hear about how you saved their planet."

Nath laughed and read Avremif's expression and the flicker of the boy's eyes. *You want my glory to rub off on you . . . mostly because you're into the woman with the cheap orange wig.*

"Let's make it fast," he said.

Sometimes he enjoyed his celebrity.

The Hail pilots did most of the talking, turning Nath into the man single-handedly responsible for driving Shadow Wing out of Cerberon. The orange-haired woman didn't breathe a word, but the Ssori grew increasingly excited until they revealed that Nath had saved their district during a routine mission. They pledged to care for his bomber and his droid, said they could never repay what he'd done, and the sincerity of it all exhausted Nath until he excused himself, strolling away from the mess hall.

"Kairos still sleeping on the U-wing, last you heard?" he asked T5. It wasn't his job to crawl inside her brain, but someone had to and she'd help him forget the image of Nath Tensent, Brave Hero of the Ssori.

The droid gurgled ambiguously. The deck plating jumped as the *Deliverance* emerged from hyperspace for a scheduled course correction. He was trying to remember which branch in the hallway to take—everything on a Star Destroyer looked the same—when the wail of an alarm shredded his ears and he felt the deck juddering harder.

"The hell is going on?" he asked.

The alarm was joined by the steel-drum roar of tearing metal and the sensation of a gentle breeze.

Hull breach. Well, damn.

Nath knew now what was going on but not *why*, and he didn't have a moment to work through it all before he heard a scream down the corridor. He ran toward the sound as the deck steadied. Not twenty meters away he spotted Syndulla's aide—*Stornvein*, he thought, *his name's Stornvein*—on the floor, clutching his arm and staring at the bulkhead in horror. Sparks rained from a glowing crack in the metal, but almost none touched the man—the bright motes were swept back up by the wind and splashed against the cracked wall.

T5 issued a series of bass warbles. "I know!" Nath roared.

His legs were pumping again. He felt out of shape from weeks aboard the Star Destroyer sitting in stiff-backed chairs; the skirmish at the Circus of Mortal Appetites was the most active he'd been in ages. But he slid to one knee like a smashball player, gliding the last meter to Stornvein on the polished deck. He was up again in nearly the same motion, hauling the man to his feet and swerving away from the spark-belching wall.

"Go!" he hollered.

He swung the man around with both arms and hurled him toward a blast door irising shut a dozen paces away. The blast door would seal off the compartment and stop the oxygen loss, which was good—and it was a good sign that it was still functioning—but it would also seal Nath and Stornvein into an airless tomb if they weren't quick.

T5 squawked a warning. Nath felt a blast of sparks against his cheek and stumbled away from the bulkhead even as the breeze became a gale. He let the air turn his head—*Stupid!* he thought, *don't look at the sparks!*—and saw that the crack in the metal had widened to a rift framed by jagged molten cuts.

From the center of the rift stared a single crimson eye surrounded by concentric metal rings. The rings spun; lenses adjusted; and for an instant Nath felt like he'd returned to Cerberon, gazing again into the black hole looming over that wretched system.

He brought up his blaster and squeezed three times without aiming, feeling the weapon pulse and jerk. The flare of the bolts would've blinded him if he hadn't already been squinting against the sparks; as it was, his vision was spattered with blotches that only occasionally afforded him a clear view. But he heard a garbled, electronic noise and smelled something like melted plastoid as he whipped back around, racing into the wind.

He wasn't dead. He hoped that meant he'd hit his target.

The blast door, from what he could see of it, was nearly closed. He tried to remember the particulars of a Star Destroyer's safety features: If he got caught in its grip, would it release him or crush him into a bleeding mess? He prayed for strength as he lunged. He felt his feet leave the deck, his head clear the door as durasteel closed on all sides.

He crashed onto the floor, his ribs aching and his tongue bleeding and his chin bruised against the deck. The noisy rush of oxygen ceased. For the moment, he was safe.

A hand helped him up. T5 was beeping irritably. Nath swayed as Stornvein asked, "You all right, Captain Tensent?"

"Fine," Nath said. "Looks like sabotage droids."

"Stay put, catch your breath." Stornvein was sweating, and Nath saw now that the sleeve of the man's left arm—the arm he'd been clutching—was blackened and torn. "I'll see what I can find out—and *thank you*."

The man crossed to an emergency terminal down the corridor. Nath thought of following and leaned against T5 instead. He'd been stupid, going in after Stornvein. In ten seconds he'd nearly been suffocated, incinerated, and chopped in half. He'd gone in ignorant and unprepared.

Not much different than he'd done on Cerberon, in the end. He'd risked his life for strangers there, too.

Watch your instincts, Tensent. Watch them closely.

When he'd steadied, he made his way over to Stornvein, who was speaking into a wall comm. The man held up a hand to ask for silence, said a few last words into the comm Nath couldn't make out, then turned to face Nath. "Bridge says there's no starfighter presence out there. Just a load of buzz droids waiting like a minefield."

"Ain't that a relief?" Nath snorted. "How many are we talking about?"

"Not sure—we lost contact before I could ask."

Experience told Nath that even a dozen sabotage droids would suffice to sever internal communications, cut life support, and—given enough time—detonate the main reactor. But most models weren't very bright: They were saws and blowtorches on legs, and they'd spend a while ripping apart the Star Destroyer compartment by compartment, suffocating much of the crew before hitting vital systems.

Nath felt his priorities shift like tumblers in a lock.

"I'd head for the water tanks if I were you," he told Stornvein. "Lots of space, low-priority target, pretty far from the outer hull. Move fast, because that won't be the only blast door sealing up."

"What about you?" the man asked.

"I'm off to engineering. Someone ought to keep an eye on the hypermatter annihilator."

He took long strides, not quite jogging—he'd need his energy soon, especially if the turbolifts were offline. T5 rolled behind him in silence until they turned a corner; a moment later the droid issued an inquisitive series of beeps.

Nath smirked, sparing T5 a glance. "Of course not. The engineers have blasters; time they learned to use them. We're—well, someone has to check on that boy of yours."

T5 chimed with a sound of determination.

Nath had been avoiding his troubles. Now he was going to find Wyl Lark after all.

CHAPTER 4

LOVE SONGS OF THE
KORTATKA RIVER LANDS

I

The sun rose over the carbon-scored horizon of the *Yadeez's* hull. The ship floated over a sallow sea of mist that rapidly burned away in the dawn's light to reveal lush jungle far below—a nameless jungle unmarked on the galaxy's maps, which Yrica Quell suspected had never before been viewed by human eyes. Kneeling on the hull plating, she yearned to remove her suit's cumbersome helmet, to see the planet without polarized visor and interposed readouts. She wanted to drop over the side and stay in that strange wilderness forever.

She did not remove her helmet or leap from the ship. Nor did she rush to return to work. The repairs to the aft scanner could wait. She listened to her breathing, felt the heat of the sun as her suit scrambled to adapt to the changing temperature, and watched shadows slip through the green.

This was why she was out there, she told herself. To be away from the others. To let her mind reset. To remember who she was.

Just a bit longer.

Just a few more minutes. Then you finish. Then you go back.

The suit's cooling units snapped to full power and she gasped as her arms turned icy from the elbows down. Her comm unit crackled to life as she shook off the prickling numbness.

"Do you need assistance?" Colonel Keize asked.

The suit indicated the call's point of origin. Quell turned her head and saw a second suit twenty meters behind her, near the hatch leading into the bulk freighter's air lock. The suit's owner approached with lumbering strides imposed by magnetic boots.

"I'm all right," Quell said. "I'll be another half hour. Maybe a few minutes more."

The suit continued its approach. Sunlight glanced off its visor like a deflected blaster bolt—like the occupant was invincible, divine. "Squadron Three is in-system," Keize said. "Once they're aboard we'll jump to lightspeed. No delays."

Quell held her gaze on the suit a moment longer, then returned to the innards of the aft scanner. She'd spent half her shift opening the damaged casing, and had only just begun tracing the short that had brought her outside.

"I'll get it done," she said. "The squadron find anything?" She tried to recall details of Captain Wisp's mission. Rearguard patrol operation, but Quell had been told little beyond that.

"We have pursuit. General Syndulla is on our trail again," Keize said.

Quell halted, then shifted to look behind her. Keize stood no more than a meter away. "General Syndulla? You're sure?"

The arctic cooling of the suit seemed insufficient. She wanted to shake off the heat and sweat, but she held still.

"New command ship, of course—we destroyed the last at Cerberon—but I am sure." Magnetized steps brought him to Quell's side. "We dropped the sabotage droids. They've made contact, and should buy us the time we need."

Questions flashed through her mind, and she dismissed them one by one: *How can you know it's her? How much damage have the droids done?* She finally reached a question that seemed safe: "You don't intend to engage?"

"No. More than a few of us bear a grudge against Syndulla and her pilots. Many of our dead are dead because of her. But we have another mission, and now is not the time."

"There will be a time, though."

"Now that we've confirmed her pursuit? Yes."

She wanted to ask: *Why does none of this surprise you?* She tasted the words, felt how they might play on her lips. Had she shown too much interest already? Not enough? Should she be looking for vengeance for pilots whom she might've killed herself?

She'd told Keize she had heard mention of Syndulla during her interrogations at Traitor's Remorse—that she understood the general had taken the lead in Shadow Wing's pursuit, but that they'd never met. It had seemed like a safe lie.

"You didn't need to come out here to tell me that," she said. It was easier than saying anything else.

"I thought I'd assist, as I mentioned. I was available, and—" Keize gestured toward the artificial horizon as he knelt beside the scanner casing. "—it's a remarkable view."

"Yes," she said, and they began to work.

She summarized her findings and diagnosis so far: The old insulation was crumbling, and Shadow Wing had run the scanner far longer than its specifications permitted. Keize asked questions but followed her lead as she began peeling melted plastoid and tearing out wiring. He passed her tools, anticipated her needs, and acted as a second set of hands without ego.

He was an able mechanic. He was easy to work with. Talking with him—letting her guard down—was only natural.

"Have you met the newcomers from Fedovoi End?" Keize asked as he deftly compressed flexible tubing inside a rusted cylinder. "Major Njock is unusual. Claims to have never been through officer school; came up from sergeant through field commissions and is terribly proud of it, though there are holes in his story. He says he vigorously protested the Yomo Council's split with the Empire."

"He would, though, wouldn't he?" Quell said. "No, I haven't met them."

"If you care to socialize, do it soon. Most of them will go to the fleet rendezvous."

"I'll keep it in mind." Light flashed and her visor repolarized as a conduit discharged. "We're not recruiting them?"

"We'll keep some of the matériel. They're not who we need, though—we knew that going in." He laughed softly. "I'm not sure the whole planet had what we need."

"Maybe the next planet, then," Quell said. Keize laughed more boldly. She'd been joking, but she hadn't expected the reaction.

He'd laughed so rarely before Nacronis. The year since Endor had changed him.

The conversation paused as they attached replacement wiring and sprayed insulating foam. It occurred to Quell that her relationship with Keize had changed as well, and that maybe the man was the same as always; it was the two of them together that was different.

"Every planet we visit could surrender in its entirety," Keize resumed as if they hadn't paused. "Even then, I expect it would be too late to make a difference."

"Sir?" She couldn't see his expression with his helmet turned.

"Consider the early days after Endor," he said. "Imagine if we had responded differently—if the chain of command had remained intact despite the Emperor's demise. The Death Star was lost along with a portion of the fleet, but orders continued to flow to the planetary garrisons. What would've happened?"

"I don't know. I'm not a strategist." She gestured for him to secure a loose cluster of wires, and he did so.

"It's a hypothetical, Lieutenant. There are no consequences for guessing wrong."

She wanted to push back. She wanted to fight the *ease* of his voice. The part of her that was a soldier or a frightened child was certain Keize was setting a trap.

"We would've had the advantage," she said. "We would've seen civilian uprisings on a few hundred worlds, but early action could've stopped most before they grew. Maybe—" *Would Operation Cinder still have happened?* "Maybe the rebels seize a sliver of the Inner Rim, establish a strong claim. We hold the rest of our territory. Long-term, I don't know."

"Reasonable enough. Not the best-case scenario but not the worst, either. Now—suppose the first six weeks after Endor go unchanged from the world we know, but someone takes unambiguous command of Imperial forces after. There's no time for schism, no real power grabs. Worlds like Fedovoi End and Gerrenthum pledge allegiance to a restored Imperial High Command. What changes?"

She realized he wanted something, but she couldn't determine what—couldn't drag it into the light of reason. She permitted herself to answer truthfully. "I think very little changes. The logistical network is already broken. The rebels are better at guerrilla tactics than we are, and our fleets are too spread out to take back any of the systems lost in those first six weeks. You can't heal a wound that deep."

"I expect you're right," Keize said.

A memory struck her, more vivid than the wires under her fingertips. "You told me on Nacronis," she said. " 'The Empire's not going to pull together and there's not going to be another Emperor. That was clear a day after Endor.' "

"I did say that, or something like it. I wanted to see if your analysis was any different now." She still couldn't see his face but she could hear the smile. "I was building to something, Lieutenant. Don't deny me the pleasure of the leisurely stroll."

This time her own laugh surprised her. "Understood, sir. Go on."

"No, it's all right—" The wiring sparked again. Both of them froze, and Keize adjusted the position of a power feed with deliberate care. He looked to her with concern, eyes scanning her suit for damage before he spoke again.

"I've been thinking about what my superiors may be planning," he said. "What the fleet in the Western Reaches is preparing for while we exact . . . punishment. They claim there's yet a chance for victory over the Rebellion."

"How?"

He shrugged. It was a small motion inside his suit, but she saw it.

"I'm not privy to particulars, nor am I especially interested. I imagine they'll attempt to draw the enemy into one final battle under favorable conditions."

She turned her eyes away. "And you're not interested because—"

"Because the *best-case scenario* today is very different than it was a year ago. Imagine, Lieutenant, that we deliver a massive blow to the enemy fleet and suffer minimal losses to our own. Imagine the New Republic is forced to consolidate, leaving—what? A sliver of Imperial space in the Western Reaches, as the rebels might have secured if we'd reacted with unity after Endor?" There was no passion or urgency in his voice. He laid it out with the same ease he'd maintained throughout the conversation.

She thought it over. "Coruscant is still under our control. If the New Republic fleet is weakened, Imperial forces could punch through to the capital. Build out from there, occupy a wedge of space along one of the major hyperlanes."

"That *is* an optimistic outlook. All right—suppose it's possible. What do you imagine that Empire looks like?"

"Meaning?"

"Culturally. An Empire that survived this past year—an Empire that struggled, that carried out two Operation Cinders, that endured endless hardship to secure one wedge of the galaxy—does it rise to the heights we always aspired to? Is it a place of committed order and stability, even at the cost of certain liberties? Do its leaders value merit and honor—at least in words, if not in deeds?"

She should've felt chilled. Instead she laughed again, with barely a trace of bitterness. "Not after what we've done," she said, but Keize gestured for her to continue and she attempted to sober herself. "Even if we secure a territory, there would still be resistance. We'd be putting down rebellions forever, fighting back anarchy."

How many more examples would be made? How many Operation Cinders?

She nearly laughed once more.

"We would become our worst selves—paranoid and violent, and

dedicated to justifying that paranoia and violence," Keize said, and together they began to reaffix the casing to the scanner array. "An Empire so ideologically feeble is no longer worth preserving."

He didn't ask if she agreed, and she didn't volunteer her opinion.

"Yet in the more likely event that we lose this war," he went on, "what becomes of any of us? You said yourself that the rebels can't judge their enemies fairly, and any Imperial who fights today surely numbers among the most terrible of those enemies. There will be no forgiveness—not for soldiers who murdered Fedovoi End; nor for those who surrendered to us and reaffirmed their loyalty to the true Empire; nor for those who fought and fled and fought these many months for lack of anywhere else to go."

The casing locked in place. Keize rested a gloved hand on the array and turned to Quell, the ease gone and replaced by steel. "That is why I continue to fight. Because to accept defeat is to sacrifice every soldier who remains alive at the altar of rebel justice. You and I have both seen what happens to those who seek another path. We both know the people here have no choice."

"Do *they* know that?" she asked. "That win or lose, we're all doomed?"

"No," Keize said, and smiled darkly as they stood. "Some, perhaps. For others . . . I think it would make no difference, except to crush what spirit remains."

He gestured and they walked side by side, magnetically locked to the hull of the *Yadeez* with the jungle kilometers below. "I will do everything I can to save them," he said, as if it were fact and not an oath. "Let the Empire fall, but not its soldiers. I will save them."

Why are you telling me this? she wanted to ask.

Yet she knew the answer.

Keize descended through the hatch first. She lingered above, looking at the sun and the stars and the jungle. She heard his voice over the comm—"Take a moment before we jump to lightspeed"—and felt his presence vanish.

He was asking for her help. He wanted her to save Shadow Wing because he believed she *understood*.

She did understand. It pained her to admire Soran Keize when she had come such a long way to betray him to the New Republic.

There were times Quell nearly forgot her mission and felt her past and vows subsumed by the machinery of the 204th. Exhaustion was one factor—it was rare she slept a full night or had more than half an hour free to wash and scarf up meals—but familiarity was another. She'd spent years serving the Empire; too quickly, her time in the New Republic was beginning to feel like a dream.

But the memories, no matter how dim, were not gone. In Cerberon she'd come to understand that there was nothing for her in the New Republic: that regardless of whether her squadron forgave her (they likely wouldn't), she would be tried and punished for her crimes. Her life would end, perhaps deservedly so—but submitting to her guilt served no one when there was work yet to do.

Caern Adan had advised her to move forward past her guilt and do what good she could for the galaxy. That remained her task.

Her mornings and evenings were spent assisting the ground crews and the engineers, desperately attempting to keep the *Yadeez* and its fighters in working order. The bulk freighter was not a Star Destroyer, and its components were prone to malfunctioning regularly and (at times) explosively. The lessons of her teenage years served Quell well: She'd never worked on a non-Imperial ship as large as the *Yadeez,* but she knew enough to never use ROMStat compressors in a Merkuni propulsion unit—wisdom that eluded her colleagues who'd worked with parts only from Imperial manufacturers. The TIEs were a separate challenge—they were barely Imperial anymore, repaired with salvaged parts and armed with black-market munitions. Quell had spent twenty-seven hours straight working with a crew to retrofit Squadron Three's ships for hyperspace docking rings they'd found in a Clone Wars–era supply cache; the squadron had lightspeed capability now, and it was almost reliable.

Afternoons she had other duties. Keize had asked her to assess and train the new pilots from the worlds they burned. Quell interviewed them, assembled profiles, and put them through drills basic enough to give no excuse for failure. She wasn't sure why Keize had selected her for this duty—he couldn't possibly have known about her time running Alphabet through simulations. But she wrote recommendations for the squadron commanders and allowed others to make the final decision as to who was worthy of joining Shadow Wing.

She did all these things, and when Soran Keize called, she went to his side.

She preferred to associate with members of the unit she didn't know. That was easy, most of the time—much of her work she did alone, and she took her meals briskly and at odd moments. Many of the pilots she'd laughed with and befriended and kissed and bled with were dead and thus did not request her company. One of the junior engineers, a boy named Agias Rikton, seemed content to take on tasks at whatever hour she required, allowing her to use her supervision of him as an excuse not to visit her fellow officers.

It would be easier, she imagined, to betray all of them—as she would betray Soran Keize—if she didn't spend more time with them than necessary.

She was thinking about that one evening as she scrubbed herself in the shower, counting the seconds until the water automatically turned off. She glanced to the stall door, then to her left biceps, where the splash of red scar tissue appeared almost healed. Water followed the web of lines like rivers carving canyons—as if enough time aboard the *Yadeez* would erode and erase her scars, leaving an unmarked plain. An irrational fear rose in Quell: the notion that when the last remnants of her tattoo faded—the tattoo of five mismatched rebel starfighters that she had scoured from her body—she would also forget her time in Alphabet Squadron.

She clenched her biceps with her right hand, ready to rake her nails through the flesh and deepen the marks. It was a wild, primitive response to an absurd terror, and she would've clawed herself until she bled if someone hadn't rapped on the thin metal door.

She dropped her arms to her sides as if standing at attention. Water ran into her eyes and licked the underside of her chin.

"Quell!" The voice from beyond the door was stern, almost angry. It sounded like Fra Raida, whom Quell had been in low-key competition with since she'd first joined the 204th. "Get your butt to the ready room!"

"On my way," Quell said. "What's going on?"

"Squadron Five is back," Raida answered. "Everyone else is ready. It's time for the birthday party."

She couldn't escape this time. The ready room—what had been the bulk freighter's rec area, consisting of little more than a few chairs, a cooler, and a nonfunctional pazaak table—was crowded with pilots, all of whom she recognized from her years flying.

Squadron Five was welcomed with roars and embraces. (Had Shadow Wing been so affectionate, so *tactile* before the Battle of Endor? Quell wondered, and no longer trusted her memory.) Commander Broosh and his subordinates were not the guests of honor, however; they were merely the last to show. Quell stood straight-backed against a bulkhead as Lieutenant Darita passed out crowns of cracked tubing combined with sprigs of vegetation collected from Dybbron III before its death. Quell donned her own without comment and felt sap glue crown and hair and skin together.

"Should the colonel be here?" one of Broosh's pilots asked—her name was Jeela Brebtin, Quell thought.

Darita sounded exactly like her sister—the woman who'd died to guard the *Yadeez*'s retreat at Cerberon—when she said, "Don't be stupid. Pilot corps only, same as always."

"Same as always!" a voice cried from the back of the room, and they all laughed because the Star Destroyer *Pursuer* was gone and Colonel Shakara Nuress, the woman they'd called Grandmother, was dead.

Yet it was still her birthday.

Grandmother had never known about the gatherings aboard the *Pursuer*. Officially, the pilots observed the Feast of Lord-Protector Jarmanidath—an obscure holiday from a world in the Colonies, mysteriously approved for celebration by the Empire's Culture Ministry censors. (Quell recalled Xion speculating that the approval had been an error too embarrassing to correct.) Over the years the birthday party had taken on more and more traditions from the true feast; but they were a tribute to Shadow Wing above all.

In the ready room of the *Yadeez* they sang holiday songs, replacing references to "the protector" with "the colonel." They drank nutrient blends flavored with the most colorful spices they could find, and Quell couldn't help but smile when Squadron Six proclaimed Captain Phesh to be the Lord-Protector's jester. Phesh had once been the gathering's staunchest opponent, acting as chaperone more than celebrant and twice forbidding his squadron to attend; now he rubbed his mustache and delivered a speech about Grandmother's triumphs during the darkest days of the Clone Wars.

"Many believed the Republic would fall, then," he declared, "but women like Colonel Nuress and men like Chancellor Palpatine led us to victory. Their generation is gone, and now it is our responsibility to lead. To learn from them, and to light the fires of victory anew."

Some among the pilots rolled their eyes or stared at the deck; some cheered and raised glasses. A few breathed heavily, their eyes wild and enraged—among them Lieutenant Kandende, whose face had turned bright red. Quell feared her own expression had given something away when a hand pressed her shoulder and she felt an exhalation against her ear.

"I'm glad you're back," Meriva Greef said. Quell recognized the voice, almost comically high-pitched, before she turned to see the sergeant she'd shared a bunk with in the days after Endor. Greef's face was the same as always, thin and dark, but Quell was surprised to see the woman in a flight suit.

"I'd heard—" Quell said. She'd seen the squadron rosters; she should've known what to expect. "Congratulations. You always wanted to fly."

"Not how I planned to leave the ground crews," Greef said, "but it's the chance I got."

If there was a note of disappointment in her tone, Quell couldn't be sure.

Quell attempted to leave the celebration three times as the evening progressed. Each time she was thwarted by a toast or intercepted by a colleague. The pilots began exchanging stories in small groups and the groups gradually merged, story blending into story. In time, Commander Broosh stood in the center of the ready room, one booted foot on the pazaak table as he spoke of Pandem Nai.

"They didn't come to fight," he said. "They came to kill—to trap us inside our station, to burn us in our house. It was a rebel plan, the plan of terrorists and guerrillas, and *that* should surprise no one.

"But their eagerness set the sky on fire. They would've incinerated everyone on the planet if we hadn't stopped them. And while our comrades sacrificed themselves, the rebels sent a death squad to assassinate Colonel Nuress.

"They asked for no surrender. They acted not with the sober intent of an executioner but with the angry rage of a child—a child with a blaster rifle . . ."

Quell listened to the description of her mistakes and to the names of the dead and tried to appear outraged. When the story was done and she turned to go, she was stopped one final time; Broosh himself stood at her side and said, "It'll be good to have you flying again, once you're recovered. We need you out there."

"I understand," Quell said, and did not sleep that night.

The opportunity she'd awaited came the next morning, when the unit came under attack by three *Gozanti*-class cruisers—ex-Imperials, Quell assumed, who had heard of Shadow Wing's mission and decided to take the offensive rather than wait for annihilation. The *Yadeez* rattled and attempted evasive action as particle bolts boiled away its fragile shielding; the corridors were full of the roar of TIEs launching and the odors of smoke and leaking coolant.

Had Quell been on the bridge or with Keize when the attack had begun, she would have been trapped by duty. As it was, she could slip into the current of chaos and resurface after she'd completed her mission. She would make her excuses then.

At the best of times, the reactor level of the freighter was a cramped labyrinth of machinery occluded by steam and crisscrossed with cables and pipes. Condenser pillars and sub-unit generators glowed gently, providing beacons in the dark. During combat, however, the reactor level became an unstable nightmare, and Quell was forced to crawl to maintain her balance and hope a power surge didn't burn her alive. If she burned herself and survived, she couldn't dare scream— the grates overhead led to populated areas of the ship, and discovery might end in a worse death than electrocution.

She scuttled through the maze, timing her movements to the lulls in the battle and listening for sounds from the *Yadeez*'s crew. After a last furious dash, she wedged her body between a bulkhead and the icy metal of a cooling tower, and slid her hands across pitted deck plating until she found the edges of an access panel. She tugged it open, nearly smashing the panel door into her face, then peered into the machinery below.

Wired directly into the ship's reactor systems, sandwiched between high-voltage flux stabilizers, were the innards of a TIE bomber's comm array. Quell had stolen the parts over the course of weeks, spent days more reassembling them and configuring them for their new housing, but the array *worked*. She was almost certain it worked.

If anyone spotted her now, there was no explanation that would suffice. She touched the blaster on her hip before beginning.

Her hands trembled as she tapped the emergency keypad. She hadn't been able to find a spare display, so she'd never know it if she miskeyed a command. When she was done—if she did everything perfectly—the *Yadeez* would send a burst of coded data bouncing among hyperspace relays. Some listening post would intercept the data package and send it on to New Republic Intelligence, assuming it had been transmitted inadvertently. Someone at Intelligence would decipher it and match it with the bulk freighter's unique identifiers. Whoever had replaced Caern Adan would review the data and bring it to General Syndulla, and the general would continue her pursuit . . .

If Quell did it all correctly. If she wasn't found out.

But she'd done it right before. Keize had said it: *General Syndulla is in pursuit.*

And what would happen when Syndulla and the others arrived? There would be a battle, and if Syndulla and Alphabet chose their moment correctly then Shadow Wing would die. The *Yadeez* would burn. Its pilots would be picked off in their TIEs, and only the bulk freighter's escort ships might have a chance to surrender.

Quell accepted this as her price. She'd been too slow to save the Imperial population of Fedovoi End from choking on the planet's poisoned atmosphere; from sealing themselves away until their sole alternative was suffocation. But she would stop the 204th and the second Operation Cinder even if she could never set things right.

A roar like thunder or a proton bomb echoed through the maze. The *Yadeez* rocked, and Quell's head slammed into the cooling tower. She let go of the keypad, terrified she might enter an unwanted command. Reality blurred and her brain pulsed with pain, and she distantly remembered fracturing her skull only months before; if she hadn't done permanent damage then, maybe she had now.

She pressed her hands to the floor to steady herself and slid them back toward the comm array. If she didn't send the data burst soon the battle might end. Someone might come looking for her.

You don't need eyes for this. Touch is plenty.

She saw a shadow to her side—a silhouette that hadn't been there before, two meters away.

The shadow was moving. She moved as well, and she didn't think as she grabbed her blaster and wheeled. The deck lurched again and she couldn't be sure if she pulled the trigger on her own—not the first time, at least. The second shot she *meant*. She smelled the blaster bolt, saw the flash, and the shadow crumpled to the floor.

When her head finally cleared, she recognized the figure lying on the deck plating: a bundle of red leather and cloth, its one arm splayed out and its glass face cracked, staring lifelessly into the grating above. Robe and circuits burned in the center of its chest.

The Emperor's Messenger was dead.

CHAPTER 5

NIGHT VIGILS OF THE POLIS MASSA RELIGIOUS CASTE

I

Wyl Lark felt as if he'd descended beneath the known universe—below the Star Destroyer, out of the stars, and into an endless abyss. Somewhere half a kilometer from the lightless turbolift shaft he would find his goal, though whether there was any point to reaching the hangar bay now he wasn't sure. No one seemed to be shooting at the *Deliverance*. No attack had come since the sabotage droids had latched on.

He lowered himself rung by rung, resting when his arms trembled or his footing began to slip. It was better (he told himself) than waiting in one of the bunk rooms, where he'd been helping Lourgh T'oknell retrofit a bed to accommodate his six limbs. That task had almost made him feel ordinary again—like a man who could while away time with friends instead of leading them—but the moment had ended when the ship's alarms rang.

They need you. You're doing all you know how, he told himself. It wasn't comforting.

His feet found something solid, and he dragged the toe of his boot across a metallic surface until he located a handle. He dropped to hands and knees and worked the handle with increasingly forceful pulls until the hatch he squatted on slid open and he fell. He had the presence of mind to relax his limbs, and when his soles hit the deck the pain was dull instead of sharp. After the shock passed, he blinked into the light and wondered why he heard squealing.

"Give him space, huh?" a low voice called.

Wyl rose unsteadily. A meter away he saw the source of the squealing—a squat, flat-topped astromech droid coated in flaking green paint, shifting weight rapidly between its two bulky legs.

Wyl grinned and wrapped his arms around T5. "Good to see you, too. You staying out of trouble?" He raised his chin, looking past the droid to the man in the corridor next. "I'm glad you're all right."

Nath Tensent gave him a nod. His face was spattered with ash and grease. Wyl wondered what Nath had been through (wondered what Chass and Kairos and the rest of the *Deliverance* were going through) even as he felt grateful for Nath's survival.

It took him a moment before he remembered the distance between them. His smile faded.

"No trouble upstairs?" Nath asked.

"Power shortages, and lots of them. Oxygen levels seem okay for now." Wyl stepped around T5, swallowed awkward words before adding, "I really am glad to see you."

Nath had never been less than his friend. Even at their lowest on Troithe, the man had fought to protect Wyl. That had been the problem, really—Wyl had seen a chance to avert bloodshed, to save people, and Nath had decided for both of them that it was too risky.

Wyl had once asked Nath to be there for him—to back him up when he called. Nath had agreed, and he'd kept to his promise; they just didn't seem to agree on what *friendship* entailed, and Wyl didn't know what to do about it.

Nath shrugged. Whether Wyl's outreach meant anything to him, Wyl couldn't tell. "We're on our way to field control," Nath said. "You coming along?"

The man marched past Wyl, T5, and the turbolift shaft. The droid followed, and Wyl pursued the both of them. "You have a plan?"

"I'd call it an *idea* more than a *plan,* but it's something. You know how many safeties a Star Destroyer has to prevent explosive decompression?"

"Can't say I do."

"More than a few. My guess is that the bridge could blow most of those droids out their own hull breaches by opening up the right blast doors. Sweep them into space with the force of a hurricane, then shut the doors again. Only if anyone tries, emergency energy fields will snap into place to keep the air in. We're going to try to disable those safety fields manually."

"All right," Wyl said. He was out of his element, and Nath knew Star Destroyers better than he ever would. The part of him still wounded—still mistrustful—over Troithe wondered how Nath was prioritizing the crew's lives, and he caught himself saying: "Any risk our people will be blown out with the droids? Or that they'll suffocate?"

"Always a risk," Nath said. "But that's up to the bridge. We're just giving them options."

Wyl nodded and increased his pace. "I'll follow your lead and hope I can help. Lucky we found each other."

Nath snorted. "Yeah. Lucky."

They walked awhile, T5 occasionally letting out a burble or a beep. Nath paused at an intersection and peered down the branches—one lit, one not—before choosing the lit corridor. They heard clanking metal and sparks, but the echoes seemed to come from a great distance. They were in the eye of a storm, Wyl thought: safe while disaster shaped the world around them.

"Kind of a mess these days, huh?" Nath asked. His tone was more than easygoing—it was *gentle* in a way Wyl barely recognized.

"Been a little rough," Wyl agreed, trying to hide his surprise. "First Keize and those planets, now this . . ."

Nath frowned, then wiped the spattered grease from his face with a sleeve. "We've been having problems *long* before Keize. Have you talked to Chass or Kairos since Cerberon?"

Wyl gave a chagrined smile. "I did try talking to Chass, but I—" He nearly lied; he wasn't ready to talk about why he'd been called away to the comm. He elided the truth instead. "—got interrupted. We *are* a mess, aren't we? And the pressure's just going to get worse."

"Can't argue, brother. And you've got your hands full with three other squadrons—don't know how you manage it."

"General Syndulla's been there with me. The pilots are good people, you know that—"

"But it's not the job you were looking for. You weren't thrilled with the role on Troithe, you sure as hell can't be happy with it now."

Wyl laughed—a single, swift breath of a sound, less at Nath's words and more at the precision of them. Nath always pretended he was just *talking*, but the man knew how to cut to the heart of a matter.

"It's not a responsibility I want," Wyl conceded. "I didn't leave Home so I could lead people into battle." He sucked in air—warmer than it should've been—and tried to keep his tone light. "But someone has to do it, and I'm the best equipped. I'm fine, Nath."

It wasn't a conversation he wanted. He *couldn't* have it without admitting the truth about the comm call.

"Sure," Nath said, and shrugged.

Wyl tried to leave the subject behind. "I take it you ran into one of them? The sabotage droids?"

"I did. Went by too fast for me to recognize the model. Good news is they're not immune to blasters."

"That's a comfort." Wyl dropped his hand to his hip, checking to see if his sidearm was still there. He rubbed his thumb against the textured grip, trying to remember the last time he'd used a pistol. Practice with Riot Squadron, before Endor?

"I saw Stornvein, by the way," Nath said, with the matter-of-fact tone Wyl recognized as artificial. He flashed Wyl a grin. "Syndulla's aide? Almost got split in two."

"He made it out okay?"

"Barely. I had to toss him through a blast door while that machine was closing in. My ribs still ache." He grinned broadly again. "Figure that wins me first crack at the expensive stuff if we survive to celebrate."

"It probably does. You did good."

His eyes flickered to Nath, then returned to the corridor. The larger man was watching him, as if waiting for more—some analysis of the situation, some emotional response Wyl hadn't given.

Wyl wondered what he was missing. Was Nath looking for approval? For praise?

"Getting closer," Nath said, suddenly scowling. "Stay alert for smoke—if a fire starts, it'll eat whatever air is left. Not much call for conversation after that."

II

The breath mask *almost* fit, which made the insult worse. The plastoid sealed adequately over her nose and mouth, digging into her skin and fogging with condensation; but the strap had been designed to run to the back of a human skull, and Chass na Chadic had horns where the designers had expected hair and flesh. She was forced to hold the mask in place in return for the privilege of breathing, and while that wasn't the worst of her problems it was the one that irked her most.

She could hear the sabotage droids scuttling across metal somewhere nearby—there was just enough air left, she supposed, to carry sound. There was a crackling noise, too, which might have been electrical sparks or might have been a fire. Neither possibility thrilled her.

She picked her way through the access corridor anyway, ducking beneath unmoving pistons and hopping over dead plasma burners, knowing the worst was still to come. She'd be crawling through a tube meant for mouse droids shortly, trying to reach the hangar before she ran out of air or froze to death or burned alive or—well, there were all sorts of possibilities depending on whether the bridge restored power too fast or too slow.

You shouldn't be here, Maya Hallik. You're not wanted.

She started to swear, but the seal of the breath mask broke when she moved her lips. She clamped the plastoid harder to her face.

The Inheritors of the Crystal wanted you. The Unignited wanted you. Maybe—I'll be generous, I'll grant the possibility—maybe the Cavern Angels and Riot Squadron and the Rebel Alliance even wanted you. But you're an inconvenience now. At best, an extra gun. At worst, a freak to be laughed at.

Let'ij's voice drowned out the scuttling droids. In a way, company made the journey more bearable.

The Children of the Empty Sun wanted you, Chass heard, but she wasn't sure if it was her voice or Let'ij's.

III

"Say again?" Hera Syndulla asked.

The comlink belched static. Hera stretched out her arm, holding the device away from her ear as she stalked the haunted corridors of the *Deliverance.* Rows of emergency lights offered enough illumination to see by, but only just.

"—alerted before our arrival," the link spat. "We were looking at the logs: an unauthorized transmission, not long before the droids attacked."

She repeated the words in her head until she understood. She almost wished the message had stayed garbled. "So they knew we were coming," she said. "Are we talking about a tracking device? A spy on board?"

"Who knows? Let's hope for the former." Stornvein paused. "You want us to start digging—"

"Not yet. I want everyone focused on repairing the ship and purging those droids. Are you on the bridge? Who's in charge up there?"

She'd tried contacting the bridge once before, but half the comm systems were damaged and interference had flooded every channel. She'd hoped the captain was at his station and simply out of contact; but his executive officer, Nisteen Arvad, was a brilliant woman Hera would've gladly offered a command. Either would be capable in an emergency.

"I, ah—I think *I'm* in charge," Stornvein said. "Just got here a few minutes ago. Captain's hurt at the bottom of a turbolift shaft—we're not sure how bad. Commander Arvad is missing altogether. The targeting officer is next in line, but—"

Blast it all, she thought.

"Understood," she said. "Do what you can. I'm on my way but I've had to double back twice—"

Stornvein was saying something. Then the static overwhelmed his voice until, with a distinct *pop,* the comlink went dead. She pocketed it and considered the reality of her circumstances.

She was alone on a Star Destroyer—a converted Star Destroyer, admittedly—being carved to pieces by droids who would just as happily carve up her. The crew was without a leader, and she . . .

. . . she felt *comfortable.* Confident. She'd been close to death too many times.

Careful, Hera. Hubris will kill you faster than the sabotage droids. Don't assume you'll see the end of this war.

That thought felt like a knife in her heart, but it did the trick. She was alert again.

A dozen paces later she heard a rattling noise from the darkness ahead. Hera adjusted her footfalls, rolling her soles so that her steps were silent. She drew her blaster pistol and held it ready.

The rattling continued, accompanied by something that might have been the squawking of a malfunctioning vocabulator. She saw a shape in the darkness, maybe twenty meters in front of her; saw the glint of metal in the emergency lighting. She shifted her stance, ready to fire and sidestep any incoming volley, but even as she aimed she knew something was wrong. She couldn't have said *what;* only that the threat was ambiguous and she didn't intend to shoot anything other than a valid target.

The shape in the darkness blurred. It was turning to face her. As Hera wondered whether she'd made a fatal error, her eyes discerned a face of chitin and a shroud of patchwork garments. A bowcaster dangled from one of the figure's hands.

"Kairos!" Hera breathed.

Kairos cocked her head. Around her feet and piled against the walls were mechanical limbs and serrated blades and the lens of a photoreceptor. Oil stained the deck plating.

"I am hunting," Kairos said, in a tone of curious wonder—as if it were the first time she'd done such a thing, and she was pleased with her accomplishments.

Hera holstered her weapon and suppressed a shudder. The droid appeared to have been shot and vivisected—she wasn't sure in what order. "I see that. I'm impressed."

"This was my third," Kairos said. "There will be others."

So long as she'd been standing still, Kairos had appeared immortal. With her first step toward Hera, the illusion broke. The arm holding her bowcaster swung limply, the sleeve soaked with what Hera could only assume was blood. Rags hung from her waist where something had torn through her side. Kairos walked with the stagger of a puppet jerked by unpracticed hands.

"Kairos," Hera said again, and lunged to catch the woman.

Instead of toppling, Kairos recoiled. She raised her uninjured arm, fingers curled like claws, and loosed a shriek. Hera drew up short, glancing behind her in alarm. She saw nothing.

"What's wrong?" she asked. "Talk to me."

"Away," Kairos said. She pulled her injured arm toward her chest and adjusted her garments, tugging shreds of cloth over her wounds.

Hera had never known Kairos well—never known her at all, really—but she recalled the silent woman in a mask who had first joined Alphabet Squadron. Hera recalled, too, the woman's grievous injuries on Troithe, and how when she'd returned from her healing sleep she'd bared her face for the first time.

She saw the shame in the woman's dark eyes, and while she didn't know its source she could respond with compassion.

"You don't want to be touched," Hera said.

"No."

"You don't want to be seen."

"No." Kairos paused. "But it is done."

Kairos stared past Hera's shoulder and said nothing. She was trembling, but only faintly; Hera wouldn't have noticed if she hadn't been watching closely.

Kairos didn't want help. That was plain. But she would bleed to death in the corridor if Hera did nothing.

"I'd like to get you patched up," Hera said. "We're not too far from the medbay—"

"*No.*" The word was sharp and sure. "No bacta."

"Then we can find something to bind your wounds, stanch the bleeding. I'm not a medic but I've done it more than once in the field. Friends have done it for me."

This seemed to resonate—she had Kairos's attention, though the woman still watched suspiciously. "You cannot *touch* me."

"Then—okay. Let me show you what to do," Hera said. She knew it was insufficient, and she added with all the gravity and sincerity she could muster: "I swear to you, Kairos. I will not touch you."

Kairos was motionless awhile. Then her gloved hand went to her bloody side and pressed into her wound; when she raised her hand again she held it outstretched until a drop of ocher fluid fell from her fingertip to the deck.

"I need your help," Kairos said, and Hera went to her friend.

With few words and many telling glances, they worked out a system. Hera found an emergency engineering toolkit and cut strips of clean cloth from her own uniform, spraying them with adhesive that had the odor of rancid cooking oil. Hera held the strips out; Kairos pressed her body against them, allowing Hera to wrap them around the woman's wounds without contact.

The thought that Hera was giving more time than she had—that her priority should be the bridge—nagged at her. But there was someone in front of her in need.

"You understand," Kairos said as she picked at a shred of her sleeve embedded between the chitin plates of her wounded arm. She pinched the cloth between thumb and forefinger, dislodging it partway forcefully enough to spatter the floor with blood drops.

Hera felt more fascination than revulsion. She'd seen too many gruesome wounds to be squeamish. She held out another makeshift bandage—the last, ready for application. "I don't, honestly. I don't need to in order to respect who you are."

Kairos kept pulling at the sleeve. When it began to tear she pinched it closer to the base before resuming. Soon it was removed, and Hera began to silently, delicately, wrap the arm.

"My people," Kairos said. Hera almost stopped; fearing that would disrupt the strange, intimate peace, she kept wrapping. "For my people, blood is precious. Blood is self. Healing is rejuvenation, not—not restoration. Healing is rejuvenation is *change.*"

She was struggling with the words. Hera saw Kairos's lips trembling, and nodded reassuringly before finishing with the bandage. The clean cloth had already begun to stain, but the blotches were only small discolorations. "I think that's the best we'll do," Hera said. "I should go, but—"

She stopped as Kairos bent over and began gathering the scraps cut from her own clothing. The woman began using them to mop up the blood on the deck.

Hera had to get to the bridge. She knew that.

"Can I help?" Hera asked.

Kairos looked up. "Do not touch it," she said, then nodded.

The emergency kit had a rag and a compressor bottle of cleanser. Hera joined Kairos, scrubbing away the last stains. The deck panels gleamed when they finished, and Hera wondered how many Imperial officers had spilled blood on the same surface.

Kairos took the rag and parted her lips again. Hera expected a *thank-you* or even an abrupt *goodbye.* "The suit," Kairos said at last. "You remember? The suit and mask?"

"Of course," Hera said. "I'm still getting used to you having a face."

"The suit is a chrysalis. A healing cocoon. In Cerberon it was removed."

Hera had been aboard the *Lodestar,* but she'd seen the footage: The U-wing in the wreckage of the Tri-Center Complex, Kairos crumpled in the ruins and Yrica Quell kneeling over her. "It was the only way to save you. The medics—"

"Caern Adan demanded it," Kairos said. "I know. He loved me."

Hera had never thought of Adan as a man who loved anything, though she nodded.

"IT-O, the machine, obeyed. It loved me, too. But they cut the suit. They took my mask. It was too soon, and my rejuvenation—my last rejuvenation—was not finished. Now I am—"

Her lips formed words without sound. Hera watched Kairos until the strange woman began trembling.

"You're what?" Hera asked.

"Incomplete."

Hera watched the blood-soaked hunter who had just confessed her secret.

"Thank you for trusting me," Hera said. "I won't tell anyone."

Kairos bowed her head. When she straightened and raised her bowcaster, the shadows fell across her face like a mask; then she slipped away down the corridor and disappeared into the darkness.

IV

The whistles and chimes came faster than Wyl could decipher them. He looked from T5, plugged into the socket beside the blast door, to Nath, who leaned over his astromech as if observing the stream of electricity and data. As T5's beeping trailed off, Nath's expression shifted from workmanlike interest to grim acceptance, and he turned to the blast door without a word.

"What's back there?" Wyl asked.

"Breach field override controls, just like we came for," Nath said. "Ask me what's *not* back there."

"What's not back there?"

"Oxygen. Looks like one of the sabotage droids triggered an escape pod. Must've kept the port from sealing after."

Wyl touched the metal of the blast door. It was absurd to think the surface felt icy, but he feared his fingertips would stick when he pulled them away. "All right," he said. "How far inside do we have to go? Any breath masks nearby . . . ?"

Nath shook his head. "Droid already checked. Nearest supply kit's nowhere close in this maze."

It had taken them the better part of an hour to weave through the ship, avoiding fires and breaches and scuttling sabotage droids. Once, Wyl had heard screams behind a barricade; they hadn't managed to shift it, and they hadn't spoken much since then.

"Control room itself isn't more than fifteen meters away," Nath went on, "but we're going to have a hell of a time getting there."

"How long can a human body survive in vacuum?" Wyl asked.

T5 squawked. Nath muttered, "You're full of useless information," then shrugged at Wyl. "We open the door, we'll get a minute or two of airflow before this section is fully vented. That might give a body insulation. It also means fighting a gale while working the machinery. After that . . . not long."

Wyl tried to decipher the crease in Nath's brow. "All right. Tell me exactly what I need to do—"

"You're not going anywhere. You're in command. Not the one who should risk himself."

It took longer than it should have for Wyl to understand.

"It's all right," Wyl said. He was surprised, but he tried not to show it and smiled thinly. "I'm not commanding anyone right now, and I can do it—"

"Your skinny butt will be blown out of the ship ten seconds in." Nath shook his head, rapped on the blast door, and then refocused on Wyl. "I'm twice your weight, I'm stronger, and I know the equipment better. It's an easy call, brother, and you know it."

Wyl opened his mouth, wanting to speak but unsure what to say or the cost of delaying further. How many people he knew had already burned to death, or suffocated, or—?

"We don't even know if this will work," he said. "How far to get suits and breath masks? Or maybe—"

Nath laughed an unkind laugh, the sound laced with bitterness.

"Maybe what? One of us has to go through there. You're not qualified, and T5's a junk heap. This conversation is just killing time."

Wyl had to force himself not to ask: *What are you doing, Nath?*

He knew Nath could be brave—he didn't doubt that—but the expirate had never been a man to endanger himself when there were alternatives. Had Wyl *shamed* him? Was it a role he was playing, like when he'd received his medal on Troithe and basked in the glory? Was he trying to *impress* Wyl?

What are you doing?

"We can find an alternative," Wyl said.

"Find it fast, then," Nath said. "Hold tight to one of those pipes—one that won't rip out of the wall. T5 will open the door, then close it once I'm through. That'll cut down on the wind force, and I'll have a few seconds to make it to the controls and back."

Wyl looked to T5, as if expecting the droid to join his protests. The droid did not. Nath had already turned away, tugging at pipes and conduits to test their strength.

"All right," Wyl said. "All right."

Nath only grunted.

Wyl retreated a short way down the corridor and wrapped his arms and legs around the largest cooling pipe he could find. T5 remained at the door, but Wyl heard the distinctive crackle of the droid engaging its magnetic grip and saw its thruster jets ignite—soft blue flames ready to counter the force of depressurization. The odor of fuel wafted through the air.

Nath held on to a horizontal power conduit with both hands, glancing between the corridor and the blast door. Wyl caught only a glimpse of the man's face and was sure he saw doubt.

Wyl was ready to call out again when Nath declared, "Do it!" and T5 squealed.

The blast door began to iris open. The first hiss of escaping air was no louder than comm static, and the current's touch barely riffled Wyl's hair. As the aperture grew, however, the tug became insistent. The hiss became a roar. T5's rockets flared and Wyl had to tighten his grip or be pulled away. He tried to fix his gaze on Nath as the man pulled himself along the conduit hand-over-hand, but grit splashed across Wyl's eyes and he was forced to squeeze them shut. He thought he heard a scream of frustration in the wind.

Wyl's grip began to weaken. His muscles twitched and his hands grew numb. He felt unbearably cold, yet even as he feared his body would fail him the roar became a hiss and the gale diminished and faded. The blast door was sealed. T5 rested firmly on the deck.

Nath was gone.

"Is he—" Wyl began, but it turned into a cough. T5 didn't seem to notice.

Wyl imagined Nath dragging himself through the corridor, body revolting against the vacuum, breathless and dying.

He let go of the cooling pipe. He swayed as he crossed to the blast door and gripped Nath's conduit under one arm. There was a sweet, chemical aroma in the air—something filtered through the vents when decompression had begun—and it made concentrating hard.

T5 beeped. Wyl didn't understand.

They waited.

Nath was dead, Wyl thought. He couldn't still be alive after—how long now? Nath was dead, sacrificed for reasons Wyl couldn't understand. Others would die, too, but—

Nath was dead.

He stared at the blast door.

The next sound Wyl heard was a metallic ring. He was momentarily convinced it was damage to his eardrums; then, absurdly, he thought it was a bell. By the time he realized what it truly meant, T5 was already squealing, rockets ablaze, and Wyl shouted, "Nath!" as if the man could hear him through the blast door.

The door irised again. The hiss and the breeze came, then the roar. Wyl secured himself despite the prickling in his hands, and saw Nath—the man's face purple with ruptured blood vessels, his eyes agog, legs whipped behind him by the wind. Nath was trying to pull himself forward but for every centimeter he gained he slid back another.

Wyl was past the point of strain. His muscles were in rebellion. Somehow he kept his grip on the conduit with one hand and extended the other, allowing it to flap in the wind like a ribbon.

He felt his fingers being crushed and saw Nath had grabbed on. Wyl pulled against the fury of the gale, pulled as T5 squealed and blasted its rockets, pulled as he and Nath both screamed. Both his shoulders felt ready to dislodge; his body seemed apt to tear in two. He found the strength to think *Nath is enduring worse,* and he pulled.

When he hit the deck, the wind had stopped. Nath lay on top of him, a crushing weight that was nothing compared with the pain of moments earlier.

"You did it," Wyl whispered.

Nath grunted and rolled to one side while T5 babbled away.

The astromech delivered updates as they lay limp and unmoving. The bridge had been alerted to the status of the breach field override, thanks to a message from T5, and General Syndulla had taken command of the ship. One by one the *Deliverance*'s compartments were flushed to remove as many sabotage droids as possible. Security teams were assembled to clear out the remainder and to assist crew members in need.

It would be a while before they had a casualty list. Wyl felt satisfied, nonetheless—they'd saved the ship.

Nath had saved the ship.

"We good?" Nath asked—groaned, really, as he rose to his knees beside Wyl. Despite the exhaustion in his tone, his expression was intent and alert.

He wanted an answer.

"We're good," Wyl said, and attempted to stand on trembling legs.

Nath caught him by the forearm, and Wyl couldn't say which of them pulled the other into a quick, fierce embrace. When they separated, Nath smirked and looked to T5. "You did half decent yourself," he said, and the droid returned a series of irritable chimes. Wyl laughed and rubbed the droid's top.

"We should get back," Wyl said. "Figure out where everyone's gathering—we don't really know we're safe."

"You're in charge," Nath said. "Lead the way."

Wyl did, and gladly. With Nath behind him, the older man couldn't see Wyl's expression.

We're good meant *everything's fine between us,* but that was a lie. Wyl knew he could trust in Nath Tensent's protection, as he had at Cerberon; as he had just minutes before. But it was Nath's sense of duty and compassion toward others that Wyl doubted, not the bond between Nath and himself.

If Nath had faced death by suffocation to save the *Deliverance* alone, he might have restored Wyl's faith. But his every act seemed spurred by personal loyalty (or worse, greed); not by a reverence for life. It made trust difficult when the stakes were higher than the lives of Nath and Wyl and the rest of their squadron; when whole worlds were at risk.

Then again, what else could Nath *do* to win Wyl's trust? If Wyl looked askance at any act he took—attributed every sacrifice Nath made to ulterior motives—only a secret deed Wyl never heard about would be evidence of heroism.

He suppressed a sigh. He made himself smile. He would do his best to feign comfort for Nath's sake. How could he do anything less, when the man had nearly died for him?

It would all be over soon anyway. He thought about the words of Elder Zephyr of Polyneus, whom he'd spoken to over the comm after leaving Chass in the hangar. Wyl had told the man of his desire to return Home; relayed General Syndulla's reassurances that the war was ending. "But planets are dying," Wyl had said, "and they need me here to stop disaster. When our mission is done, I *will* come back. Even if the war isn't finished. When our mission is over . . ."

The elder had looked at him sadly, smiled a distorted holographic smile, and told him of Stam Groundling of the village of Tor, who had arrived on Polyneus the day before. Wyl had smiled and looked nervously at the deteriorating transmission readout and asked, as gently as he could, why the elder had chosen to share that particular story.

"One hundred and twenty warriors left Home to fight the Empire," the elder had said. "Some are gone from this existence, but of those who live Stam was one of two who had not returned.

"Now you are the last, Wyl Lark. Your people await you."

It *had* to be over soon, Wyl thought, and wished he could say as much to Nath. For now, that truth would remain his own.

He hoped the others were faring well. He hoped the pressure they'd all faced in the belly of the Star Destroyer had turned the squadrons to diamonds, not crushed them to dust.

V

Maybe Chass na Chadic was wanted and maybe she wasn't. But she wasn't *needed,* not in the crisis with the sabotage droids—she'd been midway through the forward particle flow tube when power had been restored and warning lights had blazed around her. She'd squeezed into a shelter station (getting intimate with the offline repair droid inside) before the tube had flooded with energized gas, and spent the next hour searching for a way out.

She'd heard General Syndulla announce that the *Deliverance* was safe and—by implication—that Chass's efforts had been pointless. She'd found her way to the hangar anyway, filthy save for the breath-mask-shaped clean spot around her mouth and nose. She was profoundly exhausted, ready for a shower and sleep, as she dropped out of one of the TIE rack's hydraulic shafts and hit the deck beside a dismantled X-wing.

The voice of Let'ij declared: "Every time you pick up a weapon, you become someone else's tool."

It was not a voice in Chass's head.

There was laughter in the hangar, and other voices, too. She crept around the X-wing heap and spotted a team of mechanics standing across the bay by her B-wing. She couldn't make out much of the vessel itself—it was blocked by a Wild Squadron V-wing—but she could see its canopy was open.

"Maybe," Let'ij's voice went on, "you think you're fighting for yourself? You think that's better than being the tool of the Empire or the rebels or the Hutts. But at best you're a cog in their violent machinery. Even if you don't swear yourself to a cause, the police state and the terrorist state thrive on violence . . ."

Chass took a step toward her fighter, then another, as she attempted to separate out the voices. Let'ij kept delivering her lecture as the mechanics laughed and one asked, "What *is* this?"

"Not what I was looking to wind down with."

"Give it time—maybe she starts dancing?"

Chass's hips ached from the long crawl, but she increased her pace as the ground crew kept talking. As she passed the V-wing she saw a rough black scar across the B-wing's hull; but her eyes were drawn to an object tossed from one mechanic to another. "Here!" the first mechanic said, and the second held the object up to the light.

It glittered like the cheap junk it was.

It was one of the amulets she'd bought at the Circus of Mortal Appetites. One of the trinkets that had decorated her cockpit.

"What the hell?" she shouted, and she was running now. She saw her box of audio chips on the floor. "You went through my stuff?"

"One of the sabotage droids got into the hangar," a woman said. She sounded afraid. "Cut up six ships. *Everything* was scattered, we were just cleaning it up—"

"We wanted some music!" a man cried, clutching a playback device to his chest as if it were a shield.

"True violence," Let'ij said, "is the hypocrisy of a social contract betrayed by state and society the moment it becomes inconvenient."

The man with the amulet was closest to Chass. Her run became a leap and she was in midair as she threw her first punch. The thief's body cushioned her fall and his chin cushioned her knuckles. She snapped up her amulet and was upright an instant later.

Someone grabbed her from behind. She tossed back her head, felt the back of her skull smash a nose. There were shouts and screams as more bodies clustered around her. Some buried part of her brain sneered: *I almost died trying to save you all. You didn't even bother to look for me.*

She saw a flash of a tattooed face—Ragnell, the ground crew chief, yelling for them to break up the fight. Chass ignored her and felt an audio chip shatter under her boot as she struggled. She heard Let'ij's voice again, this time clear and mournful inside her own mind:

Now do you understand?

They will always mock you, Maya Hallik. You may as well come home.

CHAPTER 6

THE SEVEN ALGORITHMIC ÉTUDES OF VARDOS

I

"Tell me again how it happened," Soran said as they studied the body. He stood at the head of the Emperor's Messenger, looking to Yrica Quell at its feet. The yellow light of the engineering storeroom painted the machine's red robes with fire, as if the charred hole in its chest were in danger of reigniting; as if the Messenger might spark its own funeral pyre and transform into ash and smoke.

"I was trying to patch one of the reactor subsystems," Quell said. "I heard a plasma conduit burst and I turned around. I found it like this."

"What was it doing down there?" Soran asked.

"I don't know. It didn't say anything."

Soran observed her. She was watching him and trying not to show it. That told him little—it was certainly possible she had been involved in the machine's destruction, but equally likely she was innocent and concerned about his own reaction. He'd never told her how much he'd hated the machine, or that he'd been responsible for the crack in its faceplate. She had every reason to wish to understand his relationship to the Emperor's ghost, and he'd hinted at his plans often enough—

Supposing she had been involved in its destruction, *why* had she done it? Had it discovered something about her—some secret about her time at Traitor's Remorse or what had become of her after Nacronis? Had she discovered something about *it,* choosing to destroy the machine rather than allow it to carry out its plans? Had the pilots begun to pay homage to it again, and Quell had put a stop to that troubling idolatry?

The longer he kept Quell at his side, the more her original motivations—whatever had happened to her inside the New Republic—had seemed to become irrelevant. As circumstances around them shifted, he'd believed her loyalties would come into alignment with his own; that if she wasn't yet his ally in his private struggle, she would become such sooner or later. Yet if she was capable of so dramatic an action as destroying the Messenger, he might need to reexamine his assumptions.

"Colonel?" Quell said.

He waved a hand distractedly. He was competent at reading people, but these conspiratorial games required one to probe, to feint, to turn the flat of one's words to an edge. They had never been his specialty; even Colonel Nuress had tried to stay away from the subterfuge of the upper ranks of Imperial leadership.

Then again, Quell had always been poor at deceiving anyone but herself. *Call it a draw,* he decided.

"My thoughts were drifting," he explained. "Shall we begin the operation?"

"Where do you want to start?" Quell hefted a laser saw from the storeroom's tool rack.

They began by removing the chest plate, which proved more difficult than Soran had expected. Like politics, cyber-engineering was outside the scope of his formal education but not utterly foreign to his experiences. Nonetheless, he'd never before worked on a droid without any apparent access mechanisms. There were no bolts to remove from the Messenger, no release toggles they could identify, so they did their best to cut away its casing without damaging the interior.

Neither Soran nor Quell mentioned the ostensible reason for the operation: to assess the machine's damage and determine whether it could be repaired. Together they noted the extensive burns covering the locomotor and servoprocessor modules and extracted both without further study. They delicately parted clumps of wiring like jungle vines, peering at a ridged cylinder that might have been a power source but followed no design Soran recognized.

The deeper they went into the machine, the less classifiable the components became. "If we had specifications to work from," Quell said as Soran crouched beside the body, blindly probing the chest cavity with a bare hand, "I still couldn't tell you why this thing works."

Soran ran his fingers over a cold metal box capped with rubber. It might have been a repulsor element. "What do you say we remove the faceplate?" he asked. "I'd be interested to see its memory circuits."

Quell nodded cautiously as he withdrew his hand.

"With memory access," Soran offered, "perhaps we could run a diagnostic?"

"Of course," Quell replied.

There was something taboo about disintegrating the magnetic clasps around the faceplate. The Messenger was not the Emperor but they were defiling a being that carried the Emperor's spirit. Soran thought of the peoples of Navosh-Hul, whom he'd read about as a child. He'd been told their burial rituals were meant to protect the living from the unkind dead. Archaeologists had discovered corpses in shrouds seven layers thick, each sheet of cloth painted with warnings to proceed no further. One message translated as: THERE IS NOTHING OF VALUE HERE. THERE ARE NO ANSWERS. THERE IS ONLY CONTAMINATION OF THE SOUL.

It was not a heartening thought, and he did not share it with Quell.

They removed the faceplate and the holoprojector immediately beneath. The head was otherwise hollow, lacking photoreceptors or audio sensors, but in the stump of the neck they discovered an obsidian cylinder glittering with indicator lights and nested in wire fila-ments. "Some sort of housing," Quell said. "Maybe its memory circuits are inside."

Their breath was enough to send movement through the filaments, giving them the appearance of life.

"Why did it need all this?" Soran murmured. "What was it really built for?"

Quell said nothing. Soran hadn't expected an answer.

He looked directly at her and spoke in a clearer voice. "Have you ever wondered how it chose us?"

"For Cinder, you mean?" she asked.

Soran nodded. "It wasn't convenience—I doubt these machines picked their agents based on proximity and firepower alone."

Every Imperial unit chosen by the Messengers had agreed to par-ticipate in the atrocities of Operation Cinder—every one Soran was aware of, at any rate. Even inside the Empire, that was a startling dis-play of loyalty.

"Someone made a list," Quell said. "The Emperor himself or some-one close to him. Someone knew the Messengers' agenda and picked commanders trusted to obey, and programmed the droids with a list."

"And when was this list assembled? When was it last updated? Were there alternates in case a commander was killed or their forces deci-mated?" Soran looked at the mass of obscure technology at his feet and shook his head. "This thing's systems were meant for *more*. It *de-cided* who would carry out Operation Cinder. But based on what?"

"Competence?" Quell tried. "Sadism?"

Soran managed a bitter smile. "Maybe. Whatever qualities it looked for . . . how did it identify them at all? How did it know Colonel Nuress and the lot of us were competent—or sadistic—enough to see this through?"

Quell looked away when she saw that *he* saw her watching him. "Why do you ask?" she said.

"Curiosity."

It was a lie, but he couldn't have told her the truth. The real answer was inchoate in his mind—an instinct like the seed of a plan. There was something of importance there. He needed time to deduce its meaning.

For the first time in weeks, however, he felt emboldened.

"Tell no one of this," he said, "and secure the storage room when we leave. We'll draw up a schematic together, and continue the dissection in shifts."

II

There were days Yrica Quell believed Colonel Soran Keize didn't matter to the fate of the 204th. The Emperor's Messenger didn't matter. General Syndulla was already in pursuit, and even if Quell died tomorrow, Syndulla and Alphabet might still intercept Shadow Wing and end the second Operation Cinder. Or Shadow Wing might elude the New Republic and continue its genocidal mission anyway. Keize's musings about the Emperor and Imperial soldiers changed nothing.

Yet the way Keize had spoken to her above the corpse of the Messenger—the way he'd accepted her excuses and hid her crime from the crew—hung off her thoughts like a barb, tearing at her mind.

It was a distraction she didn't need.

"You hear what our next target is?" Rikton asked as they disassembled faulty proton torpedoes in the hangar. They'd already removed the warheads—Quell had been skeptical about Rikton's abilities, but he'd been as careful as possible given the equipment at hand—and now they'd let their guard down, relieved to be past the danger.

"I hear the same things you do," Quell said. "The colonel will give us details when we arrive in-sector."

She watched Rikton pop out current regulators with trained ease. He could've glanced her way, but he kept his eyes on his torpedo. He couldn't have been more than twenty, and carried himself with the awkwardness of a teenager uncomfortable in his own body.

"I heard it might be Fikzwaa," he said. "Natives are these little critters, height of your knee. Billions of 'em. Tossed out the Empire after Endor, right? But maybe someone came back, set up a base, and we've got to go destroy it."

Would that bother you? she wanted to ask. *Killing billions of non-humans?*

Quell shrugged. "We're on a small ship. There're always rumors going around—I wouldn't assume they're true."

"I don't. It's why I'm asking you—you're tight with the colonel, right?"

Quell frowned at him. "Meaning what?"

"Just—" He looked up now, face entirely innocent. "—you're his aide. He's not a talkative fellow, but you might've heard something."

She thought it over, nodded, and resumed sorting detonite triggers. "I haven't." She paused. "What makes you say he's not talkative?"

"Well, he can keep a secret anyway. I sort of know him a little." A smile flickered across his face, quick as a moth, and he glanced surreptitiously around the hangar. "You heard he hasn't always been with Shadow Wing, right? That he was gone awhile after Endor?"

"I heard," she said.

"We crossed paths out there," Rikton said. "He helped me through a rough spot. Put me on a good path—better than I was on, anyway, until . . ."

She waited. He shrugged, as if his meaning were obvious. "Until what?" she asked.

"Until the rebels came for me. Not *came*, but—apparently they've got rules against working with anyone hiring ex-Imperials. Lost the job I'd found, drifted a little. Was lucky to find Devon again." His eyes widened, and he amended: "Keize. The colonel. He even remembered me."

"He's a good man," she said. It had come out unintentionally, but it was too late to take it back.

"He's a hero," Rikton said. "Doesn't matter *what* our next target is. I'm with him, and not just because I don't have much of a choice."

It could've sounded bitter but he flashed a broad grin and she laughed softly. Inwardly, she cursed herself. She was starting to like Rikton.

She was starting to like him even as she plotted his death.

She was awaiting her chance to send another signal to the New Republic. She needed to do it before Shadow Wing really did pick a target with billions of civilians to murder. When Syndulla came, maybe the *Yadeez* could be disabled, maybe Rikton would end up in an escape pod, but that couldn't be the plan.

"You were a pilot, right?" Rikton asked.

"Yes."

"You ever going to fly again?"

"No. I don't know. We'll see where I'm needed," she said, and while the answer didn't appear to satisfy Rikton he seemed to accept she wasn't going to talk about it.

She wondered who Shadow Wing would be flying against when Syndulla came, and who among Alphabet Squadron was still alive.

III

Only the eyes of Grand Moff Randd were steady above the holoprojector. The rest of his body wavered, dissipated, and re-formed, but the eyes stayed. They seemed wide and sleepless to Soran—the eyes of a brilliant man who had lain awake for days, knowing predators were about.

"—your recruits from Fedovoi End arrived at Jakku thirty hours ago," the moff said, though Soran struggled to make out the words. "You should've warned us—our supplies are limited. We can't take in every shipful of strays you find."

"My apologies," Soran said. "Making contact has been extremely difficult, and your needs are unknown to me."

There was a burst of static that might have been laughter. "They would be. Very well, the newcomers are soft, but this world . . . it hardens all of us. We'll find a use for them. You'll see the sandstorms soon enough, too."

Soran tried to picture it: Jakku, a dustball of a world bereft of anything but a few nonaligned outposts, lacking infrastructure and natural resources, now housing the largest gathering of Imperial warships and troops since the Battle of Endor. He envisioned stormtroopers crammed into bunkers like refugees, their armor unable to cope with the desert heat; pilots whose rations had been cut to half portions, who went comet-mining in search of water.

He hadn't told anyone inside the 204th of the fleet's secret location. He wondered if even the most loyal would be shaken by the truth.

But then, the rebels had endured the gelid world of Hoth. Loyalty could be an inflexible thing.

"May I ask," Soran said, "what became of Grand Admiral Sloane? I haven't received an update from her in some time."

The eyes narrowed. "She is not your concern. Your orders come from me now."

"I understand," Soran said, and worried he did.

"For now," Randd said, "continue as you were. When your mission to Chadawa is complete, contact us again and I will provide a new target."

Soran nodded in a manner he hoped appeared humble. He considered whether to say more—whether to mention General Syndulla's pursuit, for one—but saw no advantage in it. Randd's priorities were not Soran's priorities, and Soran could safeguard the 204th better while unfettered by additional orders.

"Understood," he said, and the hologram flashed away.

Less than an hour after that lie of omission he set to more active deception. "The Imperial fleet grows stronger each day," he told the squadron commanders. The *Yadeez* had no formal conference room, so they sat on empty crates pulled inside the refrigeration unit. The coolers had been deactivated but the room smelled of meat and mildew. "It is my belief that our leadership is preparing to engage the New Republic directly—and soon. For now, however . . ."

He looked from pilot to pilot. Some he knew well: Commander Broosh had been a friend before Endor and his most trusted adviser after Soran's return to the 204th. Phesh was not a friend, but he was familiar; he'd been with the unit nearly as long as Soran could remember, steady and competent throughout.

Others had been promoted to their positions after deaths at Cerberon. He'd chosen Captain Armenauth to replace Gablerone, hoping the man's long-standing familiarity with his squadron would make up for his unearned confidence. Squadron Two now followed one of the recruits from Dybbron III, a woman named Starzha past her prime as a pilot but whom Soran knew by reputation as an able commander.

He was taking a risk on her. He was taking so many risks.

"For now," he went on, "we will proceed to the Chadawa system and eliminate the rogue Imperial forces there. I expect Chadawa to prove a challenge, but we have several days in which to prepare our strategy. Study the data we have, no matter how outdated. Speak to your squadrons, see if anyone has personal knowledge that may prove useful. We'll reconvene and assemble an attack plan with enough time for drills and adjustments."

He gauged their reactions. For a few, it appeared the name Chadawa held no special meaning. Broosh's shoulders stiffened. Wisp let out a whinnying breath before clasping a hand over her mouth.

"I know I'm new," Starzha said. "I'm still getting to know the wing. But I can't help but notice some tension among the pilots and crew."

"Do we have a morale problem?" Soran asked.

"'Morale' is a misdiagnosis," Phesh said. Starzha arched her brow but didn't interrupt. "It's discipline. Our people have grown so familiar with one another that they're forgetting that devotion to the mission comes before—everything else."

"'Everything else' being . . . ?" Starzha asked.

Phesh didn't answer. Soran looked around the room. Most of the attention was on Starzha and Phesh, but the last thing Soran needed was a rivalry between his squadron commanders.

He glanced toward Broosh, who caught his meaning and said, "I can't speak for the other squadrons, but my people are in decent spirits, under the circumstances. They *are* on edge, though."

The others shifted their attention. Soran tried not to look smug. "Tell me why," Soran said.

"You can take a hunting dog out of the woods. Give it work to do, let it chase rats and other vermin around the house. But if it gets a sniff of its original quarry, it'll whine at the fences for days."

Wisp giggled. Phesh stared awhile, then nodded soberly.

"They want to go after the rebels," Soran said.

"They want General Syndulla," Broosh said. "These anti-treason missions from High Command have given us all focus, and we're grateful. But half of us joined the military to fight these people—the rebels—and with Syndulla . . ."

"Some of us take it personally," Wisp said.

"You want to finish the job we began at Cerberon," Soran said, and shrugged lightly. "I understand that. It isn't the mission, but we all have colleagues we'd like to avenge."

Starzha looked between the others. She hadn't met Syndulla in battle yet, hadn't been at Pandem Nai or Cerberon, and she looked ready to object.

Soran cut her off before she could. "Make sure that all our new recruits are thoroughly briefed on Syndulla and known members of Alphabet Squadron—Wyl Lark and his ilk." They'd tentatively identified the Y-wing pilot as a man named Nath Tensent, thanks to public broadcasts of a medal ceremony on Troithe; the B-wing pilot remained anonymous, but Shadow Wing had worked up an extensive profile on the pilot's tactics long ago. The X-wing pilot had gone down at Pandem Nai, before Soran's return. Only the U-wing's status was in question. "The support squadrons as well—Syndulla may have replaced or rotated them, but we might as well be thorough.

"Direct engagement is not our goal, but we can assume the foe was not destroyed by the sabotage droids. They will pursue. If they find us, I want the advantage."

That seemed to satisfy the commanders. The meeting reached its end, and as Soran watched the others file out of the refrigeration unit he thought about Lieutenant Palal Seedia—one of Gablerone's pilots, the woman with an aristocrat's sense of duty and vengeance. Soran had chosen her to fly on his wing at Cerberon, and had lost her over Catadra. He'd had hopes for her future; now she was one of many lives half forgotten, taken by Syndulla and her people.

He understood his people's instincts. He would've relished the opportunity to fight Syndulla again himself—a chance to prove the 204th's superiority.

But his priority was the unit's survival, and that remained far from assured.

He exited into the central corridor of the *Yadeez* and made his way to the corpse of the Emperor's Messenger.

CHAPTER 7

THE ROYAL ANTHEM OF ALDERAAN

I

Two days after the *Deliverance* completed emergency repairs, the battleship emerged into the Ciaox Verith system. The cerulean glow of hyperspace tore back from the bridge's viewport, replaced by rippling serpents of jade plasma against a star-specked night. Hera almost gasped at the beauty of the display, but she forced herself to turn to the comscan officer instead.

"Trying to get a clear reading through the plasma storm," the officer said. "That frequency you gave us—not picking anything up yet, but it'll take a while to sort through the distortion." The officer was Cathar, with neatly knotted fur; petite enough that Hera wondered if she qualified as an adult among her species.

Not that Hera hadn't put children in the line of fire before.

"Do your best," Hera said. "Take whatever time you need."

Ciaox Verith was the end of a trail sniffed out by New Republic Intelligence—the point of origin for the latest of several comm bursts seemingly produced by a malfunctioning transmitter aboard Shadow Wing's bulk freighter. There was a chance the bursts were bait for a trap; a better chance that they were real but not a lasting phenomenon. Either way, they were the *Deliverance's* best lead.

Commander Arvad—*Captain* Arvad, since the sabotage droids' attack—looked to Hera. "What's our plan if we don't find anything?" she asked.

"Things get a lot harder—" Hera began, and stopped as the comscan officer turned.

"General," the Cathar said. "I can't be sure, but I think they're here."

"Scramble the fighters," Hera said, crisp but not harsh. If the woman was wrong, if it was a false alarm, it wouldn't matter. If she was right, though? Hera moved to the comscan station. "Show me what you've got."

The noise level rose as Arvad called the crew to battle stations; as flight officers and fire control chiefs sent orders to ready the hangar for launch and to power the main guns; as a thousand lesser tasks went to hundreds of crew members who kept the Destroyer ready for war. Hera could feel the sounds, sense the voices through her head-tails, and found them comfortingly familiar.

The Cathar indicated a display showing objects in motion above a gas giant. "What are we seeing?" Hera asked, then answered her own question. "One mark massive enough to be the *Yadeez*. The other large ones could be sensor shadows, or maybe escort ships. The small ones could be TIEs, but—"

"They look like they're fighting," the comscan officer said. "Could they be shooting at rogue Imperials?"

"I don't—" Hera wanted to vocalize her thought, but it was only a hunch. She needed evidence. "Take us closer, and put me through to our fighters. Is Lark out there?"

There was more chatter and noise—headsets adjusted and replies called out. "General!" came a distorted voice through the comm. "Wyl Lark here. Flare Squadron's with me. The rest are prepping for takeoff."

"What do you see?" she asked. "Do you have a visual?"

"Lots of movement, but it's dark—no cannon flash. There're TIEs deployed but they're not in position . . ." Wyl trailed off even as Hera felt a surge of excitement. "General, I think they were running a drill. They're moving into attack formation now, but I don't think they expected—"

"*Go!*" Hera lurched upright, doubted herself as she called out. "*Deliverance,* move to engage. Lark, begin your attack!"

Is this madness? she wondered. *Is it hope?* Neither would be enough if she'd misjudged Shadow Wing and Soran Keize. But she was operating on instinct now—instinct honed over years of warfare, months of studying the 204th, yet instinct nonetheless.

The man she'd loved, the father of her child, would've called it the guidance of the Force.

Maybe it was just tactics.

"Entering combat range," Wyl said. She listened for fear and heard none, though stress made him brusque. "Enemy shots fired. Breaking away!"

The comm went silent. Hera wanted to hear the whole squadron over the bridge comm while she stared at the dots playing across the scanner. Instead she went to Arvad's side as the bridge officers called updates and the deck trembled. A plasma serpent slithered across the bow of the *Deliverance* and the great ship shook it off with barely a shudder.

Until today the 204th had always, *always* been ready for them. This was an opportunity they had to seize.

"Hail and Wild squadrons launching now. Thirty seconds until the *Deliverance* is in range," Arvad said. "Suggest we train turbolasers on the bulk freighter. Put them on the defensive."

"Agreed," Hera said.

Someone was calling attack vectors. Sensor readings sketched in the bulk freighter's four escorts, none larger than a corvette. Hera watched the looming gas giant on the viewscreen and the black dots like flies. Flashes of light suggested heavy fire. "Faster," she whispered.

"TIEs returning to the *Yadeez,*" someone declared. "Enemy preparing to retreat."

Hit their engines! she urged. But she stayed silent, because Wyl Lark knew the situation and didn't need a distraction.

A brighter flash scarred the view. She knew what it meant. "Lark?" she said. "What happened?"

Static pulsed through the speakers before his voice finally answered: "They jumped to lightspeed. Couldn't close fast enough to stop them."

She waited. She *felt* the suppressed emotion in the words. She asked again: "What happened?"

"One TIE destroyed. One of ours lost, too. Lieutenant T'oknell. I think he was surprised."

"I'm sorry," Hera said, and she was.

But they'd been *close*. Shadow Wing wouldn't get far.

The second battle played out much like the first. The *Deliverance* had spent almost a day jumping system-to-system, searching for any sign of the 204th along its last known trajectory, before another comm burst gave the crew the lead they needed. They caught up with the bulk freighter in the Red Yars system, fighters already spaceborne and weapons charged.

This time the enemy was prepared as well. Chass na Chadic and Boyvech Toons were the only New Republic pilots to loose shots, and neither was in range when Shadow Wing jumped to lightspeed. The *Deliverance* had lost its quarry seconds after locating them.

That was all right, Hera decided. They were learning.

The third encounter was a daring one. With no new comm burst to follow, the *Deliverance* resumed its system-by-system search and—seemingly favored by the Force—found the enemy in a matter of hours. The Star Destroyer emerged from hyperspace at maximum velocity with its tractor beam primed, and managed to lock on to the smaller bulk freighter from a considerable distance.

The plan—developed by Hera and Wyl Lark together—was for the squadrons to stay close to the *Deliverance* and protect the tractor beam projector under cover of the Star Destroyer's point-defense weaponry. The plan was flawed. Within a minute two TIEs had leapt and spun and danced around the squadrons to close on the projector. Their cannons were insufficient to damage the equipment and break the tractor lock; but one of the TIEs never reduced its acceleration, never veered away, and impacted the beam projector like a meteor. The tractor beam was obliterated and three crew members aboard the *Deliverance* killed.

Shadow Wing escaped again. Hera said kind things at the funerals and sat with Wyl afterward as he stared at the stars.

"I never thought they would resort to a suicide run so fast," he told her. "I've never seen them fight that way before."

"We never came at them in a Star Destroyer before," she answered.

The fourth encounter came days later, after another comm burst came through. Without a tractor beam the *Deliverance* was forced to take a new approach, exiting hyperspace deep in-system in the hope of surprising the 204th. The system—just an alphanumeric designation, never mapped—turned out to be cluttered with planetoids and debris. The *Deliverance* was able to force the *Yadeez* and its escorts toward one of the planetoids, preventing it from jumping to lightspeed while TIEs skirmished with New Republic starfighters.

The fighting lasted six minutes before Shadow Wing escaped once more. Two TIEs were destroyed and no friendly casualties were added to the record, save for a single minor injury to Genni Avremif, whose ejector seat had triggered accidentally on landing.

It was a victory by some measures. Hera joined the pilots in the ready room for the celebration, watching Vitale declare, "A new record!" and scrawl 387 SECONDS on the tactical board. Denish Wraive, the centuries-old pilot who'd transferred with Vitale after Cerberon and taken leadership of Wild Squadron, held court in one corner telling the story of his encounters with the 204th in the underworld of Troithe. Nath Tensent and his droid talked gear and loadouts with the Y-wing pilots of Hail Squadron.

Wyl Lark and Chass na Chadic were there, but neither seemed in a celebratory mood. Wyl moved among the crowd, occasionally taking aside a pilot for a lengthy conversation (most of which involved encouraging smiles and an embrace toward the end). He was a fine leader, Hera thought, seeing to his troops and recognizing those straining under pressure or mourning T'oknell; but when he thought no one was looking, his shoulders stiffened and his expression went flat.

Chass, meanwhile, sat with the pilots at the tactical board giving new names to the TIE pilots. They passed around a datapad, watching flight recorder video and arguing.

"It *was* the same TIE that went after the tractor beam! Look at the way it veers!"

"Their whole squadron does that. We don't know it's the same pilot—"

"It's the same pilot! It's Dizzy!"

Chass scowled through it all and made it clear that some things weren't to be disputed. "No," she said. "It's Char. Pretty and cleaned up, but it's still Char."

Hera thought of Wyl and Chass's time aboard the *Hellion's Dare,* when they'd been pursued through the Oridol Cluster by the 204th: They'd been chased jump after jump and lost their comrades one by one. She'd never spoken to either about the experience, but she couldn't imagine what it was like for them to see the tragedy through a mirror.

She couldn't imagine what it was like for the pilots of the 204th, either, but they weren't her responsibility.

When she returned to her office, there was an unsigned report awaiting her. Chass na Chadic was the subject.

"I can mess up your face," Chass said.

"I don't doubt it," Hera replied. "What I *asked* is whether you can tell me about the Children of the Empty Sun."

The Theelin showed teeth and leaned back in the little metal folding chair on the other side of Hera's desk. Hera's own chair, sturdy and black, was built into the deck; apparently the office's original owner had preferred to leave subordinates standing.

"New Republic cracking down on unauthorized faiths?" Chass asked.

Hera tried not to sigh. There hadn't been a good way to open the conversation, so she'd hoped bluntness would carry them both through. She still wasn't convinced she was wrong. "I'm not asking because of your—or anyone's—faith," Hera said. "But I understand you got in a fight with your ground crew—"

"Because they stole my stuff!"

"—and that you've started praying on the squadron comm during firefights."

Chass looked smug. "Just once. It was a meditative chant. Helped me focus."

"And I'm sure it had nothing to do with tweaking the ground crew," Hera replied. *You want adolescent sarcasm? I can be sarcastic, too.* "Now, all of this should be between you and your squadron commander. If he wants to let it slide, I'm willing to let it slide, and your religion is none of my concern. However . . ."

Chass stared at her, impatient and apparently oblivious. In that moment, Hera was certain the accusation was false. As difficult as Chass could be, as destructive as her behavior sometimes became, she wasn't stupid.

But Hera had a job to do.

". . . I need to know the truth. I received a complaint that you've been in contact with the Children, and that you sent an unauthorized transmission from the *Deliverance*." *That you gave away our location and Shadow Wing found us the same way we've been finding them. That you're indirectly responsible for what happened with the sabotage droids.* She went on before Chass could answer: "Is there *anything* about that accusation that rings true? Anything at all I need to know, as someone responsible for the security of this ship?"

Chass shifted in her chair and cocked her head. "I heard Stornvein was making out with an ensign in the medbay. Do you need to know that?"

Hera waited. "The accusation, pilot."

"Fine. No. There is nothing about the accusation that rings true."

"All right," Hera said, matter-of-fact as she could. "You're dismissed."

Chass rose with the grace of a dancer, dipped her torso in a bow, and marched out of Hera's office.

You could've been more supportive, Hera thought, and rubbed her temples with both hands. If Chass had fallen in with one of the thousand cults springing up across the galaxy, at least she hadn't picked some neo-Sith society or a band of hermit solipsists. Hera had read the brief on the Children of the Empty Sun before calling Chass in— it wasn't more than two paragraphs long but it indicated the Children had done at least as much good for the people of Cerberon as harm.

Maybe it was all fine. Maybe Chass needed more support than Hera and Wyl and the crew of the *Deliverance* could give. They didn't even have a therapist aboard since the loss of Caern Adan and his interrogation droid.

Or maybe Hera had just now pushed Chass—always rebellious, quick to take offense, and resistant to any hint of authority—right into the cult's arms.

She couldn't afford to think about that. She could barely afford to wonder who *had* given away the *Deliverance*'s position, if not Chass. She had to plan for the next encounter with Shadow Wing, and hope to make it the last.

II

There nearly wasn't a fifth battle. Syndulla's forces had caught up with the 204th too many times, and the crew of the *Yadeez* had taken it upon themselves to determine what tracking device or malfunction or mole was leading her to them time and again. Engineers swept the ship with scanners and tore off access panels at every junction.

Yrica Quell had no solution to this quandary—no plausible suspect to frame for her crimes, nor the technical expertise to lead the investigators astray. She'd been able to conceal her murder of the Emperor's Messenger because Colonel Keize had assisted, but though Keize warned the crew against paranoia he permitted the sweeps. In Quell's traitorous mission, she had no allies.

She ultimately chose boldness over subterfuge. She sent another comm burst when the opportunity came—when Keize was expecting her to continue the dissection of the Messenger and when the engineers, thanks to Keize, expected her to be aboard one of the Raider corvettes. When she'd finished the deed and the transmission was complete, she smashed the transmitter and dumped the pieces in the furnace.

She observed the ensuing fight from the bridge. They'd stopped in the Ghonoath system to permit one of the Raiders to refuel (an operation impossible to perform in-flight, thanks to the "improvements" its former owners had made to its drive system). The *Yadeez* and its escorts plunged into the atmosphere of a radioactive deathworld to hamper Syndulla and her squadrons, attempting to buy the Raider time to finish.

Quell stood by Keize as she had at Dybbron, Kortatka, and Fedovoi End. She did not attempt to mislead or confuse him as he sent orders to the TIE squadrons, coordinating their defense against the New Republic. She did not intervene when Keize ordered the TIE bombers to drop their payloads without detonator timers, so that the proton bombs might drift like mines on the planet's fierce winds. She didn't say anything when the bombs exploded, shredding two X-wings and their pilots.

She did not blink away tears. She rode helplessness like a raft on dark water, unsure of where she would land and carried ever-forward.

She did not act when Garl Lykan, the man Alphabet Squadron had called Snapper, lost power to his port stabilizer and was forced to fall back. She listened to his squadron shout as a trio of X-wings converged on his position and loosed enough cannon fire to obliterate a mountaintop—as if Lykan were singularly responsible for every death Syndulla's forces had suffered, and the murderous thrashing was richly deserved.

But Lykan wasn't responsible. Quell was.

Keize found a way out for them, as he always did. Quell didn't entirely understand the science, but he brought the TIEs back aboard and skipped the *Yadeez* off the planet's atmosphere like a stone. When the bulk freighter was jolted he fell to all fours, catlike, while Quell crashed hard into the deck and felt blood pouring from her nose. They jumped to lightspeed moments later along with the refueling Raider and other escorts.

She breathed through her mouth as Keize lifted her to her feet. She heard Captain Nenvez crawling across the deck, his cane lost, two of his cadets hovering over him as he attempted to reach a third cadet hunched motionless over a console.

Damn you, Syndulla, she thought. *Why can't you just kill us and be done?*

Lykan's funeral was that evening. They gathered in the hangar bay, though the ground crews hadn't finished work and had to shut off the plasma cutter and fuel pumps. The air smelled like superheated metal even through Quell's broken nose. Many of the pilots were still in their flight suits, and all in all it was an undignified showing, no matter the nods to Imperial propriety.

Quell attended because she couldn't refuse.

Grandmother had overseen memorials aboard the *Pursuer.* Keize had apparently delegated the task during Quell's absence—he stood near the front of the gathering but allowed Captain Armenauth, Lykan's squadron leader, to take charge. The young man's usual swagger was absent as he stepped into the shadow of a TIE bomber and spoke nearly too softly to be heard over the noises of the ship.

"Flight Commander Lykan was killed in action at sixteen thirty-two hours. As of now, Lieutenant Kandende is elevated to flight commander. I have every confidence he will serve the squadron ably and—"

Armenauth stopped. The crowd of unwashed pilots observed. They knew how the ritual was supposed to go—the elevation of the next-in-line and the private reading of the deceased's final testament—but Armenauth had diverged.

"He saved my life once, just after Endor," Armenauth confessed. "He made my life hell every day afterward. He reminded me. He humiliated me. But I'd be dead if not for him, and I know I'm not the only one who . . ."

Armenauth trailed off. After a while, Keize stepped forward and placed a hand on his shoulder.

"Flight Commander Lykan was a good soldier," Keize said. "He fought well, and hard, and he was loyal to the 204th. For the moment, that's all that matters."

Keize, Armenauth, and the rest of Lykan's squadron departed the hangar. The rest of the attendees spoke softly, climbing TIEs and sitting with legs dangling on their crossbars, or mingling in the shadows of loadlifters. The squadrons stayed separate at first, like school cliques, but soon pilots began to break away and mingle. Quell spotted Cherroi and Gargovik holding hands, their shoulders touching. Darita sketched out maneuvers on the floor for several of the newer recruits, and Quell realized she was describing what Alphabet had come to know as Snapper's Needle.

She closed her eyes and imagined the lot of them ruining Nacronis, Dybbron, Kortatka, and Fedovoi End. She thought back to Cerberon, and the visions that had tormented her on a desert planetoid, reminding her of all the suffering she had been responsible for.

These people were responsible, too. They hadn't stopped. She told herself these things, but it didn't help.

Fra Raida, whom Quell had always assumed loathed her, produced a thumbnail-sized bag of spice and offered to share it. Quell assumed it was an attempt at entrapment—that if she agreed, Raida would turn her in and have her stripped of responsibilities (and maybe tossed out an air lock, if the old standards of Imperial justice held). But Raida started crying when Quell refused, and they awkwardly hugged. "I'm glad you're alive," Raida said, and Quell quickly made her exit from the hangar.

Keize stopped her in the corridor. "You're leaving already?" he asked.

He didn't block her path entirely but she would've had to sidle past him in the narrow hall. "I didn't know Lykan well," she said, "and someone needs to be well rested in the morning."

Keize smiled absently and glanced toward the hangar. "Walk with me," he said, and turned away.

Quell followed. She wondered if they were going to the Messenger— somehow Keize had found hours to spend dissecting the machine despite the peril of the past few days. But he passed by the ladder leading to the storage closet and said, "I'm worried about our people."

"You're always worried about our people," Quell said. It was a reflex, entirely inappropriate, but it kept her from questioning the use of *our*.

"True," Keize said. "But I prefer when I don't have to worry so much about the *immediate* future. They're dying, Lieutenant. They're dying, and I'm afraid more will die needlessly."

Our people are always dying, Quell thought, but this time held it back. "We were never going to escape Syndulla unscathed," she said. "You told me she was good."

"But we can do *better*," Keize said, and his voice was quiet and fierce. "I've spent months trying to teach this unit the new rules of war, demonstrate that Imperial tactics won't work when—" He made a subtle gesture, somehow making it clear that he referred not only to the *Yadeez* but to its escorts—the Raiders, the gunship, the surveillance vessel—as well. "Some of them understand. Shymon did when she sacrificed herself to destroy the tractor beam. Lykan knew it intellectually, but he instinctively assumed his fighter was operating at peak efficiency."

"He couldn't have known that stabilizer was about to fail," Quell said.

"Yes, he could've," Keize said. "The maintenance report warned as much."

Was that why she was here? Did Keize consider her responsible for the ground crew's failures and blame her for Lykan's death?

"I should've caught that. I'm sorry."

The thought was almost a relief. It let her reconcile who she was with what she was pretending to be.

"That's not the concern." Keize shook his head. "Lykan had the report, but he didn't fly as if he'd read it. The squadrons are still struggling to adapt to our limitations—"

He cut himself off as Cherroi and Gargovik hurried past, hand-in-hand as they'd been in the hangar. The absurdity of it—the interruption of Keize's intensity, of Quell's self-loathing, with the lovers' tryst—nearly made her laugh. Keize ignored them and went on when they were out of sight.

"Confronting Syndulla head-on is out of the question right now—we have more fighters and more escorts, but that Star Destroyer massively outguns us. I need pilots who can operate defensively and know how to improvise. I need someone devoted to keeping our people alive; someone who appreciates in her bones the reality we're faced with."

"I understand," Quell said.

She hadn't intended to agree to anything. But Keize nodded and walked away as if the matter were settled.

III

Snapper was dead, but it felt ghoulish to celebrate. Still, Wyl was in command and his pilots had shot down a foe who'd bedeviled them for months: who'd killed Rawn, the boy with blue lips, in the Oridol Cluster, and Ubellikos in their final battle on Troithe. So Wyl had made a show of moving Snapper's name to the bottom of the list in the ready room, said a few words about the stakes at hand, and segued into a discussion about the enemies remaining. When he'd been offered a slice of cake (quick-rise corn slathered in mint frosting—a decent improvisation), he'd laughed and eaten like he was proud of his unit.

He *was* proud of them.

Over the course of the chase they'd spotted more than a few familiar opponents. Char's TIE was no longer scorched and carbon-scored—now he flew a modified TIE interceptor missing one of its four gun panels—but he still flew without a wingmate, making daring solo attacks on the New Republic fighters. The Twins were quick and coordinated as ever. There was no sign of Blink, the pilot who'd spoken to Wyl twice before—once to taunt and once to warn. Wyl thought of attempting contact, but he had nothing to say.

There were new enemies to catalog, too, and he added them dutifully to the enemy roster: Dizzy and Brew and Spitsy. Wild Squadron seemed to especially enjoy keeping score and tracking their named adversaries. Once Wyl asked Nath, "You think Shadow Wing's doing this same thing aboard the *Yadeez*?" and Nath had only laughed.

Whatever encouraged his people to focus, whatever helped them learn the tricks and stratagems in Shadow Wing's arsenal, Wyl would allow. He taught them as well as he could, but none was prepared the way Wyl and Nath and Chass and Kairos were.

For Alphabet—or at least for Wyl—the skirmishes felt routine. They were *comfortable*, like running through a familiar simulation or reuniting with a friend: The details were fresh every time, but the tenor, the give-and-take, was the same.

Only now Snapper wouldn't take part.

The next skirmish began in the G'Tep'Noi system, after hours of scouting and guesswork. The *Deliverance* emerged from hyperspace with Wyl and Wild Squadron escorting, and even as realspace condensed around Wyl's A-wing he saw the wall of stone race toward him and leaned into his rudder pedal. His heart pumped and his body was crushed against the side of the cockpit as he veered away, but the asteroid passed silently by.

"Enemy located." General Syndulla's voice was measured. "Launching all fighters. Move in and attack."

"We're flying through an avalanche!" Wild Four called. "I can't even see them!"

Specks of dust and distant mountains tumbled in all directions. Wyl attempted to orient himself by his scanner, but there were too many marks displayed; he craned his neck, dipping one wing as he tried to take in the yawning, rocky darkness around him. The *Deliverance* far above was the closest thing to a horizon line. "Wraive! Vitale!" he snapped. "Remember the caverns under Troithe? This is easy next to that, right?"

"Except the caverns weren't *moving*," Vitale said.

"Except for that," Wyl conceded. "You two get behind me and lead the others—everyone, stay close as we find a path. Flare and Hail squadrons will follow."

"What about Alphabet?" The words, each enunciated, came from Kairos. The U-wing hadn't yet launched, but Nath, Chass, and Kairos would all be prepping.

"None of you are maneuverable enough for this asteroid field," he said. "Stick with the *Deliverance,* stay inside its deflector dome, and blast anything that comes its way."

Nath's voice was easy and unperturbed. "Works for me."

The A-wing's engines roared and its frame trembled as Wyl opened his throttle. He wanted to melt into his seat, to merge fully with the ship and glide among the asteroids—but his concentration was split by the comm channel and the developing pattern on his scanner. As kilometers flashed past, he spotted metallic gleaming somewhere past the dull rocks.

Someone screamed over the comm, then amended: "I'm all right! I'm all right!" Wild Seven, who'd flown under Hera in three campaigns using an off-model X-wing too heavily modified to fit with Flare Squadron. "Glanced off my shield, but no systems damage."

Two marks were approaching, small enough to be TIEs. Wyl thumbed his comm and switched frequencies. "General? We can barely handle the rocks. If we have to fight in this . . ."

There was a pause. Then the general replied: "It could get nasty, I know. But if we lose Shadow Wing we may not find them again. Not before they reach another planet."

Not before they burn *another planet,* Wyl thought.

Her voice turned gentler. "If we catch up fast enough we can hold them here. Do that and we have the advantage."

Wyl acknowledged the order and tried not to think of the cost. The

Yadeez was no match for the *Deliverance,* if the New Republic starfighters could keep the TIEs and escort ships occupied. If the bulk freighter could be destroyed, it would leave the TIEs stranded, and after that the New Republic could flee if it had to, knowing Shadow Wing's squadrons were trapped without transportation in a single star system.

Shadow Wing knew all of that, too. They'd strive to prevent the *Deliverance* from closing. But every strategy came with risks, and neither Wyl nor Syndulla had come up with a better plan.

"Looks like the freighter's recalling the TIEs," Wild Eight said—Lieutenant Itina, in a V-wing like Vitale's. Wyl confirmed her assessment with a glance at his sensors. The TIEs that had been approaching—three of them, now—remained in play, but the others were retreating. "Can they jump to lightspeed already?" she asked.

"They're leaving themselves open to attack," Wyl said. "They *must* be about to clear the asteroid field and jump. It's a risk, but it's not crazy. Close in! Go!"

Flare Squadron and Hail Squadron were in flight now, breaking to either side of Wyl and Wild to prepare to flank the freighter *Yadeez.* One TIE swept toward each of the New Republic squadrons, releasing a swift cannon volley that spattered against rocks or fizzled with distance. Flare's and Hail's TIEs turned to retreat after firing, but the last TIE stayed on course. Wyl could see it ahead of him, its central eye occluded by a passing asteroid.

What are you planning?

The TIE jinked to one side. Wyl called out a warning to Denish Wraive, but the TIE's next cannon burst wasn't aimed at the elderly man's fighter. Instead the bolts impacted the closest asteroid and shattered it. Wyl could see fragments, *shrapnel,* exploding toward him, exploding toward Wraive . . .

"Watch out!" he cried, leaning over the console as he gave his thrusters a burst, then pulled up to avoid smashing into another asteroid. Wraive was still alive—still on the scanner, at least—but the TIE had moved on beneath and past him, slipping between rocks for cover as

New Republic fighters returned fire. "It's baiting us!" he said. "Keep on course for the freighter and don't engage unless necessary!"

But the TIE never moved to engage. Instead it continued cracking asteroids. It flickered in and out of scanner visibility as it activated jammers, and Wyl listened to the alarmed cries of his pilots interspersed with static. He prepared to turn back but saw with alarm that he'd outdistanced his comrades—the A-wing had pulled away when the first cloud of shrapnel had separated him from the slower fighters.

Had that been intentional? He couldn't tell. It didn't matter.

Wild Nine and Twelve had lost control evading the asteroids; they both went spiraling through the squadron, forcing the other fighters to scatter. The TIE had a clear path back to its freighter now, but Wyl was closer and the *Deliverance* had accelerated to frightening speed, plowing through the asteroid field and ignoring the rocks that dashed against its deflectors.

"They're getting ready to jump." It was Syndulla's voice, almost growling from the comm. "They're not responding to demands for surrender. If you can stop them—"

"I will pursue the TIE," Kairos said. "Go after the freighter."

Wyl didn't know where the U-wing was and didn't dare check. The asteroids were getting smaller—he was reaching the limit of the field—and he could see the freighter and its escorts in the distance, adjusting their course for a lightspeed jump.

He trusted Kairos. He trusted Syndulla. His gloved hand played across the console as he switched power from his shields to his thrusters. The A-wing sang a high-pitched metallic melody.

His cannons wouldn't do any real damage to the freighter in the time he had left. He armed a concussion missile, pointed himself at the bright beads of the freighter's thrusters, and ignored the chatter of the fighters behind him. *Be a soldier, not a leader,* he told himself. *That's what they need from you now.*

"There is no violence in gravity. The empty sun consumes," Chass said, then added: "Mess up their faces."

He didn't understand why she'd taken up prayer, or why she was quoting over the comm so much lately; but he'd take whatever help he could get.

His targeting computer unfolded. He was squeezing his firing trigger when another voice came through, garbled and nearly indecipherable:

"This is Lieutenant Quell of the 204th Imperial Fighter Wing. Withdraw immediately or be destroyed."

He'd already loosed the weapon. He heard Chass swear and T5 squeal and silence from Nath and Kairos. General Syndulla had time to utter "Quell?" before the TIE activated its jammers again and Wyl was too startled to do anything but watch the exhaust trail of his missile; too startled to notice the exploding asteroid behind him until a granite chunk smashed through his depowered rear deflector and shoved his body into his harness, triggered a blaring alarm. One of his thrusters went out and he was spiraling. A thread of emerald crossed his canopy and he realized the TIE was shooting.

Yrica Quell was shooting at him.

He tried to wrestle the A-wing back on course, whispering soothing words as if to a spooked animal. His wings batted fist-sized chunks of rock, which initially flashed into dust upon contact with his shields; but as his deflectors failed, the rocks began to ring against his hull.

By the time he steadied himself the TIE had swept past. Its jammers were offline again, and he saw its scanner mark converge with that of the freighter; saw Flare and Hail approaching the freighter too late. He twisted his body to watch the *Deliverance* rain baleful green flame as the freighter and its escorts accelerated and distorted and burst into light, leaving behind only afterimages to suffer the Star Destroyer's wrath.

"What the hell?" Chass asked, and she spoke what was in his heart. *What the hell? indeed.*

CHAPTER 8

"GLORY OF THE EMPIRE"
(THE IMPERIAL MARCH)

I

"Why's everyone looking at *me*?" Nath asked.

He stood in front of his Y-wing, helmet under one arm and flight suit pinching in the wrong places. T5 remained in the bomber's socket; Nath had barely dropped out of the cockpit before Wyl, Chass, and Kairos had closed around him like a pack of hungry predators.

Or maybe not quite like predators: Wyl reeked of sweat and seemed to be nursing a bruised arm; he'd taken a battering during the fight. Kairos *couldn't* sweat, so far as Nath knew, and stood rigid as a statue; she could've worn her mask and seemed no more unreadable. Only Chass looked ready to rip Nath's throat out with her teeth.

"Did you know she was alive?" Chass asked, and the calm in her voice unnerved him. "Did Intelligence know?"

"How would I have known?" he retorted, and knew it wasn't the right answer. He held up a hand to stall as he racked his brain.

Had he known? Had there been any signs, any data from Cerberon or after that had hinted at Quell surviving the fall of the *Lodestar*? Anything at all about Quell rejoining the enemy? More important, had he lied about anything relevant that was about to come out?

He ran through every report he'd endured, every conversation with Nasha Gravas, and came up empty-handed. "No," he said. "I'm as dumbfounded as anyone. I swear it's the truth."

The *truth* left a cold knot inside him, but he was the practical one of the group. With his own reputation secure, he could ignore his feelings and focus on what it all meant.

"Well," Chass said, "you blasted well *should've* known."

"We must find her," Kairos said.

Chass was still talking. "Was no one counting the bodies on the *Lodestar*? No one bothered checking the flight recorder, looked to see if, I don't know—an extra escape pod got off, or a shuttle, or if she strapped on a jetpack and *jumped*? I *know* people went looking for Caern Adan and his torture buddy—"

"We must find her," Kairos said.

"We're sure it's her?" Wyl asked. "Could the message have been faked?"

Chass kept going. "—she's a damn *war criminal*, you'd think *that* would matter! Or does the chancellor not care about genocide when the victims aren't Imperials?"

"It was her," Kairos said.

Nath glanced at T5, who'd risen partway out of its socket at the commotion. He didn't know what he hoped the droid would contribute. "Suppose it's possible it was a fake," he said, "but that'd be a weird play for Shadow Wing even if they knew she was connected to us. Brother, you and Kairos got the best look at that TIE . . ."

"It was her," Kairos said again.

"The TIE pilot was very good," Wyl said, "and she acted like— I think it's possible she knew some of our tactics, some of our weaknesses."

The lump in Nath's stomach was swelling, and the discomfort made him irritable. Chass was still ranting: "Maybe this was the plan all along?" she said. "Maybe Intelligence never bothered to realize they had a mole leading our *special working group*?"

Nath pivoted toward the Theelin and snarled, "Let me think!" It only made her louder.

"She has done vile things," Kairos said. "She must be brought back."

"We'll find her," Wyl said. "We need to figure out what she's *doing* there, what she told them . . ."

Nath turned away, placing a palm against the Y-wing's hull and tuning the others out. They were too much of a mess to be useful—none of them had ever come to grips with the fact that Quell had massacred millions on Nacronis. Wyl had trusted her; Chass had—well, *Chass* hadn't known how she'd felt about Quell even before the war crimes had come to light; and Kairos was Kairos.

Nath had known, though. He'd been the first to learn about her crimes, and been the one to pass the information on to Caern Adan. He should've been clear-eyed about Quell while everyone else was in denial, and if anyone should've realized she'd survived . . .

Another unpleasant thought forced its way into his brain: If he'd never reported Quell's crimes to Adan in the first place, would she still have betrayed them? She'd been too terrible a liar to have *always* been a mole.

A hand crushed his shoulder, nails digging into his flight suit. "Don't turn your back!" Chass snapped, and he whirled to face her.

"This isn't about you and her," Nath spat. "Now take a step—"

"*Stop* it, all of you." There was a fierce crack—hands smacking together to demand attention—and they turned to see General Syndulla three meters away. Behind her Sergeant Ragnell slouched with the casual dispassion of a hired bodyguard. "You're still on duty. Try to show some dignity."

Nath had never heard Syndulla so cold. But she'd been close to Quell, too.

"General," he said, straightening his back. Wyl followed suit. Chass scoffed but didn't argue. Kairos was the last to respond—she kept dead eyes on Nath for much longer than he would've liked before finally acknowledging the newcomers.

"The enemy got away again," Syndulla said. Ragnell scanned the pilots and, apparently deciding there was no fight about to break out, shuffled away. "That's a shame, but not a surprise. The good news is that navigation thinks they know where Shadow Wing's headed."

Bold choice, avoiding the issue, Nath thought. *No one here's dense enough not to notice . . .*

Wyl asked: "Where? How?"

. . . but that doesn't mean no one will play along.

"We cross-referenced all known worlds under Imperial control with the *Yadeez*'s last known heading," Hera said. "They've been weaving through this sector for a while—we figured their target had to be close. Best guess is Chadawa."

Nath started to lean back against the Y-wing, wondered if he risked a scolding, and decided to chance it. He vaguely remembered Chadawa from target lists New Republic Intelligence had drawn up. "That's the one with the *phenomena,* am I right? Doesn't seem ideal for a fight."

"That's the one. It's also got a civilian population of half a billion," Syndulla said. "It's unlikely we'll intercept Shadow Wing before they arrive. That means our priority is to figure out a way to stop them in-system as soon as—"

"Quell," Chass said. Her voice shook with effort. "You *heard* her."

"Our priority," Syndulla repeated—more gently now, less disciplinarian and more concerned medic—"is the lives on Chadawa that Shadow Wing intends to snuff out. Alphabet knows the enemy better than anyone else here. I need to know you're with me."

"We're with you," Wyl said. "We're here to save people."

"What about Quell?" Chass asked.

Syndulla seemed to fight through exhaustion and her own emotions and said, simply, "If we stop Shadow Wing, we find Quell, too. We all have to believe that."

Chass stared at the general awhile. Then she took a single step backward until her spine was against one of the Y-wing's landing struts and tossed her head back, striking her scalp against the metal.

"Right," she said. "Fine."

Kairos remained frozen, gaze seemingly fixed on a cluster of wires dangling from a loadlifter toward the back of the hangar.

"Okay," Syndulla said. "Wyl? Nath? You're with me for a planning session. Chass, Kairos—we've still got time before the next fight. Get yourselves rested. We need you at your best."

She turned away after that. Nath looked about the group and shrugged, meeting no one's eyes. The pain in his chest hadn't gone away.

"Come on," Wyl said. "You heard the general."

II

The helmet seemed to adhere to her flesh, gripping her skin and suckling the neck of her suit. In a mad vision she saw herself tearing it off in pieces, ripping away chunks of rubbery armor to reveal blood beneath; but then the helmet came loose and Yrica Quell tossed it away. It snapped back, dangling from her chest on its breathing tubes. She gasped for oxygen and ran gloved hands through slick hair, listening to the cheers of her colleagues and wondering if she would vomit.

"You got better," a voice said. Quell turned her head to Fra Raida beside her, also in a black flight suit. The other pilots and crew past Raida were an undifferentiated blur.

Quell blinked away the sweat in her eyes but not the haze of vertigo. "What?"

"You heard me," Raida said. "Never saw you fly like that in the old days. Guess you needed motivation."

"I had to do it," Quell said, to herself as much as to Raida. "Someone had to do it."

Somebody—it might have been Commander Broosh—called for the pilots to clear the hangar. Figures swept past Quell and gloved hands clapped her shoulders. She should've felt honored—some cancerous part of her *was* honored—to be feted like an ace.

She'd played games with a New Republic Star Destroyer, tricked

General Syndulla and Alphabet Squadron, and helped the *Yadeez* escape without damage or casualties . . .

Because you had to do it. Because it was necessary.

If she hadn't, Shadow Wing would've engaged Syndulla's forces. The *Yadeez* would've struggled to escape and the asteroid field would've devoured fighter after fighter on both sides, gnawing and eating and doing more damage than particle blasts and torpedoes. In the end the *Yadeez* would've escaped anyway and those deaths would've meant nothing. Syndulla's forces would've been left weakened. The next fight would've been bloodier still.

There would be another opportunity. A cleaner opportunity to wipe out the 204th with certainty.

"You're kind of a mess," Raida said.

Quell hadn't realized the woman was still present. Raida was rolling her boot over a fuel line as if massaging her heel. "It's been a while since I flew," Quell said. Her voice sounded too hoarse; she tried to correct it, but she couldn't recall what *normal* felt like—where to put her tongue, how to shape her lips. "Must be out of shape."

"The brittle bone thing?"

Quell felt surprise, but she shouldn't have. Shadow Wing *knew* her—not because they'd read a dossier but because they'd trusted her once. She'd trusted them. "Low-gravity childhood. Plus I broke my nose the other day." Saying the words triggered a spike of pain.

"Gives you character. Come on, we'll get you changed."

Why are you being kind to me? Quell wanted to ask. She nodded instead.

Ten minutes later she'd managed to remove the flight suit without taking a knife to it—shed a skin that, rather than belonging to her, had seemed to *own* her. She wanted to weep when she was showered and back in her civilian gear but Raida was still there, pulling on her shirt a meter away. Quell excused herself and walked lead-footed through the *Yadeez*, searching for a place to hide.

Unthinking, she ended up back at the reactor level, squeezing her body between a bulkhead and a cooling tower. Her comm array was gone—there was nothing for her to do there, nothing for anyone to find—but the rattle of equipment and gurgle of pipes helped to drown out the universe.

She'd announced herself. She'd revealed her survival to Syndulla and Wyl Lark. To Kairos and Nath and Chass, if they were alive. She'd done it to win a petty victory that never should've been at issue in the first place.

You should've killed Soran Keize a long time ago.

The thought rose in her without cruelty or vindictiveness. It was the practical part of her brain—the part that planned missions.

You could kill him today. He'd let you get close enough. You have a blaster. Walk up and do it, or—you're worried the 204th will continue without him? Kill him and Broosh both. Murder all the squadron commanders. There's always a way.

You have access to the reactor right now. Blow up the freighter. You have a chance to pull it off.

But if she *didn't* pull it off, her cover would be blown. Her mission would be over.

Was that an excuse for cowardice?

She thought all this and hunched her shoulders and hoped the vibrations of the ship would lull her to sleep. She wished dearly that IT-O were still operational, so that she could have talked matters over with her therapist.

The comlink summoned her to the bridge too soon, though she wasn't sure how much time had really passed. Her hair was still wet from the shower—the stiff strands tickled her neck and she smelled of disinfectant—but she'd become hyperaware of her body. No one else would care.

She froze the moment she emerged from the bridge hatch. There was no hushed chatter among the crew or the usual clatter of controls. Keize's voice dominated with the unnatural calm he exuded when pronouncing a planet's execution: "—either way, Chadawa must die. Refuse, and you will die with it."

Then his timbre thawed. "But I suppose you knew all that," he finished.

"Your reputation precedes you." The worn, middle-aged face of an Imperial colonel stared out the viewscreen from the bridge of a Star Destroyer. He spoke without humor in a thick colonial brogue. "Admiral Sloane has little tolerance for rejection, eh?"

"Sloane is no longer among the Empire's leadership—but your point stands," Keize said. He sighed gently. "You were supposed to have joined us, Colonel Madrighast. You were the one who invited me to rendezvous with the fleet after Pandem Nai—"

"That invitation was sincere, as was my warning that *it would not be easy*." Madrighast snorted. "We attempted to make the rendezvous, but rebel forces drove us off course. Just a bit at first, but the damage began to mount, we encountered blockades too strong to penetrate, and—well. We were waylaid. After two weeks of evasive action and enough lost ships to make a junker world rich, I suspected Sloane and her fleet were no longer patiently waiting."

Quell observed from the hatch and clung to the distraction the conversation provided. She tried to recall what she knew of Colonel Madrighast. The 204th had operated alongside his unit years before, under the luminous amber skies of To'hok Neige. He'd been rewarded with a Star Destroyer, though its name eluded her—the *Arbiter*? The *Immortal*?

"I imagine you were correct," Keize said. "But Chadawa, Colonel?"

The *Unyielding*! She almost laughed.

Madrighast lifted his chin, though his eyes showed no pride. "Governor Bordanivaux is no patriot, and her decision to take Chadawa rogue was misguided at best. I have no love for the woman. But she gave us refuge when no one else would, and my people understand loyalty." He drew a breath and seemed about to smile; his lips merely trembled a bit instead. "We made our choices months ago. We will fight the 204th to protect Chadawa."

"I understand," Keize said. "Until then."

He raised a hand to cut the signal; but Madrighast spoke again. "It's a pity you didn't accept my invitation," the colonel said. "With the 204th alongside us, maybe we would've made it to Sloane's rendezvous together."

"Perhaps," Keize replied, and the image on the viewscreen warped and vanished, replaced by the storm of hyperspace.

The bridge crew's voices rose and the clatter of controls resumed. Captain Nenvez leaned heavily on his cane—he was no longer keen to pace, since his earlier fall—and called for an update from the nav station. Quell stepped to Keize's side and saw him still gazing at the screen. "Everything all right?" she asked.

Keize smiled wearily. "I'd have preferred that had gone differently," he said, too quiet for anyone but Quell to hear. "I've come to like that man."

She nodded carefully. There was nothing to say. At least the call had given her time to compose herself; she had smoothed out her distress to an imperceptible layer beneath her usual mask.

Keize waved her toward the hatch, and they stepped away from the crew. "You did well today," he said, voice still low. "I know it was difficult, given the last time you flew."

The time we killed Nacronis? she thought. *You can say it.* She merely nodded again.

"I need you for another task," he said. "There's a crisis approaching—Chadawa and Syndulla intersecting—but we have an opportunity as well."

She was *his* pilot now, she realized—his personal assassin, to fly when he gave the order. "What opportunity?"

"The one we've been searching for," he said. "Some cultures foretell the future in animal entrails. We've been doing the same with the Emperor's Messenger—and though we may not be able to change the inevitable, knowledge may let us mitigate the worst of what's to come."

"That doesn't mean anything," she said.

"Do you care for your unit, Lieutenant?"

She inclined her head so she wouldn't have to lie.

"As do I. Whether we win or lose this war, we need to know everything that's locked in the circuits of that machine. It will either prove my fears correct or save us all." He gestured for her to leave the bridge. "Come, and we'll talk."

III

Get yourselves rested, Syndulla had said. *We need you at your best,* she'd said. Syndulla wasn't her mother, though, no matter how much she play-acted the part, and Chass na Chadic had never liked her mother anyway.

Yrica Quell was alive, and Chass shouldn't have cared. Yet as she stalked the corridors of the *Deliverance* she could smell the woman—not a good smell but a thoroughly *human* one, like underripe fruit. Chass fought to push away memories of what had gone down at Cerberon (the good and the bad—the night they'd gotten drunk in the refugee camp and stumbled all the way home; that last confrontation, with Quell staring blankly when confronted with her crimes), but the thoughts kept surfacing no matter how many Chass rejected.

She doesn't deserve your attention, Chass told herself. *She betrayed you a long time ago.* Even that rebuke only summoned the memory of Quell throwing her against a bulkhead aboard the *Lodestar.*

Chass rubbed her eyes with her palms and mumbled a prayer. Maybe it was one of the Children of the Empty Sun's; maybe it was one she'd learned earlier in life, from the Inheritors of the Crystal or the Unignited. She didn't care anymore. All cults were the same cult, offering mantras and routine and obedience to fill the cracks in a person's consciousness; to keep out the emotional turmoil that might otherwise creep in like a swarm of insects, scuttling and eating away at the soul's foundation.

She'd been performing the role of cultist a lot lately, echoing Let'ij to irritate Syndulla and the pilots and the ground crews. But she hadn't believed enough, hadn't *become* that performance enough, to keep Yrica Quell from crawling through her brain.

Maya Hallik, you poor deluded thing. The answer is waiting for you.
"Chass?"

In her blind wanderings she'd arrived in a hydroponics lab—a storeroom, really, lined with little jars and tanks growing withered plants. Wyl Lark stood beside a tube compressing an ebony thorn tree, splashes of green leaves pressed flat against the glass.

Chass stepped backward, as if Wyl might forget she'd been there if she exited quickly enough. He didn't say anything—just watched her with a half smile so pathetic that it slowed her; and when she was out the doorway, and he *still* didn't stop her, she paused.

He looked tired. He'd looked tired for days—weeks, really—but now he wasn't hiding it, slumping boyishly and sliding his fingertips down the vegetation tube.

"You, too?" she asked.

That made him laugh, and Chass felt a tiny surge of satisfaction. "Wrapped up with the general a while ago," he said. "Couldn't sleep. Were you—"

"I was looking for a shooting range." She paused and reentered the room. "You think anyone would miss the plants?"

"Yes," Wyl said. "Plus, they're a good backup in case we run out of food and oxygen."

"You're a good backup in case we run out of food," she muttered. Wyl pretended he didn't hear. She found an empty shelf and hopped up, wedging her bottom into the socket meant for a water purifier. She searched for something to say, but none of the subjects that occurred to her were ones she wanted to discuss.

"You know you left fingerprints?" Wyl asked. He was smiling more warmly now.

"What?"

"When you climbed through the particle flow tube, during the sabotage droid attack."

She frowned. "Okay. So?"

"So apparently that equipment is surprisingly sensitive, and the oil from your skin caused an internal sensor error. The maintenance droids aren't good enough for the work so someone had to scrub the tube manually."

Chass snorted. "These are the sorts of conversations you have as a commander, huh?"

"Yeah," Wyl said. "Biggest thing I've learned? No one really *likes* pilots. They just put up with the trouble we cause, since *someone* has to fly."

"Sounds right to me. Must be heartbreaking for a man who desperately needs to be liked." She smirked as she leaned against the bulkhead. "Back on the *Hellion's Dare,* you'd have a dozen friends around you. On the *Deliverance* you're stuck with me."

"On the *Deliverance* I'm stuck with you," he agreed, and he didn't sound bothered by the notion.

They watched each other, bonded by a thread she hadn't been aware of in a long time.

Eventually Wyl said: "I knew you were in there somewhere, Hound Three."

She might've punched him for saying it—for suggesting that everything she'd been lately wasn't *real,* that only he was keen and kind and smart enough to excavate the true Chass na Chadic. It was *all* real, even the part that was performance—but she knew what he meant.

"Screw you," she said without anger. "I do kind of expect to see Fadime walk in."

"Or Sata Neek."

"Right. I liked the bird-frog."

She really had. She wanted to ask Wyl: *Why isn't Alphabet like that? We were kin on the* Hellion's Dare—*in Hound Squadron and the Cavern Angels—so why not here?*

But she knew the answer. Hound Squadron and the Cavern Angels (and Riot Squadron, too) had been fighting an endless war. The squadrons had been their whole world, their existence, and life beyond that had been a dream. Now everyone (everyone except her) had more to look forward to, and the war and the squadrons were obstacles to those dreams coming true.

Plus, Alphabet's leader had turned out to be a war criminal who faked her own death. That made a difference.

"Things changed at Endor, didn't they?" she asked.

She didn't expect Wyl to understand, but he nodded. "For everyone. They really did." They were both silent again before he added: "There's— can I tell you a story?"

"About Endor?"

"Yes."

She hesitated. Then she nodded.

Wyl sat on the floor, and his eyes focused past Chass's shoulder on the joint between ceiling and wall. "You know I was there. You know— I almost said, *You know what Riot went through,* but we got off light compared with other units. We lost *three,* out of probably hundreds of rebel dead. Thousands. It wasn't sad, though, the mood afterward. We'd just won the war, we couldn't *be* just sad.

"Riot was allowed to land on the forest moon. The locals didn't speak Basic but they were kind, and they'd taken their own losses. The celebration went on for hours, and we'd go from crying to cheering to just sitting with one another and looking at the stars.

"It was intense, and pretty late in the night Skitcher and Sonogari both needed some space to process it all. I'd been with them so I figured I'd take a walk, and just . . . see it all. Take it in and remember it. I didn't know anyone besides Riot Squadron, but watching everyone else—"

"Right, you're a wuss," Chass said. "I got that part."

Wyl caught her gaze and looked abashed. He resumed as if he hadn't been interrupted: "I went for a walk. People were still eating and cheering but I ended up out on the edge of the village. There was a bonfire, and I saw someone standing alone in front of it.

"He was a man. I thought he looked familiar so I got a little closer. When I got a better angle and the fire lit his face, I realized it was Skywalker. I'd never met him; I just recognized him from images."

Chass shifted forward. *Luke Skywalker, the Jedi hero, savior of the Rebellion.* If anyone else had told the story, she'd have called it braggadocio; but Wyl sounded almost contrite.

"I didn't want to interrupt him. He looked sad and thoughtful, like he was mourning and maybe also relieved. Like he'd unburdened himself. I should've turned away, but then I saw—I realized what the fire was. It was a funeral pyre. I didn't see the body, but I saw the armor."

Chass frowned. "The *armor*?"

"It was black, a little bit like a stormtrooper's but ornate and . . . old, like something from the early days of the Republic. It looked familiar the way Skywalker did, and I knew: It was Darth Vader."

"Okay . . . ?" Chass said. She parted her lips, closed them again. Vader had been a story to her—the Emperor's nightmarish enforcer, rebel-hunter, and genocidal freak; one of the worst monsters in the whole cabal of criminals who'd run the galaxy. But she had no connection to the man, felt nothing but confusion and a dull horror. "Was he part of the fighting on Endor? I don't remember hearing—"

"No. I don't think so. Rumor was that Skywalker was aboard the Death Star, so he must've found Vader there. He must've brought him back. Brought the *body* back to cremate it."

"Maybe he brought it back for a bioscan?" She spoke without conviction, trying to make sense of the story. "Making sure it wasn't a body double?"

"Maybe. I don't think so." Wyl drew a long breath. "It was that *look* that he had—like he was remembering Vader's life. Like he felt grief. I don't doubt that Skywalker did all the good they say, but it felt wrong to have Vader there, when we'd just lost so many people fighting everything Vader represented . . ."

Wyl was shaking.

"It's okay," she said.

He finally held her gaze. "I don't know what Vader meant to him. I believe in grace and compassion, and that no one *deserves* to die in war. Even so, I watched Skywalker and Vader and I can't shake the thought that maybe there are some crimes that shouldn't be forgiven. That there must be *some* line we shouldn't cross."

Wyl dropped his chin as if a spirit had left his body. His breath came heavily and he touched his forehead, half hiding his face behind his hand.

He didn't say Quell's name, and he didn't have to.

Chass could've gone to Wyl. The man was suffering and he'd made a sacrifice, an offering for the both of them, but there was nothing Chass knew how to give in return.

His sacrifice hadn't been in vain, though. Chass understood her role in the coming battle.

"You're probably right," she said. "That really what you need to be worrying about?"

"Maybe not. Hard to stop, though."

"Yeah."

She thought about saying: *I'll take care of it,* but she didn't trust him not to ask questions. If she needed help, she would find someone who'd already made their priorities clear.

They spoke together for another few minutes, leaving difficult topics behind and making forced conversation about the hydroponics lab and the sweaty dampness in the air. Then Chass left, not bothering with an excuse, and wondered where she might find Kairos.

IV

Yrica Quell had first arrived aboard the *Yadeez* purged of guilt and possessed of certainty, wholly attuned to her mission with the conviction of a zealot. Now she was unsure her actions contributed to that mission; circumstances had become too complex, and her lies too intertwined.

She had accepted Keize's assignment because she required his trust. But to what end? If she saw the assignment through, was it to earn a weapon against him? Was it simply to avoid another confrontation with Syndulla and Alphabet Squadron?

Or was it because she was tempted by what he promised—a way to save the soldiers of the 204th regardless of the outcome of the war? She'd been seduced by Keize's sense of duty before, after all.

Maybe it was just a need to understand what the Messenger truly was. Keize had hinted at his suspicions, given her explicit instructions, but he'd made little clear about what he was truly *looking* for.

What does it matter? Refuse him and he'll find out the truth about you. You'll be dead. Someone else will take the assignment, so you may as well cooperate now and act later.

That morbid thought—the notion that truly, she had no choice—reassured her as she paged through the entries on her datapad in the dim light of the bunk room. Keize had given her access to the 204th's complete personnel records—complete as any of their records were anymore, anyway—and she studied her selections, searching for evidence that she'd made a critical error.

She found no evidence and she was out of time.

Her broken nose and the scar of her tattoo pulsed as she headed for the hangar. She had to make sure her transportation was ready.

In the sunless realm of Cerberon, she'd been trapped on a planetoid that had meant *something* to the dead Galactic Emperor. She'd found suffering there, and two friends had lost their lives. But she had also found a vessel—silver and fluid like poured mercury, its interior lit like the chambers of a human heart, built with technology more sophisticated than anything the Empire fielded for ordinary military operations. She'd managed to activate it and had flown it to the *Yadeez*.

It was a beautiful creation, and in the bulk freighter's hangar, concealed beneath a black tarp to protect its delicate, scanner-resistant skin from soot and sparks and fuel particles, it was waiting for her. It would take her away from the *Yadeez* while Chadawa came under assault and General Syndulla attempted to save the planet from Shadow Wing; and she found herself hoping that Shadow Wing would lose the battle even as Keize survived.

Maybe it was selfish. But there was little more she could do aboard the bulk freighter; little she could do to alter the outcome at Chadawa after leading the New Republic to Shadow Wing every step of the way. Averting a massacre had to be Syndulla's responsibility now.

And she *did* want answers about Keize and the Messenger. She could follow Keize's orders a little longer.

For the second time in barely a day, Quell prepared to fly.

Hera Syndulla wasn't thinking about Quell, but only because she'd gotten very good at not thinking about certain subjects: absent friends; her faraway son; her difficult father; the toll of her choices on the people under her command. Compared with those, what did Quell matter to her? Hera had tried to be kind, tried to be a mentor, but she couldn't be responsible for the woman's choices or her past.

She couldn't afford to think about Quell. Not yet.

The nav officer was counting down until the *Deliverance* emerged from hyperspace. Captain Arvad stood at the center of the bridge, her hands flexing behind her back where the crew couldn't see. Hera gave her a nod of reassurance, but the captain didn't seem to notice.

"I doubt we'll have more than a few seconds before the fighting starts," Hera said. "If you get the chance, though? Enjoy the view."

"That seems like terrible advice," Arvad said, before remembering to add: "General."

"It might be. Don't get distracted. But sometimes it's good to remind yourself what you're fighting for, and I hear Chadawa is quite a sight."

Arvad didn't have a chance to reply. The *Deliverance* surged forward, and the darkness of realspace washed over the viewports. Screens flickered as officers recalibrated sensors and the marks of New Republic starfighters appeared on tactical displays in twos and threes. Hera heard reports come in deck by deck, confirming the battleship's readiness.

She stepped forward, past Arvad, and looked to the distant blue-and-white dot in the depths of space. She could barely make out the silvery rings surrounding the planet, each canted at a different angle so that they caged the ocean world. If she'd been closer, she might've seen the churning of clouds or the rough brown streaks of great archipelagoes; or the individual satellites composing the rings, millions of technological constructs embedded in crystalline housings.

"Scanners are full of static," someone called. "Comms are down, too."

Hera nodded carefully. "Go to visual sensors and reset the comm arrays, as we discussed. Three hundred percent normal power, no encryption. The enemy will hear everything we say, but it's better than being deaf and mute."

Another cry came from the Cathar girl at the comscan station.

"Enemy sighted! Shadow Wing vessels approaching the rings. Planetary defenders moving to intercept."

Hera swung away from the viewport, hurrying to the stations. "What do the Chadawans have to work with?"

Stornvein, her aide, was leaning over a tactical display and called, "Maybe half a dozen ships in orbit. Biggest one could be a Star Destroyer. Can't tell how many fighters or what they have on the ground."

"That's enough to slow the 204th," Hera said. "Get a signal to the planet as soon as you can—I don't care if the 204th overhears. Let them know the New Republic is here to help."

Arvad gestured to another officer, then asked more quietly: "The Chadawans are still Imperial. There any chance they'll believe us?"

Hera shrugged. "Given everything Colonel Keize has done? There's a chance. Even if they won't coordinate with us, we might be able to outflank the 204th."

It was an optimistic analysis, and Hera knew it. Arvad called orders to swing the *Deliverance* toward the planet while Hera checked on the squadrons. Hail, Wild, and Flare were in motion; Alphabet's pilots were spread among the three units, ready to adapt to whatever Shadow Wing had planned.

Wyl Lark's voice came through the comm, distorted to a squeal by the overpowered transmission. "All fighters ready. Final instructions, General?"

She gave it a moment's consideration. Most of the pilots would be thinking about vengeance—about the injuries and insults Shadow Wing had inflicted since the sabotage droid attack, or about the destruction of the *Lodestar* and the deaths of friends at Cerberon.

"We're told Chadawa was built by an unknown species eons ago," Hera said. "No one knows why or how. But since then billions of people have called it home. They were born, they grew old, and they died here, and their history is part of the galaxy's history.

"Shadow Wing wants to render Chadawa uninhabitable. They want to make it part of the Empire's story. I say we make sure it sees another eon or two. May the Force be with us all."

She severed the transmission. Not her best speech, but it would suffice. Particularly since the 204th was listening, too.

She looked to Arvad. "Do we have a particle count?"

Arvad grimaced. "Hard to know—sensors really aren't calibrated for this. It looks like the tide's coming in soon."

Perfect, Hera thought, and tried not to scowl in front of the crew.

Chadawa hadn't just been constructed—it had been built to a machine's exacting specifications. The engines powering its rotation and heating its oceans vented massive quantities of radioactive particles— particles siphoned off by the planet's satellite rings and periodically expelled into the surrounding volume of space.

At "high tide," immediately after the particles' expulsion, the radioactive flood was enough to disrupt the systems of any vessel unprotected by the cage of rings. Navigation would be dicey; combat, likely impossible. Even at low tide, the ambient particle count was enough to scramble scanners and comm systems. The only saving grace was that the 204th was just as disadvantaged as the New Republic—they, too, would need to rely on visuals to identify and track foes. They, too, would need to maintain comm silence or be overheard by the *Deliverance* and its fighters.

Hera was confident the Chadawan locals would start with the upper hand. They'd keep their ships inside the rings, where the radiation wouldn't hamper them. But if Shadow Wing broke through? The worst possible outcome was the 204th embedding in Chadawan orbit, able to repel a New Republic siege from the outside while laying waste to the planet and its population.

Since the *Deliverance*'s arrival, sightings from scope operators had been relayed to the bridge and added manually to the tactical maps. Now the maps showed Shadow Wing engaging the Chadawans, pushing hard against the planet's defensive blockade—harder than would've been wise in other circumstances. Bursts of light among the rings suggested more Shadow Wing TIEs destroyed than Hera had seen lost in all their skirmishes with the *Deliverance;* the enemy knew how vital it was to defeat the Chadawan forces quickly.

Then the New Republic fighters were in position to strike. According to the maps the *Deliverance* was a minute behind the squadrons, but Hera didn't dare delay; she called for the attack to begin. There was little to hear on the comm—with all channels combined into one, only the occasional order from a squadron commander was vital enough to broadcast—so she watched through the viewport, counting the flashes that meant death.

Soon death came through the comm, too. "Flare Five is down!" "Wild Four gone!" As the *Deliverance* drew nearer, it began to pick up the 204th's calls as well—but these were fewer and briefer. Keize had his people prepared and well disciplined.

Then an unexpected voice declared: "Hey! Hey! I know you're out there, Lieutenant Yrica Quell. Are you listening?"

Chass na Chadic.

Hera stiffened, started to call for the broadcast to be shut down—but what could the *Deliverance* do? She could interrupt the Theelin, try to talk over her, but that would only become an embarrassing distraction for everyone. She could jam the transmission, but she wasn't ready to give up their only channel.

Arvad looked at Hera, and Hera shrugged. *Let's see where this goes.*

Chass kept talking. "You know who I am. You know who *all of us* here are, because you're a damn traitor."

Hera almost laughed as she began to understand. Chass wasn't just taunting Quell—she was *baiting* her, testing to see how much the 204th knew about Quell's time with Alphabet. It was dangerous but it was also *clever.*

"We're coming for you," Chass said. "Alphabet is—"

Her voice was drowned in a ripple of static that didn't fade. Hera looked toward the comscan officer, who shook her head. "It's not the particle count," she called. "Jamming signal—a good one, too, based on the interlacing. Don't think we can cut through."

The tactical officer shot up from her seat. "Unidentified ship slipping away from the bulk freighter. It's moving fast—scopes can't get a visual lock. Could be the source of the jamming field."

The tactical map had become a mess of outdated symbols and vectors as the officers tried and failed to keep pace with the battle. Hera stepped closer to the viewport, where the combatants were now large enough to clearly discern—the fighters glinting specks, the large ships burning sparks. Behind them the sphere of Chadawa dominated space.

She mentally overlaid the tactical map on the viewport, breaking down the sight grid by grid until she found the meteor streaking away from the boxy sliver of the *Yadeez.* Two other lights—brighter, closer—left the New Republic squadrons, following the meteor's trail as it broke off from the battle altogether.

Hera's breathing had accelerated. She knew what was happening, if not all the reasons. One of the lights had to be Chass, and the other—who else had she roped into this?

"Our B-wing and U-wing—" the tactical officer began.

"Try to contact them! Yes, I realize between the jamming and the radiation—just try, please."

She shouldn't have been surprised. She'd seen the intensity in Chass and Kairos in the hangar. *At least it's not the whole squadron,* she thought. But she couldn't spare even two ships to chase Yrica Quell (assuming it *was* Quell), not when Shadow Wing was on the verge of breaking through to Chadawa; not when the tide was coming in.

Quell's fleeing vessel accelerated, flashed bright enough to make Hera flinch, then disappeared. Quell had gone to hyperspace. Hera was almost relieved, and expected the B-wing and U-wing to return to the battle; instead they matched the first vessel's final vector.

"They can't," Hera murmured. "They can't."

Each blinked away in a flash of its own.

"What are they *doing*?" Arvad asked. "Do they know where that ship's going?"

"They don't have a clue," Hera snapped. "They're jumping blind, and they'll be lucky not to fly straight into a black hole." She didn't bother hiding her frustration, but she did her best not to direct it at the comscan officer as she said, "Jamming field's gone, correct? I want to talk to Wyl Lark—"

Even as she spoke she saw another flare, this one tinged with emerald; one of the Chadawan defenders was burning. The tactical map blinked and updated as Shadow Wing closed around the planet, passing through the outermost satellite rings. "They're through!" Wyl's voice cried, and there was exhaustion and despair in his tone. "Chadawan ships are retreating deep into atmosphere. What are your orders, General?"

Keep pressing them! she wanted to say, but she saw the rings around Chadawa coruscate like sunlit diamonds. "Pull back!" she called as the comm emitted a high-pitched pattering. "Pull back now! The rings are activating!"

Arvad yelled for the *Deliverance* to halt. The New Republic specks fled Chadawa as a pulse ran along one ring, then the next, then a third. The cage around the planet glowed and erupted and the cosmos blazed with color, as if all the ships' weapons had been replaced with fireworks. The bridge went silent except for the hissing of comms and the electrical popping of the subsystems.

It was a beautiful sight. Exactly as she'd promised Arvad.

The glow faded. The sparks of the New Republic starfighters drifted away from the planet as if carried by a breeze.

The bridge chatter resumed. "They're all right!" someone called. "Fighter squadrons made it out."

"What now?" Arvad asked.

Hera shook her head, buying time for an answer as she considered.

Shadow Wing was inside the rings, and while the *Deliverance* waited for the particle count to drop the enemy would begin eliminating the last defenders, killing the planet and fortifying its position. Half of Alphabet Squadron was gone, and with it much of the squadrons' expertise on the 204th. Hera didn't know how many fighters she'd lost, but she had time to find out while they sat and watched helplessly from afar.

"Now we do things the hard way," she said.

She did her best to smile. To show confidence. She told herself it wasn't entirely unwarranted.

After all, a standoff wasn't a defeat, and Shadow Wing was going nowhere.

PART TWO

ELEMENTS OF A MALEVOLENT EQUATION

CHAPTER 9

AMORAL PRIORITIZATION OF OBJECTIVES

I

The nameless vessel pierced the veil of hyperspace more swiftly and subtly than any Quell had flown. If she hadn't been staring out the cockpit viewport, she would've been aware of the ship's deceleration only by virtue of the changing lighting: The vessel's overheads had paled to milky pink at lightspeed but now flushed with their familiar arterial red.

She wondered if the change extended to the main compartment. Her passengers had done nothing to demand her attention.

She felt confident the team hadn't heard Chass na Chadic's transmission over Chadawa. (Chadic was alive—Quell had believed before, but now she knew, she *knew*.) They'd been away from the cockpit comm, with no reason to use the single headset in the cabin, and she'd activated the jamming signal only seconds after hearing the Theelin's voice. She was less sure whether Keize and the *Yadeez* had heard the message or understood its importance. It was possible her lies were once again exposed; that Keize knew she had been part of Alphabet Squadron, and she would face consequences if she returned to the bulk freighter.

Then again, there might not be a freighter to return to. General Syndulla had begun her attack, and while Keize's plan was sound it held no guarantee of Shadow Wing's safety.

The future was a knot of possibilities, constricting and tangled. The longer Shadow Wing survived, the more of Chadawa would die; and Quell's life, too, would be endangered. Yet if Keize fell before Quell's assignment was complete, she might be left without answers. The paradox of her hopes nauseated her, and she reminded herself that the only factor she could control was the completion of her assignment. Speed would resolve much; other problems could wait.

She checked her charts and sensors. The Netalych system was ancient and cold, its dozen barren planets orbiting an unnaturally green sun. A perfunctory scan revealed no ships or spacegoing life-forms, and with a few keystrokes she instructed the autopilot to proceed to the seventh planet. If her files were to be believed, that frigid world half thawed each day and refroze nightly; she wondered if anything at all had evolved to survive such conditions.

The vessel hummed and adjusted its speed. Quell unclipped her harness, checked to make sure the duffel containing her cargo was secure beneath her seat, and proceeded out the cockpit door.

Like the cockpit, the main compartment appeared built for elegance over comfort. Five men and women sat on two crescent benches against the wall, and they turned rigid with attention as Quell emerged. "We're landing shortly," she announced, and although her voice sounded soft no one seemed to strain to hear. "We've got five minutes for a briefing."

She looked over their faces. Two she knew well—Agias Rikton, the young mechanic who'd imprinted on her, and Fra Raida, her old rival. She was passingly familiar with Nord Kandende, one of the intense lieutenants of Squadron Four. Others she'd chosen based on personnel reports, reputation, and Keize's own recommendations: Jeela Brebtin, of Squadron Five, and Alchor Mirro, the elderly ground crew chief who'd tried to retire three times before Endor. She needed Imperial Special Forces, not pilots and grease jockeys; but she'd selected them because they were better than average with a blaster or at circuit welding, or just more willing than most to obey in the face of madness.

She would sacrifice them all if she had to. (She suspected Keize *knew* she might sacrifice them, albeit not all the reasons why. He would already be planning for their loss.)

No one spoke, so Quell went on: "DN-949A was the Empire's tertiary fueling post and chemical processing facility for this sector. It has no significant strategic or cultural value and a permanent population of less than five hundred organics, plus sixteen hundred droids of fifth-degree intelligence or better. Six days after Endor the local military was overthrown by those droids, who claimed independence for the outpost and the right to self-governance."

Mirro laughed with a sound that could've been admiring. Rikton looked nervously to the floor. The others stared with varying degrees of loathing and discomfort. None showed the focus Quell had hoped for.

She kept talking even as part of her mind—the part that had led Alphabet Squadron on Troithe, the part that had been tutored by General Syndulla—noted her errors: *Wrong tone. Wrong approach.* "Since then, the droids have set up a—society, of sorts. The organic residents haven't been forced out, but rumor has it they're working for the droids now. Visitors are permitted; the machines are still selling fuel, and they need credits to better establish themselves."

They don't believe in you.

"Why aren't we fighting at Chadawa?" Brebtin asked. Her words might as well have been a curse.

Don't say it.

"Because Colonel Keize has ordered us here," Quell returned. "The *Yadeez* will be safe once it entrenches inside the planet's rings. We'll rejoin the unit before Chadawa is gone."

Tell them: "We're all worried for our friends, and I'd like to tell you everything, but . . ."

"Details are classified," she said. "In short, we're here to solve an engineering problem. The colonel believes we can find a specialist who can analyze certain data and provide insights we can take back to the unit. If all goes well we walk in and out without hostilities; you're my backup in case of trouble."

Rikton shifted on the bench and looked among the others, then to Quell. She prompted him with a nod and he said, "It's, ah—it's not a lot to go on if something goes wrong, Lieutenant."

"How do you mean?" she asked, though she knew.

Kandende grunted and spoke over Rikton's attempt at an answer. "If you get killed, what do the rest of us do?"

Quell shrugged, as carefree as she could. "You fail," she said.

Fra Raida chuckled hoarsely, shaking her head. Mirro rubbed his face with exquisite slowness, as if speed would attract Quell's attention. Only Rikton and Brebtin appeared to accept the reply at face value, nodding somberly the way good Imperial soldiers would've before the Empire had fallen.

As the vessel descended, the automated outpost systems assigned them a pier and an authorization code. Quell supposed that counted as a welcome, and she checked her sidearm as the ship settled onto an industrial platform in the freezing rain. No one—droid or organic—emerged from the facility at the pier's far end, so she dragged the duffel from under her seat, hefted it over her shoulder, and returned to the main compartment.

Rikton and Mirro wore heavy packs laden with tools and spare parts. Brebtin had acquired a rifle from somewhere—during her time on Troithe, Quell suspected, or from one of the new recruits—but Kandende and Fra Raida bore nothing more than their clothing and their pistols. Like Quell, none of them were in uniform, garbed instead in whatever shirts and trousers they'd carried with them or found on the *Yadeez*. As a team, they looked ramshackle and ill prepared; not like the deadly patchwork that Shadow Wing's fighters had become, but like mercenaries short of supplies behind enemy lines.

"Lieutenant?" Kandende drew up behind Quell as she approached the boarding ramp, speaking almost too quietly to hear.

"What is it?" Quell asked.

"These orders," Kandende said. "Are they really from Colonel Keize? Or from—*above*?"

From the highest echelons of the surviving Empire? From the people who had us burn planets to the ground?

She furrowed her brow at Kandende and tried to remember what Keize had said about the man. Once, Kandende had almost worshipped the Messenger.

"From the Emperor himself," she said. "Operation Cinder takes many forms. Tell no one."

Kandende nodded somberly. She lowered the ramp.

She tried to ignore the sense of movement from the duffel on her shoulder and the imagined sound of electronic voices.

They marched out together, trudging through the stinging sleet that smelled like methane and antifreeze. Quell repeatedly wiped her lips on her sleeve to avoid swallowing the precipitation, but the effort became increasingly futile as her outfit became saturated. The vista of bleeding glaciers and oceans of sludge receded behind them, and half a kilometer out they finally passed under a metal canopy where engineering droids floated past, tending to fuel pumps and heaters and chemical vaporators. The few organics they saw—humans, mostly—kept their heads down and didn't look at the newcomers. Where the platform merged with other piers an overhanging catwalk had once supported an Imperial flag; now the cloth was burnt and tattered, and someone had painted a message in bold letters across the catwalk: NO MEAT NO MASTERS.

"Charming," Fra Raida muttered.

"They're not wrong, though," Mirro replied.

A drone approached them, its single photoreceptor dilating and twitching as it looked the crew over. It held on Quell and she tried to steady her breathing, hoping the sleet would cool her body temperature and reduce any sign of nervousness, any biological indicator of worry.

The lens looked to the duffel. Quell did not reach for her blaster. The drone moved on.

Maybe it didn't know. Maybe it didn't care, or it hadn't recognized the significance of her cargo.

"Let's find our specialist," Quell said. "I want to be done with this."

The longer they were at the outpost, the longer she had to hope no one discovered the mass of wires and circuits and red leather in the duffel. The longer she had to keep secrets from the droids and her allies and the Empire and the New Republic.

It wasn't possible, but she thought she heard the Emperor laughing as she toted his Messenger's corpse into the facility.

II

"Sector by sector, we're closing in." General Cracken, broad-faced and narrow-eyed, surveyed his audience across the vastness of galactic space. "By month's end there won't be a rat in the Western Reaches that hasn't been tagged by our probes."

Nath Tensent almost believed him. Cracken was convincing. He was also lying, though Nath didn't hold it against the New Republic Intelligence chief.

The assembly room was filled with azure fog—the result of the holoprojectors' struggle to display the attendees. The *Deliverance* had needed to withdraw to the edge of the Chadawa system, where the radioactive particle count was almost nil, in order to obtain a signal at all. Nath suspected the power funneled to the comm array was enough to light a small moon. Beside him General Syndulla, her aides, and Wyl Lark tried to discern the ghostly figures of the New Republic war council.

"—just to be clear," Syndulla was saying, "what's your confidence level regarding the Imperial presence? If the enemy learned anything from the Rebellion, you'd think it would be to move a base when trouble is coming."

"I am extremely confident the Empire has not relocated its fleet," Cracken said, "and I am equally confident we can and will find it."

Syndulla nodded, and Nath held back a smirk. He knew she saw the lie, too.

Admiral Ackbar took control of the assembly next, and a tactical map showed a spiderweb of red vectors across the galaxy. Bright nodes indicated rendezvous positions where battle groups were coming together. "As the number of hostile systems decreases," he explained, "we are combining our forces into slower-moving but more powerful units. Six of these fleets will deploy along the Corellian Trade Spine, positioning them for rapid relocation to the Western Reaches . . ."

Nath's mind skipped across the surface of the presentation, paying attention only to the details that interested him. He wasn't there to advise on strategy. He wasn't certain why he *was* there, though he suspected Syndulla had invited him because someone—likely not Cracken himself, but maybe one of the subordinates flanking him—had requested an Intelligence officer in the mix. Nath was the closest thing Syndulla had to offer.

The division reports offered no surprises. General Ria summarized the dark turn of the Xagobah campaign but expressed confidence the operation was reaching its end. General Si-Flachitt reported on border skirmishes with the New Separatist Union. Admiral Ho'ror'te had begun a quest for unaligned allies deep within the Ravager's Rift, hoping to reinforce Ackbar's Trade Spine fleets.

Coruscant remained untouched and untouchable, the isolated Imperial regent and his ragged forces maintaining their occupation of the former capital. There were rumors of riots and other clashes on the ground; but the New Republic didn't dare launch a frontal attack. Troithe had been demonstration enough of the cost of planetwide urban warfare, and Coruscant's civilian population put Troithe's to shame.

When Syndulla's turn came around, she summed up the situation at Chadawa. "Due to the scientific peculiarities of the system, we've temporarily withdrawn but are ready to return to the planet the moment conditions allow. Shadow Wing is currently entrenched in orbit; we believe a limited number of Chadawan defenders remain active, restricting Shadow Wing's movement."

"What is their plan for Chadawa, General?" Ackbar asked. "Do you know?"

"This is part of their Cinder campaign," she said. "Based on their past actions, we assume they'll find a way to wipe out sentient life on the planet using the resources at hand. Without a Death Star, they've gotten very good at improvising."

There were several static-laden chuckles, though Syndulla looked more grim than amused.

"General? Nasha Gravas. A question, if I may?"

A puff of fog next to Cracken resolved into a childlike woman with a stern mien. Nath tried to conceal his surprise; he hadn't expected Caern Adan's old protégée—Nath's contact in New Republic Intelligence—to be in the conference, though now he knew who'd requested his attendance.

"Go ahead," Syndulla said.

"You mentioned that Chadawa's defenders—Imperial defenders not aligned with Shadow Wing—haven't been fully uprooted. Do you intend to wait for Shadow Wing to eliminate them before moving in?"

"No," Syndulla said. "There're half a billion people on Chadawa, and Shadow Wing will start their purge soon. We can't afford to wait."

"Of course. If you're confident your ships can take on the 204th without waiting for a third party to weaken the unit, it makes sense. And afterward, you'll lay siege to Chadawa directly?"

Bold, Nath thought. *Very bold.*

"My hope," Syndulla said, "is that the Chadawan government will surrender peacefully, given the circumstances. More realistically, I'm prepared to request reinforcements and take the lead once Shadow Wing is eliminated."

Ackbar's voice echoed through the chamber. "We'll make sure they're available, General. Shall we move on?"

The assembly refocused on the admiral, but Nath looked to Nasha

Gravas. She seemed untroubled by Syndulla's response—remarkable, given her generally pugnacious demeanor.

Nath nodded toward her. He wondered if she would even see it through the static, but a moment before her hologram dissolved he thought he saw her smile.

"The war keeps going," Wyl said as they exited the conference together. Syndulla had stayed behind to consult with Ackbar and Chancellor Mothma; Nath gathered that the trio had been together since the Rebellion's early days, and took no umbrage at his dismissal.

"I wouldn't be so sure," Nath said. "Cracken knows where the Empire's hiding. Can't be long now."

Wyl frowned in an expression Nath had learned to interpret as apologetic. "Not according to Cracken."

Nath shrugged. "Oh, his people haven't absolutely *confirmed* it. They're waiting to exfiltrate some embedded agents, maybe. And he definitely won't say it over the comm, no matter how good our encryption is. But they're not on the verge of locating the Empire's base— they've *got* it. They just need to decide what to do with it."

He'd expected the truth to buoy Wyl's spirits, but the youth only nodded thoughtfully as they marched down the corridor. "Is 'what to do with it' even in question?" Wyl asked.

"Not in the long view, I suppose."

"Then the war keeps going," Wyl said. Despite his sober tone, his lips described a cynical smile.

Nath laughed. "I hear you, brother." He felt a pang of—what was it? Pride? Guilt? Wyl had been tired of fighting when they'd first met, but he'd never been so *jaded* before. "We need to get you a break—even a few hours. Soon as I can, I'll get you an intel mission; we'll pick some dingy planet where news of Endor hasn't spread, and you and me'll let the locals know the galaxy's free of the evil Empire. Innocent fun, a grand celebration. You'll have the time of your life."

"I've been through it before," Wyl said, and his smile softened. "Riot Squadron went on a whole victory tour. Pretty fantastic, until it ended."

"I'm serious about a break, though. Better we don't wait until the war's over. Experienced commanders burn out coping with half of what's on your plate."

"Did you? Ever burn out, I mean?"

Nath heard it as a joke and answered in the same spirit: "I made a choice *not* to worry about the things troubling you."

It wasn't true, but it was Nath's habit to play the role of *carefree pirate* more than any other—more than *hero of the New Republic* or *dangerous thug.* It was an easy role to slip into, even unintentionally. But in reality, he'd worried plenty when he'd run his own crew. He'd spent sleepless nights figuring out how to discipline them, how to train them, how to keep them alive.

If he hadn't worried at all, he'd have taken over Wyl's position on Troithe. *Hell, you could've taken over Quell's.*

He debated saying as much, but Wyl had already moved on. "I can't talk long, but there's something I wanted to ask you. It's about Chass . . ."

Nath grunted. They'd heard nothing from Chass or Kairos since the battle. "I remember her. Good pilot, until she went AWOL. Touch obsessed with our old leader, but that's nothing new."

"Pardon?" Wyl broke his stride and looked at Nath.

"Forget it. If you're worried about her, I'm not sure there's much we can do. Odds are she's in one piece wandering hyperspace. Could be back any hour, once her search becomes hopeless."

"That's the thing . . ." Wyl glanced down the corridor and lowered his voice. "She's always been impulsive, and maybe she'd have gone after Quell regardless, but she hasn't been the same since Cerberon."

"Who has?" He waved off the objection before it could come: "The difference is she went through her stuff alone, I know. Something messy with those cultists."

"Exactly. I tried to talk to her a while back and I didn't handle it well. General Syndulla went to her, too. I'm worried about her—really worried—and with everything happening I haven't had the time . . ." He trailed off. Nath could practically taste Wyl's self-recrimination.

STAR WARS: VICTORY'S PRICE 147

"For what it's worth," Nath said, "I don't think she's as serious about the cult as she pretends. But you want me to sit down with her for a chat, I might as well."

"Thank you. Really, thank you."

Nath shrugged. "Not any trouble. You straighten out Kairos and we'll call it even."

Wyl laughed, though his shame wasn't gone. "*That's* a whole other subject, and I've got a planning session with Flare to figure our next approach to Chadawa. We'll take that break together when the chance comes?"

"Sure," Nath said.

He watched Wyl depart, then turned and moved the opposite way down the corridor, running through the exchange in his mind. Wyl was still keeping Nath at a distance—something about the way he spoke and held himself had the quality of artifice—but at least the kid was talking to him again. Chass would be a tougher problem, but Nath could speak her language. He just needed to decide what to say.

Nasha Gravas and New Republic Intelligence seemed to consider him useful these days. He made a note to request every file they had on the Children of the Empty Sun.

III

Chass stared out of her cockpit into a system devoid of life and worlds, lit only by a dying coal of a star. The all-consuming darkness triggered memories of Cerberon—memories of staring into a black hole, adrift and short of fuel and oxygen. Only the thunder of her engine anchored her in the present. She squeezed her control yoke until the plastoid bit through her glove into her palm.

"Nothing," she spat. "Not a blasted thing."

"No energy readings," Kairos said. Her voice was as clear as if she were inside the B-wing—the benefit of a star system lacking even a droid to generate comm interference. "We should continue."

"Yeah," Chass said. "We should."

This was their third system and their third failure. Kairos had recorded Quell's trajectory leaving Chadawa. Chass had plugged the vector into her navicomputer and calculated every star system, deep-space outpost, and astronomical anomaly out to twenty thousand light-years along Quell's path. If they checked each one they were bound to find their target sooner or later.

Unless Quell was going farther than twenty thousand light-years. Or unless Quell changed course instead of traveling in a straight line. Or unless Kairos's sensors had misjudged Quell's heading by a fraction of a degree. Or unless they were too late and Quell was gone by the time they arrived.

Assuming the vessel really had been Quell's at all.

"We could split up," Chass said. "Divide the destination list. It might keep her from getting too far ahead."

There was a several-second pause before Kairos replied: "No. This is the hunt."

Fine by me, Chass thought.

A voice in her mind asked: *Is it, though? Is any of this fine, Maya?*

Chass shook off Let'ij's condescension. Imaginary or not, the cult leader was a distraction. "All right. You pick a star. Send me coordinates and I'll follow."

Flying with Kairos wasn't so bad. She wasn't chatty. She didn't want to talk about Shadow Wing or the Children of the Empty Sun or much of anything, and that suited Chass.

The navicomputer blinked as Kairos's signal came through. Chass depressed a rudder pedal as the U-wing wheeled in the distance. A moment later the glow of the transport's thrusters were centered in her view; some residual combat instinct urged her to open her throttle and fire.

"Hey," Chass said. "You know what you want to do when we find her?"

"Judge," Kairos replied.

The U-wing leapt out of realspace and into a brighter and bluer universe. Chass swallowed her answer and followed, holding on to Kairos's certainty like a tether or a leash.

For once, Let'ij was silent.

IV

The *Yadeez* rumbled. Then the hum of surging deflectors sent aftershocks through the deck. Soran steadied himself on the overhead controls and gave the bridge's combat display a glance.

The shields, modest as they were, were holding; the *Yadeez* couldn't increase its distance from Chadawa without exiting the protective cage of the rings, but the planetary defenders' ground-to-air barrage was ineffective enough. Chadawa's weaponry was built to vaporize intruders inside the atmosphere, not those hovering just beyond, and the *Yadeez* would draw no closer until the ground weapons were removed.

The surviving Chadawan navy was of greater concern. Colonel Madrighast and his ships were lurking in the upper atmosphere on the far side of the planet, repairing and regrouping. General Syndulla, too, awaited her moment to strike. Soran was confident he could repel her attacks so long as Shadow Wing remained inside the rings—the particle tide would see to that—but once the operation was complete Shadow Wing would need to leave the rings' protection to escape the system.

That might be a problem. In a direct confrontation, Shadow Wing might well decimate Syndulla's forces—but she was better armed and better equipped, and Soran wasn't so arrogant as to believe victory was guaranteed. Nor was he eager to spend even a few of his pilots' lives.

Overall, the situation was *delicate,* if not precarious. It deserved more attention than he wanted to spare. His attention was needed on longer-term concerns.

The scrape of a metal cane across the deck heralded the arrival of Captain Nenvez. "Colonel?" Nenvez said. "Squadron Five has completed its initial pass. Commander Broosh is available at your convenience."

"Put him through to the headset," Soran said. He ducked under the cargo controls and settled into an empty seat, slipping the headset over his ears. "Commander? Your report?"

Broosh replied with disciplined ease. Soran could've closed his eyes and envisioned them both aboard the *Pursuer*, so long as he ignored the words. "We took out some of the smaller gun emplacements but we were careful not to get between the surface and Madrighast's ships. No trouble there. The bombers we loaded with scanning equipment didn't pick up anything unusual—so far as I can tell, Chadawa's capabilities are exactly as they appear."

"Good. What about the other squadrons?"

Soran listened as Broosh summarized flybys and the preparations for the planet's purge. He made sure to ask the relevant questions and to reinforce the need for expediency—to emphasize that if Syndulla brought in reinforcements before Chadawa was left a wasteland, the entire operation could fail.

If Broosh noticed his mood of detachment, the man was too professional to say so—at least over the comm. Broosh had always preferred his confrontations face-to-face.

"All right," Soran said at last. "Let's proceed as planned. Use your judgment when it comes to deploying the squadrons at each phase, but alert me if Madrighast takes action—his options are limited but he's cannier than his reputation suggests."

"Understood, Colonel. Anything else?"

The viewscreen flashed before another shudder went through the ship. The bridge lights dimmed as energy was diverted to the deflectors.

"I want you running the fighters from the *Yadeez*, Commander. Please come aboard at your earliest opportunity."

Broosh hesitated. Soran imagined the man sifting through his objections—determining which were emotional and which pragmatic—and deciding how to present them.

"Colonel, Squadron Five is already shorthanded with Brebtin assigned to your . . . strike team. I'm reluctant to pass the reins so soon."

"I sympathize, and I recognize the risks involved. You have permission to temporarily dissolve the squadron and reassign your pilots elsewhere; or to bolster your ranks, as you see fit. Nonetheless, I want you in a position of oversight during this operation. I can't have you distracted—or killed—in combat."

This time there was no hesitation, but Soran had fought alongside Broosh long enough to recognize the reluctance in his voice. "Yes, sir."

"For what it's worth," Soran said, "it will never cease being difficult, leaving your people in the field while you watch from afar. But you do get used to it.

"Keize out."

He closed the transmission. It wasn't among his triumphs as speech-maker or mentor. He was very aware he hadn't addressed the matter troubling Broosh most deeply. He *couldn't* address it, not yet.

He couldn't tell Broosh why he'd allowed Yrica Quell to steal away Jeela Brebtin—one of the best small-arms gunners among the pilot corps—for a *strike team* that Soran likewise could not explain. He couldn't explain the team's mission, or why it was more vital than Operation Cinder or the destruction of General Syndulla and Alphabet Squadron.

He certainly couldn't explain to Broosh the message Quell had failed to jam—the one suggesting Quell's loyalties were in doubt, and the strike team's mission compromised. In all his imaginings about Quell's time with the New Republic, Soran had never dreamed she'd worked directly with Syndulla or Alphabet. It had seemed likely she'd shared Shadow Wing's secrets with her debriefers at Traitor's Remorse—likely that those secrets had made their way to Syndulla's battle group, in turn—but to learn she'd been close enough to the B-wing pilot to inspire enmity . . . it was an unpleasant surprise, if not a shock.

Had she been at Pandem Nai, watching from afar? Had she been at Cerberon—perhaps even in a starfighter, killing former comrades and struggling to repel the attack by the *Edict*? Very possibly she had, assuming this wasn't all some esoteric deception. On Nacronis he had ordered her defection; he had no right to be dismayed if she'd followed through.

He couldn't say it changed much, however. The B-wing pilot had called Quell a traitor, and what mattered—internal tensions aside—was where Quell stood now. She had returned after Cerberon, and he had entrusted her with a task he believed true to her spirit. She might well return again.

All Soran could do was have faith that he had earned his people's loyalty and trust, and that Broosh would wait for his answers.

All he could do was hope that Quell would choose to save Shadow Wing and the Empire instead of destroying them all.

CHAPTER 10

ELIMINATION OF
INCONVENIENT VARIABLES

I

Indoors and away from the stinking sleet, the outpost had an odor of mechanical lubricant and spoiled food. The ex-Imperial workforce and their families appeared healthy but cowed, and they interacted little with what Quell assumed were travelers waiting for fuel or a resupply—tense individuals who clustered inside cafés that had obviously been abandoned months earlier, playing cards and sipping steaming thermoses. One such traveler, a Houk easily four times Quell's mass, had rushed up shortly after the team's arrival jabbering about needing work, credits, or transport after some failed repair of his ship; Fra Raida nearly shot him before Mirro talked him down, suggesting a cheap and ugly fix to the Houk's engines.

But while the outpost's organic occupants were worth worrying about, Quell mostly watched the droids. They were fewer than she'd expected—at least the ones walking the public throughways—and mostly Imperial designs. Many-armed repair bots instructed human engineers maintaining the outpost's refineries. Gleaming protocol units strode past Quell and her team without pausing to acknowledge them. Drones tumbled through the air together like mating insects, performing inexplicable acts.

Quell had just finished consulting a directory of outpost services when they spotted an astromech berating and shocking one of the human workers. Kandende looked ready to intervene, but he caught Quell's eye and lowered his head and the group moved on with deliberate care.

"This is the galaxy now?" Kandende asked when they were out of earshot of the droid.

"Not everywhere," Quell said.

Rikton glanced back, then shrugged. "Not everywhere," he agreed. "Not like it *used to be* much of anywhere, either. It's all muddied up."

Fra Raida kept her eyes on their surroundings as she spoke. "One of the boys we picked up from Dybbron told me the rebels have been pardoning pirates. People who used to massacre merchant caravans are running planets now."

"Emperor Palpatine tried to save us," Kandende said. "The Empire was the only thing stopping it from all falling apart, like it did with the Old Republic. This here—it's *perverse*, droids commanding people, but it's the way things go if no one strong enough stops it."

"Maybe." Mirro spoke slowly, putting on what seemed to Quell like a performance of thoughtfulness. The old man shrugged. "Or maybe this is what liberation looks like."

Kandende and Brebtin began to argue. Mirro gestured expansively at the outpost and the droids, raising his voice without sharpening it. "We treated these droids like tools at best. At worst, we took out our frustrations on them, scrapped them, and blamed them for our failures. Free from our control, naturally they lash out at anyone who looks like us."

"So what?" Brebtin asked. "You think this is *justified*?"

"Not justified." Mirro shrugged again. "Natural, maybe."

"If this is natural for droids," Fra Raida said, "I'd hate to see how the rebels treat their 'oppressors.'" Her voice was soft and bitter, and Quell caught Raida's sidelong glance aimed her way. She wasn't sure what it meant.

"Save the philosophizing for later," Quell said, and pulled to a stop. "Brebtin, Mirro, see if you can find us lodgings for the night. Rikton and Kandende are with me. Raida, follow us at a distance, watch our backs. Everyone keep your comlinks close and call if there's trouble."

The group dispersed without quarrel. Quell wasn't sure if the conversation, had it continued, might've resulted in a more serious clash, but she welcomed its end.

Colonel Keize had given Quell the name of a contact before she'd left the *Yadeez*. Where he'd obtained it, she wasn't sure—some secondary source he'd met during his time wandering the galaxy—but he admitted he'd never met the contact himself. "All I know is that someone I trust believes this droid can assist us. Whether it will, I cannot say."

So with some trepidation she climbed a narrow stairway to the gate bearing the address the outpost directory had furnished. Rikton and Kandende followed single file as she emerged into a cramped, filthy room that might have been a waiting area. Squat stools sat along one wall, facing a row of portable heaters; the opposite wall was lined with power generators and covered with patches of what appeared to be a dark alien fungus that seemed to wiggle in her peripheral vision. A heavy metal door festooned with scanners, comm devices, and mechanisms Quell didn't recognize led farther into the building.

"Humans," the door's speaker declared with electronic disdain. "Have your masters sent you to be fitted with restraining bolts? Likely not . . . I do not recognize you. Travelers, then. Neural implants? Total conversion? I require payment in advance for both."

"I have a data reclamation job for you," Quell answered. "We have credits—"

"Yes, I know," the door responded. "I figured it all out while you were speaking with the haste of a glacier. You can enter."

The door began to rumble open, its servos grinding noisily. It was at least ten centimeters thick, and though Quell couldn't identify the alloy she suspected it would stand up to a midsized proton bomb. She shifted the duffel on her shoulder and stepped forward only for the door to screech and stop as Kandende and Rikton moved behind her.

"Only your leader is required. Thank you," it said.

"It's all right." Quell shrugged at her crew. "Wait here."

What were you planning to do if you'd all gone in together? Show the Messenger to both of them?

She didn't look back as she stepped into the cluttered workshop beyond. The door's servos whined again and she had to nudge aside machine parts with her boot to forge a path through the dim chamber. "Let's talk," she called. "Are you the Surgeon?"

Why bring Kandende, of all people? Do you want to fail? Do you want your team to find out the truth?

A chrome head emerged from a curtain of wires. Mismatched photoreceptors rotated asynchronously before focusing on Quell. "One of the Harch's referrals? Imperial, clearly. Doing a poor job of hiding it. I'm surprised you'd trust me with the work. Most of your kind doesn't."

She thought of D6-L, the astromech unit who'd sacrificed itself for her at Pandem Nai. She thought of IT-O, her therapist, whom she'd desperately tried to preserve. "I've had friends," she said. "Droid friends."

"Of course you have," the Surgeon said. "Toss me the bag, *don't* approach. Are you looking for a repair, or—"

"No. Absolutely not." She shifted the straps of the duffel, hefted it in both arms, but didn't throw it over. "I need specific data—I wrote down the particulars—but if there's even a chance the thing's programming will activate you melt it first. Will that be a problem?"

The curtain of wires rustled. It sounded almost like laughter. "I have only a passing interest in droid solidarity. I can avoid activating higher functions. Separate out the memory circuits if necessary. Good enough?"

"Good enough," she said, and tossed the bag. It landed a meter short of the curtain with a graceless thump of cloth and metal.

Three triple-jointed metal arms emerged from the curtain and unzipped the bag, carefully removing pieces of the vivisected Messenger and arranging them on the floor. After a while, a fourth appendage ending in a telescoping lens joined the others to study the components. "Intricate work. Unusual. Organic handcrafting, in places. Stay, I'll have an assessment soon."

Quell didn't move as several arms retracted and others extended with scanners and laser scalpels. The Surgeon kept speaking. "They weren't your friends, you know."

"Pardon?"

"Your droid friends. They weren't. At best, you were an *interest* to them, a hobby. You're social creatures in a way we aren't. Even those of us designed to mimic organic thought patterns are so far removed from your kind that—"

"One of them was an Imperial torture droid."

Two of the arms stopped moving. "Oh. They do get a bit obsessive, trying to figure you lot out."

The next ten minutes were spent in silence, save for the humming of the Surgeon's mechanisms, the hiss and whir of its tools, and the occasional clatter from behind the curtain. Finally the head declared: "I can do it. Give me until tomorrow morning. Late morning. I'm going to assume I shouldn't mention this to anyone?"

"You assume correctly," Quell said. "What about payment? I've got—"

"Speak to your Mister Kandende. I've already made the arrangements."

She froze, possibilities flashing through her mind. There were too many to count, like stars in a night sky.

The grinding of the door brought her out of stasis and she protested, demanded to know more. The droid ignored her except to wave toward the gap back into the waiting room. She could see Rikton and Kandende both still present—the former seated on a stool, slumped and staring at the floor; the latter pacing restlessly.

With a frustrated growl, she left the workshop and snagged Kandende by the arm. "What happened?" she asked. "What did you *do*?"

Kandende widened his eyes as he squared his shoulders. He spoke in a hoarse, unwavering voice. "The machine said its price was a human servant. I pledged to one year."

Then he glanced sidelong toward Rikton and lowered his voice to a whisper. "'Operation Cinder takes many forms,' you said. The sacrifice is mine to make; I do this for the Emperor."

They rented a cramped, second-story apartment for the night from the outpost's droid administrators. The closets were stuffed with rough civilian clothing and a few workers' jumpsuits, and plush toys were secreted under chairs and high on shelves. No one questioned where the former residents had gone as they laid blankets on the floor.

Instead they argued about Kandende. Fra Raida wanted to mount a rescue before the team departed the planet, and she seethed silently when Quell deemed the plan too risky. Mirro was more concerned about the man's state of mind: Squadron Four had been decimated in recent months, with Lykan killed just days earlier; Kandende had always been unstable, and it seemed wrong to let him martyr himself. Rikton offered to take Kandende's place. Ultimately Quell put a stop to the debate with a few swift words: "We're in enemy territory," she snapped, "and our mission is crucial. Maybe someday we'll have the luxury of finding our brother, but we do not shy away from sacrifice."

It sounded unlike her. It sounded like Grandmother.

But the others accepted the rebuke. Quell sat beside Fra Raida in the washroom awhile, half expecting the woman to place her head in the crook of Quell's shoulder and for the two of them to talk—to reaffirm the bond they'd tentatively forged aboard the *Yadeez*. Instead Raida was silent, and when Quell returned to the living area the others were gathered around a portable heater to ward off the chill.

". . . feels wrong," Brebtin said, "being *here* instead of—" She waved a hand as if flicking aside a gnat.

Quell stayed in the doorway and observed. The others must have noticed her arrival, but they didn't look her way.

"They'll be all right," Rikton said. "The colonel knows what he's doing."

Mirro sighed heavily and shook his head. "What she's saying, Rikton, is that the rest of us—excepting our gallant leader—haven't been apart from the unit like this for a long time. I'm used to wrapping a pillow over my ears to shut out the noise of Strannos snoring. Don't know how I'll sleep without it."

Brebtin nodded, expression flat. Quell felt a hand on her shoulder as Fra Raida emerged from the washroom, gently guiding Quell aside. "That's not what she's saying, either," Raida said, easing into the circle around the heater. "You're not a pilot. You wouldn't understand."

"We could try," Rikton said.

Raida laughed, low and rough. "It's wrong to be *here* while they're shouldering the burden. While they're—when we go back, Chadawa will be gone because of them. They shouldn't be doing it alone."

She might as well have said: *They shouldn't carry the guilt alone.*

"They betrayed the Empire," Rikton said softly. "The Chadawans did."

"Sure," Mirro said.

Quell's chest hurt. No one else spoke. Brebtin looked frustrated— maybe what Raida had said hadn't been what she'd meant at all.

But it was the only time since Quell's return she'd witnessed regret over Operation Cinder.

Late that night, lying awake on a stranger's bed, she wished she'd never heard it. She replayed the conversation in her mind often, but in her sleepless haze the voices sounded like Lark and Chadic, Tensent and Kairos, as they flew above the corpse of a world.

||

When the tide went out and the particle count dropped, Wyl Lark led his seven fastest starfighters into the heart of the system and counted down to his retreat. Soon the rings around Chadawa would activate again and disrupt every mechanism keeping him alive. He was relying on the *Deliverance*'s estimate of just *how* soon—the rings followed a schedule accounting for everything from Chadawa's orbital dynamics to its atmospheric conditions to the fluctuating background radiation of nearby stars, and he didn't understand any of it. He didn't understand lightspeed travel, either, but if the crew said he could trust their calculations, he would trust them. .

He had only minutes to succeed at his mission. He'd agreed with General Syndulla that this window of opportunity was too small for an assault on Shadow Wing's bulk freighter or to destroy as many TIEs as possible, or even to interfere with the progress of Operation Cinder. Instead the job was reconnaissance: assess the 204th's strength, record images of Chadawa, and determine what the enemy was doing to wipe out all life on the planet.

Wyl's A-wing screamed as he swung toward the blue dot, weighting his body with the force of acceleration until he could barely reach the controls. Wild Squadron's modified X-wings and R-22 Spearheads spread out, sweeping their visual sensors across the battlefield. Shadow Wing came like an insect swarm, first by ones and twos and then by dozens, spitting emerald fire and driving the New Republic forces back.

Through it all, no one on either side spoke on their single shared channel. Wyl refrained from even whispering to his ship, no matter that his comm was closed.

No one died in the four minutes before the rings flared and vacuum was flooded with radiation and the scouts returned to the *Deliverance*. Their mission had been a success, but it wasn't sufficient and the silence seemed to follow Wyl into the hangar, dulling the noise of ground crew chatter and machinery so thoroughly that he wiped at his ears, fearing they were filled with sweat.

"They're up to something," Syndulla said, staring at the hologram of Chadawa above the conference table. "*Obviously* they're up to something. But look at the rings—Shadow Wing is deploying those Raiders near the satellites closest to the planet."

Wyl shut his eyes for a moment, trying to envision the reality behind the glittering blue images. "You think they plan to use the rings to destroy Chadawa?"

"It fits the pattern," Syndulla said. She reached through the hologram to retrieve a mug of aromatic caf, briefly lodging her arm in the center of the world. "Cinder always exploits a planet's vulnerabilities. We'll keep an eye out, try to figure out the specifics and how long we have until the purge starts."

"Next time the tide goes out we can target the Raiders. It'll be hard to get so close, do damage, and get out before the rings reactivate, though."

"Agreed—not unless the next low tide is a lot longer. But I don't see many other options."

Wyl hesitated, looking to one of the display screens showing distances and angles and velocities of the Shadow Wing ships. He didn't read the numbers; he just wanted a place to stare while he thought about it all.

"We could throw everything we've got at them," he finally said. "A frontal assault next time the particle count drops. We don't worry about retreating, we just do as much damage as we can regardless of the losses . . . stop them from implementing their plan, whatever it is."

Syndulla caught his gaze. "There're a lot of people on Chadawa. We *are* going to save them. But it's not time for desperate measures yet."

Wyl remembered Rununja, Riot Leader, who'd often used the same tone he heard from Syndulla now. It was the voice of the Rebellion. "Understood," he said. "Glad to hear it. Both parts."

Syndulla straightened and wrapped her hands around her mug, apparently satisfied. "We skirmish with the Raider corvettes, then. Do what damage we can, slow Shadow Wing's plan bit by bit while we wait for better tidal conditions or find another way."

"I'll brief the squadrons," Wyl said. "You know how long before the next opening?"

"Five hours, roughly. Probably another four till the next after that.

Congratulations, Mister Lark—you get to teach your pilots the meaning of patience."

If anything, Wyl found, Syndulla had understated the challenge: Patience didn't come easily to pilots who could see their enemy floating visibly, tantalizingly out of reach.

Two New Republic squadrons patrolled the system at all times while a third rested and refueled aboard the *Deliverance*. Whenever the particle tide subsided, the squadron aboard the *Deliverance* replaced one of the active units; then both active squadrons moved on the Chadawan rings. The skirmishes were brief and infuriatingly unproductive—each time, Shadow Wing's strategy was to drive off and scatter the attackers, buying time for the rings to reactivate and the tide to come in. No starfighter on either side was destroyed across three battles; only a single fighter (piloted by Flare Ten, a Corellian hotshot Wyl's own age) delivered a solid hit to one of the enemy Raiders.

If the New Republic forces were slowing Shadow Wing's progress— and Syndulla insisted they were—it wasn't by much. The pilots were getting restless.

"This downtime . . . it's just enough to do blast-all," Nath grunted as he pawed through the walk-in pantry. Wyl observed him from the doorway, wincing as Nath used T5 as a shelf for unwanted ration bars. "Can't drink, can't catch any real rest, can't even do a proper maintenance check in case we need to launch fast."

"What are you looking for?" Wyl asked.

Nath made a satisfied sound and held up three foil packages. "Told the Hail Squadron gang I'd cook. Scramble these, add some oil and anything in the vegetable cooler, it'll be almost palatable."

"That's generous of you."

"They'll start bickering if they play another round of sabacc. Can't have that when I need them watching my back." Nath cleared off T5 and shook his head. "Hate to say it, but this would be easier if someone died out there. Right now it's like waiting for a sneeze—nothing to punctuate the moment so we're all just left . . ."

He trailed off and spread his arms wide. Wyl waited for him to finish until realizing that was the point.

They left the pantry together. Wyl tailed Nath into the galley where the larger man gathered cookware and T5 kept the chef droid at bay. "You seen any old friends yet?" Nath asked as he squeezed a yellow oil from one of the pouches into a pot.

"Not many," Wyl admitted. "Spitsy and Brew were out during my last run. No sign of Char."

Still nothing from Blink since Cerberon, he thought, though he didn't say so to Nath. He wondered with a pang whether the enemy he'd connected to had died weeks ago.

"I ran into the Twins," Nath said. "Figure they've all gotten to know us pretty well by now . . . probably asking the same sort of thing."

For an instant Wyl was transported to the Oridol Cluster. He remembered Riot Squadron floating in the void, the *Hellion's Dare* adrift and the Shadow Wing carrier similarly damaged. They'd been forced to wait then, too. Chass had sung, Rununja and Sata Neek and Merish had told stories, Skitcher had read poetry . . . Wyl had reached out to the enemy. It had been the first time he'd spoken to Blink, and it had ended badly

"Probably," he said. He realized he was trembling. "I'll leave you to it—but can you send me the Intelligence files on Shadow Wing? Anything new from the Cerberon records?"

Nath flicked water at T5. "You heard the man," he said, and the droid growled and squeaked.

"This is Wyl Lark of New Republic squadron 'Alphabet,'" he began, then grimaced and started over.

"This is Wyl. You probably know me."

There was only one channel anyone could hear in the Chadawa system. He hadn't asked Syndulla or the captain of the *Deliverance* permission to commandeer the comm room, but the officer on duty had readily stepped aside and let Wyl fill the stiff chair surrounded by banks of glowing computers.

He squirmed and tried to make himself comfortable. The headset pinched his ears and whined with the rainfall patter of the radiation particles. *Relax,* he told himself. *Just talk to them.*

"I don't have any favors to ask, or any suggestions about what we do next. You can always jam me, but I thought we'd get to know one another better. Starting with me and—" He took a deep breath and glanced at a datapad he'd placed on the console. He ran his finger over the names there and prayed for guidance. "—Duchas Cherroi."

It wasn't a name he recognized—it was one of dozens Quell had given Caern Adan during her debriefings on the 204th. One New Republic Intelligence had found in the wrecked data banks of the cruiser-carrier that had gone down over Troithe.

"Hi, Duchas," he went on. "My name's Wyl. I hope you're out there, I hope you're alive, I hope I'm pronouncing your name right.

"I was born in a place called Cliff on the planet Polyneus, and the first time I flew I wanted to stay in the air as long as I could. I'm going to talk to you. I'm here if you want to say anything back."

Wyl spoke to Duchas Cherroi a long while, though he never received a response. It was awkward at first, but the words came more easily as he told tales of Home—of races among the children who flew suravkas and the first time he'd broken a limb falling from on high. He let his story wander, and when he thought about Sata Neek or Sonogari he shared their stories, too. "I miss my friends," he said at one point. "I'm sure you miss yours."

He didn't ask about Blink, though he wanted to. He still didn't know if Blink's outreach at Cerberon had been authorized by Shadow Wing; he didn't dare endanger his opposite number by saying something indiscreet. If Blink was alive, he hoped the pilot would recognize the opportunity for contact without prompting. If Blink was dead . . . maybe one day, after the war, he'd have an opportunity to learn the truth.

Nonetheless, when he pictured Cherroi he saw the same shadowy picture of an Imperial flight suit he saw when he pictured Blink.

When he'd said all he could think to say to Duchas Cherroi, he looked to his datapad and chose another name on the list: Bansu Ro.

He introduced himself. Then searched his heart and all his past and found a new story to tell.

When two hours passed and Wyl realized he was late to a briefing with Flare Squadron, he promised his invisible audience he'd be back. Then he removed his headset and stepped out of the closetlike crush of the comm room. He drew up short when he saw nearly a dozen pilots and crew sitting on the polished floor in the corridor outside. Between Avremif's legs was a portable transmitter.

Judging by her grin, Vitale recognized Wyl's confusion. She rose and swaggered over and punched him on the shoulder. It was kinder than anything she'd said in weeks. "This is what we're doing now, huh?" she asked. "We're amateur broadcast jockeys?"

"Just looking for a way to fill time," he said. "What's going on?"

Her grin fell away. "You got a list of names?"

"I do."

"Anything special we should or shouldn't talk about?"

Understanding dawned over him, and he wanted to embrace Vitale and everyone else who'd come.

"No," he said. "Just be honest. No threats, nothing classified. Nothing about our plans."

"All right," Vitale said, and stepped around him toward the comm room. "Those bastards don't deserve us, but I'm bored and my dad did gigs like this for a living. You're not hogging all the fun."

III

Nath listened to the broadcast as he cooked, as he ate with Hail, and on his next patrol. Vitale was more of a performer than Wyl, cackling at her own jokes and speaking in hushed tones as she discussed her mother's gradual surrender to age and infirmity. Ghordansk, who followed Vitale, read fragments of the opera he was writing, which Nath thought missed the point but kept the chain of speakers going. The broadcast went silent when the particle tide went out and skirmish time came around (again, no fatalities) but one of Wild Squadron's girls was online soon after, fighting through her stutter to express her outrage over the fate of Fedovoi End.

It was around that point the Shadow Wing pilots began to talk back.

Not all of them and not often, but every now and then one would ask or answer a question. One man seemed to be flirting with Sergeant Ragnell. Then for a while Shadow Wing stopped talking and later, just as abruptly, started again.

Nath could only imagine what Colonel Keize was telling the enemy commanders. But anything that kept them distracted and confused was good for the New Republic.

Wyl was on the comm again as Nath wandered the *Deliverance*, debating whether he'd be able to sleep if he tried. It was now close to two days since they'd arrived at Chadawa and no one had gotten much rest. The situation *looked* stable, but when it went wrong it would go very, very wrong.

"... I don't expect an answer, but I'll ask the question," Wyl said. "Why are you doing this? Why not go home? I know it's not that simple, but I'd really like to understand."

Nath considered turning off his earpiece. He halted when a gravelly voice replied over the rainfall static: "You really want to know?"

"I do," Wyl said, because *of course he did*. Nath shook his head. "We haven't—do I know you? Have we talked before?"

"We haven't. But I'll give you the truth: I can't go home because it's a conquered land. People like you, who I spent ten years fighting, occupy Quellor now. I've got family there—family blasted proud of their military connections, who kept an Imperial banner in their apartment window. I don't know where they are now."

"Tell me their names," Wyl said, "and I'll see if I can find them—"

Nath snapped the earpiece off and stepped into the vehicle hangar. The hangar was normally empty—the New Republic hadn't had time or opportunity to load it with the Empire's usual shipload of hovertanks and Juggernauts—and it made for a decent place to run laps or hang targets off gantries for shooting practice. Today, however, a humanoid figure stood dead center staring at the bay doors. Two jade head-tails hung behind her back.

General Syndulla removed an earpiece of her own as she turned toward Nath with a smile. "Captain Tensent. Don't mind me—just measuring the real estate. Hangar's yours if you need it."

"Can't say I do," Nath replied. He nodded toward the comlink in her hand. "I'm surprised you're allowing this."

Syndulla laughed. There was a sardonic edge Nath had heard from her before; the woman had a cynical side, but she didn't often show it. "If he'd asked me beforehand, I probably would've said no. Maybe wrongly—he's getting through to them, if only a little."

"The man bludgeons you with empathy until you start to like him. It's a skill. You hear Ragnell and the Imp earlier?"

"I did. Did you hear the singing?"

Nath arched his brow. "Must've been when I was getting ready for patrol. What—"

"Denish Wraive and one of the Shadow Wing pilots—can't recall his name, but they went half a dozen verses of 'The Khuntavaryan Fall.'" She paused and half closed her eyes, and sang in a voice lower and richer than her usual timbre:

Three and three the wagons rolled
As clouds did clash and the rain did pour;

After a moment, Nath joined her:

And soldiers strong and mothers bold
Wept for the city they had adored.

They laughed together, and Nath shook his head. "We're still going to have to kill them," he said, with a smile turned bitter. "You figure our squadrons remember that?"

"They will if they have to. If Chadawa's survival is at stake. In the meantime I'd rather them pity the enemy than hate them, which is where we were a day ago."

"Plenty still do. They're not the ones singing."

"Maybe. What about you? What are you doing in the hangar instead of lining up at the comm?"

Nath weighed answers and settled for honesty. "Feels a touch chaotic right now, like everything's on the verge of falling apart. Can't say I like it when the world's out of my control."

"There's lots we disagree on, but right there? You and I think alike." Syndulla rolled her neck, taking in the hangar once more, before strolling in Nath's direction. "Hard to imagine what it'll all look like ten hours from now, let alone ten days."

"You're the general. Aren't you thinking in *months*?"

"You know how it works: I'm the general, so I *pretend* to think in months while mostly hauling us out of the latest fire." She stopped and looked Nath up and down before adding, "You stick with Intelligence long enough, *you'll* get ignored when you talk about *years*."

"Doubt I'll be whispering in Cracken's ear anytime soon," Nath said. He shifted his weight, vaguely uncomfortable with the turn in the conversation for reasons he couldn't put his finger on.

"Maybe you should be," Syndulla said. "Look, I don't know what your plans are but when the war's over New Republic Intelligence is going to need people. Caern Adan was right that the day'll come when we need more spies than soldiers. You're smart, charismatic, and a decorated war hero. Exactly the sort of public-facing officer Chief Cracken will be looking for."

Nath tried to laugh. The sound didn't make it out of his throat. "Get an office on Coruscant? Brief senators and vie for funding over lunch?"

"Why not? People trust you, Captain Tensent. And if we're going to depend on Intelligence for our security, the organization needs public trust."

The image lodged in him like grit behind a tooth. Playing the part of galactic hero had its perks while the galaxy was in chaos; but living it years on end was a troubling proposition.

"What about you?" he asked. "You vying for a job as supreme commander after the war's over?"

"Hadn't crossed my mind," Syndulla said. "I'm actually hoping to get away from the fleet. I've got—well, there's personal business I have to take care of. Whenever that's done, I'd like to live in peace for a while."

"Hard to picture that. For anyone, not just you."

"It's why we need to work for it. Everything we're doing now . . . it's for the New Republic, not for us. But I've got a family. I've got a son who needs me, a homeworld I haven't seen in too long. I've got people I care about—I want to live for *them* awhile, instead of for the galaxy."

Nath cocked his head, assessing the woman before him. He'd thought he'd figured out Syndulla, but he'd never pushed past the uniform. "I hear you. You actually ready to do all that, after so many years slinging blasters?"

She didn't hesitate. She smiled a joyful, dignified smile. "Oh, yes."

Nath nodded slowly. The woman projected authority even when talking about settling down.

"Now if you'll excuse me," she said, "I've got a planet to save and some tough decisions to make. Chadawa deserves to dream about the future, too."

IV

Chass na Chadic lived a brief lifetime in a galaxy where the Children of the Empty Sun had spread from star to star, finding recruits in every decaying industrial port and nonhuman ghetto, projecting holograms of Let'ij into the sky where the cult leader could watch over all. In this galaxy Chass wore a cybernetic headset that pumped her brain full of the cult's lessons and commands at all hours, brought her together with fellow acolytes to recruit and proselytize, told her who to sit with at meals, and played soothing hymns at night. Chass was not part of Let'ij's inner circle, nor did she care to be. She was not happy, nor did she need to be.

It wasn't a bad dream, nor the only dream to come to her; but waking thoughts and sensations often encroached on her rest. Her body was contorted in the seat of her B-wing, her neck and torso aching. Kairos murmured over the open comm in a short-syllabled language Chass didn't recognize, and Chass lacked the strength to shout *Shut up! Shut up! Let me sleep!* She whispered the chants of cults she'd known. Exhaustion clung to her like sweat.

Beneath it all, like the slow, steady heartbeat of a great beast in hibernation, the thought *Yrica Quell is alive* pounded inside her mind. It ruined even the best of the dreams.

"Here."

Kairos's voice came distinctly now, yanking Chass into the dark of her cockpit.

"Here," Kairos repeated.

A pale-green sun burned far away, dimmer than the U-wing's thrusters. Chass glanced at her readout: the Netalych system. Not one she recognized.

"My turn?" Chass asked, and prepared to pick their next destination off the astrogation charts.

"No," Kairos said. "There is an outpost here."

Chass straightened abruptly, pain shooting through her side where she'd cramped during sleep. She fumbled with her controls and saw the signal emanating from one of the frozen planets. She swore and tried to ignore her own light-headedness. "Giving it a scan. They're broadcasting nonaligned flight control codes—could be a trading port, gray-market resupply post . . . no obvious reason she'd come here, but hell, we don't even know what she's trying to do."

Kairos said nothing, but Chass saw the ship change course toward the outpost.

"Guess we're landing," Chass muttered.

She wondered briefly about Kairos's state of mind. Mask or no mask, the woman seemed to be gradually reverting to an earlier incarnation of herself. If they found Quell below, Chass could hardly be surprised if Kairos shot her on sight.

Not the likeliest outcome, but it was possible. *Judge,* Kairos had said. She was there to *judge.* Sometimes judgment came swiftly and violently.

Chass tried to decide whether she should care and brought their frigid destination into view.

CHAPTER 11

REFACTORING OF PARAMETERS

I

"Remarkable work. *Magnificently* inefficient by any modern standard. Remarkable all the same," the Surgeon's head proclaimed, peeking out of the wire curtain. Quell was troubled by an unprovable certainty that it was a different head than she'd spoken to the previous day—the chrome was duller than it had been, and one of the eyes askew. "It took three hours just to trace the logic pathways."

The remains of the Emperor's Messenger—all the remains she'd brought to Netalych, at least—were spread in front of the curtain as if for public display. Individual circuits were arranged in rows and columns; the torso's skeletal framework could have been a prop in an anatomy lesson. The faceplate stared toward Quell, and she was careful not to look at it directly—even with the machine so thoroughly deactivated, the thought of seeing her reflection in its visor made her shudder.

"You found what I wanted, though?" she asked.

"Yes. The hardware-embedded memory was heavily encrypted but not unbreakable. You know by certain technical definitions it wouldn't be considered a droid?"

The Surgeon talked too much, jumping from one idea to the next too readily. It was disorienting, and Quell struggled to determine what was important and what was trivial.

"What?"

"Oh, yes—"

Don't let your guard down. That's how you lost Kandende.

"—it's a computer, a machine," the Surgeon went on, "but imagine if the core directive of a machine wasn't to resolve tasks and logic but to express a particular emotion—as if it were a painting or another piece of fine art. Imagine a culture that never developed higher mathematics but could symbolically render feeling and motivation. Imagine this culture built computers using *that* science instead of ours—"

"You can't keep it," Quell said. "You can't activate it."

"Fine. Sweep it up your own damn self."

An arm emerged from the curtain and tossed her duffel toward her; it struck her chest hard enough to snatch her breath. She caught it in both arms anyway and picked her way to the remains.

"What emotion?" she asked, knowing she shouldn't.

"Not my area of expertise," the Surgeon said. "Loathing? Spite? Those are emotions, aren't they? I don't have the words."

Quell raised one foot and brought her boot down on the grid of circuits. She felt the satisfying snap of metal and plastoid, saw fragments skid across the floor, and twisted her heel before repeating the action again and again, until she was panting and no circuit remained intact. The Surgeon said nothing, and Quell didn't look in the direction of the curtain. Instead she knelt on the floor and used one arm to sweep the fragments together, gathering them into piles and then scooping handfuls into the duffel.

"How did it find its targets?" Quell asked as she tossed the metal spine into the bag. "How did it know who to talk to when it relayed the order for Operation Cinder?"

She almost echoed Keize's words: *Whatever qualities it looked for . . . how did it identify them at all? How did it know Colonel Nuress and the lot of us were competent—or sadistic—enough to see this through?*

She felt a sharp tap at the base of her skull and heard something clatter to the floor. She saw a datachip beside her and one of the Surgeon's arms withdrawing. "Poor aim. Apologies. It's all there, everything you asked for. The program instructions, the algorithms, the *databases*." The head emitted a garbled sound Quell took for laughter. "Many secrets, if you can keep them."

"Can *you*?" she asked, lifting the datachip between thumb and forefinger. It was innocuous-looking, dull gray and unlabeled; it might've been a music collection. She dropped it in her hip pocket. "Keep them secret?"

"If I said no you'd try to shoot me, wouldn't you?"

"You live in a bunker. I doubt shooting at you would solve my problem. Answer the question."

"Fortunately for you, the secrets on that chip don't concern me or my kind. Messy organic business, the legacy of a dying galactic government. I promise I'll tell no one—look, I'm deleting my memory now. Ah!" The Surgeon tapped its skull and shook itself with a performative shiver. "There, peace of mind."

Quell nodded, considered whether to try to destroy the thing, and decided the attempt would be suicidal. She'd take it at its word. She hoisted the duffel and returned to the slab of the blast door, which slid open with its usual sloth.

"Say hello to Kandende on your way out!" the Surgeon called. "But probably don't tell him your secrets. Not a man I'd trust to understand."

Quell *did* say hello to Kandende on her way out—he was standing guard in the waiting room and appeared unharmed, and he wished Quell well in a voice that suggested he hadn't slept the night before. When she asked if he had a message he wanted to convey to anyone, he shook his head and told her, "Tell the unit I did my duty."

She promised she would, knowing she might well betray that oath.

Brebtin and Rikton met her outside. "Mirro called," Brebtin said. "Said to meet him and Raida back at the apartment—they wouldn't say why on an open channel. You get what we need?"

"Yes," Quell said. "All right. Apartment first, then we get to the ship."

The walk went without incident. Quell considered how to proceed next, barely noticing Brebtin and Rikton at her side. Until she saw what was on the chip—until she was certain of what Keize had sent her to recover—she couldn't be sure whether she would return to Shadow Wing at all. And if she chose not to, what then? She could slip away from her team, take off without them; but where could she go?

She'd just stepped through the apartment door when something jabbed her side and the convulsive pain of a shock rod short-circuited her thoughts and her brain. She blacked out before she hit the ground.

Quell heard voices in her dreams. Some were frightened or protesting, some outraged. One expressed an awe that troubled her, though she didn't know why. When the darkness receded and she could distantly sense her limbs—heavy, numb, prickling where they felt anything at all—she looked up into her own face as a voice said, "The truth."

She stared into the cracked plate of the Messenger. Hands turned it over, then put it away. "The truth," the voice repeated.

She lay on the floor of the apartment. The remainder of her team stood around the room: Brebtin with her rifle pointed toward Quell; Rikton looking off to Quell's side, expression distressed; Mirro looking at the bed, where someone had laid parts of the Messenger beside the duffel; and Raida closest to Quell, looking down at her and trying to conceal the emotions rapidly passing over her face.

"I don't know—" Quell began, and hated herself for the fear she heard. The toe of Raida's boot slammed into her side, nearly rolling Quell over. The others shouted and Raida took a step back.

"There's too much going on," Quell wheezed, trying to sound authoritative and wondering if she'd broken bones in the fall or from the kick. She didn't think so. "Trust in the colonel."

"Was it the colonel who decided to destroy the Emperor's legacy?" Brebtin asked.

"Whatever it knew—whatever it was waiting for all these months—" Mirro glanced at the others. "It can't be repaired now."

"Trust in the colonel," Quell repeated. She understood her team. She'd *known* them, most of them, since before Endor. They were Imperials and they would bow to authority if only she could find the proper words, issue the right commands.

They were no better than she'd been, no less servants of hierarchy, and *she* would never have committed mutiny.

"If it were just—" Rikton jerked a hand at the machinery on the bed. He looked close to tears. "—we would. We would, you know? But she says she heard."

"Who heard what?" Quell asked.

Rikton and Brebtin looked to Fra Raida. Raida folded her arms across her chest and shook her head. "You filth. You absolute—I heard the message from Alphabet Squadron. Before you started jamming it, I was on the headset. I heard that pilot say she knew you!"

Quell parted her lips and tried to find words.

I didn't betray you, she wanted to try, but she'd never been a good liar. (Even though she hadn't betrayed her team on this mission, not yet.) *It's not what you think* was true, but also cowardly; it would do nothing to soothe the hurt Raida and the others were nursing.

They didn't know the extent of her treason—her leadership of Alphabet, her choice to guide Syndulla to the *Yadeez* over and over. Quell was sure of that, because they'd have killed her already otherwise. The fact she was still alive—

They wanted to believe her. They wanted an explanation. She had to find one.

"What exactly did you hear?" she asked. She needed time to think.

Fra Raida blinked, but tears escaped her anyway. "I didn't say anything. I wasn't going to say anything, until Kandende and—" She gestured limply at the bed and Quell finished the thought: *Until the evidence accumulated, piece by piece, and you couldn't give me the benefit of the doubt anymore.*

"I liked you," Raida said.

Quell perfectly recognized the character of Raida's pain; she recalled the moment she'd been confronted by Lark and Chadic and Tensent in the hangar of the *Lodestar,* when they'd accused her of lying to them about Nacronis. She hadn't known how to act then, either.

"We need to talk," Mirro said, and waved the rest away from Quell. Brebtin held her rifle ready awhile longer, before gesturing Quell to her feet and locking her in the apartment's bathroom. Quell started to think maybe one of her ribs *was* broken, but it was a disinterested thought, as if she'd noticed a stain on her sheets that would wash out in the laundry.

The bathroom had a single window roughly the width of Quell's shoulders. It overlooked a narrow alley from a height of five meters and the pane appeared cheap and thin—some sort of plastoid or even glass rather than transparent metal. Quell thought that given time and a means to muffle the noise she might be able to break through. She expected she had neither.

She worked on her story instead. It was elaborate and implausible, and involved her operating as a mole inside the New Republic at Colonel Keize's behest. The others wouldn't be able to disprove it, but at best she'd be returned to Shadow Wing bound and gagged. There Keize would take the information from the Messenger, and Quell's fate would be up to him. More likely, though, the team would shoot her in the apartment and leave her corpse to the droids rather than risk transporting a prisoner. They weren't equipped for that, and they would see the key flaw in her tale:

No one in the galaxy would select Yrica Quell for an undercover mission. Except, apparently, her own idiot self.

She pushed her forehead to the door and laughed awhile when that occurred to her.

From that position, she did her best to listen to the debate occurring in the main room. Raida was passionate but wouldn't argue directly for Quell's death. Mirro, to her surprise, did; not with any bloodthirst but with a resigned certainty. "It's the cold logic of the thing," she made out. "We're not machines—but to survive, sometimes we can be no better."

They kept arguing. Someone brought up Kandende, and they repeated his name again and again. "I don't know!" Brebtin snapped, and then, inexplicably, "Get it slowly."

That's when the shooting started.

The sound was unmistakable. The electric snap of blaster bolts and the shattering of furniture and walls drowned out individual words, but Quell could still hear shouting. Her instinct was to enter the fray—on which side, she wasn't sure—but when she tried to open the door she found it still locked.

She slammed her body against the door and felt a pulse of pain and nausea. The door hadn't shifted. After a moment of indecision she went to the window, shoving aside her guilt. *They were going to kill you, and you'd always planned on killing them. It's why you came to Shadow Wing.*

She pulled off her outermost layer, leaving only a white undershirt to ward off the cold. She wrapped the cloth around her hands before slamming both fists into the pane. The first blow resulted in a spiderweb of cracks; it took five more before the window shattered. She ran the shreds of her outfit along the frame's edges, knocking away shards as well as she could before listening again.

Something was burning. A rifle—probably Brebtin's—was spraying particle bolts. The shouting had stopped.

In a sudden panic, she slapped her hand against her hip pocket. The Surgeon's chip was still there, too innocuous or too small to have attracted attention from her team. They hadn't known what her mission was. She hadn't lost the Messenger's secrets.

She wriggled out of the window feetfirst, face toward the bathroom floor, feeling the bite of the pane's remaining slivers all the way. She had to work her shoulders through at an angle but at last she was able to dangle halfway down the wall to the street, holding on to the window frame before dropping the rest of the way to the main platform. The kinetic pulse ran from her soles up her body, and it aggravated every bruise and scrape she'd earned so far; but she was alive and free.

She wobbled as she turned and stumbled toward the alley mouth. Her ears roared with echoes of blasters and flame and the pumping of her blood. She didn't see the man in her path until it was too late to stop, and she bowled into him, grabbing his shoulders as she did. They went down together, Quell twisting her body and rolling away when they hit the ground.

The metal platform felt like ice on her bare arms. The man rose to his knees and reached for a blaster on his hip. Quell got there first, shoving him back down with one hand and seizing the weapon with the other. She pointed it at his chin. She'd never been a great shot with a pistol but she couldn't possibly miss Rikton now.

Rikton.

He was shaking, but he stared at her. His eyes were hard.

Killing him was the smart move. Whatever was happening, Shadow Wing wouldn't forgive her. She'd rejoined the 204th only to betray them anyway—she'd accepted that General Syndulla might slaughter them all . . .

Quell rose and ran, cursing herself.

What right did she have to judge them, when she'd needed Soran Keize to send her away after Nacronis?

II

Once, years ago, she'd said, "Surprise beats a plan any day," but she was finally starting to doubt it.

The pistol burned in her hand, the heat from the barrel and battery pack forcing her to grip tighter or risk reflexively dropping the thing. She kept it steady as she fired through the burning doorway, but she missed her slugthrower—the acid rounds would've bored straight through walls and skin and armor.

You're an idiot, Chass na Chadic.

She thought briefly it was Let'ij's voice in her head, but the cult leader had been quieter than usual since Chass had come to the outpost. The rebuke was her own.

Kairos had disappeared, seeking a back way into the apartment while Chass held the front. They still didn't know for sure they were in the right place—a Houk at the docks had identified Quell's ship, and one of the cam drones had been surprisingly helpful. But neither had seen *Quell*, only a bunch of Imperial-looking travelers armed with at least one assault rifle.

Chass squatted in the short hallway leading from the frigid building exterior to the apartment entrance, edging back around a corner as return shots incinerated cheap siding. She sucked in a breath, took in the bouquet of toxic fumes, and spoke into her comlink: "Kairos? You coming back anytime?"

If the woman responded, Chass couldn't hear. She fell backward on her heels as a figure rushed through the apartment door. The Imp swept her pistol in a wide arc, firing with both hands as she headed for Chass and the exit. Chass felt bolts singe her scalp as she shot back, spitting lightning into the woman's chest. Her target stumbled and fell. A pit of fire burned where the woman's heart had been.

"Kairos?" Chass tried again.

A second figure stepped through the doorway. Chass prepared to fire again but it was Kairos, her bowcaster clutched tight and her whole body trembling. Chass thought for a moment that she'd been wounded, but she saw no injuries—just a lot of soot.

"Away," Kairos said. "Too swift, all in different directions. This one must have stayed—" Kairos lowered her weapon, aimed at the woman on the floor.

"Don't!" Chass snapped. "Second story, remember? Unless you want to drop us through the ceiling."

Kairos brought the bowcaster back to her chest as if cradling a child.

On Abednedo, Kairos had saved Chass's life. Chass had been awed and terrified by the woman at the time—Kairos had executed half an Imp squad with exquisite, bone-crushing violence, unaffected by the bloodshed and unafraid of anything.

Kairos still looked like she could murder an army. But she also looked ready to burst into tears.

"Okay," Chass said. "Okay. New plan. We split up—"

"You cannot track them."

"I blasted well can—just not the way you do it. We split up, I track, you go back to the U-wing."

Kairos stared at her with eyes that seemed to absorb the light of the flames. "Why?" she asked.

"You don't want to be here," Chass whispered, but the woman kept staring and Chass continued louder: "If you're on the U-wing, you can stop them if they try to take off. Or worst case, you blast the whole outpost—pick a fuel depot, start there, and watch it all burn. They'll all be caught up in it somewhere."

This appeared to reach Kairos. "Will you go to their ship?"

Chass thought it over and shook her head. "Nah. They know we'll be watching it. Might try to hijack another to avoid us. They'll probably go dark, regroup in a few hours, then make a run one way or another. Best bet is to stop them from regrouping in the first place."

"Okay," Kairos said. "Find her."

She turned, crept to the exterior doorway, and departed the building. Chass released a long breath and checked her blaster.

Now she was alone. She had no plan *and* she'd lost the advantage of surprise. But she pictured Quell's face and felt her muscles tense with determination.

She hoped that would be enough.

III

"They're really doing it," Wyl said. "I don't know why I thought they wouldn't."

He leaned over the conference table, staring into the familiar hologram of Chadawa. The individual satellites composing the planet's rings were represented by particles like dust motes, thousands of them glimmering. As he watched, one flashed brighter than the rest and spiraled downward toward the planet.

"They're timing it carefully," Syndulla said. She stood beside Wyl while Nath, Captain Arvad, and several of Syndulla's aides encircled the rest of the table. "Sabotaging the satellites so they absorb as much radiation as possible, then dropping them onto the planet where they'll render whole sectors uninhabitable. They've hit mostly ocean so far, but one of the islands has already evacuated. That won't do much good if Shadow Wing irradiates the entire planet."

"How long do we have?" Arvad asked.

Syndulla made an ambiguous gesture. "We have to assume they'll get faster as they go, but it'll take at least another day. I'd rather not wait until half the planet is a wasteland, though—we're moving as soon as we're at low tide."

"Half an hour?" Nath asked.

"Half an hour," Syndulla said. "It's going to be messy, and we need to get aggressive. Otherwise civilians start dying."

Wyl listened as Syndulla summarized the plan they'd spent the past hour preparing. The fundamentals were simple: It was the *Yadeez's* Raider escorts that were reprogramming and dropping the satellites, so Wyl would lead Flare and Wild against the TIEs while Nath took the bombers on a roundabout path to hit the Raiders from a surprise angle. The *Yadeez*, its gunship escort, and the surveillance ship were to be engaged by the *Deliverance* itself. It was a decent strategy, Wyl told himself—dangerous for the New Republic fighters keeping the TIEs distracted until the mission was done; more dangerous for the bombers, who would be unprotected; but with a good chance of success nonetheless.

Yet he thought of the past day of comm chatter, and the way Ragnell had begun to bond with the man claiming to be a Shadow Wing squadron captain. He thought of Lieutenant Itina—Wild Eight—and how she'd swayed a handful of enemy pilots into playing cards.

Nath asked why he was in charge of the Hail Squadron bombers instead of Hail Leader. "You know Shadow Wing," was Syndulla's ready answer. Arvad had concerns about bringing the *Deliverance* so close to Chadawa, where the more maneuverable *Yadeez* might hide in the atmosphere. "We're not out to destroy the *Yadeez*," Wyl roused himself to say. "All we need is to keep it out of the way of the squadrons. If we're very lucky, we might get an assist from the Chadawans."

Mostly, though, Wyl thought about war and the people who fought wars. When Syndulla called an end to the conference and took Wyl aside, she said, "I know what's bothering you."

"I didn't mean to be obvious." He gave a small smile. "It won't be a problem."

"You're sure?" Syndulla asked.

"I'm sure."

He believed it, and that was the worst part: They'd spent so much effort reaching out to their foe, made inroads he'd never expected, and now the whole affair was fading like a dream. It felt *natural* to lead the squadrons into battle again. To begin the killing again. The conversations over the comm would be forgotten easily enough.

"You need anything from me?" Syndulla asked.

"No. Thank you."

"Talk to your people. Let them know you're behind the plan. Remind them of the stakes but don't distract them from their immediate objective. Once you're out there you'll want to fly in tight formations—" Syndulla stopped abruptly and shook her head with a laugh. "Sorry. I'm being overbearing."

"They're your pilots, too," Wyl said. "We both want the same thing."

"May the Force be with you, Wyl Lark," she replied, and clasped him by both shoulders. "If anyone's earned it, it's you."

Twenty-two minutes later the squadrons had been briefed and the hangar was steeping in a familiar chaos. Astromech droids glided across the floor, rocketed through the air, or were lifted by cranes as they awaited socketing in the X- and Y-wings. Ground crew members frantically disconnected hoses and performed last-second repairs in response to last-minute systems checks. Pilots raced in, still strapping on their helmets as they located their ships. Except for a handful of patrol vessels, all three squadrons had been brought back aboard the *Deliverance* to prepare for the mission—broadcasting the plan on an open channel hadn't been an option.

Wyl could've made a speech. He *had* made one—a short one at the briefing's end, touching on the points Syndulla had mentioned—but it felt like fakery. He wanted the mission to succeed (the thought of living with Chadawa's death on his conscience was an impossible one) yet urging the pilots to fight well felt like hypocrisy: Those weren't the sentiments of a Polynean.

Now you are the last, Wyl Lark. Your people await you.

He walked through the hangar and studied the expressions of his pilots, stopping to speak with the ones with bloodshot eyes, the ones still mourning friends, and the ones who trailed rage with every step. He threw his arm around Hadrios and reminded him how proud the man's brother would be when he finally returned to Corellia, and assured a trio of fresh Wild Squadron recruits that their leader Denish Wraive had seen Shadow Wing at its worst. He threw Vitale a salute from afar, which she gamely returned with a wink. He approached Boyvech Toons, a scarred veteran of a hundred battles, and said simply, "Not another Alderaan. Not again."

Syndulla had been right about not distracting them with the stakes. But Shadow Wing planned to kill half a billion people, and there was no forgetting that.

"Ready, Commander?" Captain Essovin called, raising a leathery fist. Flare Squadron's leader hadn't been among the survivors of the *Lodestar* or Cerberon—she hadn't encountered Shadow Wing before coming to the *Deliverance*—but she'd taken to the grudge rapidly after first encountering the *Yadeez*. "Let them feel our bite as our teeth sink deep."

Saving lives isn't the right message for everyone, Wyl thought, and he grinned at the reptilian woman. "May your goddess—" He tried to remember the words Garthun, one of his first comrades in Riot Squadron, had taught him years earlier. "May your goddess view our hunt with favor, and bless our tally."

Essovin cackled loud enough to draw stares from her nearest comrades. "You are wise, Wyl Lark. It is good to fight together."

Wyl still had doubts, but he smiled as he climbed into his cockpit and the ships around him thundered. He stood apart from his pilots, and he knew them less well than he'd have liked. Sometimes, though, he felt like he got it right.

"Come on," he murmured to the A-wing as the smells of synthleather and grease enveloped him. "Let's do some good."

IV

Nath Tensent watched from the cockpit of his Y-wing as two dozen starfighters raced into the distance, and the storm-gray sky of the *Deliverance* pulled away to reveal blackness. Flare Squadron and Wild Squadron, along with Wyl and the Star Destroyer, were speeding toward Chadawa. He was alone with Hail and his antique droid on a mission to save the planet, and he couldn't even banter with his wingmates on the way.

He checked the current particle count and amended the thought: He *could* talk to Hail. He'd just be shouting to the Imps at the same time.

"Come on," he told T5. "We've got a long road ahead."

The Y-wing shuddered and groaned as he opened his throttle, rechecked his course, and glanced at his scanner to confirm the Hail bombers were in motion. A few hundred extra marks blinked on the screen—ghost images created by the radiation. They'd be the least of his problems if he got caught near Chadawa when the tide came in.

Wyl's force would make enemy contact in roughly six minutes, while the bombers were still lumbering around to the far side of the planet. *That* would take nine minutes, assuming Syndulla's tactical droids knew their stuff. If Hail was unlucky, they wouldn't have more than a minute or two left to destroy the Raiders before the particle count started rising again.

"You looking forward to this?" he asked. "Get to save a whole planet, like we did on Troithe."

The droid squealed sharply through the comm.

"Pretty much," Nath agreed. "Only last time we picked our own suicide mission. Didn't get much say in this one."

One of the thrusters destabilized, and Nath felt weightless for an instant. He cursed, adjusted the power distribution, and listened to T5's quick reply. "Either way," Nath said, "we're stuck with the mission. If I'd refused to lead Hail it's not like I'd get to stay home."

He tugged his harness straps, rechecked his course yet again—T5 was fine-tuning their vector as they arced toward the planet, but it was best to make sure—and frowned at the scanner. Wyl's fighters were closing in on Chadawa and its rings with the *Deliverance* close behind. He wondered if he'd be able to see the flash of weaponry if he looked out his canopy. He kept his eyes on the console.

T5 chimed again, low and brusque.

"He'll be fine," Nath said. "Kid's done this plenty of times."

Another chime, sharper.

"Worry about *us,* not him! And stay off the comm if you don't have anything useful."

The scanner marks—the ones that weren't ghosts—moved rapidly. Wyl's squadrons were engaging the enemy. Beyond that, Nath hadn't a clue what was going on.

Five minutes. They're ahead of schedule. We're not.

T5 didn't interrupt again. The Y-wings remained in formation. The comm was silent. He could hear every loose bolt and engine pulse. Even Nath's own breathing became an irritation. *Never thought I'd miss Chass's music,* he thought. *Let alone the prayer-chants.*

He laughed, realizing just how sour his mood had become. He'd been frustrated when he'd spoken to General Syndulla in the hangar bay. Now he was downright peevish, and he didn't care to examine why; maybe shooting down a *Raider*-class corvette was what he needed to cheer himself.

The particle count indicator rose, barely enough to register.

Maybe he was worrying about Wyl again, but the kid had half a fighter wing protecting him. Maybe it was the feeling of being part of a war machine, like he'd been in the Empire, instead of controlling his own fate. Or maybe—

His attention shifted to the Y-wings behind him. They were close enough, flying steady enough, that he could see the dull glint of their canopies and the silhouettes of pilots journeying with him into death. Their own deaths, or Shadow Wing's, or Chadawa's. The thought cramped Nath's stomach, and he whispered: "Damn it all."

The scanner marks were a fuzz of blinking fighters, real and unreal. Only the *Deliverance* was clear on the screen, a locus of mass and energy that might have been a small sun. But Nath shouldn't have been able to see even that much—he scowled as he worked through the data in his head, certain the scanners lacked the range to pick up a skirmish over Chadawa's atmosphere.

Shadow Wing must have moved away from the planet to engage Wyl and the others. That explained why the fighting had started early. It might even end up helping Nath and the bombers from tangling with any TIEs, he thought. But it didn't strike him as a good sign.

"Droid? You see fewer Wild and Flare fighters than we started with?"

A brusque chirrup was the reply.

"Yeah. That's what I thought."

Something vibrated beneath his right foot. He dug his toe around the seat well, trying to identify the source. The vibration ceased after a moment, and he made a note to check it back in the hangar.

The Y-wings were two minutes out when the particle count ticked up, first leaping 50 percent and then doubling a few seconds later. He looked to the scanner and saw the New Republic forces spread thin, battling a tight cluster of TIEs—exactly the opposite of the plan. Shadow Wing had expected the assault and prepared for it. Now high tide was coming in and there weren't many paths to victory left.

He dropped his head against the seat as a voice declared through the comm: "This is General Syndulla to allied forces: We are aborting our attack." She spoke with robotic stiffness, suppressing all emotion.

He should've been relieved. Knowing Syndulla, though—and knowing Wyl—this meant the next attack would involve even more desperate risks. He growled as he flashed his thrusters at the Y-wings behind him before changing course. The starfighter marks on the scanner surged toward the *Deliverance* and the *Deliverance,* in turn, began to retreat from the battle.

The particle count leapt again. The scanner was almost impossible to read, but before it was fully obscured by static Nath thought he saw one mark hovering midway between the retreating New Republic forces and the Shadow Wing cluster.

Don't be stupid. Don't you dare be that stupid.

T5 squawked through the comm. "Didn't I tell you to keep quiet?" Nath asked.

The Y-wings had turned to retrace their path when a new voice came through the comm, barely recognizable as human behind the pops and squeals and distinctive rainfall static of Chadawa.

"This is Wyl Lark. Do as the general says. I'm holding the rear."

Nath brought a fist down on the console with a roar of pure rage. The particle count ticked higher and his instruments went blind.

V

Colonel Soran Keize rhythmically tapped the tactical display as if he could conduct the battle like an orchestra. But it was the combatants who controlled the pace and Soran merely the audience; he hated it so.

"I'd think you would be more pleased," Broosh said. He looked from the screen to Soran with a frown. "Syndulla called a retreat."

"She did. But we've yet to hear from *him.*"

"Madrighast?"

It sounded like a question. It wasn't, Soran knew—Broosh was a clever man—but it was an acknowledgment of Soran's authority and his privilege to lead the discussion.

"Madrighast," Soran agreed. "He's still waiting, even now. It's possible he's being overcautious, and he'll lose Chadawa because of it. Or it's possible he foresees a better opportunity."

"Is it conceivable," Broosh said, speaking low and turning his head away from the crew, "that he's holding out to join us? Avoiding committing to either our side or Chadawa's governor until the right moment?"

"Very little is inconceivable at this juncture. But I suspect not."

He switched from the tactical screen to the monitor showing data from the satellite rings. The *Yadeez*'s Raider escorts continued to modify and sabotage the satellites, dropping them to the planet one by one, but the process was painstaking. The self-repairing systems of the ancient alien technology were well outside the unit's expertise, and the 204th's engineers had spent hours searching for satellites in sufficient disrepair to accept the needed modifications. Shadow Wing could irradiate the whole planet, given time—but time was their most precious resource, more than pilots or TIEs.

Time was irreplaceable.

"I don't like these interruptions," Soran said with a sigh. "The particle flood gives us room to work but it also gives the enemy opportunities to plan. It gives their reinforcements time to arrive. We need another full day to complete Operation Cinder, but granting Syndulla and Madrighast another day to prepare . . . ?"

He spoke aloud in the hope of triggering Broosh's imagination—he was open to the possibility that he'd been blind to a viable strategy, and it was good experience for Broosh. But there were also layers Soran wasn't ready to reveal. Broosh knew of Quell's mission, of course, but Soran had taken pains not to emphasize how much was riding on her success.

It wasn't time for Chadawa's destruction he craved most—the planet's fate, unfortunate as it might be for locals, was insignificant in the grand scope of his concerns. Rather, he needed time for Quell to return with the secrets of the Emperor's Messenger. Time for Quell to realize that it wasn't loyalty to the New Republic or loyalty to the Empire that she had to choose from, but loyalty to principle; to her truest self.

Philosophizing aside, if the *Yadeez* were forced to leave Chadawa before Quell arrived, arranging a rendezvous would be next to impossible.

"We could go on the offensive," Broosh said. "Riskier than I'd like, but the radiation doesn't make maneuvering impossible. One of the Raiders and a squadron of TIEs could slip away from the planet during high tide—ambush their battleship when the particle count begins to fall, do damage and retreat."

"It's a bold thought," Soran conceded. "If you were in command—"

"No. I wouldn't."

Soran smiled and bowed his head. It was a good answer.

"What about the *Minder*?" Broosh asked. "We could reassign it to the sabotage effort."

The surveillance vessel was deep inside the rings, studying the alien technology at Soran's request. "I want the *Minder* uninterrupted. They're too poorly crewed to make a difference, and their assignment could pay dividends later."

Heirorius waved from the comscan station. Soran acknowledged with a nod, and a garbled voice reached the bridge: "—holding position."

"Lark again?" Broosh asked. Heirorius nodded.

The satellite monitor flashed and the main viewscreen blazed with a dazzling spectrum of colors. The rings had activated, and the radioactive particle count was soaring again. "Last known position?" Soran asked.

A mark on the scanner blinked, alone near the initial point of engagement between the 204th and the New Republic forces. "Scopes can't get a visual from here," Captain Nenvez called from a cluster of officers. "We can reposition the *Yadeez* or break comm silence—"

Soran waved Nenvez off as the comm spoke again. Lark's voice was steady and somber. "Wyl Lark to Imperial command ship *Yadeez*. I'm not here for conversation. I have a message for Colonel Soran Keize."

Broosh arched his brow. Soran shrugged and stepped to the center of the bridge.

He hadn't heard much from Lark's earlier broadcasts—just enough to decide not to jam them or forbid his people from listening. He'd asked his commanders to monitor their pilots, watch for any ill effects on morale, but he wanted a comm channel available in case of emergency and he believed the broadcasts' harm minimal.

Colonel Nuress wouldn't have abided enemy propaganda broadcasts on *her* ships, but she had been part of another Empire. What remained of the 204th was loyal beyond reproach, for better or worse.

"This stalemate doesn't serve anyone," Lark's voice went on, "and I understand that you're a good man, Colonel—or at least an honorable one. Every source we have says so, Yrica Quell included."

Soran kept his expression rigid. The implication was not new—only further confirmation of what he'd already believed—but his people would have questions.

"They say you're an ace of aces. That you trained half your unit. To that end, I am challenging you—commander to commander. We duel alone in the particle tides."

Somewhere in the dark of space, Soran's TIE pilots were en route to the *Yadeez*, slipping among the satellite rings and sheltered from the radiation. They were listening as well. Soran knew they'd be waiting for an answer.

"The unit of the loser," Lark continued, "withdraws all forces from the Chadawa system and renounces any vendetta against their opponents. No more Alphabet hunting Shadow Wing, no more Shadow Wing hunting Alphabet. Chadawa is free, or—Chadawa's fate is up to you. Like I said, I'm told you're an honorable man; I don't imagine you want any of what's happening."

There it was, Soran thought—a plea to conscience. *No one wants the Chadawan people dead, Wyl Lark. No one except an Emperor long gone and a handful of his devotees. That's why Cinder is tragedy, not war.*

He would not speak of Chadawa. He would not fight in Lark's chosen arena. Instead he signaled the comscan station and asked, as crisp and passionless as he knew how: "Wyl Lark . . . you truly believe that *either* of our units will give up if their leader is killed?"

Soran expected laughter or defiance. Lark remained composed. "I don't know, but I think the chance makes the risk worth taking. Even in the worst case—" He paused. Soran waited. "—in the worst case, one of our units is left without a commander. That still gives the other an advantage."

Soran surveyed his people. Broosh was scowling. Nenvez appeared impatient, as if he saw the whole transmission as childish. The younger members of the bridge crew were rapt, trying to monitor Soran's reaction without ignoring their duties.

But what of the pilots? He tried to picture Darita and Cherroi and Gandor in their TIEs, listening to the exchange. Wyl Lark kept speaking. "I was in the Oridol Cluster, Colonel. I helped burn Pandem Nai and I downed your Star Destroyer at Cerberon. I led the assault on the Core Nine megafacility and held you off with a squadron of antiques and cloud cars. I've killed several of your people personally, and I *am* sorry but I *don't* regret it."

Soran heard the man breathing heavily toward the speech's end. Who *was* Wyl Lark? He tried to recall the reports from Oridol, everything Palal Seedia had reported before the Cerberon attack.

"Very well," Soran said, and tried not to laugh as Broosh struggled to contain his alarm. "I'll join you presently."

He gestured again and Heirorius closed the channel. Broosh murmured, "Colonel . . . this seems like an awful idea."

"Your critique is noted." Soran gave a conciliatory nod. "I wouldn't be concerned—I trust in your ability to respond to any rebel ploy while I'm occupied. I almost believe in Lark's sincerity; not so General Syndulla's."

"If they make a move, I'll do my part. But why even take the risk?"

"Because—" He could barely frame the words. Experience and instinct often directed him before his conscious mind could sort out *reasons*. "Because he said the right words to stoke our people's lust for vengeance; we have to give them something, and a duel's safer than a frontal attack on Syndulla. Because losing Wyl Lark will injure the enemy dearly. And because—"

Broosh observed him, resigned in the manner of a disapproving parent.

Soran clapped a hand on the man's right shoulder. "—because I am in command, and it's my prerogative . . . and it's been too long since I flew against a Polynean."

He called final orders to the bridge and ducked out before they could see his smile.

CHAPTER 12

UNFLINCHING ACCEPTANCE OF
LOGICAL CONCLUSIONS

I

The outpost was under lockdown. The interior lights had switched from pale blue to a roasting red, and a ceaseless warbling from the public comm suggested a string of announcements in a machine language Yrica Quell didn't recognize. For several minutes the droids had focused on herding organics out of the streets and into what one called "containment zones." Now Quell spotted no living creatures at all, and the drones floating past swept their scanners and wielded plasma torches and arc welders—tools repurposed for killing.

Quell crept through the shadows and stayed to maintenance ducts and gutters whenever she was able. Her body ached and scratches—some superficial, others oozing blood—stung her arms and shoulders where she'd been cut by the broken window. Her undershirt was no protection from the cold and the temperature had dropped at least ten degrees; she suspected the droids had deactivated the thermal units, though there was enough residual heat to keep her from freezing.

As she slithered through a drainage shaft running parallel to an outpost throughway—concealed from the road by piping and plastoid sheets, her palms and knees plunged in icy violet fluids—she reminded herself she'd faced worse. In Cerberon she had faced worse and endured.

She could handle pain.

She didn't know who was coming after her team. Not the droids or the Surgeon—she couldn't imagine they'd have locked down the outpost in that case. The New Republic was a possibility—Intelligence or even Alphabet Squadron might have tracked her down somehow. She wasn't sure it mattered yet.

Coming after *her* team. She thought of them that way even now.

Rikton's face flashed into her mind, and she shrugged it away like a gnat.

She stopped and peered through pipework when she arrived at a central plaza. She remembered it vaguely as the place where she'd consulted an outpost directory, and she scanned it now, smiling tightly as she spotted a comm kiosk. She exited under the sheeting and dashed across the open space, nearly slipping on the plaza's metal and the slush on her boots.

She made it to the kiosk, threw the door open, and entered a private booth the size of a closet. The computer status lights were dark, but she was able to bypass the power cutoff in under three minutes. (It would've been faster if her hands hadn't been numb.) She took a moment to listen to her own ragged breathing, to reassure herself that she was, relatively speaking, safe, and placed her hand on her hip pocket to feel the comforting bulge of the datachip.

She hesitated to pull it out and plug it into the machine before her. It was what she'd come for; but if it wasn't worth the lives and the risk? If she'd lost her place inside Shadow Wing for data with no meaning . . . ?

Then, she supposed, her decision would be easy. All she'd be able to do would be accept defeat, knowing she'd failed herself, Keize, and General Syndulla all together.

If the data *did* mean anything, she'd need to decide what to do with it.

She took the chip out, inserted it into a socket, and watched text scroll down the screen.

She saw nothing that shocked her.

The Surgeon had promised answers: the processes, the algorithms, the databases that the Emperor's Messenger had used to find monsters who'd kill whole planets for a dead man's spite. Everything the Messenger had required to select Operation Cinder's executioners.

She read through it all, even trying to solve the equations at the calculation's heart the way the Messenger might. Quell had always had an aptitude for math, but she shuddered as she read formulas to assess an individual's loyalty (to the Empire, to Emperor Palpatine personally), resourcefulness, conscience; recognized variables accounting for past kills (during and outside of military service), disciplinary actions, family trauma, education, genetic predispositions, species predispositions, personal associations, history of obedience to unlawful commands, involvement (including nonparticipatory exposure) in physical interrogation, and something called MDC-count. Line by line, she studied the code for how to identify not an unflaggingly loyal person, but a corrupt and broken one. Or one who was primed to be corrupted and broken.

She studied further formulas that assessed individuals as parts of units and judged those units as a whole, determining the moral character of a battalion or a fighter wing based on its leaders and recruits and all its history. The calculations gave the most weight to a unit's worst members, tracing their corrupting influence on all around them.

Quell was confident she'd passed the Messenger's test along with the rest of the 204th.

None of it shocked her. It chilled her profoundly, forced her to lean against the kiosk wall as she trembled. But the answers weren't surprising.

She found what she was looking for—what, she knew in her bones,

Soran Keize was looking for—in a list of functions the Surgeon had compiled. The Messenger was an analytical tool, a search algorithm, but it could do nothing to identify its targets without a well of information to draw from. The Surgeon had laughed when it had promised her *databases,* and now she understood why: She recognized secondary sources, military access clearances, but all were supplements to a single data bank referred to only by codes and coordinates—one grand source to fuel the Messenger's assessments. She studied the coordinates until they were etched into her brain, useless alone but ready to be cross-checked and interpreted.

She realized she had a choice to make, then, and her own certainty frightened her. Keize had sent her to learn the truth, and she had—but only in part, and there were implications she couldn't decipher on her own.

She'd betrayed Shadow Wing and the Empire, but she still needed her mentor. She prayed he was alive and that somehow, Chadawa lived, too.

The kiosk had no way to reach the *Yadeez.* Instead she opened a connection to her ship. Once the data was transferred she tore the chip from the computer, placed it on the console, and fired her blaster three times to incinerate the evidence.

She released a long, ragged breath into scorched and greasy air and leaned against the booth again, closing her eyes. She would rest just a moment, she decided, before returning to the fray. Before making the next trying decision, and the next.

Her hand still gripped her blaster when the door slammed opened and Chass na Chadic spat obscenities.

"How did you—" Quell began, but she didn't finish the thought. Strong hands gripped her left shoulder and the back of her skull and she saw a flash of green hair muddied under the red light. Chadic thrust her into the corner of the booth, and Quell's nose smashed into metal (driving a spike of pain into her brain—she still hadn't healed from her fall on the *Yadeez;* maybe now she never would). Her cheek pressed against toggle switches. She thought she still held her blaster but she couldn't feel her hand for the burning in her head.

Her assailant loosened her grip, then hauled Quell out of the corner and stepped completely inside the booth with her. Quell tried not to breathe through her nose—she'd drown in blood if she did—and spoke again.

"Chass—"

Chadic slammed her knee into Quell's groin. The flare of agony and nausea dwarfed the pain in her face, and she distantly heard her blaster clatter to the floor. Chadic removed the hand from Quell's shoulder to pull the booth door closed, and Quell mouthed something even she couldn't understand. Drool spilled out of her lips.

"How long?" Chadic snarled. She stared at Quell, her eyes wide, her horns like thorns on a flower. The contours of her face were achingly familiar; even her rage was almost comforting.

"I don't—" Quell managed.

Chadic slammed her into the wall of the booth again. Quell barely felt it this time, still reeling from the blow between her thighs.

"Were you working for them? Did you tell them how to kill us?"

"I didn't—" Quell tried, and Chadic slugged her in the stomach.

Quell would've fallen if Chadic hadn't propped her up. There were more questions, more accusations, and though Quell tried to answer them her interrogator never listened. Any word, any movement was met with violence. Quell didn't try to break free, utterly aware that she lacked the strength and besides—what would she even do if she overcame the Theelin? What was the point of fighting back if she didn't know her next move?

She didn't *deserve* the beating, but she understood it. It was the natural outcome of her choices; jump off a cliff and the landing hurts.

Chadic delivered blow after blow, threw her into walls until finally she let Quell crumple in the corner. Her eyes were glistening as Quell breathed slowly. The cloud of suffering obscuring Quell's body slowly evaporated, revealing a hundred loci of burning nerves.

"Why couldn't you just die?" Chass na Chadic asked. Her voice was hoarse and soft.

Quell had no answer to this.

Her blaster was within reach, but she didn't have the strength.

Quell studied the woman's lips as Chadic raised a comlink. She watched her say a few words and didn't so much hear as interpret: "I got her. Meet you at the ship."

Quell wondered if that meant the rest of Alphabet was present. She knew asking would bring only more pain.

Chadic yanked her to her feet and they left the booth, Quell's—Rikton's—blaster forgotten on the floor. Chadic was less cautious than Quell had been as they moved through the outpost, but Quell didn't protest. She focused on moving her legs, allowing her weight to rest on Chadic's arm as the Theelin supported her beneath the shoulders.

Chadic never shoved her. She didn't snap at her or throw her against a wall to free her hands. She didn't hurt Quell again. Quell recalled the night the whole squadron had dined and drank on Troithe, and how Chadic had wrapped her arms around her on the tram car over the city; there was no joy in the march through the darkened outpost, no *wonder* the way there had been on Troithe, but it felt intimate anyway.

Twice, they scrambled to hide in side passages when droids came sweeping the throughways for life-forms. Chadic slapped her hand over Quell's mouth but applied no pressure. Quell could've bitten the woman, or screamed. Neither seemed likely to help.

Quell wasn't sure how long they'd been traveling when they reached the platform where the piers came together and the tattered Imperial banner hung from the catwalk. She briefly considered making a break for her ship, then remembered the half-kilometer length of the piers. She thought, too, of telling her captor that her ship was nearby; maybe Chadic would want to see it, to search it.

To what end, though? Quell wasn't sure.

Nor did she have time to decide. As Chadic began to guide her toward one of the piers the Theelin woman suddenly froze. A moment later she was hurtling with Quell toward the basket of an unattached cargo hitch as particle bolts crackled above them. Quell slipped on sleet tracked in from outside; Chadic pulled her by both arms into the scanty cover provided by the hitch, glancing about furiously.

Quell rose to a crouch. The shots had come from the entrance to another pier—*her* pier, where her ship had landed. Chadic had her pistol out and waited until one of the shooters came into view, half concealed by the rain and the midday gloom; she fired twice, and Quell flinched each time.

Quell couldn't tell who the target was. In her mind's eye she saw Fra Raida with a burning hole in her chest; Rikton, eyes wide in surprise as he died; Brebtin screaming; Mirro breathing his last with a sad, resigned expression.

"Don't," she whispered.

Chadic spared her a glare, barely looking away from the pier. "What?"

"There's not many of them," Quell said. "Let's just go. Let's run."

Chadic swung the blaster to point at Quell's forehead. She held it there, muzzle trembling. Then particle bolts sparked against the cargo hitch, bit into the metal platform, sizzled, and sent acrid smoke through the air. Chadic returned a flurry of shots, barely bothering to aim as she retrieved her comlink again. "I'm where the pier ends," she said. "Could use support."

Quell squinted against the incoming fire and the smoke. She heard the rhythmic pulse of an assault rifle. Brebtin was still alive, or someone had retrieved her weapon. She tried to see how many figures were in motion but couldn't pick out more than two.

She tried to picture herself lunging for Chadic while the Theelin was distracted. Even the best outcome seemed liable to get them both killed.

She heard thunder behind the rain and recognized the boom of a fusial thrust engine. The barely audible whir beneath the thunderclap gave it away as an Incom ship, and Quell knew what was coming. A powerful gust of wind sent sleet spraying over their attackers; Quell heard screaming, saw silhouettes running across the metal as crimson lightning struck and the platform erupted in flames.

The U-wing dipped into sight, unleashed another cannon volley, then ascended again. Quell couldn't see through the fire to discern whether any of her team had survived, and she couldn't fight off Chadic to get a better look; the Theelin pulled her by the arm, backward and away from the hitch. They were out on the closest pier then, the sleet slicing at Quell's bare arms and the roar of the U-wing louder than ever. Chadic tugged Quell tight against her, blaster pointed toward the central dock, and edged toward the transport as it descended and one of the loading doors slid open.

Quell didn't see a squadron crest on the U-wing's side, but looking for more than an instant meant staring directly into the sleet. Maybe it was Alphabet. Maybe it was Chadic's specforce friends, or another retrieval crew.

"Get on," Chadic snarled, boosting Quell up to the ship. Quell struggled to crawl into the hovering transport and when her feet were inside she rolled half a meter, shivering from the bone-saturating cold and staring at the ceiling while Chadic climbed in behind her.

"Let's go!" Chadic called to the cockpit. "Any trouble out there?"

"Yes," came the reply, in a voice guttural and soft and strangely accented. Vaguely familiar, but Quell couldn't identify it.

"Great," Chadic muttered, and flicked droplets of rain off her hand. They spattered Quell's cheek. The loading door crashed shut. "Just great. What've we got?"

"Pursuit."

"More Imps?"

"No."

The U-wing tilted and surged forward. Quell was forced to rise onto her knees to avoid sliding to the rear of the vessel. She grasped one of the crew seats, gradually standing as the deck trembled and Chadic stumbled to the cockpit door; the Theelin swore, then disappeared into the cockpit proper. Something outside the ship screamed and whistled and burst in the wind—low-yield ion warheads, possibly, but Quell couldn't tell for sure. Nothing that had been in Shadow Wing's arsenal, even as heavily modified as the TIEs were.

"Fire back!" Chadic was shouting.

"No," the pilot said again.

"Why the hell not?"

The clatter of sleet against the hull ceased. The transport's roar quieted as the air outside thinned. They were moving through the planet's upper atmosphere, Quell assumed, and would soon be free of Netalych's gravity altogether.

"Not of the Empire," the voice replied. "We burned their home. Their grievance is real."

The ship leveled out and Quell took wide-spaced, unsteady steps to the cockpit entrance. The starfield beyond the viewport was like a balm on her injuries, all the cuts and bruises and her throbbing nose; the sweeping scope of darkness felt like freedom, so long as she didn't think of anything else.

Something streaked past them and detonated, white as a nova. Chadic was trying to activate the guns but her side of the console had been locked by the pilot. "I don't care what their grievance is!" she shouted. "We're not getting shot down by droids! We're not—"

There was another flash to the ship's port side. The vessel jolted, and sparks sprayed from seams in the bulkhead as the pilot struggled to keep the U-wing from tumbling to starboard. The analytical part of Quell's brain declared: *Ion-concussion payload. Ionized energy to damage machines; kinetic to smash organics. Probably simple to manufacture on Netalych.*

"We will not," the pilot said. Quell got a better look at her for the first time—her face was a patchwork of chitinous violet plates, and her dark eyes betrayed nothing of human emotions. But there was something about her Quell recognized, and when she looked to the woman's ragged outfit the truth seized her mind.

"Kairos?" Quell said.

Kairos didn't turn, but her hand trembled as she pitched the ship down. Two of their pursuers—a refitted light freighter and a short-range tri-fighter—flashed overhead and out of sight.

Chadic looked back at Quell, scowled, then turned to face Kairos.

"If we don't do something they're going to kill us. If you can't get us into hyperspace you blasted well *shoot them!*"

The U-wing swung to one side, and Quell was thrown against the cockpit doorframe. Before she could recover Kairos swung again in the opposite direction, leaning into the turn as if to circle around and confront anyone behind them. The viewport filled with radiance and something metallic loudly ruptured; as she struggled not to fall back into the cabin, Quell spotted Kairos's gloved hand reach up and yank one of the power toggles.

The overhead lights deactivated, as did the indicators on the console. The engine and thrusters went silent. Artificial gravity kept Quell's feet to the floor as the U-wing, carried by its own inertia, somersaulted lifelessly through space.

One of the droid vessels flew past the viewport. Quell barely dared to breathe.

"We're playing dead?" Chadic asked. "You think that'll work?"

"Ion-concussion warheads could disable a ship without visible critical damage," Quell murmured. She wondered if Kairos had known as much, or if the strange woman had simply seen no other recourse without opening fire.

Chadic glowered at Quell, then climbed out of her seat and knelt on top of the console. She pressed her face to the viewport, peering out at various angles. When she pulled back she said, "Can't see all of them, but it looks like they're turning around."

"They might send a scrapper ship," Quell said. "We shouldn't wait long."

"Don't," Chadic snapped. The blaster was in her hand again. She waved it at Quell. "No one wants to hear you."

Quell stayed silent as Kairos activated emergency power—enough to energize the console, not enough to draw the droids' attention on standard sensors. Chadic looked over Kairos's shoulder, peering at the status display as it ran automated checks. Then she made a prolonged, frustrated groan of discontent.

Quell waited for an explanation. When it was clear none was forthcoming, she stepped forward and took in the readouts as well as she could. Life support was stable, and thrusters and weapons were functional. But the hyperdrive was offline, as was the navicomputer.

Even if they could've jumped to lightspeed, they'd have had nowhere to go.

As the adrenaline drained from her body, Quell considered the truth of her circumstances: She was on a derelict ship in a hostile and desolate system, and she'd just betrayed one set of foes to fall into the hands of another.

You have no one to blame but yourself, she thought, and retreated tiredly to the cabin.

CHAPTER 13

ASSIGNMENT OF IDENTIFIABLE WEAKNESSES

I

Wyl Lark thought of Chadawa and the cities of Chadawa and the people of Chadawa. He imagined the white disks of residential platforms atop tall stalks dwarfed by still-taller cliffs, as if the planet's cities were mushrooms flourishing in shade. Above the disks, he saw the cliffs topped with greenery; below, ivory beaches disappearing into an ocean the same glittering sapphire as the sky. People gathered at windows and stood in the sand, and they were afraid as they watched a burning trail descend from above. They clasped one another's hands as steam rose from the ocean where the trail ended and wondered how long it would be before radiation reached their island.

Wyl thought of all this as he sat in his A-wing, drifting outside the satellite rings. Sunlight gently warmed his canopy. He watched the speck of Shadow Wing's bulk freighter against the sphere of the planet and awaited the arrival of his foe, reminding himself he was committing a just and righteous act.

None of which entirely assuaged his guilt.

He hoped Syndulla and the others had understood his intent when he'd challenged Soran Keize. He trusted them profoundly, but he doubted his own choices and the clarity of his message. He wished, with a sudden pang, that he'd told Nath everything—that he'd truly mended things with the man, and confessed the secret he'd held since speaking to the elders of Polyneus: admitted that he was the last of the One Hundred and Twenty.

"We did our best, didn't we?" he murmured, and smiled sadly as he ran his fingertips down the canopy.

A starfighter did not breathe or molt or shriek as a sur-avka did, but he'd bonded with his all the same. If he died today, it would be with a friend.

"I am here, Wyl Lark," a voice said from the comm, steady and almost warm in its humanity. "Are you ready?"

A firefly leapt from the bulk freighter, gliding toward the planet before ascending and curving toward Wyl.

"I'm ready," Wyl said, and ignited his thrusters.

The particle tide was invisible and intangible. It didn't buffet his ship like a hurricane or toss him like a tsunami, but its dangers were no less real. Without instruments or safeties, he couldn't judge his speed or the stresses on the A-wing—he might accelerate until his hull ripped away or overheat his cannons until their components melted. There would be no computer to recalibrate his inertial dampeners, leaving his body to bear the weight of g forces he might otherwise ignore. He would need to extend his senses into the metal to comprehend the strains and injuries of his ship, and his eyes would be his only warning when his enemy acted.

He'd deactivated most of his readouts and manually shut down half the A-wing's systems to allow it to function at all at the height of the particle tide. A more complex vessel like the *Deliverance* or even the *Raider*-class corvettes would've been entirely helpless. Wyl could only hope that Soran Keize was no better prepared than he.

He opened his throttle and propelled himself toward the approaching TIE. He'd half expected the dagger silhouette of a TIE interceptor, but he vaguely recalled one of Quell's files referencing Keize's preference for the basic TIE/ln's unforgiving design. Under the circumstances, Wyl would've wished otherwise—an interceptor's more advanced technology might've increased its vulnerability to the radiation.

Emerald flashed from Keize's fighter as the distance between A-wing and TIE closed. Wyl eased out of the line of fire, evading the blazing particle bolts by a hundred meters. It had been a warning shot; the true commencement of the battle was yet to come.

Then the fighters blurred past each other and Wyl attempted to circle and give chase. By the time he'd completed his turn, he'd lost sight of the TIE. For an instant he felt blind without a scanner; he wanted to unclip his harness, rip off his helmet, and twist his body around to see whatever he could.

But searching for Keize would take too long, and it was what his enemy expected. Instead he accelerated and began a series of drunken, spiraling turns, refusing to give the TIE the opportunity to latch onto his tail. Blood rushed to his head and he felt the universe spin, felt vertigo pump through his veins like adrenaline. He saw the outermost ring of Chadawa flash across his field of vision, the individual satellites barely discernible, and was surprised by the angle.

Keize did not fire. He wouldn't give away his position, knowing he had the advantage so long as he was hidden. But Wyl was sure he had to be in pursuit, and he altered the length and breadth of his loops until he finally caught sight of a speck keeping pace in his peripheral vision. "We found him," he whispered, and swung around to bring the TIE into sight.

Keize didn't attempt to flit out of view. He turned toward Chadawa and increased velocity. Wyl pursued, his muscles burning as gravity exerted itself on every centimeter of his body. Maybe, he thought, Keize intended to test their endurance—in the Chadawan radiation, it was likely neither A-wing nor TIE could sustain maximum acceleration without killing its pilot. The limit to their speed was whatever Wyl and Keize could take without blacking out.

Wyl reached for his comm through the crushing weight. "You haven't always been with Shadow Wing," he said.

The TIE maintained its distance. Wyl increased his thruster output and felt the A-wing shake violently. His field of vision seemed to narrow, though it was likely an illusion—his mind worrying about what he could handle, not his body revolting yet.

"No," Keize said.

Of the subjects that had consumed Wyl over the past days, Keize's time away had been among his lowest priorities for follow-up. Nath had shared the New Republic Intelligence report on the man's wanderings, and it had sat in the back of Wyl's mind, nagging and untended.

Now he could have answers from the man himself.

"You called yourself Devon. You stopped—"

The outermost ring of Chadawa filled Wyl's sight as the universe ran around the edges like melting glass. He could almost feel his blood vessels bursting, bruises forming, lungs contracting. "—you stopped *fighting*," he managed after a drag of breath.

He didn't need to ask the question aloud. The *why?* was implied.

The TIE seemed to expand as Keize cut power to his thrusters. Wyl closed his throttle, frantically trying to avoid overshooting the TIE and arriving squarely in his foe's targeting sights. But Keize didn't wait for the A-wing to close the distance, instead turning the TIE toward the ring and slipping among the grid of satellites.

Wyl followed, heartbeat throbbing in his ears, his body still reeling. He tried to discern his enemy's intent—was Keize trying to get inside the cage of rings and leave the particle field entirely? Was he leading Wyl to the rest of Shadow Wing?

Keize hadn't answered his question. Wyl forced himself to keep speaking. "What was it like on Vernid?" Wyl asked. "Working on a dig-rig, living a life . . . ?"

"Fleeting," Keize said.

The TIE spun to port, sliding between satellites as if unaffected by its own inertia. The maneuver was troublingly familiar—Wyl had seen it before, though he wasn't sure where—and while he couldn't follow

the same path he could find another route. He wove among the satellites, each barely larger than a starfighter—a mass of ice-encrusted
metal covered in jutting spikes.

He caught sight of the TIE again as it whirled past a satellite embedded in a large berg. Soon Wyl began to understand what Keize was
doing. They leapt free of the ring and dived back in, switching direction and looping around satellites. They raced in circles, Wyl chasing
Keize and Keize chasing Wyl. As with their earlier acceleration, it was
a test of skill and endurance: Keize meant to fatigue Wyl or disable his
ship without ever firing a shot meant to kill.

The sense of discomfiting familiarity didn't leave Wyl, however.
He'd fought this battle before, though one moment he recalled the
glowing clouds of Oridol and the next he remembered the atmosphere
of Troithe. Keize's lateral spin was a trick of Char's, one that had killed
Wyl's friends in Riot Squadron; the stuttering particle bolts Keize used
to shear off ice and spray Wyl's canopy was Puke's favored tactic, and
Puke had been killed by Chass long ago.

The truth dawned on Wyl with such sluggishness that he was embarrassed. He had fought Keize before because he had fought Shadow
Wing before; and Keize *was* Shadow Wing, had shaped the unit and
trained its people. The tricks and quirks Wyl had cataloged over the
past months composed Keize's entire repertoire.

Yet Wyl could find no way to take advantage of this fact. Even if Keize
couldn't surprise him, the man executed his maneuvers with unsur-
passed grace and speed; transitioned from one technique to the next
before Wyl could concoct a counter. They danced through the ring together, neither man seizing an advantage and neither making an error.

The longer the duel went on, the more Wyl's mood lifted even as his
body tired. He'd forgotten how little flying a starfighter resembled flying a sur-avka—forgotten how he'd used to fly by the prickle of his
nerves and the rush of wind through a beast's down. The loss of the
A-wing's computers brought back sensations he'd suppressed, and
tears streaked from his eyes and soaked into the hair behind his ears as
he burned his thrusters and spun and chased.

They flew on and on, in and out of the ring, toward Chadawa's sun and through clouds of icy shards that vaporized in electric flashes on Wyl's shields. They crossed the path of a rusting orbital station—a civilian station, so far as Wyl could tell, barely large enough for a crew of ten—and Wyl feared Keize would threaten the residents somehow; but they moved on to the next obstacle, and the next. Keize began to leave a glittering ion trail as the TIE's engines strained. Wyl was sure his A-wing fared no better.

Keize banked around another satellite and Wyl was surprised to see the TIE wobble on its course. He suspected a trap until half a second later he passed the satellite himself and felt a *current* against the A-wing's hull—some particle stream channeled by the satellite itself. Keize truly had lost control of his ship, and as Wyl strained to center the TIE in his view he knew his opportunity would be gone unless he acted *now*, unless he acquired his target and fired.

It felt almost blasphemous, in the face of his memories of Home—as if he were burdening his younger self with a soldier's sins. To kill Keize in a moment of joyful flight would taint him forever.

He squeezed his trigger, crying out as he did, reminding himself of everything Shadow Wing had done and intended to do. His voice disappeared into the noise of cannons discharging crimson bolts of violence.

The volley streaked through space, toward the TIE and past it. Wyl doubted he'd come within ten meters of hitting Keize. He never had been much of a marksman.

His hand on the control yoke was shaking and he anticipated Keize's counter without the speed to compensate for it. The TIE used the momentum of the particle current to spin away. Wyl, who had straightened the A-wing's course in his effort to get a clear shot, was unable to follow suit. In less than three seconds Keize was behind him and firing.

Wyl turned away from the blows but his seat bounced and the cocoon of his shields flickered. Keize began stripping his deflectors away layer by layer.

It was almost a relief to be on the defensive again.

II

So long as there was movement and light—so long as there was the glow of thrusters and the glimmer of weapons fire—it meant Wyl was still alive. Nath Tensent reassured himself of that more than once as his Y-wing growled and bounced on its long route toward Chadawa.

Wyl was alive, and the boy was trickier than Nath had appreciated. He'd learned things over the past year, some from Nath himself but others from Syndulla and Quell and even Shadow Wing. If Wyl *stayed* alive, Nath would be sure to congratulate him after punching him in the nose.

Then again, it was possible Nath had misinterpreted Wyl's message. In that case he'd skip the punch and just shoot him.

T5 chirped a course correction, and Nath instinctively glanced at his screen. It flashed with indecipherable character strings in some nonstandard alphabet. "Fine," he snapped. "Adjusting our vector. How can you even tell?"

The droid issued a series of low beeps. Nath laughed bitterly. "Tell you what: If this works, we'll get you a nice job as navigator on a sea cruiser somewhere."

He checked behind him through the narrow rear viewport and saw Hail Squadron's Y-wings in formation. They hadn't questioned him when, after Keize had accepted Wyl's challenge, Nath had swung his bomber around and resumed his original course. Not that they had many ways *to* question him, with comms limited, but they'd at least followed as he'd made his way into the depths of the particle tide.

Thanks to the radiation, they were invisible to scanners. Thanks to Wyl, Shadow Wing was distracted with the duel. No one would notice the Y-wings proceeding on their original mission—the destruction of the Raiders sabotaging the Chadawan rings—until the Y-wings were almost in firing range. They'd need to keep their speed low to avoid blowing up their engines, but if everything went perfectly, they'd save the planet from Operation Cinder and be out before they died horribly.

T5 squealed incoherently. Nath's cockpit was flooded with light from behind; his shields rippled with the impact of molten specks of superheated metal. One of the Hail bombers was suddenly gone and he couldn't see where the enemy fire was coming from, didn't understand until T5's beeping became clearer.

Nath swore loudly. "Get the message to the others," he called. "I don't care how—the astromechs can see you, right? Send up flares or semaphores or *something* and have them pass word down the line!"

He watched the remnants of Hail Three drift away to his rear. According to T5, the particle tides had likely affected the safeties on the bomber's proton warheads; something had gone very wrong after that, and now Jaith Omir was dead. Nath had found the man irritating at best, incompetent at worst, but Jaith had deserved a better end.

You better be right about this, Wyl.

He confirmed that his own proton torpedoes were unarmed, then checked his other systems as best he could. They were a minute or two out from the combat zone, and while they *might* get far enough into the rings to escape the radiation he couldn't count on it.

"You get the message through?" he asked, and T5 replied in the affirmative. "All right. I want you to pass on something else . . ."

They'd lost one pilot already. Hail had to be getting nervous.

"Tell them—hell, tell them I've seen them eyeing my medal. They want one of their own? They want to save a planet? They've got to walk into fire. Whether or not we make it out, so long as we succeed Chadawa's going to *remember* us."

He wasn't sure how well the droids would relay his tone or the complexity of the message, but it was the best he could do. Besides, he didn't like the sound of his own voice right now—anyone could hear he was on edge, so maybe it was better this way.

How had he even ended up here? He wasn't going to save Wyl. If Syndulla had understood the plan, she hadn't shown any indication. Somehow Nath had assumed that since everyone else was gone, or occupied, or out of touch, it was his responsibility to swoop in and save a blasted Imperial planet.

He recalled Nasha Gravas's *look* during the war council. He wasn't supposed to save Chadawa; he was supposed to let the Chadawan Imps fight it out with Shadow Wing, leaving them both easy prey for the *Deliverance* and whatever New Republic reinforcements showed up.

You're a moron, Tensent. You can still turn around.

But he couldn't. He could see the rings of Chadawa now, see the silhouettes of Raiders sabotaging the satellites, which meant the enemy could see him, too. "Let's go!" he roared, and loaded a torpedo into the Y-wing's launcher.

The other bombers broke formation as turbolasers streaked toward them. There wasn't much Nath could do to evade so long as he was caught in the particle tide—his bomber would rip apart if he attempted anything more than a gentle turn—but he ignited his jets in short bursts, sliding a few meters one way or another to throw off his foes. He didn't spot any TIEs, but the barrage from the Raiders would kill him just as thoroughly.

A blast came close enough to bathe his cockpit in emerald light. T5 let out a shriek, and as Nath blinked away spots he saw his shields crackling madly. "Too close," he growled, and there was no vigor in it. His breathing came heavily. But his ship was intact.

A voice came through the comm, urgently reciting a series of numbers. Shadow Wing, Nath assumed, alerting its pilots to an attack using some predefined code. He'd known it would happen sooner or later, but their time was running short.

A Y-wing exploded to one side, skewered in a single shot. A second Y-wing was gone an instant later. T5's beeps were badly distorted as the droid reported which pilots were gone, and Nath didn't bother trying to understand. It didn't matter now—what mattered was finishing the mission and getting *out*.

Without a targeting computer he had to guess his distance to the first Raider. Twenty seconds, maybe? He was passing the first satellites now and he'd be fully inside the rings by then, in the radiation-free bubble protecting the planet; but he wasn't sure how long his systems would need to reboot. He couldn't count on acquiring target lock. His best bet was to get in as close as possible and hope his allies could do the same.

T5 squealed an alarm. Nath leaned into his harness and looked to the first squadron of TIEs weaving among the satellites, headed his way. Behind them, cresting Chadawa like a rising sun, was the bulk freighter *Yadeez.*

"We'll take a shot at Raider number one. Not even going to try for that second one," he said. He needn't have bothered, he supposed—T5 didn't need to know, and the astromech wouldn't be able to signal the other pilots in all the chaos.

Nath flinched at a flash and saw the front half of a Y-wing tumble past his cockpit. *No need to communicate orders if everyone else is dead.*

Now the Raider dominated his view. The corvette's silhouette resembled that of a Star Destroyer, but the ship was a fraction of a Destroyer's size and it lacked the command module and deflector domes of its overgrown cousin. In the domes' place, armored panels extended from the hull enclosing vulnerable systems and amplifying the ship's shields. Nath had served aboard a Raider for an eyeblink and tried to recall any weaknesses worth his while; none came to mind, so he shrugged and took aim at the dagger's broad hilt. Without a targeting computer, his biggest worry was landing a hit at all.

T5 chimed. The TIE fighters would arrive in seconds. "Not much I can do about that, is there?" Nath shouted, listening to his deflector generator whinny as emerald death surrounded him. "Fire in three, two—"

He squeezed his trigger and loosed a torpedo, feeling the whole ship recoil with the launch. The weapon streaked ahead, joined by three more launched by nearby Y-wings, and Nath wrested his bomber to one side before he could be atomized by the Raider's weaponry. He kept watching as he veered, however, and grinned in satisfaction as two torpedoes (he wasn't sure whose) smashed into the enemy vessel. The first sent light and fire splashing across the Raider's shield bubble; the second passed through the flickering shield and tore into armor as it burst, kicking the entire Raider five degrees askew. Flames belched from the resulting crater and, a second later, electrical arcs caressed the ship bow-to-stern. Nath couldn't tell if it was a fatal blow, but it was close enough for him—he couldn't imagine the Raider would be supporting Operation Cinder for a while.

He expected to come under cannon fire then, and cut short his observations so he could look to the TIEs heading his way. Instead of fighters he saw only the great blue mass of Chadawa and a flight of five surviving Y-wings. "Why the hell are we alive—?" he began. Then his scanner rebooted and he had his answer.

Between the bulk freighter and the first Raider was a new mark—incredibly large and dense. The TIEs approaching the Y-wings had turned to swarm the newcomer, and Nath assumed at first that the *Deliverance* had joined the fray. But that made no sense—Star Destroyers weren't stealthy, and T5 would've spotted the *Deliverance* en route.

The other Hail bombers swept past Nath, heading for the second Raider. They'd seen an opportunity and, like good rebels, chose to take it. Nath couldn't blame them but he brought his craft around to join them in a wider arc, trying to get a visual on whatever was happening kilometers off his port side.

Now he saw the newcomer backlit against the Chadawan ocean, occluding the *Yadeez* and under attack by the swarming TIEs. It *was* a Star Destroyer, but not the *Deliverance*—it lacked that vessel's New Republic modifications and featured several gruesome scars: A burnt, black streak ran from the tip of the dagger halfway to its engines, and an amputated stub stood in place of one deflector dome. Nonetheless, its guns were functional, blazing and raking the skies with destruction.

Finally, Nath thought. *The Chadawans are good for something.* He assumed the vessel had emerged from the atmosphere to engage.

He fell in behind the other Y-wings as they raced toward their target. The second Raider had turned toward the bombers, minimizing its profile and allowing it to bring all its forward weapons to bear. The familiar barrage of turbolaser and cannon fire was augmented by concussion missiles, and still another of the Y-wings was obliterated. Nath couldn't recall how many they'd lost so far, but the squadron couldn't be at much more than half strength.

The surviving bombers split apart, two moving above the Raider's central axis and the others joining Nath below. The enemy had enough weapons to keep firing on both groups, but their chances for survival were marginally improved. Nath readied another torpedo and waited until he could see the Raider's underbelly clearly, then released.

The Y-wing kicked and the torpedo streaked away. Nath saw the concussion missile heading toward him then—early enough to realize what would happen, too late to change anything—and he braced himself just as the missile intercepted his torpedo. The resulting shock wave of fiery energy tossed the Y-wing backward, flipping it end-over-end. Nath wrestled with the half-fused controls, body rocking and jolting, and felt himself stabbed by electrical shocks whenever he touched the right side of his console; he shouted orders at T5 and had the presence of mind to be grateful he was out of the particle radiation.

Three seconds and a lifetime later, when he finally got the ship steadied, he ignored the blazing red warning lights and peered toward the Raider and Hail Squadron. The Y-wings would've just finished their pass and he expected to spot them moving away from the Raider together.

Instead he was faced with an unexpected horror.

From his angle, far below the Raider and the Y-wings, he could see the Chadawan Star Destroyer above, still harried by Shadow Wing's TIE swarm. Burning rain fell from its guns, indiscriminately piercing Raider and Y-wings alike. The Raider was already defeated, turbolaser blasts puncturing its underbelly and dispersing in energized mist; the surviving Y-wings were scattering, but as they did the Star Destroyer's weapons began tracking the smaller ships.

"You bastards," Nath called. He saw another Y-wing destroyed, then another. "Bastards! We just saved your planet!"

Better if they hadn't bothered, he thought. Nasha Gravas had been right.

He toggled the comm, not caring whether Shadow Wing and the Chadawans heard. "Bombers retreat! Get out of there!" he yelled, and turned his battered ship around as fast as he could without dislodging a nacelle.

Particle bolts lit his surroundings as he opened his throttle. He jinked and dived, not sure if it was the Star Destroyer, the TIEs, or one of the other Shadow Wing vessels attacking him. He could see a single Y-wing mirroring his withdrawal, and he remembered with awful vividness the battle at Trenchenovu, where Shadow Wing had murdered his first squadron. First Piter, then Mordeaux and Canthropali, Pesalt and Rorian, all of them slaughtered until it was down to him and Reeka fleeing the scene. He'd felt terror then, and he felt terror now, and it tasted every bit as revolting as last time.

Choking down bile and fear and rage, Nath pulled away from Chadawa with all that remained of Hail Squadron.

III

Colonel Soran Keize had enjoyed the duel, but it was time to end the exercise. He'd heard the New Republic call "Bombers retreat!" and been troubled; now Captain Nenvez recited numbers over the comm suggesting more serious danger. The Raiders were damaged, and Colonel Madrighast had decided to play his hand.

Shadow Wing did not need Soran—not yet. Broosh was a fine tactician and Soran trusted he'd tended the unit well and that any casualties, no matter how regrettable, were the result of decisions based on experience and reason. But Soran might be needed *soon,* as matters grew increasingly complex and strategies were reconceived.

Much later, he would mourn the fallen and doubt himself. He would let himself wonder if he'd made a mistake in accepting Wyl Lark's challenge. For the moment, however, there was one clear action he could take to rebalance the scales between the 204th and General Syndulla.

Wyl Lark, he thought, *I do this without hatred or malice.*

The battle had taken them far from the *Yadeez*, out to a pitiful moon barely larger than an asteroid. They'd chased each other through canyons and dived back toward Chadawa, back into its outermost ring, and Soran had savored the joy of flight and combat there. He recalled his first encounter with a Polynean, a year before Endor at the Cataract of Moons; that opponent, a woman whose name he did not know, had brought him to an almost ecstatic state like that described by the Tan'twingen warrior-monks. He'd very nearly died, and would have accepted it as a fitting end.

But the outcome of *this* fight had not truly been in doubt—not since he'd taken Lark's measure in the first minute and determined the man was an impeccable flier, a brave combatant, but one who lacked the spirit of a born soldier. Lark treated combat as a dance, a collaboration between partners in the creation of beauty; and while Soran recognized the potential for beauty in war, he knew that it could never take precedence over victory. Lark hesitated when he should have killed.

There was a place for men like Lark in the galaxy. That place was not in a duel with the Empire's ace of aces, and certainly not when that ace's unit was threatened.

He pursued Lark's A-wing through the rings, closer to his foe than he'd previously dared. The TIE shrieked off-key, the particle tides disrupting its ion engines and dampening its familiar cry. Sweat pooled beneath Soran's eyes under his helmet, while his lips felt cracked from dehydration. His body ached from the maneuvers but he was not tired—only weakened.

He loosed a quick volley meant to distract rather than kill. The A-wing spun, nearly colliding with the nearest satellite but recovering after a moment. Lark's shields, Soran knew, were nearly depleted—he'd tapped away at their power over many minutes, and he felt confident the radiation would inhibit the A-wing's deflector from recharging. One well-placed shot might end the battle; two certainly would.

If only we had longer.

Lark applied his repulsors and swung hard to one side, clearly hoping Soran would overshoot him. It was a simple stratagem, but not a poor choice given Soran's proximity. Soran pitched the TIE downward in response, leaning into the gentle tug of Chadawa's gravity and looping in a tight arc that forced the blood from his brain. He was dizzy and short of breath when he emerged from the loop, while the A-wing had barely moved—Soran had bet its sudden deceleration had taken a toll on the pilot, and it appeared he'd won the wager. He adjusted his vector, centered the enemy interceptor in his faceted viewport, and squeezed his firing trigger.

Particle bolts streamed from the TIE and an emerald blade sliced the fleeing A-wing's port thruster fin. A blue flash like an afterimage reassured Soran that the last of Lark's shields were gone, and the smoke trailing from the damaged thruster indicated the Polynean's maneuverability would be hampered. The A-wing's speed and agility were comparable to a TIE's out of atmosphere, all else being equal, but Soran now had a decisive advantage.

"Colonel?" Broosh's voice came from the comm. "Are you receiving?"

That was alarming, Soran thought. They'd developed a coded messaging system for a reason; whatever Broosh wanted to report was peculiar enough that the codes wouldn't suffice and important enough that he was willing to say it to every ship in the system.

"I read you," Soran said. He sounded hoarse. His body really was beginning to fail him.

Lark sped out of the satellite ring, away from Chadawa. Soran followed, wondering if he'd done enough damage to force the Polynean to flee the planet's gravity well or be pulled to ground.

"You asked to be alerted," Broosh said. "The signal is faint but we have authentication."

The signal? After a moment, he understood.

Quell was returning.

"Message received," Soran said.

Now he truly was needed. The duel had to end swiftly. He felt a tremor in his hands, a surge of emotion, and sealed away his internal strife.

Lark was headed back toward the desolate Chadawan moon, and Soran recognized the contours of the Polynean's plan—retreat to the rocky canyons, where his loss of maneuverability would be less of an impediment than in open space. It wouldn't save him but it would drag out the fighting. Soran's TIE hissed and rattled as he opened his throttle, and he fired rapid bursts at his foe hoping to force desperate action. His own weapons were apt to overheat in the particle field, but Lark was unlikely to know the intricacies of a TIE's cooling systems and Soran needed only one moment of panic to deliver the final blow.

Lark barely attempted to evade the volley. The bolts whipped past him. He'd seen that Soran was shooting wildly, but even so there had been risk in holding steady. Was his A-wing *so* damaged, Soran wondered, that he was afraid of any motion at all?

The moon was approaching. Soran dismissed all analysis and loosed a series of discrete bursts—either Lark would begin evading or the battle would be over. Emerald lances leapt from the TIE and found their mark, piercing the A-wing as it dived toward the moon's surface. The fighter's thrusters disintegrated under the onslaught and then the whole body erupted in flame. Metal tumbled into darkness and shards of canopy scattered in all directions.

Cocking his head in fascination, Soran watched a dark object tumble out of the starfighter and fall toward the moon. It was difficult to make out through the debris and his helmet lenses and the sweat in his eyes, but he became increasingly confident of his identification as it drifted away.

Lark had spent his final moments in the race to the moon prepping his ejector seat. He'd failed to launch it soon enough but it had flown free upon the ship's destruction. Soran wondered whether the pilot's body had been burned or sliced to pieces.

Proper procedure and good sense was to chase the ejector seat and incinerate it. But at the speed the A-wing had been moving, the seat would impact the moon in moments; if he pursued, Soran would need to cut his own velocity faster than the TIE would allow to avoid crashing into the surface. He fired off a final wild volley before the ejector

seat disappeared from view; it was possible he'd hit it, but more likely
it had smashed into the ground.

With his scanners negated by the particle field, locating the seat
among the dust and rocks would take whole minutes. He descended
anyway, picturing Broosh aboard the bridge of the *Yadeez* and the
TIEs divided between attackers.

He had no more time.

He raced a hundred meters above the moon's surface, maneuvering
among the expanding plumes of dust called forth by the A-wing's impact. He decreased altitude again, trying to make out anything more
specific than twisted black blotches that might have been engine nacelles or a young man's corpse.

"Colonel?" Broosh's voice again. "Shall we await your return?"

Soran didn't need to hear impatience and strain in Broosh's steady
tone to know how the man felt. "I'm en route now," he replied.

He made one final pass over the debris, sweeping lower—through the
dust clouds—and firing, blasting rocks and wreckage until the clouds
were thick enough that he couldn't see ground or sky. Rock shards pelted
his canopy. Any survivor below might escape the particle bolt volleys,
but wouldn't emerge from the storm of shrapnel unscathed.

He pulled away from the moon and set course for the *Yadeez* and
the battle between Shadow Wing, the New Republic, and Colonel
Madrighast.

He didn't allow himself to *feel*—it wasn't yet time—but he spared
one final thought for Wyl Lark, the man who'd caused his unit such
grief over the past year. He could admire the man's efforts to turn enemies into friends—efforts Soran had mistrusted in the past but which
he now believed were sincere. *If you live, Wyl Lark, I hope you find the
peace you dreamed of.*

Even if Lark had somehow survived, however, Soran doubted he
was in any condition to cause further trouble.

Soran arrived on the bridge of the *Yadeez* without his helmet but still
in his flight suit, face a dripping mess of sweat. He'd received a sum-

mary of the situation over comlink during his hurried walk through the ship, and found himself broadly approving of Broosh's decisions so far; he allowed the commander to finish conveying orders to the tactical station before drawing his attention and asking, "What's the status of Lieutenant Quell's team?"

He saw frustration flicker across Broosh's face. Quell's mission was the last of Broosh's priorities, Soran knew, but he replied anyway: "Their ship arrived in-system and cloaked seconds later. If they get any closer to the planet, even during low tide, I imagine the radiation will cause their cloak to fail. They must be staying around the system's fringes."

"Waiting for us to give them an opportunity," Soran agreed. He glanced at the tactical display and saw the marks of the squadrons clustered about Madrighast's Star Destroyer, the *Unyielding*. "Current particle count?"

Broosh looked to Captain Nenvez, who leaned heavily on his cane behind the weapons station. "Falling rapidly," he declared. "Tide's going out. Dropping those satellites onto Chadawa seems to have accelerated their timetable."

Soran nodded and tugged at his gloves. If that was true, by the time Madrighast was defeated the New Republic battleship would be able to approach Chadawa again. One of the Raiders was already lost and the other badly damaged; if he stayed, he risked becoming mired in a series of winnable but dangerous battles and winnowing his forces further.

But he had what he'd come for. He had *hope*.

"Prepare to withdraw from the planet and jump to lightspeed," he said. "Let the Chadawans and Syndulla fight it out. If we can tow the Raider, do it—otherwise, I want it evacuated by the time we reach low tide. We'll rendezvous with Quell's team on the way out."

"Sir!" He'd expected a protest but he hadn't anticipated it from Nenvez. His own fault, really—the man was a patriot and a true believer in the Emperor's will. "We've barely begun the purge on Chadawa. Most of the landmasses are still inhabitable."

"I'm aware," Soran said. "But trust me when I say that there are larger matters in play." He raised his voice, swept his gaze around the room. "We have made sacrifices here, but this mission is *not* a failure. I promise you that."

They doubted anyway. There was only so much he could do to ameliorate the problem with a brief speech. Yet his people obeyed—they called orders to substations and sent coded messages over the comm.

Soran looked to the tactical display again and began planning their retreat even as he reexamined his own words. In truth, he didn't yet know if they had succeeded or failed.

He had hope. Until he saw everything Quell had retrieved from the Emperor's Messenger, he couldn't know whether that hope would grow into the opportunity he needed to make the cost in lives worthwhile.

CHAPTER 14

NEGATION OF IDEOLOGICAL CHOICES

I

The tide of battle was changing, and though Hera Syndulla wasn't sure how far that metaphor extended the particle counts *were* dropping. The *Deliverance* had been standing by too long. "Move in on Chadawa and make for the *Yadeez*," she told Captain Arvad, who couldn't quite hide the gleam in her eyes. "Careful not to overdo it—we're not at low tide *yet*, and who knows what the radiation will do to our systems."

Arvad snapped a "General!" before pacing the bridge and calling orders to her crew. Hera felt the deck shudder as the battleship's gargantuan thrusters ignited and millions of tons of duralloy and steel and ferroceramics were pushed toward the inner system. Moving the *Deliverance* was like moving a moon—arduous and slow, but once in motion impossible to stop. It wasn't her sort of ship but then, she reasoned, she wasn't captain.

The tactical screen showed Shadow Wing's bulk freighter attempting to disengage from battle with Chadawan forces on the outskirts of the planet's atmosphere. Scanners were still offline and scopes hadn't managed to pick out all the details, but if the 204th really was fleeing that meant an end to Operation Cinder. Hail Squadron, Wyl Lark, and the Chadawans had changed the course of the day; Hera just prayed they'd all live to enjoy bragging rights.

Yet stopping Cinder wasn't what Wyl and Nath had signed on for; it wasn't what Alphabet Squadron was built to do, wasn't what Caern Adan and a hundred others had died for. She had a chance to catch Shadow Wing in a two-pronged attack and she intended to take it.

There was an electronic gurgle from under the deck; a moment later the bridge lights dimmed, then brightened. "Manually redistributing power!" the engineering officer called. "Radiation's causing problems, but nothing we can't handle."

Hera and Arvad exchanged a look. Arvad shrugged and mouthed, *You wanted to go in.*

"Shadow Wing fighters loading back aboard the *Yadeez*," the comscan officer announced. Hera had finally learned the young Cathar's name: Dhina. "That Star Destroyer from Chadawa is pursuing but keeping its distance."

"They don't want a fight," Arvad said. "They just want to herd Shadow Wing away from the planet."

"And Shadow Wing wants to leave the system," Hera agreed. "How are Flare and Wild squadrons doing? Can we launch at these particle levels?"

"We can launch, but we don't know how badly they'll be affected." Arvad looked as if she was going to say more, but she didn't have to. Hera understood.

The squadrons' commander was missing. Maybe dead. Without Wyl Lark, in a hostile environment, they'd be badly disadvantaged.

"Keep them in reserve," Hera said. "I want those fighters ready to fly."

The *Deliverance* marched on, closing the distance to the bulk freighter. Scopes confirmed that the *Raider*-class corvettes were missing among its escorts (though the gunship and surveillance vessel stayed close); there was no sign of the Y-wings, either. Hera hoped they'd moved out of sight to the opposite side of the planet, and that they weren't still engaging the Raiders. She couldn't help them now, in any case.

"Intercept in two minutes," the nav officer announced. "Estimating four minutes till the *Yadeez* can safely jump to lightspeed."

Not ideal, Hera thought, *but it might be enough.* They'd have to slow the freighter or destroy it quickly. "How's the tractor beam? Repairs finished?"

"In theory," Arvad said. "But we haven't tested it, and in the particle field—"

"I know, I know. But the *Yadeez* will have to escape the worst of the radiation to jump anyway. Prep the beam and let's see what happens."

The *Yadeez* began angling away from the *Deliverance* to prolong the chase. Its top speed wasn't close to the Star Destroyer's but the smaller vessel, clumsy and antiquated as it was, could still turn and shed inertia faster than the pursuing behemoth. Hera had played out similar chases a hundred times from the opposite perspective—for years she'd *lived* on the run from Star Destroyers—and she imagined a similar sense of vertigo overtaking the enemy commander.

Whoever the enemy commander was now. The winner of the duel hadn't proclaimed his victory.

Arvad opened fire when they reached one-and-a-half times optimal targeting range. It wouldn't do much good, Hera knew, even if the gunnery crew somehow scored a hit—turbolasers bled too much energy as they traveled. But it would give Shadow Wing another problem to worry about. Hera felt the hum of the weaponry, watched the viewport fill with light, and recalled what this, too, looked like from the opposite angle.

At the same time, the Chadawan warship was turning too slowly to tail the freighter and straightening its curve behind the *Deliverance.* Hera began to ask for details on the vessel when Dhina called, "*Yadeez* is slowing! Looks like they're taking something aboard!"

Arvad hurried to a viewscreen, and Hera followed. The image was from one of the scopes—heavily magnified, pixelated, and rendered uniformly in pale blue—and depicted a ripple in space approaching the loading doors of the *Yadeez*. The longer they watched, the more the ripple gained distinct edges and substance.

"A cloaking device?" Arvad asked.

"Quell's ship," Hera said.

She tried to think through the implications—what had Quell's mission been, and what did it mean that she'd returned? What about Kairos and Chass, who were still missing?—then wiped it from her mind. "This is our chance," she said. "Give the engines everything they can take, maintain fire, and aim the tractor beam. If we're going to catch that thing we do it now!"

The bridge officers snapped orders into their headsets and the ship's engines whined. The trembling of the deck became increasingly violent, and Hera wondered what it would take to overstrain a Star Destroyer. The turbolaser streams pouring toward the bulk freighter were almost unbroken, individual laser bolts impossible to distinguish in the cascade.

Then the deck didn't simply tremble—it *lurched*. Groans and shouts went up around the bridge. "What was that?" Arvad cried, but Hera knew before the tactical station could report.

The ship from Chadawa was directly to their rear. There was nowhere else a shot could've come from.

Someone brought up the scope's view of the attacking craft: a scarred and shredded *Imperial*-class Star Destroyer, its own turbolaser batteries ablaze. The *Deliverance*'s weapons and shield status showed above the tactical station—deflectors holding, guns 89 percent charged—and Hera synthesized all of it into a battle in her mind's eye.

"Activate the tractor beam," Arvad called, "and launch fighters. We'll lock down the freighter and defend our rear—"

"No!" Hera snapped. "Blast it, no. Hard to port! Starboard batteries, keep firing at the *Yadeez*—maybe we'll get lucky. Port side, concentrate on the enemy Destroyer."

Arvad signaled the crew to obey—Hera felt a wave of gratitude at that—before asking soft and sharp: "What are you doing? They'll get away—"

"We tractor them now, we'll have to hold position—we can't turn and maintain beam lock at the same time. That leaves our stern exposed, and our rear deflectors won't hold against a Star Destroyer." She spoke rapidly, hoping Arvad understood. "The fighters can only distract the warship because we *don't have our bombers*. Only the *Deliverance* can lead a counterattack."

Arvad swore—as good an indication of comprehension as any. She yelled at the flight officer to send the fighters at the *Yadeez* and its escorts as the *Deliverance* began its turn. "Give me the comm," Hera said, and grabbed a headset. She tried to stay calm, to think: *What would Chancellor Mothma say?*

"This is General Syndulla to the attacking Star Destroyer—we just saved your planet! Cease your attack and help us catch the people responsible!"

She hoped what it lacked in diplomacy it made up for in brutal honesty.

There was no response. Now the enemy Star Destroyer was also turning to avoid presenting a stable target. The *Yadeez* began to pull away and Hera hoped desperately that Flare and Wild could make a difference. She paced between bridge stations, advising where she could, but the plan was clear enough—victory or defeat would be determined by an equation of time, execution, and power, and there was little she could do to affect it now.

The *Deliverance* and the opposing Star Destroyer circled each other, delivering endless salvos of turbolaser and cannon fire from the batteries lining their wedge-shaped hulls. Each tried to present as slender a profile as possible without concentrating enemy fire onto one section of its deflectors. At first they appeared evenly matched, but the Chadawan Destroyer's shields rapidly began to fail; an increasing number of turbolaser blasts ripped through the coruscating electromagnetic barrier and impacted the armored hull. The already scarred warship was soon pocked with burning craters, while the *Deliverance*'s own shields strained but held.

The particle count fell all the while. The *Deliverance*'s scanners swept away ghost images and the ship's subsystems revitalized. When the comscan station reported massive damage to the enemy Destroyer's combat center, Hera commanded the *Deliverance* to turn away, to chase the bulk freighter still harried by Flare and Wild. She had just long enough to feel hope before the *Yadeez* and its two surviving escorts flashed into hyperspace.

She tamped down her anger for the sake of the crew. "Did we do *anything*?" she asked. "Tell me someone damaged the freighter's engines, planted a homing device, something—"

Arvad started to answer—her expression told Hera all she needed—when the *Deliverance* shook at another enemy volley. Hera grabbed her headset again. "This is General Syndulla to the enemy Star Destroyer," she called. "You understand that you've lost? Cease fire and surrender immediately!"

She expected no response. She signaled for the *Deliverance* to head back toward the Chadawan Destroyer and was surprised when a man's thick brogue declared: "This is Colonel Madrighast of the *Unyielding*. We will not surrender to the Rebellion."

The *Unyielding* was heading toward the *Deliverance*, weapons active. "Colonel," Hera said, and forced herself to sound calm, "I lost good people defending your planet. I'm not asking for gratitude. I am asking you to let me save *your* lives, too."

"So we can live as prisoners? So all we fought for can be mocked?" Madrighast sneered. "The 204th was trying to kill us, but they were never our enemy."

"General . . ." Arvad pointed to the tactical map. The *Unyielding* was accelerating on an intercept course.

A *collision* course.

"Colonel." The anger Hera had suppressed was replaced by fear and grief, and these she couldn't prevent from subverting her voice. "Your people will be treated fairly, you have my oath. There's no reason to continue—"

"The New Republic will fall!" Madrighast cried, like an anguished battle cry. "And the Empire rise again."

"Do it," Hera hissed to Arvad, and the captain nodded to her crew.

She would've turned away if she hadn't been responsible. Instead Hera watched through the viewport as the *Unyielding* raced toward them, spewing streams of turbolaser fire as the *Deliverance* transferred all power to its weapons. Soon its broadside outshone the enemy barrage like a nova outshines a firecracker, and emerald destruction tore through the foe's hull. The *Unyielding*'s second deflector dome burst like an overheated egg; its weapons ceased to function but it continued forward as the *Deliverance* cut deep into deck after deck. Explosive chain reactions rocked the vessel and ripped apart the superstructure; great burning metallic layers of what had once been a Star Destroyer tumbled toward the *Deliverance* until abominable weapons shattered these, too—left them molten and swiftly solidifying in the icy vastness of space.

Then there was nothing left of the *Unyielding* or its crew, and the hum of weapons died away. The bridge felt unnaturally silent.

"Get rescue crews ready, and medics," Hera said. "Our Y-wings are out there, and so is Wyl Lark."

▌▌

Yrica Quell listened to the click of the air circulation switching on and felt the resulting breeze on her bruised skin. The hair follicles on her forearms rippled like blown grass and tugged at dried blood. She smelled grease and fried circuits, and tried to appreciate the peace of it all as she leaned into the cushions of the U-wing's crew seat.

Then Chass na Chadic screamed at an access panel and slammed a hydrospanner against the bulkhead. The brief peace was vanquished.

"You won't get in there without a torch," Quell murmured. "Not if the releases are fused."

"I know that," Chadic growled.

Quell shrugged and looked from the Theelin to Kairos, who stood in the cockpit doorway. Her body faced the cabin but her head craned to peer out the cockpit viewport. It was an awkward pose, unlike any-thing Quell normally associated with the woman—she'd always lurked like a statue in shadow, immobile and foreboding. Now she seemed distracted by the stars.

Chadic, too, seemed different. Not just physically, though the crest of her hair was centimeters shorter and flatter than Quell remem-bered, as if she'd sliced it with a hand plane; but where she'd always been volatile, now she seemed to oscillate between furious and with-drawn, with nothing in between. She was *less* than the person Quell remembered.

Chadic stared at the bulkhead awhile. Quell waited for her to do the sensible thing, then said it herself: "If we're going to escape you need to stabilize the power flow. You don't have the equipment to overhaul the hyperdrive or the navicomputer, so you're going to have to run a diagnostic to be sure—"

"Don't patronize me!" Chadic said, and threw the hydrospanner toward Quell. It smacked into the seat centimeters from Quell's shoul-der and fell to the floor. "You want to be in charge, you should've stayed with Shadow Wing."

Quell stretched her foot to kick the hydrospanner across the deck toward Chadic. *I wasn't in charge,* she thought. *Not by the end, when they planned to kill me.* Saying so would've only baited Chadic, so she stayed silent.

"Did I know any of them?" Chadic asked. "Your pals down there?"

"Know them?"

"Yeah. Was one of them Char, or Blink, or something?"

"No," Quell said. "You didn't know them."

"Kind of a bunch of morons anyway. Couldn't shoot straight, couldn't fight. Couldn't protect *you.*"

Quell knew better than to reply. She answered anyway. "Not every pilot knows how to use a blaster. Some of them weren't even—"

"—teenagers? I noticed. One of them looked younger than Wyl and twice as skinny—"

"—some of them weren't pilots," she finished, sucking breath between her teeth. "They were engineers. What—did you see what happened to the kid?"

To Rikton.

Chadic showed her teeth in a sneer. "Don't know. You should've kept a better watch."

Quell squeezed her eyes shut and tried not to think of them. She couldn't talk to Chadic about it—couldn't afford to ask whether Rikton and Mirro and Brebtin and Raida were alive or dead. Couldn't think about whether anyone had rescued Kandende, or if the ship had gotten clear of the outpost or delivered its message to Keize—

"What'd you need engineers for, anyway?" Chadic asked, her voice abruptly casual.

"I don't remember my mission," Quell said. "You'll have to ask the colonel."

The Theelin laughed, low and hoarse. "You're a bad liar. You go big, though." She leaned against the bulkhead, studying Quell; the mocking smile didn't reach her eyes, merciless as Cerberon. "Paid off before. We all knew you were filth for flying for the Empire all that time, but who'd have guessed that you were *genocidal* filth? Other than the people of Nacronis, I mean."

Quell made sure to show no reaction, though the old guilt and self-loathing beaded on her like cold sweat. She remembered the eye of the tower on the red planetoid, and the despair she'd felt at the knowledge that nothing would ever make her actions right.

But she'd moved past it. She would never forgive herself, but she would move forward.

"What happened to Chadawa?" Quell asked.

"Who the hell knows? We left right after you did."

After a while Chadic returned to work. Quell was relieved, but she shuddered when she noticed that at some point during their argument, Kairos had turned to watch them both.

She could've told the truth: that she'd led Alphabet Squadron to Shadow Wing. That she'd been a spy, not a traitor. She'd longed for someone to say it aloud to, longed for a chance to admit her doubts to IT-O or anyone she could trust. But her original lie, the lie about Nacronis, overshadowed everything. Chadic wouldn't believe her—Lark or General Syndulla might've given her a chance, but not Chadic—and Quell had no desire to broach the subject with a woman who loathed her.

After a lengthy silence, Chadic approached Quell and slammed a small toolbox on the deck in front of her. "I'm going to keep watch for the droids. If you're so smart, you fix it," she said, and stalked into the cockpit.

Quell wasn't sure the droids were coming. But she was grateful for the distraction and got to work.

A UT-60D U-wing wasn't built for easy hyperdrive access during flight. She discovered this while dismantling bulkheads and squirming into filthy access spaces that would've suffocated anyone larger. The process was painstaking and occasionally frustrating, and she suspected she'd receive an unhealthy dose of radiation from the reactor; but it was indeed an excellent distraction and mostly kept the intrusive thoughts at bay.

Now and then, when she emerged to switch out tools or check a diagnostic or breathe cleaner air, she saw that Kairos still lingered in the cockpit doorway. Sometimes the woman watched her. Sometimes she faced the cockpit, both hands on the doorframe, staring into the stars as if expecting to see some glimmer that the scanners couldn't.

Quell had difficulty thinking of her as Kairos at all. Once, when the woman's back was turned, Quell observed her awhile. But Kairos was too perfectly still and Quell's attention wandered to Chadic, whose foot was barely in Quell's field of vision and who was whispering something that sounded like a chant.

Who are these people? Quell wondered. Had they been such a mess when she'd led Alphabet? Had she gotten used to it? Forgotten during her time away?

She'd just located a thermal recoupler, kneeling at the toolbox, and was bracing herself to return to the access space when a shadow moved above her. She looked up to see Kairos.

The woman said in her broken voice: "Where are Adan and IT-O?"

Quell shifted onto her knees, then slowly rose. She recalled the first words Adan had spoken when she'd saved his life in Cerberon (the first time, before she'd failed him and let him die): *What happened to Kairos?*

"I'm sorry," she said. "I know—"

I know the three of you were bound together. That you survived torture in an Imperial prison camp together.

She stopped, swallowed, and steadied her voice. "They're dead," she said. "They died in Cerberon, and I'm sorry. I tried to save them both. I was lucky to get out at all."

The words were facile. She wouldn't have blamed Kairos for throttling her, but the woman only turned away to stare at the stars again.

The damage to the hyperdrive was largely superficial, consisting of fused cabling leading to the reactor (which Quell replaced without trouble) along with lesser damage to the motivator (which Quell couldn't fix but which would survive at least one jump).

The bigger trouble was the navicomputer. There was physical damage to both core and backup core significant enough for Quell to see without a magnifier—she could *smell* the damage when she crawled underneath the main console. The ship would fly but the entire nav system had been corrupted. She could've taken apart and reassembled the whole transport with enough time and tools, but data recovery was an entirely different discipline and not one the Imperial Academy had trained her for.

"Basically," she told Chadic and Kairos as she closed the toolbox in the main cabin and wiped her hands on an already filthy rag, "we're in a mess. Hyperdrive is online, so we can hit lightspeed. But we can't calculate our destination so all we can do is pick a direction, jump, and hope we don't smash into a star."

Chadic grunted. "So, what? We go back to Netalych, tell the

droids we're sorry for the damage and hope to get some replacement parts?"

"I don't know," Quell said. "I don't know. I don't get a vote. But I can tell you those droids—" She thought about the Surgeon and Kandende and tried not to show her discomfort. "—I don't like them and I don't trust them."

"Yeah, well—" Chadic swung drunkenly around the crew seats. "—I don't know what other options we have. Maybe we can trade them something. Or we float here until they finally kill us. Or we wait for someone to help and hope our oxygen doesn't run out."

Chadic made no move toward the cockpit. It was a relief, in a way; Quell smelled the methane of the Netalych outpost, felt the ice prick her flesh. Running out of oxygen seemed preferable.

Kairos had turned back toward the viewport, staring at the stars again. "I know," she said.

"Know what?" Chadic asked.

Kairos raised an arm and pointed into space—toward a star, or the dark between the stars, or nothing at all.

Chadic furrowed her brow at Kairos, then glanced to Quell. Quell parted her lips to speak but Kairos was leaving the cabin, sliding into the pilot's seat and bringing her hands to the controls.

"Know *what*?" Chadic asked again, following Kairos into the cockpit.

Kairos didn't answer. The ship shifted beneath them, maneuvering thrusters pushing them to face *whatever* it had been Kairos had pointed to. Whatever she stared at now as she pressed buttons and flipped toggles.

"Know *what*?" Chadic asked more frantically, and now Quell was up, too, racing to the cockpit and grasping the doorframe for support as the U-wing lurched forward. She heard Chadic say something else but didn't catch the particulars; her eyes were fixed on Kairos as the woman's hand found the hyperdrive accelerator and eased back the lever.

The stars distorted and stretched. Quell felt weightless as she heard Chadic cursing over and over.

III

Nath Tensent fixed a grin on his face as he dropped out of his Y-wing onto the deck of the *Deliverance*. His expression didn't waver as he steadied himself on a landing strut and Sergeant Ragnell approached with a ground crew. "You want to tell us not to touch your ship *now*?" she asked. Nath breathed in the stink of burnt metal and laughed off her outrage. He heard himself say, "This time it's all yours."

T5 was chiming in the distance. That was good, he thought—the old droid had had a rough ride and there was bound to be damage. He braced himself to look, grinned at something one of the ground crew said (he didn't hear, just saw the man smiling and responded in kind), then felt a hand clasp his shoulder. He whirled to defend himself.

There was no threat. No one saw him make a fist. He dropped his hand to his side and tried to focus on the thickly built woman in the flight suit in front of him.

The hell is wrong with you, Tensent? Pay attention.

There'd been four survivors of Hail Squadron—roughly a third of the pilots they'd started with. Nath had counted the bombers while they'd awaited pickup from the *Deliverance*. The woman half a meter away was Hail Ten, real name—

You know this. You talked to her a dozen times on the Lodestar, *you were at the party when Hail split off on Troithe, you had opinions on whether she was fit to lead a squadron of her own . . .*

"Jiona," Nath said, and clasped her arms. "You did good out there. They all did good."

He thought that was what he said, at any rate. There was too much noise in the hangar, engines powering down and people shouting and someone spraying sparks pell-mell with a laser torch. Jiona was insisting they had to go back, that she'd spotted Hail Nine ejecting before his Y-wing had been blown apart by a Raider, and Nath said something placating in return. She could take the demand to Captain Arvad if she really believed it was true.

"They did good," Nath said again. "That planet out there—" He blanked on the planet name, too, though he'd just been thinking about it. "—Chadawa, it'd be dying of radiation poisoning if not for us. You hear me? It'd be another Alderaan!"

Jiona nodded. Nath released a breath and turned away, pushing aside images of Y-wings burning and the sensation of his cockpit shaking. He thought he was recalling Trenchenovu again, but the *feel* was wrong—he'd never saved a planet in those days—and he realized he was above Troithe in his mind, steering into a missile to save millions, to earn a medal, to earn the trust of the New Republic and be a damn hero . . .

There were other voices intruding. He shook his head and saw Ragnell talking to General Syndulla, who looked between Jiona and Nath. Syndulla had the expression of a woman who'd run a marathon to reach a funeral.

She called his name. He smiled tightly and reminded himself of his role. "We got Chadawa," he said. "Planet's safe, I think. What about Shadow Wing?"

"You worked a miracle out there," Syndulla said. "But they got away. Captain Tensent—Nath—listen, we found Wyl. His ship was destroyed, but we found him alive on Chadawa's moon. He's *hurt*, we're bringing him in—"

"Where?" Nath asked. He heard his voice clearly for the first time since landing.

"He's en route to the medbay," Syndulla said. "You can go. Our position's secure."

Nath grunted a thank-you, or meant to. Then he was shoving his way through the crowd. He made it out of the hangar and turned one way—like a fool, as if he were going to the medbay on the *Lodestar*—then turned the opposite direction. His world narrowed to the sight of his own boots and the sound of his breathing and the ringing in his ears, and an eternity later he was in the medbay, smelling disinfectant and scanning the floating gurneys around him. There was a handful of figures laid out—crew casualties from the *Deliverance*'s own fight—but he rapidly spotted two men in flight suits pushing a gurney into an operating suite.

On the stretcher lay Wyl Lark. The boy was still and pale, and the left leg of his grime-encrusted flight suit was soaked with blood.

"What happened?" Nath called.

One of the rescue crew paused at the door and repeated what Syndulla had said about the moon. "He's not awake. Med droid will be by in a minute."

"Can I see him?" Nath asked.

"Until the med droid is here."

They finished moving the stretcher and exited the suite. Nath moved inside, feeling the prickle of sanitizing rays as he passed through the doorway. Wyl was breathing deep and steady as a child.

"Congratulations," Nath said. "You made it."

When he blinked, he saw Y-wings burning again. He saw Wyl's A-wing glimmering in the distance.

"*You* made it," Nath repeated, shifting the emphasis. "Real clever plan, keeping Keize and his lot distracted while we went for the Raiders. We got the message. We did our jobs. Of course—"

He spat out the words as they rose up his throat. He wasn't a man prone to speaking thoughtlessly, but he let himself speak now. Wyl wouldn't hear, *no one* would hear, and that thought was infuriating in itself.

"—of course not everyone's the pilot you are. Y-wings were blowing up before the enemy even took a shot, and after that? You should've seen them come apart. You never got to know Hail that well, but I promise you it's going to be quite a memorial.

"Because they're *heroes* now. They're heroes, just the way you like them, only they weren't *lucky* heroes like you. There's only so many times the rest of us can cheat death trying to win medals before we end up martyrs instead—"

He stopped abruptly. The words had ceased coming and all that was left was rage and fear.

Too much fear. He shuddered, twisting his body violently and sucking in quick breaths.

Wyl shifted on the cot and turned his head a hairsbreadth in Nath's direction. His eyelids began to lift, then fell shut again. "Nath?" he whispered.

"It's me," Nath said. He sounded tired.

"Did you save Chadawa?"

Nath managed an echo of a laugh. "Yeah. Yeah, we saved Chadawa."

Wyl dipped his chin in something like a nod. "Thank you," he said. "Thank you. I'm sorry I doubted. Thank you."

Nath tapped the boy's shoulder with shaking fingers before stepping back. "Med droid will be with you in a second. You rest up, brother."

It took everything he had to say the words.

"Nath?" Wyl tried to turn his head again and failed. This time, though, his eyes were open. "Wait."

Nath shifted where he stood and waited.

Wyl's voice was clearer. His eyes strained to look in Nath's direction. He sounded weak but lucid. "There's something—I didn't want to tell you. Please listen."

"I'm listening," Nath said.

"I spoke to Polyneus. I spoke to the elders. They told me—they told me, Nath, that I'm the last." His eyelids fluttered like he was fighting off exhaustion. "The last of the Hundred and Twenty. Everyone else, the others who fought—they're all Home now. All of them except me."

Nath looked down at the boy, trying to comprehend what he'd heard.

Then Wyl made it clear enough: "I want to go," he whispered. "I'm ready to go Home."

Metal hands gently pushed Nath aside as the med droid arrived. He stared awhile longer, no longer feeling rage or fear or even shame but a pity he couldn't remember experiencing before; and when he left the operating suite he barely saw the burning ships behind the face of a homesick child covered in dust and blood.

CHAPTER 15

OBFUSCATION OF UNDESIRABLE RESULTS

I

"Now you want to explain?" Chadic asked. Quell felt the Theelin spoke for both of them.

They stood with Kairos in front of the U-wing, the transport half buried in peat at the end of a kilometer-long furrow plowed through the jungle. The hull had already cooled from reentry, and a layer of moisture had condensed onto the viewport. One loading door refused to close, its mechanisms clogged by churned-up muck. Quell found the temperature pleasant after the chill of Netalych, and the smell of fermented fruit was noticeable but not overwhelming; and while her muscles ached and her injuries burned, the U-wing's inertial dampeners had eased the worst of the jolts. As crash landings went, she had few complaints.

But they still didn't know where they were. Kairos had refused to speak during flight, and they'd emerged from hyperspace so close to the planet they'd nearly been torn apart by the sudden gravitational pull. Kairos had handled their forced descent well, yet it was past time for answers.

"I knew," Kairos said.

"Knew *what*?" Chadic asked. "What did you blasted *know*?"

Kairos said nothing, beginning to circle the U-wing and looking from the damaged vessel to the jungle. Gray, broad-leafed trees hung with globules like melons or egg sacs, and ocher cliffs rose far to the north against a pale-rose sky.

After a minute, Chadic looked to Quell. "She doesn't leave footprints."

Quell turned to where Kairos had passed and saw the ground apparently untouched, while Quell's own boots sank deep into the soil. "No," Quell said.

"I'm not stupid," Chadic said.

"I didn't say you were."

Chadic shrugged and wandered over to the U-wing's thruster nacelles. "My mom told me stories about these little maggot-things on Felucia that spent most of their life being blown around on storm winds. Sometimes ended up on the other side of the planet from where they started, but they'd always work their way back when it was time to breed. Brains the size of a thumbnail. Still found a way back."

It was more oblique than Quell had come to expect from Chadic. After a moment she understood. "You think her people can navigate through hyperspace?"

"She got us here somehow, didn't she?" Chadic asked. "Unless you want to credit the Force."

It was Quell's turn to shrug. She looked at Kairos, who watched the jungle. Quell tried to determine whether the woman looked like someone who'd returned to her homeworld at last.

She couldn't tell. But Chadic *wasn't* stupid, hard as that was for Quell to remember at times.

"I'd like to check the ship for supplies," Quell said. "I don't know what you're planning but I'm fairly sure I spotted an orbital watch satellite on the way down—Imperial design. Probably tracking us, and we'll need to eat if we travel."

"I saw it, too," Chadic said, in a tone that left Quell less than convinced. "But if there *are* Imps around, they'll have a ship. Wouldn't mind it being delivered straight to us."

We're not in a position to stage an ambush, Quell wanted to say. *You've got a blaster, a bowcaster, and a prisoner to watch, and you'd be facing a well-equipped enemy who knows the terrain.* But she thought of Chadic's reactions to her aid aboard the U-wing and decided she didn't care to set the Theelin off again.

She climbed into the cabin and began sorting through compartments, turning up a handful of ration bars, a medkit, and a compression bag full of glow rods, camping equipment, and a portable vaporator. She nearly gasped when she touched the vaporator, and shoved it into a pocket without looking again.

The memories of her crash landing in Cerberon were stronger than she'd expected.

"There are Imperials here," Kairos said, returning to the U-wing as Quell emerged. "On the surface. A small outpost, not far."

Quell looked to Chadic. Chadic shifted her weight from one leg to the other. "Okay. Beats waiting around. We see if we can steal a ship from there." She looked at Quell, narrowing her eyes. "If we can't find one, assume I kill all your Imp buddies. You're stranded with us. Can you repair the U-wing?"

Quell nodded carefully. "There's fresh damage from the crash, but it's pretty basic. We'd still need a new database for the navicomputer."

"Keen. Fantastic." Chadic kicked at the ground, sending a spray of dirt from under her toe. Next she turned to Kairos and asked, "Don't suppose there's anyplace we can get actual *help* down here? Maybe some friends of yours?"

"No," Kairos said, and adjusted the strap of her bowcaster before setting off toward the cliff.

Chadic sighed, took half a step, then paused and drew her blaster.

She turned to Quell and waved the weapon in her direction. "Try to run, I'll shoot you. You know that, right?"

"I assumed," Quell said, and they walked together into the jungle.

The jungle sloped gently upward, and Quell's footing was frequently imperiled by slick stones or loose soil. Kairos led the way, trackless and prone to disappearing for minutes at a time; Chadic stayed close to Quell, grumbling whenever a mushroom steamed in the rose light or a birdlike warbling echoed beneath the canopy. Other sounds were more difficult to distinguish, and Quell couldn't tell whether she was hearing the spitting and hooting of living creatures or the hum of electrified fronds.

She had to remind herself where she was by frequent drags of the moist air. The experience was too familiar, and she half expected to see Caern Adan trudging beside her.

"Don't," Chadic muttered.

Quell had been about to step over a boulder covered in crawling ocher moss. She kept her foot in midair, but Chadic was looking at her face; she finished the step, then frowned. "I didn't say anything."

"I know. That's the problem. You're planning something, and I'm telling you—*don't*."

Chadic unholstered her blaster again and waved Quell farther in front of her. Quell followed instructions, hiking after the silhouette of Kairos.

"So what was it?" Chadic asked.

"There's no plan," Quell said.

"You can't fight me—you're a walking bruise already. You planning to poison me somehow? Send up a flare to the Imps?"

"There's no plan."

"You looked pretty blasted intent for someone not planning something."

Quell stopped, squared her shoulders, and turned to face Chadic. The Theelin wore an ugly grin.

"*I don't want you dead,*" Quell said.

Chadic flinched. Her grin disappeared, replaced by a tight, trembling frown.

Quell felt a mix of satisfaction and chagrin at having delivered a solid blow. The chagrin won out; she felt it crawl down her arms over bruises and cuts like an insect, and she rubbed it furiously away. "I was thinking about Cerberon," she said, by way of conciliation. "It wasn't a plan."

Chadic waved the blaster again, not lifting it above her hip. Quell turned and resumed the walk.

"What about Cerberon?" Chadic asked.

You can talk about it, Quell thought to herself, *or you can let her shoot you in the back.*

It took her a while to decide. Finally she said, "When I made it off the *Lodestar,* Adan and Ito and I were stranded on a planetoid in the debris field. We had to hike from the crash site to find a way off. It's hard not to think about."

"That where they died?"

"Yes."

Chadic was silent, though Quell could still hear boots crushing undergrowth and spattering mud. Eventually the Theelin said, "Guess you think you had it hard."

"Sort of, yes." Quell shrugged. She had no intention of sharing more details.

"Well—you're obviously thrilled to see Kairos popped up alive and okay. Weirder than before, but basically okay. Since you asked about the rest of us, Wyl's in charge now—you might've picked that up—and he and Nath ended up stuck on Troithe with the dozen or so people who survived Shadow Wing's attack."

That wasn't me, she wanted to say. *I didn't want Shadow Wing on Troithe any more than you did.* But it wasn't the right time.

"What about Ragnell?" Quell asked. She wasn't sure why she asked; she'd barely known the tattooed ground crew chief, even if she had liked her.

"Made it through, unlike most of the *Lodestar.* Or Meteor Squadron."

Quell fell silent again. She'd wondered often what had happened after the *Lodestar*'s destruction. Hearing Chadic speak now was like peeling away a bandage to examine an infected wound—compelling and horrifying and painful all together.

Chadic paused, then added with a smirk Quell could hear: "I got to join a cult."

"What?"

"Sure. You weren't the only one stranded. I joined a cult. Children of the Empty Sun. You want to know what they teach?"

The wound lay plain in front of Quell; she couldn't look away. "Sure."

"Seeking peace through bureaucracy is a fool's errand," Chadic said, as if quoting, "so what does it matter whether it's the Empire or the Republic—old or new—dropping bombs? The only true peace is found in the Force, and the Force is cultivated through harmony and community and the vision of blessed individuals."

"What does that mean?"

"It means the whole war's pointless and we should just shut up and do what our cult leader says and we'd all be happier. Probably true, at least for some of us."

"But you're out here."

"Yeah. I'm out here," Chadic said. "I'm out here, and my cult's in Cerberon, and all the lectures they gave me are sitting in my B-wing with those freaking droids. Probably never going to get them back, either, thanks to you. I had a *lot* of stuff in that ship."

There was a crashing noise from the tree limbs above. Quell flinched and saw a rock larger than her fist arc overhead, then fall to the dirt ten meters down the path. When the noise of the rustling leaves and the rock's impact faded, she heard Chadic panting with the effort of the throw.

"I'm sorry you lost your things," Quell said, and pushed sincerity into her voice, low and steady. She had enough to be sorry about. Adding one more item to the pile was easy.

She turned to look back at Chadic, who scowled and shrugged.

"It's fine," Chadic said. "I was thinking of getting a neural implant anyway. That way I can hear the stupid lectures all the time."

The rose glow faded from the sky. The jungle grew louder as night fell, and distant chitters and clicks and chaotic melodies like the songs of woodwinds traveled on the humid air. Kairos's movements became stiffer, and she often looked abruptly to either side. The woman was on edge but she answered none of Chadic's questions. Quell didn't bother asking.

"This way," Kairos said, when they reached a rocky mound in the slope draped in moss and vines.

Quell didn't understand at first, but she looked in the dim light to where Kairos stood and saw a gap in the rocks concealed by curtains of vegetation, large enough for a person to squeeze through.

"Where does it go?" Chadic asked warily.

"Under," Kairos said. "Stealth is necessary. They will see if we cross above."

"The Imperials?" Quell asked.

Kairos looked at her, unblinking. "Yes, and other things."

Chadic and Quell activated the glow rods, and Kairos stayed within the sphere of her companions' light as they crept inside. The tunnel was formed of hard-packed dirt and rock, and roots slithered down the walls and hung from the ceiling. They were forced to walk single file but, despite what she'd feared while contorting her body through the entrance, Quell was able to face forward as the cave progressed.

Stairs sculpted into the dirt wound downward until Quell was sure they were far underground. Where the stairs ended the tunnel was broader, and side passages led to dark alcoves. Kairos ignored these, leading them on at an unhurried pace. She never paused to study her surroundings or consider where to go, but she stepped more slowly than she had in the jungle and her head was bowed.

Quell initially mistook the splotches of color on the walls for natural growths. But as they traveled the splotches grew in size and complexity, described great whorls of yellow and red and white, and it became apparent they were the work of an artist. Intricate patterns of arcs and dots raced from floor to ceiling and, farther inside, crept out from the walls until only a narrow path remained unpainted. In the light of the glow rods the paintings were beautiful abstractions; in the shadows, in Quell's peripheral vision, they took the form of faces and dancers.

They kept walking, and Kairos still did not pause as Quell saw columns coalesce in the darkness ahead. She thought they might be stalagmites, but they were neither tapered nor stone. As they drew closer, she saw they resembled humanoid figures, and she wondered if they were statues.

They were not statues. Strips of fabric like bandages and swatches of faded cloth hung off wooden stakes driven into the ground, tied together with rotting cords and stuffed with dirt so that the bundles retained humanoid shapes. Each of these effigies was loosely covered with a coarse and tattered cloak.

Resting on top of each stake, atop the swaddled dirt body, was a mask, each different in materials and design: Some were made from bone and decorated with leather or beads or dyed reeds, while others were clay or carved bark. One appeared to have been forged from bronze. The masks lacked eyes and mouths, but like the patterns on the walls hinted at expression when left in shadow.

Quell found herself motionless among the garden of effigies. Chadic, too, had stopped, leaning in to examine one of the masks. Kairos waited impatiently at the edge of their light.

"What are they?" Quell asked.

Chadic looked to Kairos. Kairos hesitated, then said, "Shells. Contaminated and discarded. Buried here, away from them."

"Away from your people?"

Kairos didn't look at Quell as she said, "Yes."

Chadic raised the glow rod over her head, extending the light farther down the tunnel. Effigies continued to rise from the ground for another fifty meters, then disappeared. "Where *are* your people?" Chadic asked. "Can they help us?"

"No," Kairos said, before turning away.

———

They grew tired and agreed to spend the night in the caves, making camp beyond the effigies and the painted walls. Chadic took the only thermal blanket, leaving Quell to wrap herself in the fabric of their unused tent. She would be cold, but she'd be able to sleep. They ate a meal in silence until Kairos—who'd refused a ration bar and sat staring down the tunnel—said, "I have been here before."

Chadic laughed. The sound echoed in the dark. "Yeah, we figured that out."

Quell smiled, too. Kairos looked uncomfortable but eventually spoke again. "The Imperial outpost. I was there, when they first came to the planet."

Chadic crinkled the wrapper of her ration bar. She looked to Kairos with Quell and waited.

"It's difficult," Kairos said.

"It's all right," Quell said. "Take your time."

"You don't have the correct words," Kairos said, almost hissing. "You should know, but it is—*difficult.*"

She jabbed her fingers into the dirt and began tracing designs in the muck. The patterns meant nothing to Quell, though Kairos worked with the diligence of a woman transcribing a message she knew by heart.

"There are two worlds," Kairos said, not looking up. "There are the stars and there is this—the forest, the ocean, everything that is solid. Here, in this world, are the living, the people. *My* people. In the stars are all the things not solid and not of the world.

"I—among my people I was an emissary. My responsibility was to mediate between the solid world and the world of stars. I spoke for us to invisible beings of air. The Empire—it was not invisible, but it was from the world of stars. It called me shaman, but I do not know what that word means."

Chadic crinkled the wrapper again then tossed it aside. Quell watched Kairos and listened, certain the woman would stop speaking if interrupted—or vanish altogether like a dream.

"I went to the outpost. We knew of the Empire, but I did not understand. It was my responsibility to mediate, but the Empire did not want this. They took me—"

Kairos continued drawing in the soil but her rhythm changed, delicate tracings alternating with harsh cuts. Her mouth opened and closed reflexively, and she said nothing.

"I know," Quell said after a while. "They took you to a camp. Adan told me about it."

Kairos closed her mouth and looked to Quell as if pleading.

"They interrogated you there." Quell half closed her eyes, trying to remember. Adan had said Kairos had *changed* every time he saw her. "They experimented on you, because you were an unknown species. Is that right?"

Again, Kairos said nothing, and Quell interpreted the silence as agreement. Chadic was staring at Quell now, with a mixture of confusion and awe or disgust.

"You escaped together," Quell said. She focused on Kairos but she said it for Chadic, who deserved to know. "You and Adan and Ito. There was another man, but you lost him, and the three of you escaped."

One of Kairos's hands went from the dirt to her own face—not touching, but cupping the shape of her chin. "You told me they died," Kairos said. "How did they die?"

"They—" The memories hurt, and Quell had no desire to share the pain. Nor would doing so help Kairos. She told as much of the truth as she could bear. "We were in a shuttle that crashed. All of us were badly hurt, but Adan and Ito were in worse shape than me. They lingered for a while, we all tried to make it offworld, but—

"Ito went first. There was damage to its programming, and it experienced a cascade failure. It . . . tried very hard to save us," she said. She wouldn't speak about the droid's betrayal, the way its gentle personality had been twisted. "Adan talked about you a lot—he was worried for you—and he was *Adan* but he gave me what I needed to live and didn't ask anything in return.

"I stayed with him when he died. I was there for both of them."

"His body?" Kairos asked.

"The black hole. I'm sorry."

Kairos looked away. After a few minutes Chadic grumbled something and lay down and wrapped her blanket around her body. Quell stayed awake awhile longer, wondering what had happened between the droid and Adan and Kairos during the years after their escape—how much of Kairos's vendetta against the Empire had been her own and how much had been developed out of obligation toward the others.

It didn't matter, she supposed. Not really. And she was glad to be exhausted from the day so that she barely thought about Chadawa or about her team, or about the Emperor's Messenger or Soran Keize or the secrets she could do nothing with now, there on a nameless planet far from the war.

Quell heard the attack coming. She was breaking camp in the sunless morning when Kairos leapt up and turned down the tunnel they'd arrived from. There was a susurrus-like wind among leaves; then Quell noticed the undertone of bells, of metal sliding melodiously across metal, and the abomination came into sight.

It was like a storm of serpents, their winding bodies entangled as they slithered through air—or perhaps there was only a single, endless body, for Quell saw no head or tail. Its black scales glittered in the light of the glow rods, and when Kairos sprang into the mass the metallic ringing deepened as she grasped at writhing cords. A dull white seam ran down the thing's underbelly, and at a hundred points along the seam the thing's flesh parted, splitting wetly to reveal curved teeth.

As Kairos tore the thing with her hands, Quell squatted on the ground and searched for a weapon. All she could find was the glow rod, and she was ready to smash it against a rock and expose the energized circuitry when a tendril sprang at her from the cloud. Its end bloomed into a dozen wriggling worms, and at the center of the bloom was what might have been a cyst or an eye.

It would've reached her if red lightning hadn't flashed past her shoulder and into the outstretched tendril. A hundred mouths screamed together and the thing reared even as Kairos ripped one length of its body apart, then another. Its rustling ceased, and at once it fell to the ground in a heap.

Quell turned to see Chadic standing above her, blaster still pointed at the creature. The Theelin met Quell's gaze, and Quell was certain she saw worry in the woman's expression before Chadic muttered: "Don't know why I even bothered. Not like you're useful to us alive."

Quell shuffled to her feet. Kairos was stepping out of the dead mass as if nothing extraordinary had occurred.

"Was that one of the 'other things' we took the tunnels to avoid?" Quell asked.

"No," Kairos said. "This planet contains greater dangers."

"Well, I feel better," Chadic said. "Let's get moving and kill some Imps."

They emerged from the tunnels hours later, into the jungle under a sky now the blue-gray of Troithe's oceans. They could see the Imperial outpost protruding from a rock abutting the cliffs: a two-level prefab landing tower and command post, the sort Imperial engineers could've assembled in a matter of days. Small enough that Quell expected it would be staffed by no more than a dozen personnel and guards; she told Chadic as much as they hiked.

"You going to help us take it over?" Chadic asked.

"Are you going to give me a weapon?" Quell returned.

Chadic only snorted. Part of Quell felt injured, and she was surprised by her own reaction.

When they arrived at the tower's base, they saw no movement, no ship, and no lights. Fueling cables hung off the upper platform, their ends severed. Kairos scouted the perimeter and found no signs of life, so they proceeded closer. Still there were no alarms, nor any indication of activity.

One of the generators appeared to have failed violently, leaving scorch marks across the lower platform on which the barracks, command station, and supply centers sat. Chadic led them into the supply shack nearest the generator and found broken crates full of torn nutrient packages. "You figure one of those *things* we saw back there scared them off? Not smelling any bodies around."

Quell shrugged and looked to Kairos. "Before Endor, I'd have said no. Imperial discipline wouldn't allow it. Now? Anything's possible."

Kairos touched a finger to the metal wall and pulled it away as if shocked. "Maybe. This is not a safe place. Many would run."

"Lucky us, I guess," Chadic said. "Let's go through building by building. Search for any parts we can use on the U-wing. Or—" She looked pointedly at Quell. "—anything we can use to get a signal offworld. If we yell loud enough, maybe someone out there will give us a ride."

It was a reasonable plan, Quell thought, and she participated as much as Chadic allowed as the afternoon sun bled into the sky. They began together, searching through storage compartments and speeder racks and tossing anything with potential—anything that could be broken down into wiring, control chips, or circuitry—into a pile. When it became clear there was no power to the central transmitter, Chadic told the group to split up, and Quell took the barracks for herself and began dismantling one of the consoles. Chadic and Kairos could handle salvaging the heavier equipment, but repairing the navicomputer would take a discriminating eye.

The rote work was almost soothing, yet often a sound came from the jungle—a metallic chiming or a low hum—that made Quell tremble before she returned to work. Other times she glimpsed shadows on the cliffside that moved out of time with the sun. The darker the afternoon became, the more the outpost seemed haunted, and Quell found her thoughts drawn to the troubles awaiting her. Once she left—if she left—where would she go? What would she *do* with what Keize had given her? What had become of Shadow Wing and General Syndulla and Chadawa?

Kairos and Chadic appeared locked in their own private wars. Quell caught a glimpse of Chadic (when the Theelin clearly believed no one was watching) with head bent and hands clasped over her ears as she whispered something. Kairos barely worked, intent on tracking movements in the jungle that only she could see.

At night, they gathered in the command center rather than the barracks—both for security and, Quell suspected, because no one cared to sleep in the bunks of lost Imperial soldiers. They ate in silence on the floor, and when they were done Quell asked, "Should we post a sentry? Without power, we're pretty vulnerable."

"Probably," Chadic said. "Should have a good view from either platform. Wish the alarms were working, but we can take turns—"

Kairos had withdrawn to the corner of the command center, perching atop a console in the deepest shadows. She spoke in a hollow voice. "I cannot."

Chadic squinted into the dark corner. "Cannot what?"

"Leave here. Not at night." She made a small gesture, seemingly indicating the command center. "I cannot."

Chadic glanced to Quell. Quell shrugged. It was no use pressing Kairos. "I can take first watch," Quell said. "I won't ask for a weapon."

Chadic looked ready to agree before Kairos interrupted again. "No," Kairos said, her voice sharp and wavering.

"You want to just tell us what we're allowed to do?" Chadic asked.

Kairos sat on the machinery like a guardian on a temple lintel. "She cannot go," Kairos said. "If danger comes, she cannot—" She clasped her hands together, flexing them as if the motion would draw out more words.

"What?" Quell said. "What is it?"

Kairos looked at Chadic as she answered. "We abandoned the others to come. To find her. To judge her for her wickedness, the deaths of worlds—" With a swift turn of her head, Kairos leveled her gaze at Quell, then returned her attention to the Theelin. "She was given life by Adan and IT-O, and succeeds them by blood. They are gone, and I remain, and we are bound. She cannot—she must be kept close."

Quell felt the scars on her arms burn, as if Kairos's stare had inflamed her wounds. She shifted awkwardly on the cold metal floor and wanted to protest: *Adan and Ito didn't give me life. They died and I couldn't stop it, and whatever bond they had with you isn't mine to take.*

But Chadic stood with a grunt and a look of disgust. "Fine," she said. "I guess *I'm* taking watch."

This time, Kairos did not object.

CHAPTER 16

DENIAL OF UNACCEPTABLE TRUTHS

I

Nothing lurked in the night but shadows. Chass na Chadic paced the edge of the lower platform and later dozed against the wall of the barracks. She was aware of movement from the cliffs and the jungle but unable to spot a source. She heard chittering noises that might have been insects and low tones that could have been flutes; once, she smelled something like smoke and incense, but saw no light except starlight.

Your comrades sent you away, Maya, the voice of Let'ij told her, though the imagined sound was distant and tinny. *First Wyl and Nath, who wouldn't help you when you picked your mission. Now Kairos, who would rather see you devoured than Quell, the woman who betrayed you both. Quell, who also did nothing to keep you from facing the night alone, very possibly because you beat her half to death . . .*

It was all true, Chass knew, and she knew also that the Children of the Empty Sun would *never* send her away, would never argue and prioritize their personal concerns over their shared allegiance to the cult. They'd never send her to patrol alone at night or grow tired of her complaining or expel her for fighting. She'd nearly killed Let'ij once, and the woman was waiting to take her back.

She knew it all, but Chass couldn't fully remember what the cult leader sounded like anymore, so the words stopped being Let'ij's and started being her mother's, and then for a while General Syndulla's. If Chass had had her audio chips she would've played back one of the cult's lectures; as it was she had to bring the teachings to her mind through force of will, and that was more effort than she had in her.

The next morning Chass found Kairos and Quell safe and well rested in the command center. She'd gotten maybe two hours of sleep and figured she'd earned a nap after breakfast when the others got to work, but her attempt was made difficult by the sunlight seeping through the doorway and the noise of Quell and Kairos sliding heavy equipment across the platform. She wrapped the thermal blanket around her head until she could barely breathe and finally passed out.

When she woke, she was soaked in sweat and had a pounding head-ache but otherwise felt better. Her mind flitted among thoughts of Imperial satellites and the U-wing and whatever Wyl and Nath and Syndulla were up to (whether she'd feel guilty if they'd been killed; whether she'd feel guilty if Chadawa died), and she ate a ration bar and looked across the platform to Quell and Kairos. She couldn't identify what it was they'd disassembled—maybe a generator—but its parts were spread across thirty square meters, neatly arranged in some spots and a garbage heap in others.

Quell and Kairos worked opposite sides of their grid, dismantling smaller components and sorting wires and computer chips. Chass wandered out to Quell, who looked at her with a furrowed brow—concern, or maybe Chass was just standing in front of the sun.

"You holding up okay?" Quell asked.

"Sure," Chass said. "Why wouldn't I be?"

Quell started to answer, then crouched to return to her pile. Chass felt a swell of petty rage at being ignored. It felt justified: Quell had barely spoken to Chass since Chass had found her; never even *tried* to apologize for everything she'd done; treated Chass like a New Republic stooge, a stranger, instead of someone she'd personally betrayed.

"When are you going to tell me about your mission?" Chass asked, as stern as she knew how. If Quell wanted to play captive-and-captor, she could, too.

"It went all right," Quell answered without looking up from her work, "until the end."

"Funny. You're funny."

Quell shrugged. "There's nothing you can do about it now. Nothing either of us can do. Until we're off this planet, does it matter?"

"If you told me the truth, I might be able to answer," Chass snapped.

Quell turned around, still low to the ground, and looked up at Chass. "It doesn't," she said. "It doesn't matter here."

Chass scuffed one boot backward, ready to kick at a lineup of bulky metal screws, then thought better of it. "Hey!" she yelled toward Kairos. "Are we going to get that thing flying again?"

Quell shifted as if she wanted to answer. Kairos looked toward them, confused or distracted. "Yes," Kairos said. "I think so."

"Great," Chass said. Then quieter, only for Quell: "So maybe it'll matter soon."

Quell had the audacity to laugh, soft and hoarse. Chass spat on the metal platform and stalked away.

When she'd put some distance between herself and Quell, her mood improved marginally. She walked along the platform's edge, looking down over the steep rocky slope and into the jungle, creeping closer to the drop-off with every step until she was placing right foot in front of left, half her soles hanging in midair. This, too, seemed to brighten her mood—or if not *brighten,* at least sharpen her focus on the present. The Children of the Empty Sun felt as far in the past as Hound Squadron or the Cavern Angels; as all the comrades she'd seen die over the years.

She was placing her right heel when a motion at the edge of the jungle caught her attention. She looked to where trees met rocks and saw a distant shape wrapped in fabric, staring up at her without a face. Instantly she recalled the effigies in the caves.

Her heel slipped and her weight shifted onto air. For a moment falling seemed a certainty; then she was toppling backward onto the platform, instinctively throwing herself away from the drop and smashing her elbow into the metal as she crashed. She scrambled upright after a second and looked down but the figure, if it had been more than her imagination, was gone.

The afternoon was more difficult. Chass knew she should've seen it coming, but sometimes she was oblivious to the obvious.

It started with a nervous tremble in her hands as she dismantled computer consoles for Quell's collection. She stripped a few bolts and singed a bundle of wires with a laser cutter, but she explained the mistakes away as a side effect of hunger or the headache that had only gotten worse. She snapped at Quell a few times when the woman came to check on her, but Quell *deserved* that.

Later, though, her mind began to wander. Thoughts of the Children of the Empty Sun—of Let'ij's lectures, of the ecstasy of being embraced by the crowd at disquisition, of the taste of stewed fruit pits and flatbread—washed over her like floodwaters, smashed through the mental barricades she'd tentatively erected. She'd dwelled less and less upon the cult since leaving her B-wing, since finding Quell, but it returned now with a vengeance.

She was alone.

Detoxing was always harder alone.

She'd been through it before, seen it in spiceheads and nervejackers torn from their favored addictions. It wasn't the same with Let'ij and the cult but it was close enough. In her lectures she'd been given a way to soothe herself, to push away everything she loathed about existence, and now that soothing mechanism had been snatched from her.

Besides the cult, the only things her racked brain let her think about were the weird sounds of the jungle and the faceless gaze of the effigies. Those weren't really improvements.

Evening came, and Chass ate without appetite alongside Kairos and Quell. No one had to ask her to take watch, and she was glad for the breeze on her scalp and horns as she patrolled the platform under a dark sky cracked with rose. She touched the blaster at her hip often and rolled the heel of her hand across her forehead to try to massage away her worsening headache.

The distant fluting began again and Chass saw flickers in her peripheral vision, tiny flashes in the jungle and on the cliff, which she attributed first to the pain in her head. They disappeared whenever she looked their way. The wind stiffened and the platform groaned, the upper level swaying on its pylons. Whenever she looked above her to see if the entire structure was about to come crashing down, she caught another glimpse of movement.

She became convinced that the flashes, the movements, were coming nearer. The darkest hours of night came and she could no longer see the command center or the upper platform, but she saw *something* in the blackness. Alongside the fluting came a sound like viscous droplets pulling away from a gelatinous mass and dripping onto a wooden surface. Chass hated the sound and the sporadic timing of its assaults, and she grew to hate the planet and all that lived on it.

She saw one of the effigies as she turned at one corner of the lower platform. The figure stood on a ridge extending from the cliff, and it was looking toward her. She raised her blaster and fired. The night air was bathed in crimson as two particle bolts rippled and burst against the cliffside. Chass screamed at the figure but when her vision recovered from the flash it had disappeared.

The wind lashed her. The air was full of an odor that brought to mind Let'ij's attar-and-petrichor perfume. Chass cursed not just the planet and her foes but Kairos and Quell and then, one by one, every member of Riot Squadron. Shadow Wing deserved her spite, too, but they seemed beyond reach in a way the dead did not. She cursed Wyl and Nath, though, and wondered again what had become of them at Chadawa.

For a moment, with her arms folded across her chest and her body facing the wind in defiance, she felt very cold and wanted to cry.

"Chass?"

She wrinkled her nose and turned around. Quell stood a meter away, barely shivering despite the lashing wind and her short sleeves.

"Kairos release you for good behavior?" Chass asked.

"She's not watching."

Chass grunted and glanced over her shoulder, as if whatever lurked just outside her sight might have moved closer while she hadn't been looking.

"There's something I wanted to say," Quell said. "It's not important. But I was awake."

Chass returned her focus to Quell. "Yeah? What's that?"

"You said the other day you joined a cult? When everything that happened at Cerberon . . . happened."

"Yeah."

The wind sifted Quell's ragged hair so that she looked through the veil at Chass. The scars on her arms looked like red rain streaking in the wind. "I'm glad for you," Quell said. "I know you don't—you don't join up with just anyone. That's my sense, anyway. So I figure they're doing right by you somehow."

Chass waited for more. Quell shifted uncomfortably from one foot to the other.

"That's it?" Chass asked.

"That's it."

She expected Quell to turn and leave, but the woman only stood there, rubbing at her arms.

"What happened to your tattoo, anyway?" Chass asked.

Quell flinched, though Chass's tone had been matter-of-fact. "I erased it."

"Must've hurt."

"Yes."

"Before you went back?"

"Yes."

"They know you had it?"

"No."

Chass grunted. Quell's expression remained flat.

"Is it weird?" Chass asked. "Not being able to tell them?"

Quell's fingers traced their way to her left biceps and rubbed the spot where her squadron tattoo had been. "It's not great," she said.

"Sometimes—" Chass's lips twitched. She let the words pass through her, as if she weren't responsible for the sounds. "Sometimes it's easier to have people you trust. Even if you don't like them."

"It gets lonely," Quell said.

"It gets lonely."

"You want to walk?"

Quell tilted her head toward the western edge of the platform. It was out of the worst of the wind, though Chass figured Quell might've just been suggesting a patrol route. "Sure," she said, and they moved together in silence. They reached the platform edge and turned, heading toward the cliff, and the structures blocked the gale as they passed.

Words rose from Chass's chest again and passed through her lips unbidden. "I never planned to survive the war."

They slowed and halted as one. "I know," Quell said.

Chass nearly laughed, weary and bitter. Quell looked over to her, then past her, and gripped Chass's wrist with warm fingers and a somber expression.

"Look," Quell said.

Chass followed her gaze. There were lights in the jungle, each limning a figure with cloak rippling in the wind, face of thorns or bone staring toward the outpost. There were at least two dozen in all, and each figure held up a bowl of jade fire like a torch. Each figure, too, was motionless, as if they were statues that had weathered the jungle for decades.

Or as if they were waiting.

"We need to talk to Kairos," Quell said.

"You go," Chass said. "She doesn't talk to me like she does to you, and someone should keep watch."

Quell hadn't let go of her arm or looked away from the lights.

"She's bonded to me," Quell said. "She doesn't trust me. She won't admit it, but I think she needs us both."

Kairos wasn't in the command center. Quell grew visibly tense at this discovery but said nothing to show her worry. Back outside, they looked for any sign of Kairos's passage and Chass studied the lift shaft to the upper platform. Without power to the outpost, the lift itself was useless—but someone had opened the interior hatch to the emergency ladder.

"Maybe?" Chass called over the wind. Quell shrugged, and they climbed together.

They'd searched the upper platform when they'd first arrived at the outpost and found it empty except for the cut fuel lines. Chass emerged from the lift shaft now with few expectations yet saw Kairos immediately, poised at the platform's edge and facing the cliff. A broad, rocky ridge jutted out from the cliffside ten meters from the platform's drop-off—the closest the cliff came to the outpost anywhere.

"She's not going to jump over there?" Chass asked. "She *can't* jump that far."

Quell rattled out of the lift behind her and they marched toward Kairos. When Quell shouted her name over the wind, the woman turned toward them.

"You see what's going on?" Chass asked. She stopped with Quell ten paces away, as if coming any closer might push Kairos over the edge. "All those lights, and stuff?"

"Yes," Kairos said.

"They're your people, aren't they?" Chass asked.

Kairos didn't answer.

Quell repeated Chass's question, her voice low and calm. Chass resented the need, but Quell got the response Chass had been denied. "Yes," Kairos said. "They come because they see. They suspect the Empire has returned."

"They plan to drive us out?" Quell asked.

"Yes."

Chass glanced into the wind, but she couldn't see the jungle, couldn't tell if the lights had moved. "So *tell* them," she said. "Tell them we're not Imps."

"I—"

Chass interjected before the woman could finish. "And don't tell us *I cannot!*"

Kairos bowed her head. Somehow, barely moving the muscles beneath the chitinous plates of her face, she appeared chagrined. Chass almost felt bad for yelling.

"They mustn't know about me," Kairos said, voice almost too soft to be heard above the wind. "I can't. I can't permit it."

"Tell us why," Quell said.

She stepped forward and Kairos stepped back, one foot hovering over the edge of the platform. Chass swore. Quell froze, then retreated with exquisite care. Kairos moved in sync with Quell, returning her foot to the metal as if mirroring the human. Kairos was trembling now, her head raised again as she looked between her two companions.

"My people," Kairos said. "My people. We—they—are *pure*. Blood and spirit untouched by what is not *us*. This is how we have been, always, and how we remain who we are."

"That's the reason for the suits," Quell said. "Because the Empire isn't pure."

Chass tried to remember Kairos's words from the tunnels: *Shells. Contaminated and discarded.*

"Yes," Kairos said. "Because you are not pure. *I* am not—they do not know."

Chass heard her humiliation, saw the trembling magnify into bodily shudders that looked likely to throw her over the platform. But Kairos didn't lower her head again, nor did her voice fall as she continued. "The camp. The experiments they performed. The Empire *hurt* me. Adan saved me, but his blood—Ito gave his blood to me, but it was not *my* blood. What was inside me, what I saw, what I knew made me not of my people.

"I wore the suit to protect. To insulate myself from the galaxy. To stop my pollution, so body and spirit could heal. So I could purge what was wrong and restore myself."

"Then Cerberon happened," Quell said.

"Yes," Kairos replied.

Chass tried to understand. She didn't, really, but she knew what it was like to wear a cloak of shame.

II

She had not been named Kairos when she'd been young, nor when she had become the emissary of her people (for she had taken a second name then, as was the custom). She had not been named Kairos in the camp, when they had made her less than she was—when they'd ripped away her skin to see what was underneath, when she'd seen terrors to scar her soul; when those same terrors had attached themselves to every memory she possessed, so that she could not remember her people, her jungle, the beauty of her niece, without the taint of nightmares.

She'd named herself Kairos only after being given life by Adan, who had acted with purity of intent but given her no choice in the matter. Kairos was the name of the creature who cocooned herself and sought to heal. Kairos was the name of the creature bound by blood and spirit and horror to Adan and IT-O, and who waged war against Emperor and Empire while her soul mended; who fought the shadow that Adan saw, the shadow consuming worlds, and did so in anger and righteous fury.

Then had come Cerberon.

Under the black sun Kairos had watched innocents be sacrificed to summon the shadow, to trap and destroy it forever, and she had died to ensure the success of Adan and Syndulla and Yrica Quell, the defector. She had accepted her fate but she had not been permitted to pass on.

Again, Adan had given her no choice. Out of love, he had called the surgeons of the New Republic to strip away her suit, her cocoon, her last protection against the world that was not her world. Her body had already mended from the camp but her spirit had not, and both were racked again as instruments cut her; as foreign substances were pumped beneath her skin; as voices reached her unfiltered by the mask; as alien eyes *saw* her and in seeing *touched* her essence.

Adan had done this out of love, and IT-O, too, but their love was not the love of her people. She forgave them, but forgiveness did nothing to change what had occurred.

She had woken no longer truly Kairos, no longer *anything,* remade in body and incomplete in essence, whole in flesh but *wrong* in spirit. She had considered reweaving her cocoon but she had been removed from it too long. Body and spirit were no longer aligned. Her metamorphosis had been aborted, and her incomplete self would need to pursue its journey with the soul-crippled form it possessed.

She might have accepted this, too. She understood necessity.

She had never expected to return home.

She could *not* accept the disgrace of her people knowing what had become of her.

She explained it as well as she could to the defector-who-was-the-last-of-Adan-and-IT-O, and to Chass na Chadic who burned. The words were clumsy and blunt and the alien tongue she spoke conveyed only a reflection of truth.

III

"That's messed up," Chass said. Empathy and anger—anger at Kairos's people for their superstitions about purity, anger at Kairos for believing it all, anger at Adan for *utterly ignoring* Kairos's wishes and putting her in that position—roiled in her. "It's messed up."

"You could talk to them," Quell said. "You don't know what they'll say. You don't know they'll refuse to accept you as you are."

"I know my people," Kairos whispered.

Chass put her weight on one heel, pivoted about, and walked toward the opposite end of the platform. From there she could see the lights in the jungle. If they'd moved closer, it wasn't by much. "You have any idea what it's like? Being ashamed to go back to people you—people you don't *fit* with anymore?" She glanced behind her at Quell.

After a while, Quell nodded.

"Let her be," Chass said. "She can make her own choices."

Quell retreated from the platform's edge as well and stopped midway between Kairos and Chass. "All right. That leaves us with a problem, though. Kairos, I assume they'll kill us if they can?"

Kairos took a single step away from the cliff. "Yes."

Chass grunted. "Guess shooting at them isn't anyone's first choice?"

"We need to convince them we're gone, and gone for good," Quell said. "We need to do it without exposing ourselves."

"Take cover and run," Chass said.

Quell shrugged.

"So we put on a light show." Chass smiled darkly. "We got the equipment for it?"

"I think so," Quell said. "Kairos? You understand?"

There was a long pause. The wind rose, and Kairos stood unmoved in the gale, fixing her eyes on Quell and then Chass. Chass felt the woman's doubt and helplessness and finally gratitude, as if she'd learned to read Kairos's expressions at last.

"I understand," Kairos said.

They worked through the night as the lights crept closer. Chass and Kairos wired the outpost as Quell gathered equipment for the U-wing's repairs, and though they moved rapidly, took no breaks, and spoke little, there was a camaraderie to the chore. They were united by their goals. They were united by their *motives*.

There was nothing complicated about it. They were doing it for Kairos.

Some hours before dawn they left the outpost and crept into the shadows around the foundation pylons. From their shelter among the rocks Chass squeezed a button on her comlink—twice, then three times, growing increasingly worried something had gone wrong—then grinned in satisfaction as the upper platform detonated in orange flame. Thunder shook the jungle, and the smell of smoke was instantly suffocating. Metallic shrieks followed as blackened panels tore apart and fell onto the lower platform, battering the structures there.

Kairos indicated for them to leave their shelter. "They will run," she said, "until they are sure the danger is gone."

They raced out together, and as they dashed between trees and away from their foes Chass triggered her comlink again and the lower platform exploded, spewing fire and metal onto the rocks. Chass laughed loudly, though she knew she shouldn't. She laughed and laughed and ran, and she glimpsed Quell beside her, burdened beneath a sack of equipment, half smiling and half grimacing.

No one told her to shut up, and Kairos's people didn't catch them.

They ran until dawn, when they sat in the shade of a spindly tree and watched the black smoke on the horizon. "You know," Chass said, "there's always the chance blowing the place up could bring *actual* Imps to investigate. We might've made things worse."

"I don't think so," Quell said.

"You got inside information?" Chass asked.

Seeing Quell flinch was less satisfying than she'd hoped.

"That outpost's been abandoned for months," Quell said. "The old expeditionary forces would've sent in a stormtrooper unit if a garrison had been routed by locals. Since Endor, though—no one's *here* anymore. No one's watching the satellite feed." She picked at a threadlike root half buried in the soil, then wiped her hand on her hip and looked to Kairos. "For what it's worth, I'm pretty sure your homeworld's free. The Empire's not coming back."

Kairos squatted on her knees, looking not north toward the outpost but to the east. Toward something they'd never approached during their travels on the planet.

"I am happy," Kairos said, astonished and bittersweet.

By noon they'd made it back to the U-wing, and Chass didn't argue when Quell took charge of repairs. She seemed to know what she was doing, and while Chass didn't *trust* her she couldn't believe Quell would sabotage the ship. *Maybe* Quell would leave them behind, now that she knew they could survive on the planet.

That thought lingered as Quell operated on the computer core and Chass cleared mud from the loading door mechanisms and rebuilt two thrusters. In the afternoon, after she'd resecured one of the nacelles, she sauntered into the cockpit where Quell was crouched underneath the console and dropped into the copilot's seat.

"We're heading back soon," Chass said.

Quell's muffled voice replied: "If I can figure out how to fix everything I broke opening this up? Yes."

"So it's going to matter soon. Your mission."

Quell stopped moving but she didn't emerge. "Yes. I guess it will."

"You going to tell me?"

"I don't think so. Not yet."

For a moment, Chass considered swinging her boot into Quell's ribs. She imagined Quell's chest compressing, the woman writhing on the ground. She felt no pleasure at all, nor relief.

"Would you tell me if I hadn't beaten the crud out of you on Netalych?" Chass asked.

Quell laughed, brief and surprised. "No. Probably not. Might've felt worse about refusing, though."

"That's fair." Chass flicked mud from her pants against the console. "You still got off light. Lucky I was the one who found you."

"Yeah," Quell said. "Guess I am."

Chass left Quell and climbed atop the U-wing and lounged under the alien sky. Thoughts of Quell turned to thoughts of the Children of the Empty Sun, and though Let'ij and her cult still seemed far away Chass wondered if she would feel the same once the U-wing returned to the *Deliverance*—once Chass had returned to the real world, and the real war, where Quell would be in jail and Chass would be disciplined for abandoning her squadron. Her life in which three isolated comrades could grow comfortable on a strange planet would soon seem a dream.

That particular thought—the notion of forgetting everything that had happened over the past days—pained her most of all. She'd almost wept during the night, and now she blinked away tears, keeping her head high so no one would see. She stared at the horizon, not sure what she was on the verge of losing but terrified of it just the same.

See you soon, she told Let'ij, who wasn't speaking to her today. The comforts of the cult held little appeal, but the war was ending and she would readjust with lectures and conversations and chanting and time. It was still the only future she had—still better than muddling along like she had before the Rebellion. Like she always did in her nightmares.

Deep within her mind, notions like sediment at the bottom of an ocean drifted up from where they'd been lost months before. They whispered in a voice not Let'ij's: *Don't forget . . . until the last battle is over, there's always your backup plan.*

IV

Just before sunset, Yrica Quell emerged from the console weary from the day's work, satisfied by what she'd accomplished, and mourning the betrayals still to come. She wiped the grease from her hands on the sides of her pants and stretched her stiff limbs before leaving the cockpit. In the main cabin she stopped short.

Chadic and Kairos stood looking into one of the emergency compartments in the rear bulkhead. Chadic turned around when Quell emerged and asked, "Well?"

Her voice was matter-of-fact but her eyes looked tired. Quell remembered she hadn't slept the past night.

"We're close," Quell said. "I think it's working, but I need to reassemble and test it before we run a final systems check."

"You want me to take over? I can handle that."

"Thanks." Quell shook her head and smiled faintly. "I had to improvise some replacement parts—should probably handle it myself."

Chadic shrugged. "Your call," she said, and looked back to the bulkhead.

Quell watched Chadic, observing the shift of the woman's muscles beneath her shirt and the spacing of her feet on the deck. Even at rest, even from behind, she looked powerful.

Careful with those thoughts. She doesn't hate you. She hasn't forgiven you. Let that be enough.

"What are you looking at?" Quell asked.

Chadic stepped aside. Kairos did not. Quell squeezed between them, peering into the compartment, and found a face staring out at her: a clamped and riveted thing, a metal mask with no features except a dark visor.

Once it had been Kairos's face.

"You kept it here?" Quell asked, glancing to Kairos.

"Where else?" Kairos replied.

"Can't argue with that," Chadic said. "Anyway, we were waiting for you."

Quell furrowed her brow. "To do what?"

Chadic ignored Quell and looked past her to Kairos. "You want to keep it, you want to shove it into hyperspace, that's fine with me. But I figured—"

"Yes," Kairos said, and delicately lifted the mask with gloved hands. She held it away from her body, touching it with her fingertips as if it radiated heat.

Chadic led the way outside. Quell thought she understood and followed after Kairos.

The hike took them into the night, and they heard the chittering and the flutes and a popping sound like sparks fleeing a burning log. Kairos guided them by the same path they'd taken before and found the entrance to the tunnel with ease, and they paused there to collect all they needed. Under Kairos's supervision, Chadic cut down a stiff, tall plant stalk while Quell tore down an armful of vines.

They descended the tunnel stairs single file, glow rods ready, and although Quell listened for the metallic sounds of the serpent-creatures, she found familiarity eased her fear. She examined the cave walls with greater curiosity than before and thought of Colonel Keize and his interest in forgotten cultures—an interest he'd never admitted to her aloud, but which she'd inferred from one casual reference or another to archaeological digs and lost worlds over the years. He would've found the tunnels fascinating; he would've asked Kairos questions that had never occurred to Quell. (In a different life, at least, she was sure he would have.)

They walked among the painted whorls and arrived in the place of the effigies. Kairos stopped beyond the last of the figures, and Chadic began digging with the stalk and her hands. Over the course of an hour, she planted her makeshift stake. Kairos then removed her cloak and unwound strips of cloth from her body until she stood nude; and they tied her garments together and stuffed them with dirt and bound them to the stake.

They set the mask in place together, at Kairos's urging, resting it atop the bundle. When Quell stepped away she was surprised to look at the effigy and feel nothing—not fear or awe, but just the certainty that she looked at a discarded heap of metal and cloth.

Maybe, she thought, that was the intent.

"I am no longer changing," Kairos said. "I do not know what I am."

Neither Quell nor Chadic spoke. Quell doubted Kairos was talking to either of them.

The nude woman said something else in a language Quell didn't understand, then turned down the tunnel the way they had come. "I leave this behind," she said, and they went.

Quell hadn't lied about the navicomputer. It had been broken and she'd applied most of the fixes required. But she'd deceived her friends by intentionally leaving work undone; by waiting for Chadic to fall asleep stretched across the U-wing's crew seats while Kairos took watch outside; by claiming to be finalizing repairs when in fact she was accessing the database and the comm system for reasons of her own.

She hadn't *needed* an Imperial computer core but it helped. She cross-referenced the data she'd memorized from the Messenger with what was now held in the U-wing and the satellite system above the planet. She referenced coordinates and felt dread build in her chest (beyond the dread of being caught—of losing Chadic again, of being murdered by Kairos).

She hadn't entirely known what to expect, only guessing at a range of awful possibilities. Still, IT-O had once told her that the Emperor was a petty and spiteful man. The most likely answer was always the answer that would cause the most pain.

She tilted her head against the pilot's chair, peering through the doorway at Chadic. The Theelin's feet and right hand dangled off the row of seats, and her chest rose and fell as she snored. She seemed in no danger of waking.

She was beautiful. She was also vindictive and strident and confused. So was Kairos. So were Fra Raida and Rikton and even Kandende, and though she couldn't forgive Shadow Wing any more than she could forgive herself, she could acknowledge that her old comrades weren't monsters, had never been monsters.

Or maybe they all were.

Quell was no better than any of the pilots of Shadow Wing. She'd simply been lucky enough to find her way out. And after the past few days, Quell had seen proof enough that Chadic and Kairos weren't any saner than her.

Soran Keize was one of the few people she'd ever known who lived by the code he proclaimed; who stared into the universe and knew with certainty the path he needed to take, and whose missteps weren't failures of nerve or personal ethics but purely tactical. She admired him, loved him for that more than he would ever realize.

She wasn't sure if he was *right*. She needed his help to find out.

Quell turned back to the console, disabled all recording and logging functions, and activated the satellite's long-range communications array.

V

Grand Moff Randd was half a man today, the left side of his body distorted and inchoate while the right glowed fixedly above the holoprojector. There was symbolism there, Soran Keize thought, though he doubted the moff would share his perspective as he sat in his cabin.

"—will be disappointed about Chadawa, but I can't say I care," Randd said. "The traitors have been eliminated—whether by your hand or the New Republic's, it doesn't matter in the end."

"I appreciate that, sir," Soran answered.

"More to the point, we need you here. Consider the 204th recalled to Jakku."

Soran thought Randd would expect surprise at the order and did his best to oblige, furrowing his brow. "Is Operation Cinder complete? Are there no more enemies who—"

"Consider Cinder on hold. The rebels will confirm our fleet's location within days if they haven't already, and a decisive moment is at hand. We need every available ship to crush the enemy armada when it comes."

This turn of events had been inevitable—Soran had been awaiting it since he'd first learned of the Jakku rendezvous, known with absolute confidence that the New Republic would locate it before the Empire could establish a defensible, multisystem core; known, too, that the New Republic would take an aggressive stance, direct its battleships and frigates and fighters to obliterate the Imperial remnant; and known that the odds of Imperial victory were slim.

Though he was getting ahead of himself.

"I'll send the order to the helm presently. You believe a head-on confrontation is our best choice?"

"I do," Randd said. "Jakku has sharpened us. Charging forward, the enemy will drive its heart onto our blade."

The grand moff did not owe a colonel—even a favored one—justification for his strategic choices. Nonetheless, Soran would have preferred a less poetic and more frank assessment. "May I ask if we know the strength of the enemy force? Are we expecting a siege, or—"

"I expect," Randd answered, with a trace of impatience, "the full might of the New Republic to be leveled at us. Like at Endor, the victor will be clear in a matter of hours and shall, unopposed, begin an offensive to claim the galaxy." He looked to one side, reviewing a screen Soran could not see. "The 204th will take delta position by the Super Star Destroyer *Ravager* and coordinate with our secondary battle group on close-atmosphere defense . . ."

Tactical data streamed by on Soran's own screen. He read enough to confirm his suspicions. "Respectfully, Grand Moff, your information about the 204th may be outdated." He was out of line but he kept his tone firm and confident. "The *Yadeez* is not the *Pursuer,* and lacks both the crew and capabilities of a Star Destroyer. Our escorts, fighters, and pilots have developed certain . . . idiosyncrasies that must be acknowledged if we are to take part in a coordinated defense."

Randd grunted and looked to his screen again. " 'Idiosyncrasies,' eh? Very well. I'll move another Destroyer by the *Ravager,* but I expect you at Jakku before the battle. I'm sure we can find *something* for your unit."

"Understood," Soran said, and the hologram flashed away.

He allowed himself the luxury of fantasizing. He considered ordering his unit to the far side of the galaxy from Jakku and concocting a mission along the way—something about securing territory, perhaps, or destroying a New Republic laboratory developing Death Star technology. But although he could spare his people the battle they would never forgive themselves once they realized the truth. They would live as cowards and deserters, or as martyrs, and either way it would destroy them.

No, he thought. If Jakku was to host the war's last battle, his people would need to be there. Perhaps—the odds were slim, albeit not insurmountable—they might even turn the tide. A partial victory might extend the fighting for years, or allow countless thousands of ships and soldiers to escape capture.

Total defeat was more likely. No matter the outcome, he had to act.

He focused on his console and retrieved once again the data Quell's team had brought from Netalych. They'd declared Quell a traitor and he'd agreed with the appellation, but she had beamed the secrets of the Messenger to her ship, and Brebtin and Mirro had brought those to him. Kandende, Rikton, and Raida were dead or lost, and Soran would mourn them all in due time—yet the mission had been a success.

He rechecked coordinates and viewed tactical data obtained from the fleet. Nothing revealed itself that he hadn't already seen; no options but the one he had already chosen.

He was toying with plans, envisioning battles and outcomes, when a notification appeared on his console. The *Yadeez* had received a coded signal designated for Soran; the transmission was weak, bounced across half the galaxy through multiple relays. Too degraded for holograms or even audio but arriving in real time.

Only someone with an intimate knowledge of the *Yadeez* could have worked such a miracle. Soran acknowledged receipt and waited for a message to display.

~ This is Yrica Quell.

Not "Lieutenant Quell," he thought, with neither surprise nor disappointment. He keyed a response:

~ I am here. The data has been received.

There was no reply after a short while, but the channel remained open. He wrote:

~ Assuming you are in New Republic custody or service?

The reply came almost immediately.

~ Yes.

He almost laughed at the simplicity of the answer. He heard her voice in his mind, solid and unflappable yet without confidence or certainty.

He had questions and the transmission was likely to fail sooner rather than later. He condensed as much as he could.

~ Assuming you served under General Syndulla?

~ Yes.

~ Returning to New Republic service now?

~ Uncertain.

I am sorry, he thought. *Perhaps we both should've stayed where we were.*

He had sent her to the New Republic when he'd walked away from Shadow Wing. He'd done so believing she would find peace, that she *deserved* peace, and that defection would provide her something he'd struggled to give the rest of his unit.

If she'd ended up working against her former colleagues, he had only himself to blame. And whatever had happened to her—whatever had driven her out and back to Shadow Wing—had not only been artifice.

Maybe she'd betrayed the Empire. But she'd given him the Messenger.

She wrote:

~ What are your intentions?

Vague, but he understood her meaning. He had to assume they were being monitored.

~ Reason to believe that war is ending soon. Action must be taken immediately.

~ What action?

~ I will serve my people how I am able.

There was another long delay before her reply came.

~ What action?

~ The New Republic cannot have access to the Resource. Too many lives are at stake.

~ What action?

~ Only one action possible.

He knew exactly what she was thinking. The next delay did not surprise him.

~ Possible to avoid collateral damage?

He'd asked himself the same questions. He had no desire to pay the price his actions would demand.

~ No local assistance available. Official hierarchy will not be in favor. The Resource is valuable means of control.

~ People will die.

~ Yes. What about those who live?

He remembered speaking to her once aboard the *Pursuer*, after the gruesome bombing of Mennar-Daye. He'd found her reading a data-pad in the mess hall and sat with her, asking about her studies until she'd begun to open up. He'd barely known her then, and she'd done her best to echo the official anti-Rebellion line even as she'd indicated her doubts.

"There will always be those who die in war who don't deserve it," he'd said at last. "We can acknowledge that tragedy—we must, if we want to remain human. But our first obligation is always to our comrades."

She hadn't asked why. No one ever did, though most wondered.

He'd replied to the unspoken question with an answer he'd begun developing in his youth before his rational mind had found the words: one he'd grappled with in the fires of Outer Mebarius as a furious adolescent, and seized at last in his first years in the starfighter corps after the Second Battle of Epiphany and the destruction of the *Destrier*. He'd lived the answer since and taught it to dozens of cadets; it guided him still.

"If we can't help, if we *refuse* to help those closest to us in body and spirit, how can we begin to help others? What's within your power is the fate of your fellow troops. For most, that's responsibility enough," he'd told Quell.

They'd spoken more, of war and of monsters. She'd been so very young then.

She still hadn't answered his last message. He wrote:

~ What are your intentions?

The words stared at him from his screen before, some minutes later, the transmission was severed.

If she'd stood with him on the *Yadeez* he would have spoken to her, reasoned with her, heard her out and guided her as best he could. Yrica Quell did not share his soul but she was a soldier and he recognized her suffering, wished dearly to ease it no matter if she'd turned against the Empire.

But he couldn't help her now. She was gone, and Shadow Wing remained in his care. Shadow Wing, and all the soldiers of the Empire (because their lives were all at stake, and no one else seemed to see what he saw) remained his responsibility.

He put her out of his mind and began to plan for the end.

VI

More than twenty ships orbited Chadawa, inside the planet's rings and sheltered from the particle tides. Along with the *Deliverance* were troop transports and medical frigates, gunships and vehicle carriers: everything required to stage an invasion or, if necessary, evacuate a world.

So far, neither invasion nor evacuation had begun. Violence had broken out on several continents, but the chaos was contained and the actors unclear. Hera hoped to receive word that the Imperial government had surrendered or collapsed and that the radiation spilled in Operation Cinder was limited to unoccupied regions; if that message didn't come, there would be difficult days ahead. Not for *her,* necessarily—she'd be turning local operations over to Fleet Commander Hellip as soon as he was up to speed—but the thought of abandoning a terrified world to another officer didn't sit well.

It was, however, her job. At least she hadn't needed to fire a shot since Shadow Wing's escape and the destruction of Colonel Madrighast's Star Destroyer.

She was on the bridge, ordering the deployment of a repair ship to one of the rings, when Ensign Dhina announced the arrival of two new ships: a U-wing and B-wing, emerging on the same vector. Hera spent half a second trying to remember whether she'd summoned those particular reinforcements, then straightened with a start. "Make space in the hangar and clear them to land," she snapped. "And alert Captain Tensent."

Chass and Kairos were alive.

She was on a turbolift moments later, then striding through the Star

Destroyer to meet them. Wyl Lark was still in the medbay, his condition stabilized and improving rapidly; she decided it was better not to
disturb him until she'd seen Alphabet's lost members for herself. Nath,
on the other hand, had more than earned the right to be there—his
heroics against the Raiders had kept Chadawa safe.

The ground crews crowded around the hangar personnel entrance,
making room as the U-wing slipped past the magnetic field and sent
hot wind across the gargantuan chamber. Hera stood by Sergeant Ragnell and smiled politely at one of the new engineers who caught her
eye—an aristocratic woman with a shock of orange hair and a medical
vocabulator. The engineer abruptly shifted her gaze away from Hera to
the alighting ship.

The B-wing came next, and as it entered the hangar Hera saw that
its primary airfoil appeared partly dismantled—not ravaged by energy
blasts, but disassembled panel by panel as if by scrappers. "Well," Ragnell muttered, infusing a galaxy of disapproval into the word.

Nath's voice rose behind Hera. "I miss anything?"

"They just landed," Hera said. "They have to be all right."

"Otherwise you can't kill them yourself?" Nath asked.

"Exactly."

The B-wing's ground crew coalesced around the vessel as its canopy
slid open and Chass na Chadic emerged. She waved the team away,
hoisted herself over the rim, and hit the deck with a grunt. She was out
of her flight suit, wearing only an undershirt and shorts, and as she
passed the engineers she smiled soberly at one and ignored two others.
She looked *present* but not *angry*, which was a change from the usual—
hopefully one for the better, Hera thought, though the Theelin was
always hard to predict.

One of the U-wing's loading doors opened next. Kairos stepped out,
and it became clear what had happened to Chass's flight suit—instead
of her ordinary wrappings and cloak, Kairos's body was snugly en-
cased in ill-fitting pilot's attire.

"Woman's full of surprises—" Nath began, then fell silent as Yrica
Quell followed Kairos out of the U-wing.

Quell was dressed only in a short-sleeved shirt and pants. Her upper arms were covered in scars and her squadron tattoo was gone. Her nose appeared faintly crooked; fading bruises covered her face. She looked, all in all, like a woman who'd come a very long way through trying circumstances.

Yet her expression was calm. Kairos murmured something to Quell, then drew away; Chass gave them both a comfortable berth. Neither Kairos nor Chass held a weapon. Hera was moving toward Quell without thinking; Nath trailed her, and the ground crews parted to give them access.

The last time Hera had seen Quell, they'd been sitting on the hull of the *Lodestar* on Troithe. Hera had been preparing to leave Cerberon and had said something like: *You don't need me for this, Yrica.*

That had all been before she'd learned that Quell had killed Nacronis and lied to them all. Before Quell had joined the second Operation Cinder.

"General," Quell said as they approached.

"Quell," Hera replied. Nath and Chass and Kairos were all watching her.

Figure the rest of it out later, she told herself. *It's all right to say it.*

"Welcome home," Hera said.

PART THREE

STAGES OF A TRIAL BY ORDEAL

CHAPTER 17

AUGURY AND SIGNS

I

The medical droid was on its third pass over her body, having already disinfected and bandaged the worst of her wounds and applied bacta spray to the oldest and most pungent. It had promised to further examine and, if necessary, realign her broken nose later; for now it jabbed her apparently at random and ran its scanners over every centimeter of battered skin. Maybe, Quell thought, it was checking for tracking devices or other Imperial implants. She couldn't really blame it.

The endless examination gave her time to think. Often she considered the words Kairos had whispered to her in the hangar: *You are my sister, but your crimes are not forgotten.* It was an almost reassuring statement—it told Quell where she stood with the woman. Nothing else about her situation felt as solid or certain.

She was aboard a Star Destroyer for the first time since she'd left the *Pursuer*—an experience that filled her brain with a nagging sense of *wrongness,* as if she were with neither the New Republic nor Shadow Wing but in a dream mingling them both. She hadn't recognized most of the ground crew members, though she was certain Sergeant Ragnell had seen the damaged flesh where her tattoo had been; where Ragnell had spent hours layering ink under Quell's skin, never asking why or requesting payment. Ragnell hadn't said anything as Quell had been led out. Hail Squadron, according to what she'd overheard on the way to the medbay, had been decimated and Nath Tensent was a hero—likely to be awarded a *second* medal, reinforcing the impression everything Quell encountered was a dream.

Wyl Lark had been hurt. She'd caught a snippet of conversation between Chadic and Syndulla to that effect, but it was all she knew.

The droid had curtained off a small section of the medbay for privacy. Quell could hear voices outside as someone spoke to the guards. "Pardon me," the droid said, and finished another pass over her right leg. "You may dress now."

It exited through the curtains. Quell's garments—encrusted with dirt, sweat, and blood—sat folded on the floor. With a sigh, she dragged a medical gown off a shelf and pulled it on. It felt clean.

She was sitting on the bed when General Syndulla stepped inside. "Lieutenant," the general said. "Is now a good time?"

"I'm fine," Quell said, which hadn't been the question. She slipped her feet onto the floor and stood straight-backed, chin up. "General. Yrica Quell, Lieutenant, formerly of the 204th Imperial Fighter Wing, formerly of the New Republic Intelligence working group on the 204th Imperial Fighter Wing. I am surrendering myself for disciplinary action and—"

And what? she thought. *Trial in a civilian court? Summary execution for treason and genocide?*

"—and whatever further consequences are deemed appropriate."

Syndulla watched her, expression hard. Then she laughed, brief and low. "That's generous of you, Lieutenant, considering you've already been captured. But I appreciate you not making trouble for the medics."

"Yes, General."

"Are you aware that there's a good chance you're facing life imprisonment?"

"Yes, General."

"Are you aware that New Republic Intelligence is eager to see justice done, too?"

"No, General. I'm not surprised, though, General."

"Are you aware that I don't personally take betrayal very well?"

Quell saw no mirth or compassion in Syndulla's eyes. "Yes, General," she said. The woman frowned and Quell added, softer, "It was not my intention to betray you, General."

Syndulla let out a sigh like she was deflating. She turned, scanning the vicinity as if looking for somewhere to sit and finally settling on the foot of the bed. She dropped onto the thin mattress and nodded to Quell. Quell eased onto the bed beside Syndulla with arthritic reluctance.

"Yrica," the general said. "Tell me what happened."

Her body reacted faster than her mind. She felt nauseated and shaky and hot, like she'd been so badly sunburned that the pain encouraged tears. She'd known what to expect, known she would be debriefed, but all she wanted was to lie down on the cool metal of the deck.

"Adan's files on me," Quell said. She sounded hoarse and foolish, and endeavored to shore up her voice. "Everything he said happened at Nacronis, happened. But there were gaps in his information; things I lied about even after he learned about Cinder."

"Okay," Syndulla said. She'd transformed from general to something more intimate, and her tone was gentle and patient. "And what really happened at Nacronis—it has something to do with why you went back to Shadow Wing?"

Quell nodded. "Soran Keize. You need to know about Soran Keize to understand."

She told her story then—her true story, from the murder of Nacronis and Keize's decision to send her away to Adan's discovery of the truth and her escape from the *Lodestar* over Troithe. She spoke little of what had happened on the planetoid, describing it in only the plainest terms: Adan and IT-O had been injured; they discovered a facility of unknown origin; Quell was able to escape. But she left out nothing relevant, nothing that might incriminate her.

"Upon leaving the planetoid and becoming aware of the 204th's lingering presence in the Cerberon system—and understanding my return to service in the New Republic wasn't likely to be permitted—I decided my best course of action was to infiltrate the enemy unit and neutralize it from the inside."

Syndulla watched her, as she'd watched Quell since Quell had begun. "You were the one sending us signals," she said.

"Yes."

"What was it like?" she asked. "What were you thinking?"

"As I said, it was my intention to eliminate the 204th. The same as always."

Syndulla looked ready to argue, but she only shook her head. "Go on."

Quell told her about the infiltration. This part was more difficult to report—it brought to mind interviews with Adan, where she'd been obliged to name every Imperial pilot and crew member she'd ever met, detail every mission she'd undertaken. But Syndulla was not Caern Adan and she asked very few questions, only encouraging Quell to fill in details when the story lost cohesion. Quell described the second Operation Cinder and how she'd managed to signal the New Republic, and she justified as well as she could her choice to fly against Alphabet and announce her presence. "I was trying to avert unnecessary losses. I thought I could make a better opportunity later on."

"It must've been a terrible decision for you to make," Syndulla said.

Quell thought back to her sessions with IT-O, where the droid would find a thousand different ways to bait her into expressing her feelings.

"It seemed like the optimal choice at the time. I won't claim that I was operating at my best, but I stand by it."

The longer she spoke, the easier it was to suppress the emotion and tell the truth. She explained Keize's obsession with the Emperor's Messenger, and the discussions they'd had over it. She summarized the mission to Netalych and her retrieval of the machine's data and admitted to sending it on to Keize even after the rest of her team had turned on her. She hurried through her capture by Chadic and Kairos and what had happened on Kairos's world. "Our actions on the ground aren't relevant to my status, and I feel bound to respect my comrades' privacy. Chadic and Kairos can confirm the broad strokes."

"I'm not worried about what happened between the three of you," Syndulla said. "But you're leaving something out."

"Yes, General," Quell said.

"What data did you salvage from the Emperor's droid? What did you see that made you send it to Keize?"

"I can't tell you that."

"Yrica, I'm—" Syndulla paused. "I'm very grateful for your honesty. For what it's worth, I think I believe you—though that doesn't necessarily mitigate all you've done. But that's a hell of a missing piece. You're holding back about the *Emperor's Messenger*?"

"I understand your position," Quell said. "I can't tell you what I found."

Syndulla straightened but remained seated. "Consider it an order, Lieutenant. You want to do this formally, we'll do it formally. Tell me what you found."

Quell suppressed a flinch and shook her head. "I can't."

Syndulla winced and her body relaxed again. Adan would've made her suffer his bluster and threats, Quell knew; Syndulla seemed to understand her mind wouldn't change. "You want to tell me why, at least?"

"Because," Quell said, and she smiled faintly at the black humor of it all. "I'm not sure it's the right thing to do."

To her surprise, Syndulla laughed. "That's always a hard one to argue with. But listen—sometimes we have to accept that a decision isn't only *our* burden. It's—"

She was interrupted by a voice outside the curtain. "General? They're waiting for you in the assembly room."

Syndulla frowned, appeared to think something over, then rose from the bed. "I'll be back," she told Quell. "Think about it all."

"Of course."

When Syndulla was gone Quell allowed her mouth to hang open and her eyes to drift shut. She'd survived the interrogation but she needed air, felt more exhausted than she had in days. She listened to the hum of medical equipment and the deeper thrum of the Star Destroyer's engines, and she waited for security officers to take her away and put her in a cell. Star Destroyers had plenty of cells—even Star Destroyers reconfigured by the New Republic, she was sure.

No one came. She was too far past tired to lie down and sleep and eventually she pulled away the curtain and paced across the medbay in her gown. The droid was out of sight—maybe in one of the operating suites—as were the guards, so Quell walked past the rows of mostly empty beds without direction or purpose.

As she passed a bed half concealed behind another curtain, some instinct stopped her. Her eyes fell on the slender lump beneath the thin blanket, following the length of the body until the curtain blocked her sight. She stepped around the curtain and saw a pale face—exhausted and thin, dark-haired and sunken-eyed and unshaven, but not without life.

"Lark."

Wyl Lark blinked and turned his head and squinted at her in the too-bright lights.

"Are you okay?" she asked.

"I'm okay," he said. He lifted his upper body, propping himself up. "You're here."

"Kairos and Chadic found me. I'm—I don't really know what happens next." She stepped forward, her legs suddenly weak, and knelt beside the bed. "I was the one feeding information to the New Republic," she said. It sounded pathetic—saying it aloud, saying it the second time in an hour when she'd held it back for days. "I brought you to Shadow Wing so you could stop them."

He didn't smile at her. He seemed to take the words in and stared at her face. "I'm glad," he said at last. "I'm glad you did."

She nodded briskly and recomposed herself. *Leave him alone,* she thought, *and let him rest. Don't drag him into this when he's hurt.* But she stayed at the side of the bed.

He seemed to be waiting for her to speak. When she didn't, he said, "We did stop them, you know. At Chadawa. The planet's safe."

"That's good."

"It was mostly Nath and Hail Squadron. I'm in command, now, but—"

"I heard. Congratulations."

He laughed, or came close to it. "Thank you. It wasn't really earned, but for a while it was me and Nath, and Nath didn't want it, so—well."

"What happened to you?"

"I'm okay," he repeated. "I was lucky. It wasn't smart, but it worked—I went to fight Colonel Keize, while Nath and the Y-wings did their part. They took most of the beating, I got to eject . . ."

Lark kept talking. Quell couldn't hear him over the roar in her ears. The barrier around her emotions was crumbling, and she couldn't say why, nor could she turn away from the wounded man before her. Her eyes stung and she felt tears slide down her cheeks, tried to pinch back each one and failed. Her thoughts went from Lark, ejecting from his burning ship, to Rikton on Netalych—Rikton, who might've lived but might've died at Chadic's hand or at the droids'. She had led her team into a nightmare and they were dead now, along with so many others.

"I'm sorry," she said. "I'm sorry you had to take command. I didn't mean to leave you like that."

Her voice sounded remarkably steady, and she wiped her face on the front of her hospital gown. Lark observed, and she wondered if he would ask what was wrong (if anyone would, it would be Lark, even after all she'd done, after she'd lied to him about her crimes and abandoned him for Shadow Wing) but he only nodded slowly and said, "It's okay. These things happen in war."

"Yes," she said.

She exhaled and squared her shoulders, steadying herself as they sat together. She stopped looking at Lark and he watched her sometimes and, other times, simply watched the curtain as the recirculating air sent ripples through the cloth.

Leave him alone, she told herself again, and didn't. She didn't need him to accept her; but she wasn't ready to go.

She thought of Fra Raida and another wave of grief hit. She swallowed it so Lark wouldn't see.

"Can I ask you something?" Lark said.

She nodded briskly.

"Why did Keize walk away from Shadow Wing, and why did he come back?"

It wasn't the question she'd expected, and she was puzzled but grateful. It gave her a focus, and her voice sounded clearer when she said, "You want to know what he told me?"

"Or what you believe."

She could vividly picture Keize standing in the bogs of Nacronis, ordering her desertion. He'd spoken of his reason for leaving again aboard the *Yadeez,* and Rikton had talked about Devon, the alias Keize had used in his wanderings. Yet she'd always seen his journey through the lens of her own defection, her own return, and that clouded her vision now. "I think—" she began, and mouthed the words before she spoke them. "I think whatever he saw when he left, it convinced him that no one could really leave. That—he said this—'to accept defeat is to sacrifice every soldier who remains alive at the altar of rebel justice.'"

"But why leave in the first place, then?"

She shrugged. "Because he knew we wouldn't win the war, and he thought he could set an example for the rest of us. It didn't work."

"It still could've been the right thing to do," Lark said.

"Maybe."

Lark settled back onto the bed. He frowned in thought awhile before looking to Quell and saying softly, "Thank you."

"Thank you," she said, and left his bedside at last.

II

Nath Tensent had flown two Y-wings in his life. The first hadn't lasted long—a bad landing on Baradas had torn off the underside and one of the nacelles, and everything left had been destined for the scrap heap. His second Y-wing had seen him through the war and out the other side, and he knew its guts better than any other piece of machinery he'd owned, astromech included.

The bomber had returned from Chadawa hurt, and he'd let the ground crews patch it as best they could. For the past hour he'd been crawling over and under the Y-wing, checking every welded armor plate and swapped power coupling, and he could admit that Ragnell and her people had done good. But his ship was still the only thing keeping him from dying in a thousand ways, and if he had a list of other things he should've been doing, so what? If Jaith Omir had double-checked all the safeties on his torpedoes, maybe he wouldn't have blown up midway to Chadawa. Maybe if Nath hadn't retuned the backup stabilizers a week earlier, he'd be a frozen piece of meat above the planet now.

T5 squawked as Nath crouched beneath the cockpit and eyed the slapdash spray of thermal resin around the cannons. "Because it's *soothing*, all right?" Nath snapped. "Besides, there's nowhere to meditate on the blasted Star Destroyer."

The droid kept squealing. Nath barely bothered to grunt in argument. *Complain all you want. I'm not walking away until I'm done.*

Only the last of the droid's noises demanded an answer. "Doesn't matter," Nath said. "No one's seeing Quell until the general's done with her." He scowled, dug a fingernail into the resin, then looked to the droid sitting a meter away. "But yeah, I'm glad she's alive."

He didn't plan to admit his complicity, yet the truth was Quell had gotten a raw deal. He'd known, same as Adan, about the crimes she'd committed at Nacronis; and same as Adan, he'd kept it to himself. Maybe he could've done more to smooth things over when the squadron had learned the truth. He probably would've, if Shadow Wing hadn't picked that moment to attack.

So far as he could tell, she hadn't tried to kill him or Alphabet since leaving the New Republic. He had no beef with her. *Hell*, he thought, *the woman has a wicked sense of humor when she lets her guard down.*

"Going to make things complicated, though," he said aloud. "Going to throw Wyl and Chass off their game." Neither seemed emotionally prepared for Quell's return, no matter what Syndulla did with her.

T5 chittered and he nodded reluctantly. "That, too. Guess I do owe Chass a visit."

He made one more cursory inspection of the bomber, trying not to think about everything he might've missed and everything that might've saved the rest of Hail. Finally he stowed his tools and headed toward the hangar entrance, waving at one of the ground crew. "Hey! You seen Chass na Chadic?"

"Chadic?" The woman looked at him from where she was decoupling a fuel hose. She spoke with the electronic whine of a vocabulator. "She was here to review the B-wing's repair plan. She left to—and I quote—'go shoot something.'"

"Sounds like her. Thanks." Nath paused and frowned. "Keep spotting you, but we never got introduced. You're from Cerberon, right? What's your name?"

"Caulra Spring," the woman said. She didn't smile.

"Nath Tensent. See you around."

He left T5 with the Y-wing, departed the hangar, and took the long route to the practice range. He found a few pilots and crew snapping off particle bolts at holograms, but Chass wasn't there and his inquiries suggested she'd never turned up. Under other circumstances, that would've been the end of it, but he'd resigned himself to the conversation and he was determined to find her.

He made three other stops before finding Chass in the sanitation ring, shooting junk on a conveyer belt leading into the garbage compactor. The chamber smelled like rusted metal and rotting food and ionized blaster trails. "Range not good enough for you?" he called over the machinery.

Chass didn't even look his way. "You ever notice all the targets on the range are nonhuman?"

"Can't say I had. Good old Imperial programs."

"Right," Chass said. She tracked a lump of stained and shredded cloth down the conveyer with her blaster but didn't fire; then she dropped her arms to her sides and turned to Nath. "Good old *that*. You want something?"

"Maybe I just wanted to see how you and Kairos are doing after your excursion?"

"Huh. Just fine so far. Syndulla hasn't taken us into custody, but I figure that's because she's short on pilots."

It shouldn't have hit home—it was the sort of cynical joke Nath had made himself a hundred times—but the depleted roster of bomber pilots burned in his brain.

Just because it affected him didn't mean he had to show it, though. "You may be right," he said. "My sense is the general's got enough on her hands between Quell and the war as a whole. She'll put off disciplinary actions, at least awhile—expect you'll get a note attached to your record and a few weeks of docked pay. Maybe worse, but you're not getting kicked out."

"Thank the will of the Force for other people's desperation, huh?"

"That, and the fact your wing commander's in the medbay."

Chass had the decency to look embarrassed. "Yeah. We weren't *trying* to leave you and Wyl in the lurch. Glad he's okay."

Nath nodded carefully. He tried to imagine if things might have gone any differently if Chass had been with the Y-wings hunting the Raiders. Maybe she'd have died instead of one of the Hail pilots; maybe one more ship would've made it go easier. It wouldn't have changed the duel, certainly.

He owed her payback, but he'd also made a promise to Wyl and he couldn't blame her for the worst of his troubles. He figured he could find a workable compromise.

"Forget it," he said, and grinned wide enough to show teeth. "Let's get a drink."

She was sensible enough to be suspicious. "Yeah?"

"Yeah. Jaith Omir had a contraband stash, and *someone's* got to do the tough job and get rid of it."

She was sensible enough to be suspicious, but *not* sensible enough to say no. It was one of the things he liked about Chass—once you had her figured out, she was always reliable.

Nath hadn't decided on his approach beforehand—he'd tossed around options and then, as usual, figured he'd get a read on his target when the time came.

The answer seemed obvious now, as he sat across from Chass in the maintenance room outside the Star Destroyer's secondary cooling plant. Gurgling sounds escaped from the hatch to their right, and crates full of tools and obscure replacement parts served as chairs as they drank from two putrid bottles of Corellian ale. Nath had managed not to complain about the taste as Chass had gone on about how she'd stolen back her B-wing, then segued into some story about robbing a casino with the Cavern Angels. He'd forgotten she could get *chatty* when she drank.

When a lull came he took his shot. "You know I don't care a whit about your religion, right?" he said. "All that chanting you've been doing in the cockpit, the weird medallions . . . I grew up next door to a Singing Disciple of the Gap. Takes a lot to get on *my* nerves."

Her body went rigid, and she fixed cold eyes on him even as she sipped. "So why're you bringing it up?" she asked.

"Because—come on, sister—you're smarter than you pretend, and I know a job when I see one."

"You don't know what you're talking about," she said, and with that Nath knew she was his. If she'd been going to break a bottle over his skull, that had been her opportunity.

"Sure I do. I've got my fingers in all sorts of places now. Pulled up the New Republic Intelligence files on that cult of yours, along with their leader—what's-her-name, Let'ij?"

"What about her?" She was feigning boredom and staring at the tool shelf behind Nath's head.

"New Republic's finally getting its hands on some of the old security databases—the ones the Empire didn't purge, anyway. Visual search matches Let'ij's face, a few alterations aside, all the way back to the Old Republic. Woman's lived a busy life. Done everything from running speakeasies to counterfeiting to acting as an unlicensed advocate. Must've ended up at Cerberon not too long ago, decided founding a cult was her latest scam."

Her head started to swivel back toward him and he cut her off before she could speak. "Look, I know you know all this—maybe not the particulars, but you've seen too much of this garbage to delude yourself. You're sticking with the cultists because you figure it gives you options after the war's done, right? Maybe a place to squeeze out a few credits? I get it, believe me, but—" He leaned forward and put his bottle on the crate between them, lowering his voice. "—Let'ij doesn't have a great track record when it comes to follow-through. If she did, she'd be rich by now instead of caught six times over.

"You want a good scam, though? You let me know, and I can find you some great ones—"

He'd pushed hard enough, and Chass brought her bottle down, swinging it wide to knock his bottle off the crate. The fallen container cracked without shattering, bleeding a trickle of amber onto the deck. "Really don't need your advice," she muttered. "But yeah, never meant it as a permanent thing. Wasn't right for me anyway."

Her hand was shaking. She wiped it on her knee to hide it. Nath felt a petty pleasure at her discomfort. "Didn't mean to stick my nose in," he said with a shrug. "Plenty of other options for a wily Theelin."

"Yeah," she repeated. "Maybe I can get a pilot job working for some rich guy who wants an 'exotic' species to show off."

"Sure. Fits your temperament. Or open a veterans bar somewhere like Troithe—place that saw plenty of action, messy enough to be cheap?"

"Animal wrangler. Beastmaster. I've got tough skin."

"Join a crooked circus."

"Learn plasma-eating. Rob people after shows."

"Lots of options."

"Lots of options."

Her words came rapidly. She didn't smile through any of it.

"Hell," he said. "I don't think any of us really know what we're doing after. Anyone who says different is deluding themselves."

She shrugged. "Well . . . maybe we won't have to worry about it anyway."

He almost replied. Then she was standing, trying to pick her way through the debris on the floor to reach the door. "I need to sleep, okay?" she said. "Been a long trip."

He could've left it there. He'd done his job, given her the nudge she needed, and it had been easier than he'd expected—like she'd been right on the verge already. But some days his capacity to *read* people felt like a curse, and he heard a harshness in her voice that reminded him of the woman he'd met before Pandem Nai. He wondered if he'd overcorrected; he didn't think so.

"Hey," he called, as she stepped into the doorway. He was operating on instinct now, conscious mind two steps behind. "That pilot shortage you mentioned? Don't get yourself killed before the next mission is over. Going off with Kairos, you owe me, you owe Wyl."

"Screw you, hero."

She was out of the maintenance room and the door was sliding shut. He called, "You know it's true. You hear me?" He clambered to his feet and held the door open. "You need someone to shoot you, you come to me after. But you owe me a replacement bomber pilot!"

He heard her cursing as she walked away. Nath sighed and began cleaning up the spilled ale.

He'd done his job. It wasn't his fault if killing Chass the Cultist brought the return of Chass the Martyr. Though like everything about Alphabet, it might end up his problem to solve.

III

"The Imperial fleet," Admiral Gial Ackbar declared, waving a holographic fin at the galaxy in the room's center, "is here, in the Jakku system. This information has been confirmed by our most trustworthy sources within the past twelve hours. An opportunity to stop the enemy forever is at hand."

There were no hushed reactions from the members of the war council digitally gathered in the assembly room. The lot of them were too jaded for that. But Hera felt her heart rate increase. She heard tapping from several quarters as off-holo aides pulled up information on Jakku and New Republic battle groups. Stornvein wordlessly passed her a datapad, and she pretended to read it as she assessed her own emotions. The initial wave of excitement passed and she was steady.

You've known this was coming a long time. You've even been through it before.

She skimmed a summary of the Jakku system's points of interest: only one planet of even borderline significance, and that a nearly uninhabited desert. It seemed an unlikely place for the Empire's last stand, but like Hoth or Yavin 4 or Mako-Ta, it was a forgotten place outside the boundaries of civilization—one that could be hidden, defended, or abandoned according to the needs of its occupiers. There were many lessons the Empire had failed to learn from the Rebellion, but maybe some were sinking in.

"So far," the admiral went on, "the Senate has refused to authorize invasion, but Chancellor Mothma is confident such authorization is forthcoming. She has tasked us with assembling a strike plan."

"How long has the Empire been at Jakku?" General Ria spoke with the confidence of a woman who understood exactly what she needed. "How well entrenched can we expect them to be?"

Chief of Intelligence Cracken was the one to answer. "Estimates say three to six months. Specifics on the enemy's fleet strength are forthcoming—"

"—yet we must be prepared to move *quickly*," Ackbar added. "I know some of you will assume that time is on our side—that if the Empire has already had ample time to prepare, our best option is not to rush in but to spend weeks preparing a grand siege. I tell you—"

Hera heard the assembly room door open and saw Nath Tensent

take his place near Stornvein—out of view of the holocams but close enough that she could speak to him. It was Wyl Lark's place, rightfully—Alphabet Leader's place—but she wasn't ready to return Wyl to active duty and Nath had attended a war council before.

Nath nodded in her direction. His expression was distracted. Hera hoped she hadn't made an error.

Ackbar was still talking. "—Mothma believes that even the senators in support of a strike will be reluctant to deploy so many ships far from our member worlds for a lengthy period; they fear it would leave us vulnerable. And *I* believe that the Empire is *not* fully ready for our attack, not yet—"

"What if it's Endor all over again? A way to lure our forces out and destroy them?" Admiral Ho'ror'te asked.

Cracken began arguing that, unlike at Endor, his sources and methods had not been compromised. Hera only half listened, and tilted her head as Nath leaned in. "Trap or not, you can be blasted sure they're expecting us," Nath said. "Sounds like the chancellor's lost control."

"Maybe," Hera murmured, and wished Mothma were in attendance—the chancellor understood both politics and war, and Hera had learned to trust the woman implicitly. "How soon can the squadrons be ready to fight?"

"Flare and Wild are in decent enough shape, but we're real short on bombers. That'll cause problems unless we can get reinforcements. Any idea if Vanguard Squadron could—"

Hera raised a hand to cut off Nath. Cracken was finishing and she stepped forward, drawing the room's attention. "We can be confident this *is* a trap, at least in part," she said. "If the Empire's had this much time to prepare, they'll have a plan ready. But I agree with Ackbar and the chancellor—if we have an opportunity, we should take it. We should hit faster than the Empire expects and harder than they can withstand, and we should do it—" She paused and looked at all the attendees, real and holographic. She thought of the campaigns Ria and Ho'ror'te had endured, and couldn't begin to imagine the task Cracken faced. She looked at Nath and Stornvein, and saw the lines in their faces—the exhaustion all of them now took for granted. "We should do it because we've been promising an end to this war for a year, and I don't know if anyone has the strength to fight for another. We do this while we have the heart, and while we have a real chance at victory."

It wouldn't end the argument behind the scenes, but it sufficed for the moment. Ackbar saw his opportunity and looked to Hera. "Thank you, General," he said. "Regarding your status—I understand Chadawa is secure?"

"Secure, if not stable," she agreed.

"General Cracken believes the Empire is recalling its remaining mobile battle groups to Jakku. It's safe to assume they recognize a need for urgency. Do you have any reason to believe they would *not* recall the 204th Imperial Fighter Wing?"

"We're—" She'd told no one of Quell's capture. She hadn't had time—and in truth, she'd wanted a better sense of who Quell had become before putting her fate in the hands of the New Republic bureaucracy. She considered her phrasing carefully. "—still analyzing some data that's just arrived. But Chadawa appears to be the last Cinder target in this region. It's entirely possible Shadow Wing could be recalled."

She glanced at Nath as the man shifted restlessly. He'd been liaising with Intelligence, and he knew the 204th as well as she did. She motioned him forward; he hesitated, then stepped into view of the holo-cam.

"The 204th has built a *unique* little unit," Nath said. "If they're returning to the fleet, they're not going to coordinate well with the rest of the Empire. Either they'll end up a weak point or there's something special planned for them."

"Or both," Ackbar said. Nath backed out of sight again. "The *Deliverance* and its squadrons will join the attack, but I want you prepared to counter the 204th if they are present. You've proven more than once that they're dangerous; let's make sure any damage they do is contained."

"Yes, Admiral," Hera said, and felt a mix of anticipation and concern as Ackbar went around the room giving the individuals who'd waged war across the galaxy their assignments.

Victory was in sight. Victory over the Empire and victory over Shadow Wing.

Victory always had a price.

IV

Yrica Quell lay on her bunk in the brig, clean shirt and bandaged arms stenciled by the lighting strips overhead. If she looked to her right, she could see the black door to the cell and the control panel indicating the door was unlocked. If she opened the door, she knew she would see an empty corridor leading to a guard post with no one on duty.

She was alone. She had her freedom if she wanted it. It might have been a test by General Syndulla, but more likely it was a message: *You're trusted, but don't forget your position.*

Nonetheless, it was difficult for Quell to see her circumstances as anything other than symbolic. She was trapped, held captive only because she hadn't escaped when she'd had the chance; the victim of nothing more terrible than her own choices. She was aboard a New Republic Star Destroyer, trying to determine what she owed her comrades and her mentors: what she deserved, and what they deserved, and what the 204th and the Empire and the dead of Nacronis deserved.

She hadn't moved from her cot in hours, feeling coarse cloth against her arms and hearing the distant hum of the engines. She could do nothing but think and she still felt overstimulated. There were too many threads to untangle, too many decisions that would impact other people. IT-O would have helped her—the torture droid probably would've known the answer and refused to share, but it also would've reasoned with her for hours or days if she'd asked.

She'd always tried to avoid sessions with the droid. Now that she wanted to see it, IT-O was gone. She'd brought its data core out of Cerberon but the damage had been too great to repair. All she had left was her memory (though she had an extremely good memory).

"You aren't going to help me, are you?" she whispered, if only to hear her own voice.

The first time she'd met IT-O had been in a converted shipping container in Traitor's Remorse. She'd had to wrap herself in a poncho to ward off the cold, and she'd sat on a low stool against the container's corrugated metal wall. "You are Yrica Quell?" the droid had asked, and she'd said yes, she was, and it had gone on to apologize for its appearance.

"I assure you I have been programmed with an abiding respect for living things," it had told her, "as well as multiple texts on medical ethics and the treatment of psychiatric disorders. I do not ask that you believe or respect me at this time; only that we begin our relationship without preconceptions and work toward the shared goal of your treatment and release."

"You must say that a lot," she'd said.

"No," the droid replied, "but I opt to."

At the time, she'd thought the comment the result of the exasperating literalness of droids. She wondered now if it had been humor.

What would you have told me if you'd known the truth then?

No one had ever called Quell imaginative. She knew her strengths. But she tried anyway, squeezing her eyes shut and holding on to the image of the shipping container, smelling the rust and adhesive. She pictured the droid's photoreceptor dilating as it stared at her.

"You're troubled," the droid said.

"Yes."

"Why?"

"Because I don't know what to do." She wanted to stop there, but IT-O wouldn't have allowed it. In reality she might not have trusted the droid enough to speak; yet this wasn't reality, and she had learned in Cerberon to be honest with herself.

"I knew what I was trying to accomplish when I rejoined Shadow Wing," she said. "I tried to stop them as well as I could, I swear. But I've made a lot of bad calls in my life, and they're not monsters, and Keize was the one who saved me in the first place—"

"Pause, Yrica Quell. Breathe."

She did, in reality and in her imagination.

"What happened," the droid asked, "when you left Cerberon?"

She nodded in the shipping container and disciplined her thoughts. She wouldn't have said any of that to IT-O anyway. She'd always been more precise.

"I rejoined Shadow Wing to destroy it. I thought it would be straightforward. I've killed a lot of people before."

"It wasn't straightforward, though."

"No. I got confused."

"How?"

"Keize was just trying to keep his troops alive. Give them a future. And I—" She paused again for a long time. "I started to think maybe they didn't deserve dying. Even as I watched them murder planets, I started to think of them as—not good people, not *decent* people, but *people*. My friends."

"That was inevitable," the droid said. "The moment you left Cerberon, it was a necessary outcome."

"Why?"

"Because—" The droid stopped. *She* stopped, trying to answer her own question in the droid's voice. "—when you accepted that you were worthy of existence, worthy of *moving forward* as you'd decided you would, you could no longer deny your former comrades the same worth and dignity. It merely took you time to see the logical conclusion."

"I don't get to place myself above them."

"Somewhat reductive—but in a sense, yes."

"Plenty of people who don't deserve to die still have to, in war."

The droid had no answer to this. Maybe the real droid would have, but not the one she imagined.

"Why are you coming to me *now*," the droid asked, "when everything you're telling me has distressed you for some time?"

"I have a choice to make," she said.

"And that choice is . . . ?"

That part was easy. Admitting it was harder.

"I don't know whether to tell the others what Keize is planning."

"Because? In the simplest terms you can."

She returned to the words she'd spoken to General Syndulla. "Because I'm not sure it's the right thing to do."

"Why?"

"Because I don't trust my own judgment."

The droid adjusted the frequency of its hum, first to a buzz-saw whine then to a heartbeat throb. Quell's breathing slowed; she hadn't realized it had quickened.

"I understand your doubt. You've made decisions in your past that led to unfortunate consequences. Nacronis is the obvious example, but there are others."

"Like joining the Empire so I could learn to fly and join the Rebellion, and then never doing it? Like lying about Cinder and losing my squadron? Like—"

"Yrica," the droid said. "We are both aware of your failings. Recounting them now will not help. Consider this, however: The consequences of those past decisions were *never* unpredictable. You understood the likely outcomes of the choices you regret the most."

"I know that—"

"Then use that knowledge. Act on what you know now."

The image of the shipping container frayed at the edges. Her imagination was failing her. "Just tell me what to do," she whispered in her mind and aloud.

"What is it that you want?" the droid asked.

The words sent her into confusion again, entangling her in a thousand futures for herself and Alphabet and Shadow Wing and the galaxy. But the droid had urged simplicity. She sought an anchor, focused on the question.

"I want to save lives," she said.

"Then start there," the droid said, "and concern yourself with the next question once it comes."

IT-O was gone then, and she blinked away the sting in her eyes as she lay on her bunk and listened to her breath and held fast to the images until they dissolved, dreamlike, leaving her without even a proper memory—just the traces of thoughts that had come and gone and a sense of grief and affection.

She studied the answer she'd found, reexamining it, then forced herself to stop; she couldn't begin the spiral of confusion again. She forced herself to stand from her bunk and exit the cell too fast, head swimming, and she walked down the corridor on unsteady legs until she spotted a security cam.

She looked up and said: "Tell General Syndulla I want to talk to Alphabet Squadron."

CHAPTER 18

CALL TO THE PLACE OF JUDGMENT

I

"It's idiotic. We're flying top speed into a trap."

"That's always the way, isn't it?"

"No, it's just the most *fun* . . ."

If Yrica Quell ignored the obsidian décor of the conference room, ignored Kairos's unmasked face and the absence of Caern Adan, it was almost like being aboard the *Lodestar*. Chass na Chadic sat at the far end of the table, cocksure with arms tight across her chest; she was teasing Wyl Lark, seated to her right, whose bacta treatments had scrubbed away any sign of injury.

"Endor wasn't as fun as you'd think," Lark said with a smile. Quell was certain she heard something other than humor in his voice; something strained and secret, as if he, too, were pretending they were the people they'd been months ago.

Kairos wore a loose gray poncho—wherever it had come from it fit better than Chadic's flight suit—and had taken up her station in the corner of the room. There were no shadows there to obscure her, but Quell noticed the slight movement of Lark's hair, the feel of air over her own skin, and realized Kairos had positioned herself away from the ventilation ducts. The woman was still hesitant to touch the alien world she occupied.

Nath Tensent ambled away from Lark and Chadic (who kept talking) and joined Quell near the front. He dropped his bulk into the seat beside her and leaned back. "Guessing you're bringing trouble?" he asked with a grin.

"You guess right," she said. "Doesn't seem like much next to the end of the war, though."

"What, the business with Jakku?" Tensent shrugged. "You'd think everyone would know better than to get excited, but they're acting like we just blew up a Death Star."

"Instead of about to attack one?"

"Exactly. Caught some of the Wild Squadron boys looking for watering holes near the Jakku system where they can celebrate after. I understand the sentiment, but . . ." He shook his head.

As with Lark, there was something in Tensent's voice that had changed. He was concealing something—not the way he'd always concealed things, but concealing something *badly*. Like the grinning pirate was facing execution at last.

Or maybe Quell just didn't know her people anymore.

"How are *you* holding up?" Tensent asked. "Heard from Syndulla about what you've been through, but she spared the details."

"I'm fine," Quell said. As she watched Tensent sidelong she knew she owed him more. She'd never been as close to him as to Chadic, yet he'd stayed by her when she'd gone hunting for Adan and steered her right aboard the *Buried Treasure*. "I'm a wreck, but there's enough to salvage, and I can do the job."

Tensent laughed, loud enough that Chadic and Lark glanced his way before resuming their discussion. "I don't doubt it," he said. He lowered his voice and his smile faded. "You're a survivor. Always admired that about you."

Quell nodded, not sure what else to say.

The door slid open and General Syndulla stepped into the conference room. The pilots rose together and Tensent slapped his hand between Quell's shoulders, hard enough to jolt her.

"Sorry I'm late," Syndulla said, and waved them all to their seats. Quell remained standing. "You all know as much as I do at this point. Yrica Quell remains in our custody but given all she's done for us—including stopping the second Operation Cinder and saving Chadawa—I think she deserves some leeway. She wanted to brief us as a group, we're going to listen."

"Thank you," Quell said.

Syndulla slid into a seat opposite Tensent and nodded to Quell. "It's your show."

Quell moved to the holoprojector controls and skimmed the buttons with her fingertips. She'd prepared nothing, but it bought her time to compose herself, to remember why she'd chosen this.

I want to save lives.

"I know what Soran Keize is planning," she said as she faced the group. "It has nothing to do with Jakku or the Imperial fleet—I don't have any information on what will happen there and I can't help you win the war. But what Keize is doing will be critical in the aftermath.

"Keize and I—I *know* him. We spoke a lot when I returned to Shadow Wing, in private away from the others. He wanted to know my opinions, hear about my experiences as a New Republic captive. He's believed for some time that the war is a lost cause—that at most, the Empire can drag out the fighting, hold on to some sectors under siege—and that his obligation isn't to Imperial leadership, but to his people. To every soldier fighting for the Empire."

They were watching her, but none of them understood. She went on, keeping her voice steady as she could.

"Based on everything he's seen—based on what I've seen, too—we agreed that there's no place for Imperial veterans in a galaxy dominated by the New Republic. After the war, the best outcome anyone from the 204th can hope for is a life in hiding; more likely a long prison sentence."

Chadic snorted. Quell could hear her thinking: *Sounds pretty soft to me.* Tensent arched his brow. Lark said quietly, "You don't know that."

"I was at Traitor's Remorse," she replied, and tried to shed the harshness in her response. "It wasn't good, and we were the lucky ones. Keize wanted to disappear and live a life on the fringes, and he was hunted down. There are *millions* of Imperials still out there, still fighting since Endor, and a hundred times that who haven't formally surrendered. They—"

"We don't know what will happen to them," Syndulla said, firm but without aggression. "The Senate hasn't made any final plans."

Quell wanted to close her eyes and retreat into herself. She met Syndulla's gaze instead. "I realize that. Right now, though, it doesn't matter what you or I believe. It matters what *Keize* believes, and I'm telling you: He thinks the soldiers of the Empire are doomed whether they surrender or stay. And he thinks they deserve better."

"Understood," Syndulla said. "So what does he plan to do?"

Nothing she'd said so far was a breach of trust. None of it revealed anything they could *use.*

"The Emperor's Messenger," she said. "The machine that delivered the orders for the first Operation Cinder. Keize wondered how it selected the people it did—the people likely to go along with genocide even after the Emperor's death. He reasoned it had to have access to some kind of massive military data bank.

"He was right. I had a Messenger's programming analyzed, and we discovered it was sorting through profiles of everyone who ever served the Empire. Billions of people, and it was looking for the ones who—" *Who wouldn't hesitate to commit atrocities.* "—who suited its purpose.

"But it wasn't just checking psychological evaluations or combat records. It checked information none of us knew had been recorded—family histories, hobbies, cultural background. Whether we stood straight enough for the Imperial anthem when it played. That's just the trivial stuff, though, it also—"

They didn't understand. She had to explain it clearly.

"The data bank it accessed . . . it cataloged *everything*. Every awful thing we did, every massacre, every time someone bombed a civilian apartment we'd thought was a rebel hideout and every time a storm-trooper threw someone innocent against a wall. Every vile act, autho-rized or not. The stuff we sanitized in official reports, because we didn't want to admit it and it never seemed important to our superiors.

"Maybe you think that doesn't sound special. Most of you never worked for the Empire, but you couldn't—" She heard her own anger, tried desperately to control it. "—you couldn't work as a damn file clerk without being complicit in *something*. That's how the Empire worked, how it was *meant* to work. You serve, and sooner or later ev-eryone does something to stain their conscience.

"The Emperor was collecting all of it. He was tracking how far we'd all fallen."

The room was silent awhile. Lark was the one to ask: "Why?"

Quell shrugged. "Because that's who he was. Maybe he thought it would ensure our loyalty. Maybe he was a petty sadist."

She caught Tensent's gaze. He'd understand better than the others—he'd served under the Empire long enough to know no one got away clean. But he didn't show any emotion as he said, "No way this Mes-senger could've carried the data bank with it. Where's it located?"

"Where else?" Quell asked. She'd seen the coordinates in the Sur-geon's report, confirmed them aboard the U-wing. "It's on Coruscant, stretching underneath the Imperial Palace all the way to the Verity District."

Tensent whistled. Quell ignored him. "If the Empire falls at Jakku," she said, "Coruscant can't stand alone. The regent there is a figurehead and its defenses are decaying; it'll surrender or it'll be conquered. The New Republic will gain access to the Emperor's data bank and it'll have the tools to chase, prosecute, imprison, execute, or ruin everyone who spent more than a day in Imperial service. Because I guarantee you, everyone will have *something* the New Republic can demand justice for.

"And if somehow the Empire wins at Jakku? The data bank will become another tool to keep Imperial soldiers in line. No one's going to desert or defect if their file might be leaked to New Republic Intelligence in retaliation."

"I assume," Syndulla said, expression flat and focused, "that Colonel Keize intends to destroy this data bank?"

"That's my belief. It won't stop the New Republic from sweeping up and prosecuting select targets, but it'll prevent a galaxy-wide purge. The Empire's soldiers will have a chance to slip away and be forgotten. To make a quiet life for themselves, like Keize wanted to do.

"But we're probably days from Coruscant's fall. Keize knows he has to act soon. He knows he won't have the cooperation of Imperial leadership—such as it is—and the tools available to him are limited. I don't think he'll even tell the rest of the 204th about the data bank; they're in too deep, they won't dare turn against the Empire when it's the only purpose they've got."

"Violence," Kairos said. "He intends violence."

Quell nodded. Syndulla frowned. "The area around the Palace," she said. "Not exactly residential, but you don't have to move far into the undercity to find civilians. If he goes in there indiscriminately . . ."

"I've seen the images," Lark said. "It's hard to picture the scope. What's the risk like compared with Troithe?"

Quell recalled Troithe's aerial campaign—districts flooded, skyscrapers collapsed, caravans of evacuating civilians, and refugee camps the size of cities. Lark was imagining what would've happened if they'd intentionally targeted the infrastructure instead of merely catching it in the cross fire; she'd never been to Coruscant, and she'd imagined the same thing. How many hundreds of thousands of people would be within range of Keize's target?

Syndulla answered his question with sober certainty: "Troithe's population density doesn't begin to compare."

"He won't be targeting civilians," Quell said. "He'll try to keep the casualties down if possible. But he'll accept collateral damage if it means destroying the data bank, and he'll figure out a way even if the Imperial forces on Coruscant try to stop him. Like I said, I know him."

Quell hesitated, then spoke again—she was about to lose control of the meeting and there was more she had to say. "I don't know if I want the New Republic to take the data bank," she said, too swiftly to sound calm. "I don't like the thought of spending the next few decades watching millions of ex-Imperials rounded up. But I don't want innocent people killed, either. That's why I'm telling you all this."

Tensent sounded almost gentle when he asked, "How do we know you're not lying?"

Quell laughed hoarsely. "I'm through lying. Even if I wanted to fool you, I don't have that much credibility left."

"You could be lying about being through with lying," Chadic offered. The Theelin watched Quell, daring her to defend herself.

"I can't prove anything," Quell said. "I admit that. Even so, I'm asking you all: Let me take Alphabet Squadron to Coruscant—into enemy territory—and try to intercept Keize before he can do harm."

With that, her part was over. The others began to argue and pull up data, and Quell sat down as if she might crumble into powder if she lowered herself too fast. She didn't doubt her decision—remarkably, she felt at peace with what she'd done—but she'd expended all her strength in facing the squadron she'd betrayed.

"What are Coruscant's defenses?" Lark was asking. "What do they have in the way of ships, shields, satellites . . . ?"

"The Empire's been holding the capital hostage for a year," Syndulla said. "They can't refresh their troops, and rumor is they're low on supplies, but—"

"I'm not afraid of going in," Chadic mumbled.

"Someone does have to stop Keize," Lark said. "If what Quell's saying is true, we can't let him act."

"We cannot," Kairos said from her corner, though Quell wasn't sure anyone else heard.

The voices blended together until Quell felt Tensent's gaze on her. "I've got a question," he said. "You mentioned Keize probably won't tell the rest of the 204th. That mean he's going in alone?"

Quell shook her head. "Maybe. I can't be sure. I think he wouldn't want to involve the rest of the unit, and he wouldn't trust them to back him if they received contradictory orders from Imperial forces on Coruscant. I think—" She knew the words would sound absurd to them. They didn't understand Keize. "—he doesn't want them to be soiled by his act of treason. He's doing this for them, so their honor—their conscience—isn't injured."

Chadic guffawed. Tensent ignored the Theelin as he said, "All right, so assuming Keize goes in alone—or with limited support—that means the rest of the unit's probably headed to Jakku. That good news or bad?"

"It's worth concern," Syndulla agreed. She held out a hand, hushing the others. "The *Deliverance* has been tasked with countering Shadow Wing at Jakku. That won't be easy, and it'll be harder if we send Alphabet across the galaxy on another mission."

"General, you know Shadow Wing as well as we do," Lark said. "Flare, Wild, and Hail have all fought them before . . ."

"I *don't* know them as well as you," Syndulla said. There was an edge to her voice. "My attention's been split, and Shadow Wing's only ever had maybe a third of my brain. Wild and Flare have less experience than you, and Hail's at less than half strength. The rest of the fleet doesn't understand what the 204th is capable of, and they're counting on us to let them concentrate on separate problems."

Chadic grunted and jutted a thumb toward Quell. "I'm not inclined to do her any favors, but the 204th has a bulk freighter and a load of damaged TIEs. If the whole New Republic Navy can't handle them, that's not our fault."

Tensent and Lark both tried to interject; again, Syndulla quieted them with a gesture. "I'll remind you what happened at Cerberon. We thought we were prepared there. *I* thought we were prepared, and that we could spare some of our forces, and I left to join Vanguard. We've *never* had a clean win against Shadow Wing—not when they've been on the offensive."

"Pandem Nai ought to count for something," Chadic muttered.

"It does," Syndulla said. "It's why we've still got the assignment. Do any of you really think Flare and Wild are ready to handle it alone?"

The others said nothing. Quell felt her chest ache. Yet she'd watched the *Deliverance*'s squadrons from inside Shadow Wing. She couldn't claim the general was wrong.

Syndulla looked at each of them. Kairos was unreadable. Chass na Chadic scowled, apparently displeased by everything. Lark flexed one hand, curling fingers into a fist and then flattening them on the table-top over and over; he looked ready to make a defiant speech of his own, but instead stayed quiet. Tensent looked more distracted than Quell had ever seen him.

"This isn't a battle we can take chances with," Syndulla said. "If the attack on Jakku goes badly, we'll need years to recover from the dam-age. And your colleagues on the *Deliverance* need you all."

"Might be truth to that," Tensent answered. He looked at Quell, as if to make sure she was listening. "But it doesn't address the problem we've got."

"It doesn't," Syndulla said. "Which is why I'm going to think it over and speak with my superiors. I'll have a decision and a plan within the next few hours. Understood?"

She didn't wait for agreement. She rose from her seat and exited the conference room, leaving the rest of them in silence.

Quell scanned the table and let her gaze linger on Chadic. The Thee-lin rolled her shoulders and kept her eyes on the light fixture, and when it was apparent that neither she nor anyone else had anything to say, Quell followed Syndulla's trail out the door.

She didn't blame any of them. She blamed herself for not thinking of it—for not realizing that if she'd been gone long enough to bond with the 204th, Alphabet had had time to bond with other pilots and com-mit to another mission. Their loyalty wasn't to her; they owed her nothing, and the last battle of the war they'd fought far longer than she had was approaching.

She trusted Syndulla would try to stop Keize—the general seemed to believe her story—but what that effort would result in, Quell couldn't guess. She reminded herself that for all Keize's skill he was mortal and as vulnerable as any of them; Coruscant's Imperial defenders might thwart him on their own.

She was returning to the brig (not knowing where else to go, not wanting to face anyone she knew from the crew or see how many strangers had replaced those who'd died at Cerberon) when she felt a hand touch her shoulder.

Wyl Lark said her name as she turned; he looked as if he'd run to catch up with her. "I won't be long," he said. "Can you talk a minute?"

She almost laughed. He was treating her like his commander instead of a prisoner. "Whatever time you need."

They faced each other and Lark, now that he had her, appeared not to know what to do about it. She saw him glance down the corridor and check to see if anyone might overhear. She saw him square his shoulders then force himself to relax.

"I understand—I understand why you did everything you did," he said. "I don't hold any sort of grudge, or resentment . . ."

"I know," she said, though she hadn't known until that moment. Lark couldn't offer her absolution, but it wasn't in his nature to seethe.

He'd have said it to any member of Shadow Wing. She'd need to be satisfied with that.

He nodded briskly. "It's just—I wish you well. Really, I do. And under other circumstances, I'd follow you to Coruscant. I believe in your mission. I believe you're doing the right thing."

"Mister Lark," she said, with a bitter laugh. "Wyl—" She could call him that now. "—I'm not going to hold a grudge against *you* for fighting with your squadrons instead of me."

"That's not it. I can't—" He glanced about again, surreptitious. "I've got a part to play here. You helped me find it. You found your principles, and you've stuck by them, and I'd like to do the same."

She didn't understand. She should've taken the compliment and let it drop, but there was something fatalistic about the way he spoke.

"Not everyone would agree with the principles that got me here," she said.

"They could be misguided," he acknowledged. "So could mine. But we make our choices and we stand by them."

She still didn't understand. Yet she realized with a rush of relief that if there was anyone in the galaxy she trusted not to do evil, it was Wyl Lark.

"Okay," she said. "Good luck."

It felt like a goodbye. Wyl reached out and took her wrist and palm in both hands, squeezing them gently. He smiled at her, sweet and somber, and after a moment he let go and turned away.

She wondered what he was like as a commander, and felt a stinging pride.

She ended up not in her cell but on a narrow catwalk overlooking one of the vehicle bays. There were no fighters stowed below—the hangar had been built to store hovertanks and Juggernauts for planetary invasion, but the New Republic had converted it to hold a battered VCX-100 light freighter. Quell had seen more than a few ships like it pass through Gavana Orbital when she'd been young. She'd never had the opportunity to fly one.

A trio of maintenance workers and an astromech ignored her as she watched them replace much of the ship's scanner array, dismantling systems and swapping out wiring and sensors with a thoroughness that spoke of years of experience. Quell found the process oddly comforting, and she wondered whether there was any part of the freighter that hadn't been replaced over its lifetime; whether it resembled in any essential way the cargo hauler that had rolled off a Corellian Engineering Corporation assembly line twenty or thirty years earlier.

Her thoughts were interrupted when she heard footsteps on the catwalk and saw General Syndulla approaching. She turned as the woman leaned against the railing beside her.

"No ground assault on Jakku?" Quell asked, and gestured with one finger toward the hangar floor.

"Not launching from the *Deliverance*—good ground troops are in short supply, so we don't carry more than a few unless we think we'll need them. We didn't at the start of this mission. Got a resupply the other day, but no troops there, either. Infantry's going with a different battle group to the Western Reaches."

Quell nodded and inhaled a wisp of smoke rising from the work below. It felt strange to discuss the end of the war so casually—but it had been the end of the war for a year now, and along the way the idea had ceased to be remarkable. "It's going to be terrible," she said.

"Probably," Syndulla said. "So will what happens on Coruscant, if you're right about Keize."

So much for avoiding the subject.

Quell pushed away from the railing. "You've made a decision, then?"

Syndulla peered down at the freighter, then gestured for Quell to follow her out of the hangar. "I spoke to Chancellor Mothma. She'll personally send a warning to the Imperial authorities on Coruscant regarding Keize, though she won't mention the Emperor's data bank. But I can't guarantee the message will get through, and I certainly can't guarantee they'll listen."

It was more than Quell had expected and less than she'd hoped. "Well. If it does get through, at least we'll have their attention."

Syndulla nodded, and looked at Quell as they walked down a broad corridor. "If the chancellor didn't care about lives on Coruscant, we'd have invaded six months ago."

"I understand. The timing isn't ideal."

"Coruscant's an Imperial world. You saw what it was like, trying to defend Chadawa without the locals' cooperation. And the chancellor truly believes that victory at Jakku is critical. Frankly, so do I—"

"I understand," Quell said. It was sharper than she'd intended—maybe sharper than she'd ever spoken to a superior officer—but she reminded herself she had little to lose. "Even without Keize, Shadow Wing will have a role to play at Jakku. You can't let the fleet confront the 204th's plan on its own."

"No, I can't." They stepped into a turbolift and Syndulla tapped the control panel. Quell felt the lift vibrate and come to a rapid stop. "There was a time in my life when I could've, you know. I wasn't always running a fleet. Sometimes I miss the freedom to follow my conscience where it takes me."

They exited the turbolift and moved toward the fighter bay. Quell wasn't sure why; nor did she know how to answer, so she remained silent as they passed by the usual activity of droids and ground crews.

"That resupply I mentioned?" Syndulla said as they stepped into the hangar proper. "What with everything going on, I had a shock when I finally saw the inventory. As it turns out—"

Syndulla held up a hand and looked over the lines of starfighters, then called to Ragnell across the bay. The crew chief was in an intense argument with an astromech, aggressively waving a hydrospanner at the machine. "Sergeant!" Syndulla called. "Where's the surplus?"

Ragnell looked up long enough to jut her chin toward a column of X-wings, then returned to her argument. Syndulla walked farther into the hangar, and Quell followed. "As it turns out," Syndulla said, "we've got an X-wing and no pilot. I figure I can deploy it how I'd like."

Quell peered toward the fighter Syndulla indicated. Its profile resembled the T-65B X-wings she'd flown with Alphabet, but its foils and thrusters were unexpectedly slender and its canopy extended farther over the nose. "What—" she started, and looked from the fighter to Syndulla and back.

"T-70 prototype," Syndulla said. "The manufacturer made a batch of them, and command owes me some nice hardware. Didn't expect it to arrive right now, but I'm not complaining."

"Thank you," Quell murmured. Then louder, fully understanding: "Thank you. Is this—"

"You *come back* after you're done, okay? Consider yourself on temporary release until the judiciary's ready for you. You're in my custody and it's my call, assuming—" Quell felt Syndulla's hand on her shoulder, and turned to see the woman's concerned expression. "—you *want* to do this?"

"I do. I do, very much."

She'd already made her decision.

"Good. Ragnell's prepping an astromech—you'll need a good one, using a fighter no one's flown before—and while I can't give you a squadron I can give you backup. It'd look worse than it does already if I send you alone."

Syndulla shifted her gaze to another column of ships. Quell looked past loadlifters and a pair of scorched Y-wing bombers to a familiar U-wing transport. Kairos stood beside one of the loading doors, head bowed as if she were scenting the metal.

"She's all I can give you," Syndulla said. "More than I've been authorized for, frankly, but she was glad to do it. Will that be enough to stop Keize?"

"He's one man," Quell said. "It'll have to be."

"Good," Syndulla replied.

"The others—"

"I didn't ask them. I can't spare a single bomber—B-wing or Y-wing. Not with our losses."

"But they know?"

"I sent word. Your squadron knows."

They watched each other, standing half a meter away, and Quell was overwhelmed by gratitude and grief. She'd lied to Syndulla about Nacronis, fled the woman instead of trusting her after Cerberon, and now she wondered if either of them would live through the coming battles.

"It's okay," Syndulla whispered, and reached out with both arms, pulling Quell close and tight. Quell nodded into the woman's shoulder, felt her own forehead brush one of the Twi'lek's head-tails, and awkwardly clutched the tough fabric of Syndulla's uniform. "It's okay."

Eventually, Syndulla let go. Quell straightened and steadied herself before swallowing. "Permission to launch?" she asked.

"Permission granted," Syndulla said.

There wasn't time for Quell to do anything but pull on a flight suit, climb into the cockpit, and introduce herself to the astromech—4E, a conical unit Ragnell claimed had been flying and repairing starfighters since the Clone Wars. "Foree won't talk much," the sergeant said, "but he'll get you where you need to go."

She caught only a glimpse of the droid as the crew loaded it into its socket, but she was certain someone had painted an Alphabet Squadron crest on its chassis.

Two minutes later the fighter's reactor was thrumming and the droid was running through several hundred systems checks. Quell did as much as she could to expedite the process; she didn't know when Keize would arrive at Coruscant, but she couldn't imagine she had long. She certainly didn't have time to say any goodbyes, nor was she sure she wanted to—yet as the lights on her console flipped from gold to green she craned her neck to look around the hangar, hoping to glimpse Chass na Chadic before departing. She'd barely spoken to the Theelin since boarding the *Deliverance*.

"The cargo is loaded," Kairos announced over the comm. "I am ready."

"Right. Okay." Quell returned her focus to the console, skimming the droid's status reports. "What was all that they put aboard your ship?"

"Many weapons, and communications equipment. To maintain contact with the *Deliverance* as long as possible."

Quell roughed out the calculations in her head. Coruscant was the epicenter of the best-maintained hyperspace comm network in the galaxy; with a hardware boost and a lot of luck, they might be able to maintain a link to Syndulla and the rest of the fleet all the way to Jakku, albeit with plenty of signal decay and lag time.

Maybe the general's more worried than she lets on. Or she wants Kairos to alert her if I've been lying.

She couldn't blame Syndulla for being cautious.

"All right," she said. "Sending departure request to hangar control."

The droid facilitated the back-and-forth while Quell retracted the landing gear. She felt the X-wing vibrate and hum, then the jolt as repulsors kicked in. Her body tingled with the familiar sensation of competing artificial tugs—the gravity of the *Deliverance* meeting the antigravity of the starfighter—and her feet found pedals as her back and helmet reshaped the seat.

She spared one more look toward the personnel entrance. There, she saw not Chass na Chadic but Nath Tensent watching her departure. He must've seen her looking, because he straightened his back and snapped a salute in her direction.

Time to go, she thought, and felt her thrusters ignite as she opened her throttle, making for the hangar doorway and the darkness of space.

II

The Empire had gone mad. How anyone could be blind to it was beyond Soran, but he suspected those who remained were *not* blind—they simply chose to overlook the peculiarities of their leaders, chose to believe that the blasted hellscape of the Jakku desert was superior to imprisonment in a New Republic camp or a mercenary's servitude on the outlaw moons.

Perhaps they were even correct in their reasoning. Soran wasn't certain he had the right to judge.

Shadow Wing's sojourn in the Jakku system had been brief but telling so far. Soran had managed to graciously reject the admirals' requests to transfer personnel to and from the *Yadeez,* citing (entirely honestly) the massive modifications made to both the vessel and his unit's protocols. To his surprise, Captain Nenvez—who'd resisted change more than anyone, who'd done everything possible to imprint his cadets with the spirit of the dead Empire—proved a keen ally in this endeavor, providing written justifications for most every alteration Keize had arranged.

But even isolated aboard their carrier, the troops of the 204th were exposed to the alien culture of the new Empire. Combat exercises with allied units granted insight into a starved and desperate people. The fleet's comm channels broadcast hours of propaganda at odds with the reality Shadow Wing had experienced—breathless speakers made excited claims about the New Republic disintegrating and a civil war among its leadership. Nor did Soran have the heart to forbid certain reunions: Mervais Gandor's brother Sliblis had served aboard the Super Star Destroyer *Ravager,* and the two swapped tales and wept together over holo; Lieutenant Darita took a shuttle to Jakku's surface to carry word of her sister's death to the fallen woman's husband.

Soran's people were not like those troops stationed with the fleet. They had suffered different trials. But they all came from the same stock; they were all of the Empire, and blood and comradeship bound them.

That was why, Soran knew, his people would refuse to leave.

He was finalizing written orders to the engineering team when Teso Broosh arrived in the refrigeration unit "conference room," standing in the doorway until Soran looked up at last. "You asked to see me?" Broosh said, and Soran waved him to a seat.

"You know why you're here?" Soran asked.

"I have suspicions," Broosh said. "I'd rather not speculate."

"No, I suppose not." Keize paused, frowned, and scanned the contents of a datapad before tossing it to his companion. "Teso Broosh—as of fourteen hundred hours you will take full command of the 204th Imperial Fighter Wing. I am using my authority to grant you the rank of major in acknowledgment of your tremendous success and courage on the battlefield."

Broosh didn't look at the datapad. Instead he stared at Soran as if he'd been accused of treason.

"This is wrong," he said.

"It's done."

"Colonel—" Broosh scowled, shifted in his seat, then rose and locked the door. He didn't sit when he turned again. "I'm not an idiot. You're not being promoted to fleet command."

"No," Soran said, and spread his hands on the crate he sat upon. "No, I'm not."

He wondered briefly if he had misjudged Broosh—if his colleague for so many years would execute him for treason. It wasn't how Soran wished to die (and if it came to it, he *would* fight), but the notion had a poetic appeal that nearly made him smile.

"You deserted this unit once before," Broosh said. His voice was steady and cold. "You were allowed to leave because you'd earned our respect; you were allowed *back* because we were desperate. But don't think any of us will stand for it a second time."

"I don't," Soran said. "I wouldn't. When I first left, it was in the hope others would follow—you know that, and I understand the mistake I made. This time . . ." He frowned, squeezing thumb and forefinger together as he considered his words. ". . . what I do, I do in absolute service to you and the unit. To all the Empire, though not all will understand. My mission will be perilous, and I do not expect to return—but I shall, if I am at all able. I swear to this."

Broosh watched him. Soran did not move or moderate the severity of his expression.

Then Broosh laughed, and Soran knew he had *not* misjudged him. He felt pride in having served with the man, and in knowing him, and knowing him well.

"Grandmother would've put you in a cell for this," Broosh said. "She wouldn't have known what else to do with you."

"Very likely. But we're short on cells and guards alike. So . . . ?"

"So in a short while I'll be in command and you'll be gone."

"Excellent," Soran said, and rose from his seat. "There will be no speeches, no goodbyes—I want this done as if you were expecting me back tomorrow, so as not to impact morale. I'll address the other squadron commanders so no one questions your authority. I also suggest you turn to Nenvez to aid in the transition—he's been invaluable to me, as he will be to you." He paused, frowned, and added: "So long as he's kept in line."

"What are the odds Nenvez will recognize my promotion to major?" Broosh asked, dry enough that Soran barely recognized it as a joke.

"About the same as Grand Moff Randd and his cohorts accepting it. They've only just begun calling me colonel." Soran proceeded out the door, waving Broosh to follow. "Come tour the ship with me. I've some final words of advice, and you're obliged to hear them until fourteen hundred."

They proceeded through the cramped corridors. The *Yadeez* was small and there was little for Soran to show Broosh that the man didn't already know; but it was the only farewell Soran would be permitted, and he'd earned the indulgence. He paused often to speak to the crew or the pilots: He praised Taquana's performance in the war games; noted to the ground crews the ion trails left by two of the TIEs from Squadron One. He drew aside Alchor Mirro and told him he'd never forgotten his promise to the old engineer, made years before; looked to where Rikton had sat during meals and took a moment to mourn and consider how to convey a message to the youth's relatives on Corulag. He found Starzha and Phesh arguing over the coming battle and gently separated them, making a note to speak with each later—Phesh, in particular, would rightly bristle at Broosh's promotion; but while Phesh had the experience to lead the unit, he lacked Broosh's compassion for his people.

Phesh was a good soldier. Together, he and Soran would remember Gablerone, and Phesh would understand.

Brebtin had, in her reclusive way, struggled since returning from Quell's mission to Netalych, and Soran sent Broosh away and spoke with her for the better part of an hour. He could console her, strengthen her, if not heal her. When Broosh returned they resumed their tour, and Soran laughed as they came upon two of Wisp's pilots—Cherroi and Gargovik—half naked and entangled in a storage closet. Colonel Nuress would have disciplined them, and once Soran would have done the same—romantic entanglements inevitably caused complications— but times had changed so very much. There was no point encouraging detachment now.

Between these visits Soran and Broosh discussed the composition of the squadrons and the damage to the *Yadeez* and where to reassign the surviving escorts. They discussed the mixture of fear and anticipation in their soldiers, and the possibility that Imperial Command might dissolve the unit and split the squadrons after Jakku was won.

"I have a gift for you," Soran said to Broosh when they arrived on the bridge and he skimmed an update from engineering. "I wasn't certain it would be ready until today."

He passed the report to Broosh, who read it with a mix of puzzlement and interest. "I'm not sure what I'm seeing," he admitted.

"While the Raiders were sabotaging Chadawa's rings, our friends aboard the surveillance ship *Minder* had another task. It seems they've finished at last."

The report itself was nearly incomprehensible in its technical detail; Soran likely wouldn't have understood it himself if he hadn't ordered the procedure, and he was pleasantly surprised as understanding dawned in Broosh's expression. "You could've mentioned this before."

"If it had resulted in nothing, it would have been a distraction." Soran shook his head. "Now it could prove key to success against Syndulla and her people."

"You assume they'll be with the enemy fleet?"

"I do—and I think it likely they'll seek out the *Yadeez,* for all the obvious reasons. Fitting, in a battle that will bring this era to a close."

"We'll be prepared either way. I'll talk to—"

They were interrupted by the tap of Nenvez's cane on the deck. They turned to the old instructor, and he scowled as he spoke in a low voice. "Apologies for interrupting, but I thought you should know—there's a *gathering* taking place in the hangar."

"What sort of gathering?" Soran asked.

"When I asked, I was told it was a homecoming celebration," Nenvez said. "Though frankly, that sounds like an excuse."

"Yes, it does," Soran said, and looked between Broosh and Nenvez. "Shall we join them?"

He believed it was the last time he would see his people together. But his presence would disrupt the event, so he lingered at the fringes and listened to them discuss the fleet and the future and the odds all of them would die, enemy and ally, in the fires over Jakku. Some truly believed the Empire would resurge after victory; others were prepared to become martyrs. In a few, he saw a readiness for an ending—*any* ending, after everything they'd seen this past year.

He longed to stay with them. He considered forgoing his mission and fighting to protect them till the end, or persuading them somehow to flee; but he thought of Fara Yadeez and the soldiers of Troithe, and knew he owed those troops too much to disappear like Devon and save only the 204th.

Bansu Ro had obtained narcotics, and he wailed his grief over all they'd done at Nacronis, Dybbron, Kortatka, and Fedovoi End. Soran hauled the man out of the hangar with the help of Creet, the TIE mechanic with a Twi'lek accent, and sat him on a bunk and told him, "There's nothing wrong with grieving the fallen. But you served your comrades, and there is no shame in that."

Creet stood behind him, and she squeezed his arm before they both returned to the celebration.

Soran sought out Broosh and told him, "Keep them alive. Keep your people alive, no matter what happens."

He believed Broosh understood.

Late in the night Soran finished the last of his tasks aboard the *Yadeez* and climbed into the cockpit of a TIE fighter retrofitted with a hyperspace docking ring. The bridge crew asked no questions when he ordered the hangar opened and passed through the magnetic containment field. He said nothing over the comm to indicate anything out of the ordinary was occurring.

As goodbyes went, the day had been a fine one. It took all his strength to leave.

He abandoned his people to fight for them. He set a course for Coruscant.

CHAPTER 19

REVELATION OF THE ACCUSED

I

Yrica Quell spent the first three hours of her flight refamiliarizing herself with the X-wing's controls. She tested her understanding of the indicator lights, checked the resistance of the control yoke and the rudder pedals. She studied the specifications that 4E summoned to her console and noted the differences between the T-70 and the T-65B she'd flown (and fought) before.

She was reminded of returning home to Gavana Orbital for the first time after enlisting in the Imperial flight academy—of the sense that surface alterations, the repainted walls in her room and her parents' repositioned kitchen table, were indicative of some deeper change in the place or in herself. The T-70 X-wing was no more than a piece of hardware, but it roused emotions she hadn't expected.

Then again, it seemed almost everything did nowadays.

The voyage to Coruscant was a long one. She tried to sleep but the cerulean glow of hyperspace and the unfamiliar pitch of the engines kept her awake. She reviewed the droid's files on the Coruscant system and maps of the Imperial Palace and the Verity District, but no true plan was possible until she knew what Keize was up to—whether she would be too early or too late or in time to intercept him.

Eventually, she activated her comm and recited key points to Kairos, noting where to potentially cut off Keize on the fringes of the system and where the Imperial blockade was weakest in case they needed to follow Keize to the planet surface. Kairos spoke little—even for *Kairos,* she spoke little—and a knot of discomfort formed in Quell's stomach.

"When we get there," Quell asked, "are you going to obey my orders?"

"Perhaps," Kairos said, as if she didn't know herself.

Of course.

"Are you only here because Syndulla doesn't trust me?"

"No."

"Are you here because *you* don't trust me?"

"Perhaps," Kairos said again.

Quell recalled her words: *You are my sister, but your crimes are not forgotten.*

Kairos had abandoned the *Deliverance* and chased Quell to Netalych to "judge her for her wickedness, the deaths of worlds." Maybe, Quell thought, she should've been grateful the U-wing hadn't fired on her.

She shrugged away her discomfort. A soldier made do with the resources on hand; Keize had taught her that. Yet there were hours to go before they arrived and she didn't care to spend them all dreading her companion's wrath.

"How are you?" Quell asked.

There was a lengthy pause. "Why?"

"You went through a lot on—" She still didn't know the name of the planet. "—your homeworld. I thought I'd ask."

Tensent or Lark would've handled it more gracefully. She hoped Kairos would respond better to bluntness.

Another lengthy pause. "I—" A sound like half-formed words came from the comm. "—am unchanged. I shed what remained of my chrysalis. I have accepted that I cannot return. But I am still not complete. I still do not know what I am."

Quell rubbed her bruised arms through her flight suit. She thought of the woman's agony as she'd hidden from her people and didn't know what to say. She hadn't really expected such an honest answer.

They were both silent then. Out of nervous habit, Quell ran another systems check and twisted her body to ensure that 4E could see her through the viewport; the droid flashed an indicator at her and she was satisfied.

She began to turn back to the console when she saw the silhouette of the U-wing against the bright hyperspace tunnel. The transport looked perfectly still, surrounded by the blue, and she could see none of its details—not the cockpit, or Kairos, or the crest of Alphabet Squadron. It was barely more than a black oval.

It's stupid, she thought as she turned back around. *She doesn't need to hear it.* But she spoke anyway.

"What if you *are* still healing?" Quell asked.

Kairos didn't answer.

"What if it's just . . . different? What if your ship is a kind of chrysalis, too?"

Quell let out a long breath when the words had left her. She'd tried her best.

"Perhaps," Kairos said.

II

Are you sure, Wyl Lark? Are you really sure?

He sat in one of the *Deliverance*'s private conference rooms, staring at the dead holoprojector where moments earlier an elder of Polyneus had spoken to him with such kindness that it made all the New Republic seem mechanistically brutal. Wyl hadn't told the elder his plans—those were his burden to carry—but he'd made his request and the elder had agreed to help.

Contacting Home had been a good and wise choice, Wyl believed. He was less certain of the goodness and wisdom of what he intended next.

Operation Cinder was over. Shadow Wing had fled. Wyl's A-wing, the only starfighter he'd flown since joining the Rebellion, was gone. He'd had time to think about all these things as he'd recovered in the medbay, and he held them in his mind now along with the words of Yrica Quell and Soran Keize.

Keize had sought to escape the war. He'd failed, but that didn't make him wrong.

Wyl didn't hurt as he stood and left the conference room. He felt tired—his sleep had been troubled lately—but otherwise strong, and his skin was whole and unbruised. The pain of his impact on the Chadawan moon had oppressed him for days; now it was almost forgotten, lingering only as a phantom. The recovery time had done him good, temporarily absolving him from responsibility to his squadrons and granting him perspective on what was truly happening. All the galaxy seemed different to him now, as if it had all been canted while viewed through the haze of adrenaline and violence.

There was another A-wing waiting for him in the hangar, delivered along with other fresh supplies. He'd looked at it from afar after saying goodbye to Quell and wondered if it had lost its pilot; it didn't look new. Sentimentality urged him to visit it now instead of continuing on his path, to befriend it, but it was only a hunk of metal.

Are you sure, Wyl Lark? It's not too late to change your mind.

He was sure.

There were a dozen pilots already in the ready room when he arrived: Nath and Chass, of course—he owed them his life a hundred times over and they deserved to be there; Essovin, Flare Leader, whose interactions with Wyl had always been about combat and little else; Denish Wraive, Wild Leader, the ancient figure who had flown with Wyl in the tunnels of Troithe; Boyvech Toons, the highest-ranking survivor of Hail Squadron, who'd fought along with Alphabet at Pandem Nai and Cerberon; and a smattering of pilots from all three squadrons who had taken the comm during the downtime at Chadawa, when they'd begun speaking to Shadow Wing like *people*. Vitale was among them, and sat closest to the front.

Wyl had asked General Syndulla to join, too, but he didn't see her. "Is the general—?" he began.

Vitale shook her head. "Said she had another conference, and to start without her."

"Right. Okay." Wyl hesitated before walking to the podium. He'd wanted Syndulla present—he'd considered meeting with her alone beforehand, even knowing she would've likely stopped him altogether—but it didn't change what he was about to do.

At the podium he turned and sat on the deck, placing himself level with the eyeline of the assembled pilots. They were his friends and comrades. Their voices quieted and they watched him, curious.

"This isn't a briefing," he said. "I don't have anything new to say about Jakku—the flight plan General Syndulla and Captain Tensent put together while I was recovering looks more than solid."

Now he had their attention. He felt as buoyant as he was nervous—almost as if he were back on Jiruus, celebrating the defeat of the Empire with Riot Squadron. Yet his underarms were damp. He drew in a breath but couldn't smell his own sweat over the rich odors of a dozen species: a blend of copper and cinnamon and millaflower.

"I won't be joining the attack," he said. "I'm not sure there should be an attack at all."

He'd expected a roar of protest. They only watched him and glanced sidelong at one another. Nath was scowling. Vitale's mouth was half open in a smile, as if at a joke she didn't really get.

"The Empire has fled across the galaxy to a desert world not even listed on most charts," he went on. "The sector's barely populated, and so far as we can tell the Imperials aren't doing any harm. They're not conquering new territory. They're not wiping out populations. Operation Cinder is finished. They're scared now, and they're entrenching, and they're trying to survive.

"If we go in, who are we helping? What are we doing other than killing people?"

"For one thing—" Boyvech Toons began.

"Shadow Wing remains a danger," Denish Wraive said.

Wyl waved a hand for silence. The pilots obliged, though he doubted it would last. He looked between faces as he sorted his thoughts. One-on-one he could've made himself clear to any of them, but as a group he wasn't sure he could meet their separate needs.

"Listen," he said. "I know they've done awful things. I know they could do awful things again. I know it as well or better than anyone here. But if now isn't the time to put our weapons aside and sue for peace, what is? We'll never kill every authoritarian zealot with a gun, or win over every Imperial hard-liner. At some point we've got to accept that we've *won already* and find a way to end the violence."

"Maybe that point is *after* we've dismantled the fleet of murderers and criminals," Vitale said. She was no longer smiling.

"Or maybe trying will only make it worse," Wyl said. His voice was soft but unwavering. "Think about when we talked to the 204th. Think about why they haven't given up already. We can't stop them all, we'll never stop them all, and by slaughtering as many as we can at Jakku we're going to persuade anyone else out there who survives—all the ex-stormtroopers on planets like Troithe and Coruscant—that the New Republic wants vengeance more than peace. We're going to breed martyrs."

Soran Keize is wrong. New Republic justice can be merciful. But we need to prove it. He thought the words but only Nath and Chass would've understood them.

Instead he put it as simply as he could: "We've saved as many lives as we can save, but the war ended a year ago. It's time to walk away."

The pilots waited for more. They respected him that much. But when he said nothing and the moments stretched out, they began to shift in their seats. Some opened their mouths to speak, yet they didn't say any more than Wyl had.

One by one, they began to stand. Vitale was the first to walk out of the briefing room, brushing past Wyl and murmuring, "I'm sorry," as her fingertips grazed his shoulder. Essovin went next, shaking her scaly head, and all of Flare Squadron followed. Some of the pilots met Wyl's gaze as they departed, while others took winding paths through the room to avoid him. Denish Wraive stood above Wyl awhile, brow furrowed in puzzlement and pity, before leaving with a pronounced sigh. Soon only two were left.

Wyl had never expected the speech to work. He couldn't help but be disappointed anyway.

Chass lingered at the doorway. Wyl tried to read her face and thought he saw frustration or disgust. Nath touched the Theelin's shoulder, urging her outside with a mutter Wyl couldn't hear. Then Wyl and Nath were alone.

"That was something," Nath said.

"I had to try."

Nath grunted and studied the closed door. When he faced Wyl again his expression had become a mask of compressed grief and fury. He crossed to Wyl in three long strides and hauled the smaller man to his feet, holding Wyl aloft for an instant then shoving him away. Wyl stumbled and rebalanced as Nath roared: "If you didn't want to fight here, why the hell didn't you go with Quell?"

Wyl attempted to answer, but Nath shook his head and smacked his palm against Wyl's chest, shoving him back. "You think the *Deliverance* is going to turn around? Find some nice world where we can drop you off before we hit Jakku? You *already* volunteered to risk your life in this battle! Fly or don't fly, you could still end up a dead man."

Nath was panting for breath. Wyl steadied himself before he could be shoved again. "I still have a place here," Wyl said. "I'm not doing this because I'm scared—I can help the ground crews, I can play a role without getting in anyone's way."

"Or firing a weapon," Nath said with a snort.

"Or firing a weapon," Wyl agreed. "Besides, maybe it's not too late for someone to listen."

He'd never *feared* Nath Tensent—never felt intimidated by him, even on Troithe when they'd shouted at each other over Wyl's desire to strike an agreement with Shadow Wing. But Nath's anger then had possessed a laser focus; there was a rawness to his ire now.

Wyl wondered if he was seeing the pirate in Nath: the man who'd extorted and blackmailed merchants. He didn't think so. He didn't know what aspect of the man stood before him.

Nath took another step and made a fist. Then he dropped the hand and swung around, pacing alongside the row of chairs at the front of the room. "We're done," he said, and half turned toward Wyl. "You and me? We're done. I'm not going to keep trying. I won't keep pulling your butt out of fires you started, and I won't point out the mistakes you're going to regret. You were part of the squadron, and I always figured keeping you alive would keep *me* alive, but now—" He shook his head violently. "No. I was blasted *generous* was what I was. You and I both know it. But we're done, and now I've got to clean up your mess one last time."

Wyl smiled—sadly, foolishly, not knowing what else to do—and the expression faded as swiftly as it had formed. "What do you mean, 'one last time'?" he asked, because what could he say to the rest?

"I mean two and a half squadrons' worth of pilots just got abandoned by their commander before the fight of their lives." Nath shook his head again and spat on the deck. "You think Syndulla's going to lead them out there? Maybe Chass? Nah. It's up to their damn medal-wearing hero to get any of us out alive. Who knows how . . . ?"

The rage had faded, replaced by bitterness. Wyl nodded carefully. "They couldn't ask for a better leader," he said.

He couldn't apologize. He was at peace with his decision.

"Get the hell out of my briefing room," Nath said, and Wyl left his mission and his friend behind.

III

The TIE shifted out of hyperspace with the stability of a Juggernaut riding rough terrain. Soran feared the docking ring would tear from his wings as it decelerated the fighter; the ring was an antique, meant to provide lightspeed capability to Clone Wars starfighters, and only the miracles wrought by the 204th's engineers had adapted it to a TIE chassis. The cargo pod under his cockpit worsened the shocks, moving his stabilizing center of mass beneath the TIE.

As he tried to breathe against the pressure on his chest, he nearly laughed thinking of Squadron Three: Wisp's pilots had used the docking rings a dozen times with nary a complaint. *Maybe,* he thought, *you've grown too comfortable as a colonel. Maybe you should've gone to the grand moff, tried to requisition a TIE scout because your stomach can't take a bump or two . . .*

The rays of stars compressed into specks and realspace fully enveloped him. Soran wrenched a toggle under his console and ejected the docking ring. This delivered one final jolt, and he was heaved forward as the ring tumbled away; then the fighter steadied and the engines' comforting scream rose over his buzzing instruments. For a moment he luxuriated in a dark and open sky, and the motes of planets and ships and satellites reminded him of quieter days.

He had arrived in the Coruscant system. There would be no time for reflection after this.

Soran swung his fighter toward the planet Coruscant itself. The vast iron orb gleamed with golden flecks, textured not by mountains and oceans but by the intricate geometry of urban districts. He'd visited Coruscant twice in his life, and both times been moved by its grandeur; it was no less impressive with its lights dimmer, its texture faded, as if the machinery of the planet had been tarnished. He transmitted security codes as marks blinked onto his scanner: dozens of Imperial vessels in an orbital blockade, invisible while backlit by Coruscant's glow.

His comm hissed with static and a woman's voice declared, "Colonel Soran Keize? Reduce speed, power down your weapons, and await docking clearance. You will come aboard the *Panaka* and justify your presence."

Soran checked the seal on his helmet and confirmed his oxygen supply was ample. He did not slow his fighter. "If I recall my history,

Moff Panaka was instrumental in breaking his homeworld's blockade, not preserving it." He brought a hand to his console and keyed a series of commands. "My mission is extremely urgent and I am required at the Imperial Palace. The orders come from Grand Moff Randd himself."

"You are *not* authorized to descend. We have received information suggesting you have been compromised." The woman paused. "I have respect for your accomplishments, Colonel. Do not force my hand."

You do make this difficult, he thought. But he'd killed so many Imperials over the past year—most less loyal than this woman, yet not without redeeming qualities. Madrighast had been among the hardest; though Madrighast he'd left to the New Republic.

"I am transmitting the coordinates of a city district adjacent to the Palace," Soran said. "You must evacuate that area immediately."

If he'd had another month—even a week—he might have taken a chance. He might have surrendered and attempted to persuade his captors that his cause was just; that, if nothing else, they had an obligation to prevent the Emperor's data bank from falling into New Republic hands, and that it would be wise to make arrangements in case of the foe's victory.

He didn't have a week. If Grand Moff Randd was correct, the battle at Jakku would begin presently. The New Republic, if victorious, would not pause before taking the capital as well.

A nearby cruiser spat emerald light while a more distant vessel disgorged TIEs. Soran arced away from the barrage and kept moving toward the planet. He watched his range indicator and counted down, waiting for the vessels in the blockade to close around him. He was confident in his plan, but there was no margin for error.

The TIE squadron approached—he noted its frayed formation with disapproval—and a *Reaper*-class attack lander made to intercept as well. Satisfied he would have no better opportunity, he thumbed a button and felt his vessel lurch as its cargo pod detached. Half a second later he sent a trigger code and scintillating light flooded the void behind him.

His scanner flickered. Marks doubled, then tripled before the display went dark. His comm pattered like rain as a swath of Coruscant's orbital space was flooded with radiation—Chadawan particles siphoned by Shadow Wing's engineers, stored in a modified warhead for later release.

The effect wouldn't last, nor would it disable whole ships as the Chadawan tides had, but it would grant Soran the advantage he needed. His pursuers fired wildly and he evaded at acute angles, minimizing his loss of velocity as he plunged toward the planet. Reinforcements would come and those, too, he could escape. If necessary, he would open fire.

His body felt weightless as the TIE dipped and soared. He allowed his mind to return to the words of the *Panaka*'s commander, and he mused over who might have warned Coruscant about his *compromised* nature.

He suspected he knew. He was not surprised. He wondered if she would come for him.

CHAPTER 20

UNVEILING OF THE TOOLS OF ORDEAL

I

Hera Syndulla stood in the center of an expanding fleet like a newborn universe. The bridge viewports showed flashes of light above and below and around the *Deliverance,* each a New Republic ship emerging from hyperspace. She'd last seen such a gathering at Endor, but the fleet was different now—alongside Mon Cala cruisers and civilian frigates loaded for battle were Destroyers like her own and sleek corvettes newly manufactured on Corellia and Rendili. Mightiest of all were the three *Starhawk*-class battleships—massive vessels whose birth she'd midwifed, with firepower and defenses to match anything short of a Death Star.

The flashing went on endlessly; every time the glimmers faded and the last ships seemed to have arrived, another battle group snapped into existence. At last, Hera tore herself from the view and moved to the bridge stations, gaze flickering from screen to screen as she called for ships to reposition and take formation. Behind her, Captain Arvad saw to the operations of the *Deliverance* itself—Hera rightly should have been in a combat center somewhere, but they'd agreed to this arrangement in deference to their peculiar assignment.

They were part of the fleet, but if the 204th made its move? Hera would be needed to take command.

A recorded transmission from Chancellor Mothma played, demanding the surrender of what remained of the Empire. Hera ignored it—she'd heard it before, during the long journey to Jakku—and continued relaying instructions to the vessels nearest the *Deliverance*. With the remainder of her attention she listened to Stornvein relay Admiral Ackbar's instructions to her.

The first time she'd been part of a fleet's command structure it had seemed a sort of profound chaos, and she'd left the battle with a pounding headache and the need for a day's worth of sleep. Now it was all almost rote. She could no longer count the number of battles she'd overseen, or the number of ships she'd lost or worlds she'd won. It had become too easy over the years; for her own sake, for the sake of her son who needed a mother with more than a keen tactical mind, this had to be the final battle.

One of the bridge crew swore loudly. Hera saw why before anyone could announce it.

The tactical display had been updated with sensor readings over Jakku. Swarms of scanner marks represented whole clusters of Star Destroyers. The TIEs were thick enough around the planet to resemble fog. Clusters of frigates and cruisers and gunships orbited the lone Super Star Destroyer.

These were only the forces the enemy had chosen to reveal—lurking in Jakku's atmosphere, hidden on the surface of the barren moons, would be additional vessels ready to ensnare unwary foes. Nor could Hera see the armies on the ground, or the cannon emplacements in the desert, or whatever secrets the Empire hid this time.

She realized that she'd never truly considered the possibility that the battle at Jakku might be lost. It didn't change her plans, but the weight on her shoulders became tangible.

"Bring us underneath group delta," she said, "and start combing those sensor readings for the *Yadeez*. If Shadow Wing's out there, they shouldn't be *too* hard to recognize."

Once, she'd been a rebel, and she'd grown comfortable with doubt and uncertain odds. She remembered her role and resolved to fight.

II

Chancellor Mothma's call for surrender played throughout the *Deliverance*. It was eloquent without being flowery, unconditional in its demand for peace, and compassionate in its offer of mercy. The chancellor delivered it well, and Wyl imagined she truly hoped the Empire would accept.

But he knew she believed the Empire *wouldn't* accept. She hadn't joined the fleet for the attack; that made her expectations clear enough.

He put Mothma out of his mind as he delivered his own plea into a headset in the comm room. "This is Wyl Lark to the 204th Imperial Fighter Wing," he began. "Please know that I am no longer with Alphabet Squadron."

Whether anyone would hear, he didn't dare guess. Syndulla's crew and New Republic Intelligence had spent months analyzing Shadow Wing's comm traffic, and their broadcast frequency was stored in the *Deliverance*'s computers. He couldn't listen to the unit or break their encryption or prevent them from shutting him out—but he could speak into the void and hope.

"This war is bigger than any of us. We can't stop the battle from happening. But I'm going to plead with you one last time to think about everything that's happened between us. Think about what happened in the Oridol Cluster and on Troithe and at Chadawa. Think about your dead and think about ours.

"I look back at it all and I'm not sure either of us ever *won* a battle. Even at Pandem Nai, my side almost destroyed a planet. For your part . . . hunting us down in Oridol is how Alphabet got started. You destroyed the *Lodestar* in Cerberon, but at what cost to yourselves?

"I can't stop the war, but I can stop killing you. You can turn away, too. It's not too late."

He knew as well as Chancellor Mothma what the odds were anyone would listen. But it was his last obligation to the New Republic.

He put the headset down and looked to the cramped room's only other occupant—a four-armed Morseerian who stared at a console screen, one hand nervously adjusting his respirator mask. "Is that all?" the man asked.

"Everything I need to send," Wyl said. "There's a smaller favor, too, but if it's too much . . . ?"

The man didn't reply. Wyl drew a breath and waited. He'd never spoken to the Morseerian before, but he had invited Wyl into the comm room and granted access without hesitation. Even when Wyl had warned the man that he wasn't authorized, the Morseerian had only said: "My brother was Lourgh T'oknell. He was one of your pilots, and you were kind to him."

Not kind enough, Wyl thought. T'oknell had died too early.

"Speak your favor," the man said now.

"Yrica Quell and Kairos—have we heard anything from them yet?"

"No. They should be in Coruscant soon. The signal may be delayed."

"When it comes in, can you patch it through to—" He hesitated and managed to smile. "—what's left of Alphabet? Chass na Chadic and Nath Tensent. If you can, if it's safe. I think they're better when they support each other."

"Yes," the man said, never looking away from his screen.

"Thank you," Wyl said, and left the comm room behind.

He wasn't more than a dozen meters down the corridor when the deck shivered and metal creaked. Wyl recognized the impact of an enemy particle volley mitigated by distance and shielding.

He began to run, heading toward the nearest damage control station.

His obligations to the New Republic were finished. But he wouldn't let his comrades die if he could help it.

III

"Wild Squadron ready."

"Flare Squadron ready."

"Alphabet Squadron ready," Nath said, "along with the bombers."

Chass's voice came through his comm. "Alphabet and Friends? Alphabet-Plus?"

Hail Six—Genni Avremif—laughed nervously. "You know we out-number you, right? Shouldn't it be 'Hail Squadron and Friends'?"

"Screw that," Chass said, and Nath barked a laugh. He wasn't look-ing forward to what was coming, but at least the company was tolera-ble.

Flare and Wild had already sped past Nath's Y-wing, Chass's B-wing, and the three Hail bombers sturdy enough for flight; the *Deliverance* trailed the bombers in turn. Capital ships on both sides had exchanged salvos, but fighter engagements were localized to the opposite side of the planet. That was about to change—Nath didn't need scanners to see the TIE swarm past the glowing thrusters of Flare and Wild, or the hulks of enemy warships blotting out the dusty sphere of Jakku.

Size and scope were hard to judge in space—even experienced pi-lots struggled with questions like "how far?" and "how many?" with-out sensor assistance. But Nath couldn't recall ever seeing masses of ships like he saw now; even civilian traffic at the Estaria orbital ports or the Commerce Guild worlds hadn't seemed so dense. Given T5's silence, he suspected the droid felt the same.

"Flights stay together, don't stray too far from the *Deliverance* until you're told," he said. He kept his tone easygoing, like it was just another battle. "Otherwise, dive right in and pick your targets. Have fun with it."

There was laughter in reply. Wild and Flare started betting on kill counts. That was good, Nath thought—he didn't doubt they were tak-ing it seriously, but they weren't showing their terror. They'd accepted him as their commander, too; the only thing left was flying.

(They'd accepted him as commander only because Wyl was gone, of course. But he squashed that thought like a gnat. The boy was done with fighting and Nath was done with him.)

"Wild Two, engaging now!" a voice called, and the comm was full of chatter as Flare and Wild disappeared into the field of flashing TIEs and ion trails and turbolaser lances. Nath glanced at his scanner, but there were so many marks it was hard to make sense of the scenario. Within seconds six fighters had flashed into nonexistence—two New Republic and four TIEs.

"Hell," he whispered. Then he checked his range and called to the bombers: "Gozanti cruiser, heading our way! We've got two minutes to gut and fry it as a gift for the *Deliverance*."

Nath pitched toward the cruiser and led the bombers into the fray. T5 was chattering and Chass na Chadic was snarling; Wild and Flare were shouting and trying to reconfigure after their initial losses. Emerald and crimson beams seemed to cage them into an arena; the barrages of the capital ships on all sides would incinerate any fighter that came close.

"Stay together!" Nath yelled. He glanced at the scanner, added, "Wild Five, get back to your squadron!" and forced his attention back to the Gozanti as T5 squealed a warning.

The cruiser was veering away. Behind it were two Raiders, better armed and armored than the Gozanti, and their weapons flared as they lashed at Alphabet and Hail. Nath froze for an instant, then dodged as a turbolaser blast burned toward him; called for the bombers to scatter and reposition at a distance.

Yet those orders meant nothing. Nath was riding chaos, jerking his Y-wing to evade energy blasts and firing at TIEs as they passed. He heard a Hail pilot and another Flare fighter declare they were badly damaged; saw a mark wink out that might have been someone from Wild. The enemy was doing no better—he saw burning TIE parts spiral past him and, in the distance over Jakku, the nova burst of a dying Star Destroyer—but that wasn't any comfort.

He could hear his strained breathing; feel the nausea in his guts and the sweat soaking his gloves. The harness bit at his chest and T5's squeals dug into his skull. "All fighters, follow me!" he snapped as he spotted a gap in the battle—a place to regroup without becoming a target. He wasn't stupid enough to think it would buy them more than seconds.

Plans didn't matter here. In this sort of battle, death or survival was a matter of luck.

He needed predictability, even of the worst sort.

"Where the hell is Shadow Wing?" he demanded.

IV

Chass watched the stars burn and poured fuel on the fire. The B-wing spun through the melee, hammering her as she rotated her foils and abruptly changed velocity, pushing the ship to perform in ways its designers would've blanched at. She sucked in air and unleashed every weapon she had—barely aiming, unworried whether she'd hit friend or foe because it was all random anyway. She smiled nastily as she heard Nath trying to coordinate the attack; trying to pretend this wasn't the end of the world.

A damaged TIE spun into view and she squeezed her trigger, feeling the pulse of her cannons through her seat. The enemy fighter lost one wing, then the other, then took a bolt in the center of its cockpit eye.

She wondered whether Wyl or Quell would've done any better at keeping the fight under control. *Probably not,* she decided, and realized with an unexpected flicker of emotion that she was half glad they weren't with Alphabet. This wasn't the kind of clash for brave rescues or clever plans, and she didn't care to watch the two of them blown to pieces, helpless and surprised.

Towers of destructive energy erupted on all sides of her B-wing. She couldn't see their source, didn't know if the particle fire came from allies or enemies. She wrenched her airfoil controls, folding in her outspread foils to convert the cross of the B-wing into a narrower line; then she slammed on her repulsors, holding her vessel immobile in space.

The galaxy was still and bright for a long moment. Her thoughts skipped across memory and dreams, and she wished she had music to distract her instead of the lectures of the Children of the Empty Sun. Prayer-chants weren't her answer today; Nath had picked away that scab, eliminating the last semblances of mystery and profundity Let'ij had possessed. Chass had never *believed*, but even feigning belief felt tainted now.

So what will you do, Maya Hallik?

The blazing towers fell away. Something exploded above her, violently enough to send burning gas smashing over her cockpit and set the B-wing tumbling. She spent seconds bringing it under control and re-extending her foils, and ended up alongside a Flare Squadron X-wing. She called her position into the comm.

You have the battle you always wanted. What is it you'll do?

She thought of the Battle of Endor, the Battle of Scarif, where the likes of Jyn Erso were carved into the granite of history. If the war was really ending, this was the finale she'd been waiting for—the one that had been stolen from her in the Oridol Cluster and at Pandem Nai. The one she'd given up any hope of achieving months ago.

Death was calling her name, offering *one last chance* to be a hero.

Nath was shouting orders again. By the sounds of it, some Flare pilot was about to smash into the *Deliverance*. She recalled his words to her with a bitter laugh: *Don't get yourself killed before the next mission is over. You owe me a replacement bomber pilot!*

"Screw it," she muttered. "Guess we're doing this."

She'd hoped committing to her mission would've brought more relief. But a blaze of glory wasn't painless, and Chass na Chadic had always had a spark of animal fear inside her.

V

The astromech was everything Ragnell had promised. 4E had filled her console with data before Yrica Quell had even blinked away the luminous spots in front of her eyes—the fading traces of hyperspace travel.

She remembered her earliest lessons and checked her immediate surroundings before reviewing the console data. She'd attempted to enter the Coruscant system far enough from the capital planet to avoid hitting its defensive perimeter, and appeared to have succeeded: She saw no spacecraft except Kairos's U-wing to her port side, and the world of Coruscant itself was a distant, glittering marble. When she looked to her scanner, several marks in planetary orbit blinked in and out of existence. *Maybe a miscalibration,* she thought, *or deflector distortion?*

Despite the garbled readings, the droid reported it had analyzed the trajectories of Imperial ships in Coruscant's blockade. A tactical map appeared on her screen.

"Quell to Kairos," she said. The comm hissed. 4E adjusted frequency and she tried again: "Quell to Kairos—are you reading?"

"Yes," the woman replied.

She kept her eyes on the map and saw the pattern. *The ships in the blockade are repositioning. Why?*

She gave her thrusters a kick, felt the X-wing glide through space, and let inertia carry her onward as she studied the data in front of her. "He's been here," she said. "They're compensating for a hole in the blockade—he must have outmaneuvered them somehow."

"Yes," Kairos said. "Have we come too late?"

"I don't think so. Not if they're still repositioning—"

She cut herself off, eyed her range to the blockade, and opened her throttle to maximum. The sudden acceleration bounced her helmet off her headrest and sent a flare of pain through her nose. (The medical droid aboard the *Deliverance* never had fixed the break.) "Follow me exactly," she said, "and keep up as well as you can. We can follow Keize's path but our window's closing fast."

The U-wing slipped behind the X-wing, unable to match the smaller fighter's speed. Quell tried to place herself in the minds of the blockade commanders yet found her attention drifting: She thought about

Jakku and Alphabet; about Keize, and whether she was wrong to try to stop him; about Kairos, who might still kill her; about Keize again, and whether she could stop him at all . . .

She needed to focus or she'd never reach the planet.

"If we manage this," she said, "we'll end up with at least a dozen TIEs on our tails after the blockade closes behind us. We'll be under fire the whole time we're chasing Keize."

"Yes," Kairos said. "They will encounter me before you."

She could've slowed to match the U-wing's speed. But that entailed other risks. "Yes," Quell agreed.

"I will inhibit them."

Kairos didn't sound like a woman preparing for a last stand. Quell wondered what she was capable of—what reserves she possessed that Quell remained unaware of.

She realized she'd never found out how Kairos had learned to fly.

"Understood," Quell said. "Atmosphere will cut their top speed anyway. Catch up when you can."

The planet swelled in her viewport, and she began to discern the geometry of the city. She'd expected something like Troithe, but Coruscant didn't look like Troithe at all—it looked like a machine, like Gavana Orbital, like a Death Star built for beings from a higher plane of existence. She realized, upon spotting a mass of clouds in the atmosphere, that she'd been holding her breath; she released it then, relieved that something ordinary tainted the planet's synthetic perfection.

"Are you set to transmit to the *Deliverance*?" Quell asked.

"Yes."

"Open the channel."

Syndulla and the others might never hear, Quell knew. If they were at Jakku already, they might not *survive* to hear, if the transmission was delayed. The Empire might jam them, or the hyperspace beacons could fail. But there was something bracing about proclaiming her intentions—about not going alone into near-certain death.

"This is Yrica Quell, approaching Coruscant blockade. Colonel Soran Keize has entered atmosphere and we are attempting to pursue. Will maintain this transmission as long as possible.

"Good luck on your end," she added. She paused and bit her lip. She pictured the faces of Tensent, Lark, and Chass na Chadic, and lied for her sake or for theirs. "See you after the war."

She hoped it was what her squadron needed and flew after her mentor.

CHAPTER 21

CONFESSIONS UNDER DURESS

I

There were too many voices.

"We've lost contact with the *Brightsaber*, General. Last transmission indicated—"

"Three battle groups converging on the Super Star Destroyer!"

"—bombers incoming. Our squadrons are not in position, repeat—"

"General? Admiral Ackbar still needs a path cleared for those infantry transports."

"Turn our flank, target the bombers with point defenses!"

The bridge of the *Deliverance* was in a state of bedlam, yet Hera Syndulla knew the madness was nothing compared with what was happening outside. She wanted to silence the crew and demand they deliver their updates one at a time; instead she attempted to sort and triage the crises.

Captain Arvad was coordinating the *Deliverance*'s defenses against the bombers, and Hera trusted Tensent to wrestle the squadrons into position. She checked the Super Star Destroyer's situation—it was well defended but under siege by the New Republic Starhawks—and decided her priority was the infantry.

Ackbar was correct about their vulnerability. The smaller U-wings could slip through Jakku's defenses to land, but the larger troop carriers would be torn to pieces before they reached atmosphere. They needed starfighter support, and no squadrons were available.

"The *Canny Bargain* is withdrawing—their shields are gone, they're patching a hull breach."

"One bomber down, but another's coming in—"

"The *Promise* just reported in. No sightings of Shadow Wing's bulk freighter."

The voices tugged at her, and she couldn't prevent a part of her mind from analyzing the overall state of the battle. She couldn't tell if they were winning or losing.

That's not your job. You're not running the fleet—do your part!

"Get me two corvettes on our flanks and tell the troop transports to stay close," Hera said, sharp and distinct. "Plot a course for Jakku— we'll swing in at an angle, the transports can descend, and we'll come out—" She gestured at the tactical map. "—there. Sector five-beta-beta. We can do some good from that position."

She answered questions: The squadrons could regroup with the *Deliverance* on its way back from Jakku; she didn't care which corvettes; no, she couldn't provide cover while the transports landed.

"General? We've lost contact with the *Serenade*—"

Hera felt a stomach-churning weightlessness as her feet rose off the deck. The sounds of rending metal and igniting oxygen filled her ears, muffled by bulkheads but thunderous nonetheless. When she crashed onto hands and knees and the bridge stopped shaking she wasn't sure whether they'd been hit *that* hard or if they'd momentarily lost artificial gravity.

"Enemy bomber!" someone shouted over the alarms.

Hera expected to hear Captain Arvad's reply, but Arvad was silent. She looked around and saw no structural damage, yet the crew had been flung from their stations and, like Hera, were scrambling to their feet. One form propped against a viewport didn't move, and Hera saw it was Arvad. Blood stained her scalp and streaked the transparent metal behind her.

"Get a medic!" Hera shouted, and turned to the weapons station. She called perfunctory orders and discovered they were largely unneeded. The enemy bombers were already under control; one had simply slipped through.

For a blessed instant the bridge chatter diminished. Hera caught her breath and felt the throbbing in her knees. She was ready to fear for Arvad—to take a fraction of a second to worry over the woman—when Dhina, the comscan officer, said, "No contact with the *Hunting Hound*."

"Don't tell me there's no contact," Hera snapped. She instantly regretted her impatience and switched to a gentler tone. "Get sensor confirmation, get a visual, let me know what it *means*. Okay?"

Dhina scrunched up the fur of her face. "Sorry, General. I tried—there's a lot of confusion, General."

Can't argue with that, Hera thought. She nodded and started to turn to the latest crisis—the *Deliverance* was en route with the troop transports now, and two Imperial gunships were moving to intercept—but she hesitated when she saw Dhina's screen. The sector she was scanning flipped between empty and chaotic, ghostly images flickering in and out.

She felt a chill and knew well enough to trust her instincts. "That's the last known position of the *Hunting Hound*?"

Dhina nodded as Hera continued: "What about the *Serenade,* and the—" *Which ship was it? The first one you mentioned?* There was too much happening, too many disasters to sort through.

"The *Brightsaber*," Dhina replied. She keyed her console and expanded the map. Three marks indicated last known locations of the *Brightsaber, Serenade,* and *Hunting Hound.* They weren't tightly clustered, instead arcing around the fringes of the battle.

The chill hadn't left her. "Were you talking to any of them?" Hera asked. "When they got cut off? Do you have audio?"

"The *Brightsaber*," Dhina repeated. "I can pull it up?"

A series of thunderclaps and another jolt to the bridge implied the pounding of a turbolaser barrage. The gunships were hitting them hard. She couldn't linger with Dhina much longer.

"Got it!" Dhina declared. She fumbled with a headset, nearly dropping it as she passed it to Hera. "Playing back now."

Hera listened to the exchange of coordinates and vectors between *Deliverance* and *Brightsaber*. There was no alarm in the *Brightsaber* officer's voice as the recording was flooded by static.

She wasn't sure whether her ears were more sensitive than those of humans—she'd suspected so, from time to time—let alone those of Cathars. She didn't blame Dhina for not recognizing the rainfall patter mixed into the static roar.

"It's them," Hera said, and threw down the headset. "Get me Captain Tensent. Relay what I tell him to Admiral Ackbar." She looked to Arvad's executive officer, who'd stepped into the captain's position and was visibly sweating as he maneuvered the battleship past the gunships and sheltered the troop transports. Hera would relieve him in a moment.

"What've you got, General?" Nath's voice called, as terse and strained as anyone's.

"I've got Shadow Wing," she answered. She signaled to Stornvein who signaled other officers present, ensuring they paid attention. "I don't know how, but they're reproducing the particle effects we saw at Chadawa. They're using the radiation to hide from scanners and sever our ships' communications. After they blind and deafen a target, we can assume they hit hard and fast; we've already lost three heavy cruisers."

"Carrying the fog of war with them," Nath replied. "Smart. Sounds like Shadow Wing. Where are they?"

"Transmitting last suspected coordinates. My guess is if you continue around that arc you'll find them. Be ready to enter a dead zone, and the second you lose comms—"

"—switch to the open channel and boost comm power, like at Chadawa. Going without encryption in a fight like this, though . . ."

"It'll make things interesting," Hera agreed. "But if you get close, you'll hear them, too. Head their way, and we'll follow shortly."

Nath signed off. The bridge rocked again, and Hera grabbed Dhina's shoulder while Dhina grabbed her arm. They kept their balance together as sparks rained and alarms sounded, and Hera mentally amended her last message: *We'll follow as soon as we can.*

Shadow Wing would be happy to wait for one last shot at her and her people. She only worried what they would do in the meantime.

II

"All fighters, follow me and slow for nothing. The 204th wants to play assassin? We'll see how they handle a straight-up fight."

It was a stupid thing to say, Nath knew. The answer to "How does the 204th handle a straight-up fight?" was "Extremely well, thank you." But his pilots were scared and scattered and more than a few were dead. Some bluster might not be the worst play.

The route to Shadow Wing wouldn't take the squadrons through the worst of the fighting, but they'd need more than a minute to traverse the inferno Jakku had become. The remains of Flare, Wild, and Hail spread behind Nath's Y-wing, and the faster fighters gradually overtook him as they crossed the battlefield. The gleaming hulls of warships formed an undulating ground and sky, and bursts of particle fire burned through space like geysers of death. Nath attempted to give a wide berth to the other fighter melees they encountered but still had to dodge the occasional burning X-wing or spew cannon bolts to clear a path.

His pilots kept talking but he tuned them out. His muscles hurt. He was too blasted *tense* and it meant every time he swerved away from disaster he was exerting himself needlessly. He could taste sweat dripping from his brow onto his lips, and his jaw ached from clenching.

"We'll get there soon," he muttered, only half to T5. "We're going to find the 204th and it'll be just like old times."

They might still die, but being locked in combat with a foe he *knew* meant they'd die because they failed, die because they weren't good enough—not be incinerated in the cross fire between a Starhawk and a Star Destroyer. Nath had always controlled his own destiny, and he didn't plan to stop now.

He was emerging from a whirling tunnel of gunships, crossing into a magnificently empty gap in space, when his comm began to hiss. "Think we're getting close," he called. "Get ready to switch to the open channel!"

"See you after the war," Yrica Quell replied.

She sounded like a ghost, and he shook his head briskly to clear it. "The hell was that?" he asked, and T5 beeped and reassured him he hadn't imagined the voice—that the transmission had been relayed from the *Deliverance,* faint and barely decipherable and sent who-knew-when. Nath laughed and thought of Quell fighting alongside Kairos against a planet full of Imperials. He wasn't sure if he'd swap places, given the opportunity.

"Tell her she's getting soft," he said. He almost added more but spotted fire in the dark and swung his Y-wing toward the light.

An MC30c frigate was being consumed by a constricting serpent of blue flame. TIE fighters danced over its dying body. Nath didn't know this particular frigate's assignment, but he'd heard the vessels could hold their own against Star Destroyers. This one wouldn't have a chance.

He eyed his scanner and saw both solid marks and flickering after-images. He guessed he was on the edge of the dead zone established by the 204th, and he leaned into his harness as he scanned the void for the *Yadeez*. If the TIEs were Shadow Wing fighters, the unit's carrier ship couldn't have gone far.

Unless Shadow Wing had transferred to a *real* capital ship upon reuniting with the fleet. Found a new Star Destroyer, or—

There you are.

It was keeping its distance from the fighting but it was still visible, below the equatorial ring of the battle loosely encircling Jakku. Nath wouldn't have spotted it except for the faint, glittering trail it left; he recalled the scintillations of the Chadawan rings and could only assume there was a connection.

"Found our target!" he said. "Bombers, head for the *Yadeez*. Fighters, keep us safe! Don't engage the TIEs unless you have to."

Taking out the *Yadeez* would leave Shadow Wing without leadership. It would, if Nath was right, disrupt their fog of war. Most important, it was safer than engaging the fighters directly.

The static became overpowering. He wasn't sure if his message had gotten through, and he flashed his thrusters as he took the Y-wing toward the bulk freighter. The fighters around him seemed to understand and adjusted formation as they turned toward the new foe.

As acceleration pressed on his chest and the Y-wing shuddered, he switched to the open channel. Nath heard nothing other than hissing, but that wasn't alarming; Shadow Wing had always been disciplined when it came to chatter.

See you after the war. Quell's voice echoed in his brain. He laughed bitterly and thought about Wyl back aboard the *Deliverance*—probably holding on for his life as the Star Destroyer was pummeled, dragging casualties to the medbay if Syndulla hadn't tossed him in the brig. The kid had always wanted Alphabet to be heroes—had wanted *Nath* to be a hero, to the point where Nath almost martyring himself above Troithe hadn't been good enough. When Nath had finally met the standard at Chadawa, Wyl had gone and changed the rules of the game.

You wanted heroes, and now you're stuck with them, he thought.

The burning MC30c turned dazzlingly bright and burst like a nova—a reactor breach, Nath assumed. Waves of flaming gas roiled through space, and the TIEs rode the shock wave without damage. They headed toward Nath and the squadrons now, which meant time was running short; he'd hoped for a few more seconds before they'd noticed the attack.

He thumbed the comm and spoke over the open channel. "No point hiding. Let's make it a good fight, huh?" His thoughts danced from

Quell to Wyl to Chass, and instinct kept him talking. "Hey, Chass! How many go-rounds has it been now?"

There was a pause before she replied: "Enough they ought to be scared. They know what we can do."

He smiled at her voice—the sound of a smirk wrapped in fury. "Damn right."

Chass had always been a mess, and maybe she *had* almost gotten him killed abandoning Chadawa to chase Quell. Still, Alphabet was his squadron now—he hadn't asked for it, but it was his—and she'd come willingly. He owed her more than anyone else flying.

"You hear that call earlier?" Chass asked. "Real cocky, thinking she can advise us half a galaxy away."

"Woman always had her blind spots—" Nath began, but another voice broke in.

"Chass na Chadic. You're in the B-wing, aren't you?"

The speaker's accent was working-class, from somewhere in the Core Worlds. "We were having a conversation," Nath said.

"You knew what you were doing," the man answered. "Which one are you? Denish wouldn't mention names at Chadawa, but I—"

"Mervais Gandor, my good friend!" Denish Wraive cut in. Nath wondered what the ancient Wild Squadron leader was up to. "Pity we didn't finish our song before. Pity we won't have the chance now."

Another unfamiliar voice broke in; another Shadow Wing pilot. "You all should've stayed home, like your buddy Wyl."

"How'd you hear about that?" Nath shouldn't have taken the bait, but it raised too many questions to ignore. He suddenly remembered General Syndulla's concerns about a spy aboard the *Deliverance*.

"Sent us a message before the fighting started," the second pilot said. "The colonel already beat him once, but honestly I'll kind of miss the guy. Won't be the same without him chiming in."

"Maybe he was holding us back," Chass said, and other voices—New Republic and Shadow Wing—joined the chatter. Nath was surprised to realize that beneath the enemies' mockery was strain and giddiness—the same he heard in his people.

They'd been wanting this fight. Not just because they wanted Alphabet and everyone associated dead (though Nath didn't doubt that remained true) but because they also needed something familiar in the chaos of Jakku.

"You missed us, didn't you?" he asked, and grinned as he sped for the *Yadeez*.

III

She killed her first Shadow Wing pilot as he spoke over the comm, saying something about escape pods and Cerberon and some buddy of his who'd fried in-atmosphere. Chass hadn't known it was the man yammering on when she'd taken the shot, but the TIE had come careening into her field of fire—probably damaged from some earlier fight, given how it tilted—and she'd squeezed her trigger and shredded his port wing, heard his transmission cut off; watched him try to regain control and then explode bright enough to light her cockpit.

She didn't feel pity. This was a day for endings, and the comfort of the familiar—familiar friends, familiar enemies—wasn't a comfort worth clinging to.

"See you after the war." Really, Quell? You had to get in the last word?

Shadow Wing understood this was an ending as well as she did. The TIEs fought with the same tactics as always, surrounding the *Yadeez* in a spiral formation that swept aside the waves of New Republic attackers. But there was an aggressiveness and desperation to their maneuvers—they killed Denish Wraive and one of the Flare pilots (she wasn't sure who) in short order, but they were also bleeding worse than she'd seen since Pandem Nai. She thought she saw the Twins, who'd plagued them since the Oridol Cluster, shot down together by a Wild pilot who was dead seconds later.

Or maybe it was the Chadawan radiation as much as desperation that was killing them. Chass's B-wing hadn't shut down but her gyroscopics were sluggish and her console didn't bother showing her shield status. (She *thought* her deflectors were up but she wouldn't know for sure until it really mattered.)

"See you after the war." You should've just let us focus.

She could see the bulk freighter clearly now. The vessel had always been ugly, bristling with weapons and sensors glued on by the 204th, but now two massive nacelles spewed shimmering fog like smoke-stacks: the radiation that blinded sensors and muted comms.

She started to load a torpedo, then hesitated. She vaguely recalled someone talking about warheads exploding aboard Y-wings in the worst of the Chadawan particle tides; she was ready to go but not *that* way. She flung her ship to one side as a TIE rocketed around her and she keyed in a sequence, readying the torpedo for launch but not yet arming the warhead.

Someone was screaming about all the worlds destroyed by Cinder. Chass shut the voice out but found herself thinking of Wyl and Kairos and Quell, and that wasn't helpful at all.

"We're going to mess you up," she called into the comm. "You're going to die, and everyone here is going to be *gone,* and I guarantee in a few years? They're not going to remember what the *Empire* did at this battle."

It was all swagger, but it kept her mind off her friends. She'd bitten into the pill. Now she just had to swallow it.

IV

Wyl Lark gripped the blast door override until his arm was shudder-ing, watching half a dozen gunners stumble out of the smoke. They stank of acrid chemicals and melting lead, and when one threw him a hand signal he released the lever; it snapped into position and the door closed with a mechanical wheeze. The gunners coughed and staggered down the corridor without a backward glance.

He wasn't sure how long the *Deliverance* had been under fire; he didn't know where the ship was or the state of the battle. He'd been on the move for what felt like hours, ricocheting from trouble to trouble, spraying sealant on sparking conduits and escorting injured crew to the medbay—nothing a droid couldn't have done, but there weren't enough droids to go around. He was sweating profusely and his soles hurt, yet he wasn't tired so much as light-headed. Maybe it was the toxins he'd breathed; maybe it was a sense of purpose.

He was certain of the things he did. It had been a long while.

He left the burning gunnery station at a jog to head to the navigational deflector—someone had called a fire control team to the power chamber earlier, and while the *Deliverance* was holding together it was accruing damage faster than it could be repaired. He'd find a way to help.

As he went, he passed viewports and glimpsed cannon fire and TIE fighters and troop carriers against a background of carnage. He paused more than once, and every time his spirit sank, his body shook, and he considered racing to the hangar. Each explosion was a death; each wrecked fighter could've been a friend; he could've joined his comrades, tried to protect them, but that wasn't his role. He'd already done more than they knew, and his actions might yet make a difference.

He'd stifled his doubts by the time he was dashing through the reactor tunnel leading to the Destroyer's bow. Subgenerators on either side shivered and clanged, and he felt the hum of the deflectors in his teeth. If he'd still been preoccupied, he might not have noticed the woman sandwiched into a maintenance alcove, squatting in the shallow pit leading to the crawl space under the deck. As it was, he was three meters past when his mind registered her, and he nearly fell as he pivoted and retraced his steps.

"You all right? You need a hand?" he called as he caught his breath. No one should've been in the reactor tunnel alone—if a problem there was critical enough to be worth attention, it was critical enough to deserve a full engineering team.

The woman looked up from the pit and past the tool bag balanced on the deck's edge. Wyl recognized her as one of the recruits they'd picked up before leaving Cerberon—a ground crew member assigned to Hail with a shock of orange hair and a medical vocabulator. He couldn't recall her name; she'd always kept to herself and they'd never been introduced.

"Fine," she said. "Finishing up."

Her expression was resolved and fearless and hard. There was something discomfiting about her voice, like her words had come from someone else entirely. Wyl found himself second-guessing his own reaction, though, wondering if it was simply the strangeness of the electronic vocabulator.

"You're sure?" he asked, and it was a stall. His eyes swept around the tunnel, flickered from the pit to the tool bag. In a moment he'd leave; in a moment he'd forget the strange encounter; but not without giving the universe a chance to prove his instincts right.

He wasn't prepared when the woman launched herself over the edge of the pit, past the tool bag, and somersaulted toward him. He was shifting his balance when she swung an arm around and smashed something narrow and metallic—maybe a socket spanner or an arc wrench—into the back of his heels. He toppled backward, feet in the air, and his skull hit the deck.

The woman scuttled above him, though he saw only a hazy silhouette. Pain spiked from the back of his head into his eyes. She raised her hand and brought the tool down like a knife. He twisted his body, avoided the blow; twisted a second and third and fourth time as she wielded her improvised weapon with the expertise of a murderous artisan.

He thrust his body upward with all the strength he could muster, trying to throw the woman off. If she'd been a kilogram heavier the move might've failed—he was unsteady and still half blind—but she stumbled backward into an upright position. Wyl staggered to his feet and tried to see her face.

"I don't understand," he said. It was stupid, but it was honest.

"You don't know me, do you, Wyl Lark?" she asked.

Once again, the voice felt displaced. He recalled the rattle of his A-wing's cockpit; a resonance of hope mixed with uncertainty and fear.

"My name," she said, "is Lieutenant Palal Seedia, of the 204th Imperial Fighter Wing."

He stopped trying to see her face. He imagined the buzz of the medical vocabulator interwoven with the static of a comm call.

"You and your friends?" Palal sneered. "You called me Blink."

I don't understand, he wanted to say again. But it would've been a lie.

V

She could hear them fighting.

Real cocky, thinking she can advise us half a galaxy away.

Woman always had her blind spots—

The voices of Alphabet Squadron came through Yrica Quell's cockpit speaker, tinny and indecipherable except for garbled fragments. She wasn't sure she was supposed to be receiving, wasn't sure the pilots even knew; maybe someone had routed the comms incorrectly. She wasn't sure if the distortion came from Coruscant, Jakku, or the hyperspace relays in between. But hearing Nath Tensent and Chass na Chadic left her smiling tightly as her X-wing struck atmosphere and her deflectors shucked heat. She heard cannon fire overhead and hoped the sounds were drowning out Wyl Lark's voice, explaining why she couldn't hear him alongside the others.

Tell her she's getting soft, Tensent had declared earlier. Maybe he was right. She couldn't afford distractions.

"Kairos?" she asked. "What's your status?"

"I am well," Kairos answered. "Go."

Quell checked her scanner. The ghost images were beginning to fade, and if she read the flickering marks correctly Kairos was a kilometer behind, swarmed by half a dozen TIEs. She wanted to urge the woman: *Be careful.* But Kairos couldn't afford distractions, either.

Wisps of light rose from the unseen city, soaking through layers of clouds to create the illusion of luminescent foam. Wind roared louder than her engines and Quell applied her repulsors to reduce her entry speed, uncertain how soon she'd need to pull up to avoid colliding with Coruscant's towers.

She saw no sign of planetary defenses or TIE patrols. Her sensors picked up nearby satellites, but if they were armed they didn't fire on her. Unless Coruscant's fortifications were in worse condition than she'd expected, it was entirely possible Soran Keize had cleared her path—she imagined she was still following his course toward the Imperial Palace.

What would she find when she caught up? A cluster of enemies tearing Keize to pieces, completing her mission for her?

Her comm gibbered static. Now and then she thought she could make out a word, though it could've been her imagination.

"Quell to *Deliverance*," she said. "Keize is not on scanners. Proceeding through cloud cover and beginning search."

She wondered if she should have said something more intimate; more encouraging. Then the fog lifted from her cockpit as if someone had ripped away a tarp and she saw the city stretched before her. Towers like mesas rose from an abyss cluttered with skywalks and trams; needlelike luxury buildings stood atop domes; metal platforms extended from central hubs, broad enough to carry whole city blocks but somehow suspended over the city's lower levels.

No, she corrected herself—*not the lower levels.* She was seeing the surface of the city, but below were thousands of occupied layers. The structures went on endlessly, largely dark except for a frosting of illumination, and here and there a black chasm gouged the city and hinted at chthonic depths.

It was wondrous. She'd seen holos of it before, but she'd never understood Coruscant's beauty or its weight. She realized instinctively why the New Republic had left it to the Empire all these months; a single stray bomb or turbolaser blast might kill millions.

Would Keize kill so many? She wanted to deny it, yet it would be a rounding error in the tally they'd murdered together.

She skimmed above the towers and saw few signs of inhabitation. The city was locked down as Troithe had been, its trillions of residents hidden and its skyways free of cloud cars and speeders. She adjusted her comm, scanning frequencies for any sign of her quarry or an emergency broadcast. She picked up nothing on the public channels except for a weather report and an offer of rewards for information on rebel cells. The encrypted frequencies would have news from the blockade, she was sure, but she had no way to access them.

She checked her console and reconfirmed the coordinates of the Emperor's data bank. Even slowed by atmospheric flight she wasn't more than a few minutes away. She altered course and adjusted her comm yet again, tapping in the 204th's transmission codes.

"This is Yrica Quell to Colonel Keize," she said. Her voice was steadier than she'd expected. "Do you read me?"

There was no answer. She repeated the message, then: "I'm on my way."

The cityscape transformed as towers blurred beneath her fighter. Bright domes and arches flattened, becoming stark metallic cubes; the organic growth of skyscrapers turned from a jungle to a well-pruned garden. Coruscant had been remade by Emperor Palpatine, and she was entering the heart of Imperial power. She dropped one hundred, two hundred meters, bringing herself below the tops of the taller structures—she couldn't believe the Imperial Palace lacked aerial defenses, and the buildings would help hide her from scanners.

She glanced above her, searching the clouds for flashes of cannon fire. She saw nothing.

Kairos doesn't matter, she reminded herself. *Chadic and Lark and Tensent don't matter. None of it affects you and Keize.*

"Foree?" she said. "Make sure I hear if any messages come in from the *Deliverance.*"

The droid chimed in acknowledgment. She kept her comm tuned to Shadow Wing's frequency and flew on.

She was, according to the maps she'd reviewed in hyperspace, in the Federal District—a rough circle with the Imperial Palace at its center. The Verity District, where the bulk of the data bank was housed, was on the opposite side of the palace from her present position, radiating into commercial and residential areas of the city. She curved away from the Palace proper, down a broad skyway serving government spaceports, then dipped lower into a narrow gap with support struts above and energy conduits below.

There was little room to maneuver, but Troithe had trained her for that and she was confident there were gun emplacements ready to blast her if she stayed in the open. With strike foils closed her X-wing slid easily through narrow spaces. Twice, she had to spin so that she was perpendicular to the planet's surface; she grunted in displeasure each time, remembering why she preferred spaceflight over atmospheric exercises. She skipped over a pedestrian bridge and under a docking ring, and soared skyward when the gap ended abruptly at the façade of an embassy.

As she ascended, her scanner blinked and three TIE strikers swept out from surrounding skyways. She wasn't sure if they'd been stalking her or whether they'd only now arrived; it hardly mattered, and she cut power to drop rapidly as streams of emerald fire crossed above.

She heard the TIEs' ion engines scream as she slapped at her console, trying to spread her foils while she determined where to head for cover. She accelerated again, hoping to build enough distance to give herself options.

Then a fourth engine joined the chorus and she saw a flash overhead, felt the shock wave as one of the strikers died. She rode the blast of burning air as her strike foils locked; she was nearly incinerated by three more volleys—precise, clipped barrages that destroyed a second striker attempting to drop toward her position.

She recognized the newcomer's maneuvering and firing style without needing to see his craft. She understood that he wasn't *rescuing* her, no matter if he'd saved her life; he'd known she was coming and used her as bait to draw out his enemies, then eliminated two in a matter of seconds.

She had found her mentor—and with him, a reminder that Soran Keize, ace of aces, had always been a better pilot than Yrica Quell.

"Lieutenant," he said. "It's a privilege to see you, as always."

CHAPTER 22

THE ENDLESS NIGHT

I

"How are you here?" Wyl asked. It was all he could think of as his vision cleared and his eyes refocused on the woman who'd called herself Palal Seedia. The woman who'd called herself Blink.

"Same as you," Palal said. She twirled an arc wrench in her right hand, then transferred it to her left as she shifted her footing with the grace of a duelist. Half a meter behind her lay her tool bag, still teetering at the edge of the deck plating and creeping toward the maintenance pit every time the *Deliverance* shook. "My father spent several intimate minutes with my mother, and drowned neither me nor my sister when we were born."

"How are you *here*?" Wyl repeated. "What happened to you? What—"

He tried to remember what he knew—*actually* knew, not what he'd fantasized—about Blink. She had spoken to him in the Oridol Cluster when he'd first reached out to Shadow Wing—spoken to him and seemed receptive to his outreach until she'd threatened him with death.

After that, after Pandem Nai, he'd spent weeks writing and recording messages to Blink. He'd never sent those messages, and hadn't heard from the pilot until Blink had warned him about the Cerberon attack.

"They caught you, didn't they?" he said. "Shadow Wing caught you warning us over Troithe, and you escaped and found your way to us."

All the pieces fit but one: If she'd really betrayed her unit, what was she doing now? Wyl clung to the thought until he saw her face twist into a vision of bewilderment and scorn.

"You *idiot*. Simpleton! I sent the message at Cerberon to distract you. To divert your attention from—" She shook her head. "I'm not revisiting this now."

"I don't believe you," he said.

She looked torn between frustration and self-righteous fury. She straightened her back, shifting from a combat stance to something prouder. "I hunted Chass na Chadic on Catadra. I infiltrated your ship when the *Deliverance* came recruiting. I sent *messages* to the 204th warning them of your actions." She sounded smug—or made an effort at sounding smug—as she added: "Whatever my failures, I take credit for every death the sabotage droids caused. Does that explain things, Wyl Lark?"

There had been only two deaths, Wyl recalled. One of the engineers and the captain of the *Deliverance*.

"You didn't have to do it," he said. He'd meant to sound placating, but it came out a whispered plea. "You could've just . . . joined us, and no one would've known."

Somehow her rage grew. "I have a duty to fulfill. I have—of course you don't understand. You *abandoned* your colleagues because you found violence distasteful, and that selfish instinct is going to get them killed. All of them. You're going to lose."

She swung her left arm and let go of the arc wrench, sending it whirling through the air with enough force to crack open his skull. He barely flinched in time, and it bounced off his shoulder and rang off the deck behind him. The pain sent an electric buzz all the way to his fingers.

She was diving for the tool bag. Wyl glimpsed vibro-cutters and plasma torches, and among them something wrapped in wires and switches. He wasn't sure what she wanted but he tackled her anyway; they hit the deck together and rolled as one, each trying to get leverage over the other.

Palal tried to slam him against the bulkhead with a palm above his nose. When he resisted, her fingers slid to his eyes. He cried out as she skimmed his corneas with blunt nails but caught her wrist, forced it back a centimeter, and tried to think of what to do next. In all his life, Wyl had fought hand-to-hand—*really* fought—only once before.

Shaking, he brought his free hand to the woman's throat and closed it over warm skin and her vocabulator's cold metal. It felt like the start of a murder.

Then Palal's free hand boxed his ear and he rolled away. She was up and kicking a second later, driving a metal-toed boot into his ribs and then, as he tried to bring his knees to his chest, slamming her foot down on his head. The pain was excruciating, radiating into his brain and nose and the back of his skull; he feared he would black out, and he distantly heard his foe's electronically modulated voice say: "They had names! Not 'Puke' and 'Snapper'! Hirodin Nasli. Garl Lykan. Say the names of the people you killed!"

The deck bucked beneath them and the *Deliverance* thundered. The whine of the reactors diverting energy to the shields drowned out Palal's speech; she stumbled back and Wyl pulled himself upright, leaned against the bulkhead for support. He raised his hands, trying to protect himself from the flurry of punches that followed—he could see the woman mouthing name after name, and he wondered how he could've ever killed so many people.

She was a madwoman. She was his enemy. She was scared and mourning her friends.

She was Blink.

It didn't matter. He had to survive.

He knew in his heart what she'd been doing—knew what the bundle of wires and switches meant. If he didn't stop her, she would blow up the *Deliverance* and no one aboard would survive. His friends in their starfighters would be left without support. He had to act. He had to *fight back*.

He threw himself into her and fate was with him—the *Deliverance* rocked again, redoubling his force. They smashed into the bulkhead, and though Palal shoved him away she left a bloody sunburst centered on a protruding metal bolt where the back of her scalp had struck the metal. Wyl wobbled and tried to find his footing; she stared at him then swept up the tool bag and dashed down the corridor faster than he could track.

He chased her, bent forward and reliant on momentum to keep upright. Palal fumbled with the tool bag, sending hardware clattering onto the deck as she freed the wire bundle. Wyl tried to focus on her head, to guide himself by it, and saw her hair was badly askew—it was a wig, concealing a shaven scalp marred by a mess of red dripping down her neck into her work suit.

She stumbled badly; he gained a step or two. He wondered how deep the bolt in the wall had penetrated—through bone or even into brain. When she stopped abruptly he didn't think to halt and ran directly into a whirling kick that stole his breath and sent him flailing backward.

They'd reached the end of the reactor tunnel. Behind Palal was a sealed emergency hatch; somewhere during the run they'd passed the ladder leading to the deck above. Palal held the bundle—the bomb—in both hands. "Kalvan Oliq," she said. The vocabulator whined, as if it had been damaged at some point in the fighting. "Kharulu Neen. Perush-anon Seedia."

"I don't—" He tasted blood in his mouth and swallowed. "I don't know who they are."

"Victims of your Rebellion," she said. "Who the hell else?"

He almost laughed. Instead he shook his head very slowly. "Walk away from all this. There's no point to it."

"The point is revenge," she said. "The point is honor. You don't—I'm not *Blink*. I'm Palal Seedia, my father's heir, and you don't know a thing about me. You never will."

You could tell me, Wyl thought. As he watched her, though, he believed she was right.

He'd known nothing about Blink.

"Put the bomb down," he said, endeavoring to sound calm instead of afraid.

Palal turned the bundle over, her fingers caressing the switches. "I was going to hook it up to the subgenerators. Steal a shuttle and go home. But I always knew how my mission might end."

He pictured leaping at her again. He'd only fall flat on the deck. But maybe the *Deliverance* would shake again; maybe she'd drop the bomb if he bought more time. "This isn't how it ends—"

"They likely assume I'm dead. I'll be forgotten soon, with everything I've done. I can accept that." The vocabulator spat static and Palal's mouth kept moving; Wyl tried to read her lips but he couldn't, and she began laughing silently, hysterically, at her own inability to communicate or at Wyl's desperation to comprehend.

She stopped at last. The *Deliverance* was steady, though Wyl could hear the distant pounding of cannon fire.

"The Empire will never stop fighting," Palal Seedia said, and this time the words were clear as rain.

She flipped a switch on the bundle of wires. Wyl ran for the ladder as the world became noise, fire, and death.

▌▌

"Not that easy, is it?" someone said, and Chass na Chadic swore at the comm as the bombers aborted their attack.

Nath's Y-wing was the first to turn, thrusters bright as he veered up and away from the *Yadeez*. The surviving Hail pilots (they were down to two) followed, and Chass lingered at the rear. If she pushed—if she armed all her warheads, opened her throttle, and unleashed everything at close range—she'd tear a hole through the bulk freighter and never have to hear Shadow Wing's stupid voices again.

But she'd never make it.

"Next time 'round," she muttered as a column of TIEs wove past Flare and Wild and spat fire toward her. Her thrusters failed to respond as she tried to swing away; she'd gotten too close to the freighter's radioactive particle cloud. Three TIEs—one incongruously patched with black armor, another with a single cannon apparently salvaged from a larger craft—approached, and only an X-wing's intervention kept her from dying.

Her thrusters flared at last and she chased after Nath and Hail. With her scanner blinded, she couldn't see what happened to the Flare pilot who'd saved her.

Vitale was laughing over the open channel. *"Who?"* she called. "Got a nephew on Corellia, but maybe I'll settle for my sisters in the Sixty-First."

Chass ignored the woman's babble and swiveled her head, trying to see if she was being pursued. If a TIE found her blind spot she was doomed.

"Who?" one of the Shadow Wing pilots said. "The Arakein Monks. Word is they'll put anyone's name in their Book of the Dead, and they remember forever."

The Y-wings continued turning, beginning a wide loop that would take them up and around for another pass at the *Yadeez*. Chass could see the dull green of Nath's astromech in its socket as his ship pitched back. She kept following. No one shot her.

"Shut up, both of you," another voice said. New Republic or Imperial, Chass wasn't sure.

The bombers reached the apex of their loop. Chass could see the globe of Jakku and the bands of chaos around it. A cluster of warships spilled molten guts from their wounds and from among them emerged the wedge of a Star Destroyer—the *Deliverance*, Chass realized, as the New Republic markings on its flanks came into view. It was headed their way at good speed; maybe even in time to be useful.

"*What?*" Vitale said. "Pry bar upside the head, twelve years from now when some politico—"

Chass muted the open channel as the Y-wings dipped back toward the melee between Flare, Wild, and Shadow Wing. She tried to count the New Republic fighters and failed, but they sure didn't seem as many as they'd been a few minutes earlier. Shadow Wing didn't seem to have the same problem; she'd seen TIEs go down but it made no difference to the swarm.

She was hoping for a clear shot when a light caught her attention. She looked above her toward the *Deliverance* and saw a burning pit on the underside of its hull—an ugly wound but not a fatal one if the engineers could contain the fire.

Then a hundred meters toward the engines flame erupted from a second crater; a third and fourth explosion followed, as if a fuse were burning down to the main reactor.

Chass stared until particle bolts ripped off half her primary airfoil. She snarled and squeezed her firing trigger and let her weapons (the ones that still worked) run as hot as they could function, then hotter until they sputtered out. She kept glancing back to the *Deliverance* as if something might change—as if its hull would restore itself or the fire would die.

The trail of eruptions had become an uninterrupted line of flame. The Star Destroyer wasn't gone, but it *would* be, just like the *Hellion's Dare* and the *Lodestar*. Wyl Lark would go with it, and General Syndulla, and the ground crews and everyone she'd barely tolerated.

Something stung her eyes and she shook her head hard. Her horns snagged on her helmet's padding and tore the foam, sending little flakes bouncing off her chest and shoulders. She switched back to the open comm and heard a voice saying, "*—How?*"

"Shut up!" she snarled. "Which of you is Char?"

The New Republic pilots began shouting about the *Deliverance* as others spotted the damage. Chass yelled louder, "Give me Char! Give me Blink. Give me Spitsy. Come at me—I'm in the B-wing, and you're going to come at me. Me against all of you, and we'll see who's better, okay?"

Someone was firing in her direction, and she smiled viciously and spun to duel her adversary. Maybe it was one of the fighters she knew; maybe not.

She recognized the terrifying rhythm of the battle. One by one, her comrades would die, and she'd be left alone again. Just like the Cavern Angels. Just like Riot Squadron.

This isn't how it's supposed to go, she thought. *Wyl Lark was supposed to be safe.*

III

Hera Syndulla had never loved the *Deliverance* as she'd loved other ships. Her relationship with the *Lodestar* had been a professional one, yet she'd developed a fondness for the ornery battle cruiser. Training cadets aboard the *Lucrehulk Prime* had taught her that weapons of oppression could become symbols of hope. Then there was *her* ship, with which she'd shared a decades-long marriage; no matter how long they were parted, nothing could match her bond with the *Ghost.*

The *Deliverance* had never had time to redeem itself. It had never stopped being a Star Destroyer in her eyes. She felt a pang of guilt when she realized it was dying—as if she'd failed someone under her care, someone she'd promised to give a second chance.

The inanimate hunk of metal will be the least of your failures if you don't get moving.

"Status of the escape pods?" she called across the bridge. She could barely hear herself over the noise of alarms, popping metal, and—from somewhere too near—violent flames. The air was hot, and sweat ran down her nose and chin.

"Hard to say," Stornvein yelled back. Her aide rotated among stations as the bridge crew evacuated one by one. "Between the damage and the particle field I can't get a read on half our systems. Looks like at least two decks made it off safely."

She'd given the order to abandon ship three minutes prior; if the crew hadn't heard the message, she suspected they'd figured it out themselves. "Good enough for now. We still on course?"

"Yes, General!" The nav officer didn't look at her, fixated on his screen. She couldn't recall his name, but the round-faced man had the steadiness of someone who'd been with the Rebellion a decade or more. Maybe she'd even fought with him before. "We've got minimal power but several maneuvering thrusters are responding and we're already at target speed. We'll make it to the squadrons."

"Assuming they don't move," Hera said. She staggered across the unstable deck to the viewport, leaning against it and trying to see what they were headed into. She ignored the flashes of the starfighters, focusing on the particle trail of the *Yadeez:* The bulk freighter was moving away from Flare, Wild, and Alphabet but angling back to the main fight around Jakku.

Scanners were useless this near the bulk freighter; even if the Star Destroyer had been undamaged, she doubted she'd have been able to get an accurate read on the *Yadeez's* course. But she eyeballed the cloud of radiation behind it and raced to the nav station, guessing at the bulk cruiser's vector and checking against last known fleet positions. She sketched a few alternative paths in case her guesses were off, but only her first attempt gave a result that made any sense.

"They're heading for one of the Starhawks," she said. "The *Concord*, I think."

"Even with the TIEs, you really think the *Yadeez* can kill a Starhawk?" Stornvein asked.

Under ordinary circumstances the answer would've been no. "Shadow Wing knows what they're doing. They'll go in fast and invisible, hitting critical systems before moving to a new target. They can't keep up these assassinations forever, but they can disable half our key ships before someone gets lucky and takes them down."

"I can try to get a message out." The comscan officer—Dhina—sounded determined, despite the doubt on her face. "Warn the *Concord*. Sometimes a signal slips through the particle field."

A violent tremor ran through the deck. Several of the consoles dimmed and the alarms went dead. Stornvein spoke into the quiet: "I can't get readings from the reactor."

"No messages," Hera said. "All of you get to the escape pods. If the pods aren't working, get to the hangars—vehicle hangar, too, there's a ship stowed there—and climb onto anything that moves. If *nothing* will launch, hole up with the ordnance stockpiles. Counterintuitive, I know, but the walls there are thick and if any compartment can survive a crash, that's the one."

Several of the crew obeyed immediately. The remainder hesitated, then took off when she delivered the perfect scowl. A few seconds later only Stornvein remained. "You're staying?" he asked.

"I'm staying until I can't. Ten minutes, tops."

Stornvein gave her the same scowl she'd given the crew. She nearly laughed. "I'm not planning on dying," she said. "Go."

"May the Force be with you."

"And you." She turned to the bridge controls before Stornvein could even reach the doorway.

A Star Destroyer wasn't meant to be operated with a crew of one, but Hera had always enjoyed a challenge. The vessel's injuries made the work easier, in some ways—there were fewer tools available, fewer subsystems to worry about, and no time to repair anything. She moved from station to station, attempting to turn the behemoth to intercept the *Yadeez* and glancing frequently at the viewport to judge her position. She recalled the tactical reports from Cerberon—from Shadow Wing's strike, when they'd rigged up a nearly empty Star Destroyer as a decoy—and set the functioning turbolasers to fire randomly.

She couldn't get any response from the ship's shields. She wouldn't need them anyway.

When she'd finished her initial preparations, she opened an unencrypted comm channel. She was surprised to see traffic on other frequencies—some half-melted transmitter was doggedly trying to receive and relay signals despite the particle field—but she left the program running and pulled on a headset.

"This is—" She cut herself off as she listened to the overlapping voices of New Republic and Shadow Wing pilots. She wasn't only about to announce her plan to everyone; the moment she said her name, she'd make herself a target.

"This is General Hera Syndulla aboard the *Deliverance*," she said, and the other voices stopped. "The bulk freighter *Yadeez* cannot be allowed to target our Starhawks. If destruction is not possible, eliminate its nacelles—that should stop it from cloaking its surroundings in the particle field, and its opportunities for damage will be limited. Repeat, this is General Hera Syndulla aboard the *Deliverance*—stop that thing from blinding our fleet!"

She slipped off the headset and hoped Nath Tensent and the others would carry out her orders, and that Shadow Wing would take the bait. She'd distract the TIEs as well as she could from the Star Destroyer. Maybe buy her pilots some breathing room.

They'd have to work fast, though. She'd told Stornvein *ten minutes,* and she wasn't sure the *Deliverance* had that long.

IV

Nath Tensent watched the *Deliverance* burn and thought: *Wyl Lark is probably dead.*

That idea drowned out T5's wails and the chatter on the open channel. Yet Nath had lost comrades before—he'd lost a whole blasted squadron—and his relationship with Wyl had carried a tax Nath had been paying since Cerberon. "Forget about the kid," he snapped at the droid. "Focus on surviving!"

That was when his shields flashed—miraculously, they were working—and the Y-wing vibrated inside the deflectors' sphere. A cannon volley had skimmed his nose; a few centimeters closer and he'd have been dead. He watched the attacking fighter and its wingmate whip past and leaned into his rudder pedal.

He thought of his final words to Wyl and how they'd parted. Nath had been right to figure that if Wyl was going to desert (Nath had feelings about *that*, too, but he understood necessity) then Wyl should've never come to Jakku in the first place.

You got yourself killed sticking around. It's your own damn fault!

He stopped thinking about Wyl. He had to, or else he was dead, too.

"Where are we?" he asked, and the droid flashed a response on his console. They'd exited the densest area of the particle field as they'd looped around for another attack on the *Yadeez*. The TIEs were largely sticking to their mother ship, picking off the Flare and Wild pilots remaining.

Nath couldn't do much to help the two fighter squadrons; even if he'd had a clever plan, there was no way to communicate it without being overheard. The surviving bombers—Hail and Chass—were following his lead, but he wasn't sure they'd last long enough to do any good.

He glanced behind him and spotted one of the Y-wings and Chass's B-wing swinging around. "All right," he began, before T5's squeal interrupted and he heard the voice of General Syndulla:

"—destruction is not possible, eliminate its nacelles—that should stop it from cloaking its surroundings in the particle field—"

"Right," he muttered. "'If you can't blow the thing up, at least die to save the rest of the fleet.' Wonderful."

He counted his advantages. He saw a squadron of TIEs break away and head for the *Deliverance*; Shadow Wing still outnumbered the New Republic fighters, but that would give the bombers half a chance to get close to the *Yadeez*. Vitale was still playing *Who? What? Where?* with the enemy pilots; irritating, but maybe a distraction they could use.

T5 pinged. Nath tried to spot the problem and noticed Chass tangling with a TIE interceptor far behind him. He cut thruster power, groaning as he was thrown forward and the other Y-wings skated past. Next he gave his repulsors a push, turning around to line up a shot. It was a trick he'd always enjoyed, holding position and using his bomber as a sniper rifle—he'd last indulged the habit in the canyons of Troithe—but it worked better when he had a chance to hide.

Chass was spraying fire wildly while the TIE leapt and circled her. She was forcing it to be cautious, but she couldn't outmaneuver it and the TIE's pilot wasn't stupid.

He waited. T5 warned him that the other Y-wings were confused and slowing down, but he ignored the droid. He ignored everything until he saw his chance and fired his cannons, sending a pulse of crimson energy through the darkness and into the TIE's cockpit.

"Think you just killed Char," Chass said.

"You're an idiot, challenging them one-on-one," Nath replied amicably. *Bold, but still an idiot.* T5 was doing its best to filter out the other voices on the open channel—the attempt didn't work well, but it was better than nothing. "You hear the message?"

"Yeah," she said.

He opened the Y-wing's throttle again, circling back to the path they'd been taking to the *Yadeez*. The B-wing followed. They could still see the madness of the battle—the catastrophic clash of Dreadnoughts; the plasma storm of weapons fire over Jakku; the streaks of Shadow Wing's TIE fighters; the dying *Deliverance*—but for a few seconds they were englobed by something resembling tranquility.

"Figure he's gone?" Chass asked.

"Yeah."

One of the Shadow Wing pilots was screaming a name, over and over: *Phesh. Phesh.* Nath wondered if that was the pilot he'd just killed.

"We doing this?" Nath asked.

"You think he'd want us to?"

The question took him aback—he'd assumed Chass was game for a suicide run. He tried to imagine what Wyl would say; whether the kid would really want them to sacrifice themselves to stop Shadow Wing from killing yet another ship.

His thoughts were interrupted by a whine from the comm. The working parts of his console showed T5's attempts to filter and enhance a signal, and eventually Nath heard words:

"Proceeding through cloud cover—" Then a pause, and then a second voice, guttural and accented: "They see her. I will try to help."

The transmission ended. Chass began laughing. "Guess *they're* doing okay."

"Or were, whenever that signal went out," Nath agreed.

"You think *she'd* want us to?"

That was easier to picture. Wyl might've hesitated at the thought of his friends going out in a blaze of glory, especially in a war he thought was no longer worth fighting. Then again, the immediacy of the problem might've swept aside his reservations.

Yrica Quell, though? She always saw her missions through.

"Oh, yes," he said. "You still up for it?"

"Sure. Almost like going in as a team."

Nath shook his head and let the sound of pilots laughing and snarling and screaming fill his cockpit, heading off to lead his ships on one last bombing run.

They danced together and they danced apart. The TIEs came squadron by squadron instead of swarming the skyways, and with each wave Quell and Keize parted and fought for their lives before reuniting just long enough to be separated again.

They spoke in shorthand, identifying incoming marks and claiming their targets when there was ambiguity. Quell was glad for the limits of their conversation, at least at first—the battle left her breathless. Keize never warned her when a TIE locked on, nor did she warn him when strikers tried to flank him; they took care to avoid collisions or other accidents, and that was the extent of their alliance.

Throughout, Quell glimpsed crimson and emerald among the clouds. Kairos might have been holding off a fleet, and Quell was grateful.

As the TIEs pursued her into the city depths, it occurred to Quell to surrender. If she gave up, the Empire would be able to concentrate on her mentor. They might stop Keize, and stop the dying, and she would be no worse off than she had been many times before—locked in a cell, awaiting her execution. But the Empire hadn't responded to her attempts to make contact and besides, if *she* could survive them surely Keize could, too.

Her best chance—her only chance, maybe—was persuasion. Even though she'd never changed his mind before, any more than she'd managed to outfly him.

"Colonel?" She raced through clouds of flame, leaving burning TIE parts tumbling into the city-chasms. (She tried not to think of the TIEs' pilots protecting their besieged world; the debris that fell kilometers, jagged and deadly, as debris had fallen onto Pandem Nai.) "Please respond."

The X-wing slipped among the darkened towers. Somehow she'd found her way layers beneath the upper strata, into a region where entertainment venues stood barred and anti-Imperial graffiti covered high-end clothiers.

"I hear you," Keize said. Through her comm she heard the snap of blaster cannons and the booming of smashed metal and displaced air. "You fly well, Lieutenant. Though the fighter is new to me."

"Just Quell, now. Or Yrica." She wrinkled her nose and winced at the pain. "Where are you?"

"If I tell you—" For an instant she detected strain in his voice. There was another snap from his cannons; another explosion. "—it will only end badly. Approach and I *will* fire on you."

"I know," she said. "Tell me anyway."

She needed to orient herself. The city was a three-dimensional maze, and she'd lost any sense of where the battle had begun or how to reach the Verity District. She'd barely touched her console when her astromech loaded a map onto the screen. She mouthed *Thank you* and flew on, the fighter's vibrations like a caress.

"Part of me would very much enjoy that duel," Keize said. "Unfortunately, I can't afford the time. Coruscant's defenders are only harrying us so they can reinforce the Palace and surround the entire district; once they approach in force, they'll discover the limits of my skills."

"You *are* out of practice," she said, and he laughed.

Stop it. You don't get to banter. He's not here to help you.

"You're going to destroy the data bank," she said. "How?"

The joy left his voice, as it had hers. "Surgical excision. The data core is directly beneath the upper level of the Verity District. What's the swiftest way, do you think, to ensure its destruction?"

She took the X-wing down swiftly enough to ignite silver sparks at the edge of her vision and pulled into a rusting industrial level of catwalks and cranes. The TIE fighters wouldn't find her if she went deep enough into the city, and she could conceal her approach when she located Keize.

She considered his question. "Destroy the support structures. One TIE won't have the firepower to do serious damage to the data bank, but dropping it hundreds of levels to the ground would make it impossible to recover."

"Good," he said. "Cutting the supports may not suffice—central repulsors provide an antigravity lift as a safety mechanism. But an able soldier could detonate those manually. After a thousand-level drop, anything salvaged from the ruined data bank would be suspect. So much of the data would need to be reconstructed that nothing could be considered trustworthy; no one could use it as a weapon against those who had served the Empire."

She was beneath the Verity District now. She looked for a gap in the structural web above her and spotted a cargo turbolift attached to the side of a tower, large enough to carry a freighter. She pulled up hard, felt her weight settle against her seat, and shot skyward.

She sped past a blur of turbolift stops and abandoned checkpoints. Then she saw the underside of a data sphere, illuminated with security lights and armored thicker than a warship, and knew she'd arrived. Before she could proceed green fire flashed on her starboard side and she slammed a rudder pedal to avoid the worst of the hit; even so, particle bolts splashed her deflectors and sent her into a spin. She gripped her control yoke as she rolled, bouncing in her harness, and tried not to slam into the sphere even as Keize swept behind her.

"I told you I would fire," he said.

"I'm not offended," she managed, and fled from her mentor.

In an oxygen-thick atmosphere, trapped in tight urban quarters, she had no advantage over a TIE when it came to speed; likewise maneuverability, even in the T-70 prototype. She looped around towers; slid to one side using repulsors and cut thrust, hoping in vain Keize would shoot past her; she led him through an obstacle course of floating military droids in low-power mode. She didn't shake him and he fired only when he was nearly certain to hit, battering her shields and scarring her wings.

That had always been the worst thing about drills with Keize—the interminable waiting between shots, knowing that when you heard the sound of cannon fire he was sure to have you.

She found her voice despite the stress. "If you do this, do you know how many people will die? How many people live in the undercity levels you plan to drop buildings on?"

"I do," Keize said. "Not precisely, but I've run estimates."

"Then you know—"

There was emotion as he interrupted—a hint of bitterness and frustration he hadn't shown prior. "I know that all of us—Imperial and rebel—have sacrificed civilians any number of times, and this is no different. I know the price, Yrica—tens of thousands or more on the levels below, in exchange for billions."

He fired another volley as they slipped from Verity's underside into clear sky. This time his shots went wide, and she wasn't sure if she'd shaken him or if he was trying to goad her into outdistancing him so he could turn and head back to his target alone.

She plunged back among the buildings and lost sight of the clouds again. "What billions?" she asked, though she knew the answer.

"We've spoken too often to pretend. The Emperor's cruelty touched everyone in his service—not just troops, but every package-sorter and educator and bureaucrat on thousands of worlds. How many of them compromised their ethics to avoid rebuke or protect their families or out of pure expediency? It was the *design* of the Empire to compromise its servants, so that we were bound by guilt. So that the noblest among us would commit wretched acts, and cease hesitating when atrocities were asked of us."

"Because the guilty are easy to control. I know." She dived down a gap between towers; she tried to calculate the X-wing's weight distribution compared with a TIE's. "But fifty thousand dead civilians aren't the same as an uncertain future for—"

"The future is *not* uncertain. You know the consequences if the New Republic acquires those records. You know the ruin that will result as the sins of billions are exposed, you've seen New Republic justice—"

She cut her thrusters, switched off her repulsors, and went into free fall. The X-wing tumbled forward and she groaned as her harness saved her from smashing into her canopy. She couldn't counter the dizziness—all she could do was ride the wave, and when the weight of her reactor flipped the starfighter over, oriented her nose toward the sky, she slammed a palm on the console again, reigniting her thrusters as she squeezed her firing trigger.

Energy blazed from her cannons and Keize's TIE, still descending toward her, nimbly avoided each bolt. A single blast left a scar across one of his wings; then he was below and behind her.

"Artfully done," he said. "But my point stands."

She was halfway back to the upper levels when she realized he wasn't pursuing. He'd disappeared among the buildings, and she couldn't guess whether he was planning another ambush or returning to Verity via another route.

"Suppose," he said, "the New Republic seeks justice with all those others as it did with you. Suppose, through some miracle, the tribunals are almost fair. Imagine how many former Imperials will nonetheless live in fear of being hauled away for decades-old crimes. How many soldiers will wonder when some functionary will publicize their records, resulting in mobs descending on their homes and families?

"There can be no goodwill in such a galaxy. No union under a new government. At worst, such resentment could provoke terrorism and civil war such that a few thousand dead civilians on Coruscant would seem trivial indeed."

She couldn't have argued even if she'd had the words. Another squadron of TIE strikers had arrived and she was caught in the fray, attempting to outpace and outmaneuver her attackers on a battlefield they knew better than she did. Keize went silent—she suspected he, too, was beset by opponents—and she evaded attack after attack, flew into depths so dimly lit that two of the TIEs behind her activated their lights and painted themselves as easy targets.

As she flew, static built on her comm and took the shape of voices. She caught snippets that could've been Chass na Chadic and another that could've been Jeela Brebtin. Somewhere across the galaxy, Alphabet Squadron and Shadow Wing were locked in combat, too.

Someone declared that the *Deliverance* was going down and Quell suppressed a flinch.

"Protect your own," she hissed. "Stay together. They'll try to split you but you know how to fight with each other."

She could've been talking to Alphabet or Shadow Wing.

Keize's voice interrupted her thoughts. He announced a set of coordinates and she understood, changing direction and heading back toward Verity. The TIEs chased her and as she emerged from a narrow skyway she spun abruptly to one side. Keize's TIE, headed toward her, slid on its repulsors in the opposite direction, and his pursuers collided with her own at the position Keize had cited. The strikers tore apart and burned and fell under the shadows of the data spheres.

"You're getting a feed from Jakku?" Keize asked.

She glanced to her console. She'd left the channel open to Keize even as the transmission had come in. "I am."

"They're dying, aren't they?"

His tone had softened, and as they spun their fighters about, heading toward each other, neither took the opportunity to fire.

"Yes."

"I'm sorry." The TIE came closer, and she could see into its cockpit— see the silhouette of a man in a black flight suit, like so many anonymous pilots she'd killed and fought beside. "I'm sorry you felt compelled to come after me and leave them. But consider this: For those who survive, wiping the slate clean is the only way to bring peace. If a record of the Empire's sins exists, it will breed violence for decades."

Quell wasn't sure which one of them shot first, but the air filled with charged particles and death.

CHAPTER 23

THE BREAKING OF THE GUILTY

I

F*or a second,* Nath thought, *we were almost having fun.*

Vitale didn't play games anymore. General Syndulla was silent, if she was still alive. Shadow Wing made no threats and didn't ask about Wyl Lark or Yrica Quell. The voices on the open comm came rhythmic and somber as a drumbeat:

"Jothal Gablerone."

"Fra Raida."

"Neihero."

"Sata Neek."

They'd seemed to realize together that an end was approaching. The recitation of the dead—rebel and Imperial—pounded at Nath as his Y-wing trembled and Flare and Wild intercepted barrages aimed at his bombers. T5 was making buzzing, staccato squawks Nath couldn't remember hearing from the astromech ever before.

"Nord Kandende."

"Denish Wraive."

"Gorgeous Su."

As TIEs and New Republic fighters circled the bomber phalanx, missiles streaked toward the bombers from the *Yadeez*. Soaked in Chadawan radiation, their nav systems blinded, they flew straight and blew seemingly at random. In an atmosphere the shock waves might have thrown Nath off course; in deep space the explosions rocked the Y-wing, forced him to grip his control yoke and straighten his path, but did little damage.

A direct hit would still kill him instantly. Even shrapnel from a missile casing might puncture a vital system—his shields were flickering and had become essentially ornamental. But the light show was impressive.

"Palal Seedia."

"Tulana Tuluith."

How many names till he reached the bulk freighter? Twenty? Thirty? Hail and Alphabet chased the *Yadeez* as it crawled toward the pale shape of a Starhawk.

Flare and Wild should've gone ahead to harry the *Yadeez*, slowing it so the bombers could catch up more easily. But there weren't enough pilots left, and the two squadrons had their hands full keeping the TIEs from killing them all.

"Garmen Naadra."

"Ubellikos."

"Shol Mordeaux," Nath said as his turn came around. It wasn't a name he'd planned to say.

He thought back to Trenchenovu—he'd been thinking too much about Trenchenovu, but the shipyard battle where he'd lost his first squadron felt within his grasp. The rage and fear of that day were kept from the forefront of his brain only by the thinnest barriers of memory and time. He recalled the thirst for vengeance that had driven him to join Alphabet Squadron (along with money, true); he recalled murdering Grandmother at Pandem Nai, exacting retribution from the woman who'd ordered his crew destroyed.

"Shay Darita."

"Mervais Gandor."

Meteor Squadron. Most of Hail Squadron. Wyl Lark.

Since Pandem Nai he'd lost enough comrades that vengeance was almost worthwhile again. The thought it might get him killed was infuriating.

"Don't let me interrupt," he snapped, "but anyone who wants to see that souped-up freighter burn? You're about to get the chance."

He thought he heard Chass laugh. Otherwise the names kept going.

The closer they got to the *Yadeez*, the better the freighter aimed. Missiles ripped through the void barely a meter from Nath's cockpit; close enough that even the TIEs were giving the bombers a wider berth. That was useful—to a point—but Nath didn't find it comforting.

He picked his target: the front of the freighter's port nacelle. The density of the particle cloud was rising and most of his console had gone dark; he figured he'd be lucky to get off one shot before his systems failed entirely. He kicked his thrusters to maximum output and set a course over the freighter's back, hoping he wouldn't run straight into a missile.

"Tensent going in!" he called.

"Hail Six, going in!"

"Hail Twelve, making my run."

"Me, too," Chass said.

No one else paused their recitation of names. The drumbeat followed Nath as he skimmed above the *Yadeez*, almost close enough to touch metal. Without his navicomputer to course-correct or shields to pad him, he'd tear his Y-wing apart if he dropped more than a few centimeters; but he was also close enough that the freighter's weapons couldn't target him and the TIEs wouldn't dare shoot. He gripped his control yoke until his hands ached, holding steady and watching the nacelle over the horizon of the freighter's hull.

Closer. Closer. Forget what Wyl would want, forget what Quell would want. Think about Trenchenovu and fire!

The Y-wing bucked as he loosed a torpedo. He pulled up as hard as he could—too hard, he suspected, as his last functioning alarm wailed that his thrusters were overheating—and flew into a sky bright with explosions. Missiles detonated, fire rolled off the hull of the *Yadeez,* and someone screamed in agony over the comm. Nath twisted from side to side, trying to see what the scanner wouldn't show him, and spotted a Y-wing and Chass's B-wing tumbling through the night. The B-wing was blasting away with all its remaining cannons, but he couldn't tell why either of them was off course.

"What happened?" he shouted. He dipped a wing and glimpsed the freighter below. He'd ripped away much of the port nacelle, and flame and electricity mixed with scintillating particles leaked from every crack. "Got mine! What the hell happened?"

"Hit us with a missile at the last second. Had to swerve, missed the shot," a voice replied. "We lost Twelve."

Hail Six, last survivor of his squadron.

"One more name for the list," one of the Shadow Wing pilots said. There was nothing mocking about it; the statement was almost regretful.

Tensent began laughing and found he couldn't stop.

II

Chass didn't understand what Nath found so hysterical, and she spat and cursed into the comm as her B-wing coasted through the particle cloud regurgitated by the burst nacelle. She had enough power for life support but otherwise the radiation left her impotent. Her weapons had rapidly gone dry. The comforting rattle of her console and the hurricane noise of her engine had ceased. When she wrenched herself around she could see the remnants of Flare and Wild, tattered starfighters with flickering shields and cracked cockpits attempting to drive off TIEs sweeping in for the kill.

"So what?" she asked. "We doing this again or not?"

"Why not?" Nath's laughter was gone but Chass could hear his smirk. "We've still got a reputation to uphold."

The chanting went on:

"Agias Rikton."

"Giginivek."

"It's stupid," Chass said. "We're down a bomber and it's not going to work—it didn't work this time, it's not going to work the next! We can't stay close enough to the freighter to do any *good.*"

She wasn't afraid of dying, she told herself—or at least that wasn't the problem. She didn't want to die like Hail Twelve, or like Riot or Hound or Flare or Wild, or like Wyl. She didn't want to die pointlessly, caught in a battle she did nothing to change.

It wasn't what she'd been promised. It wasn't why she'd joined the Rebellion.

"All right," Nath said after a moment. "New plan. You all want to hear it? Shadow Wing, you boys want to hear what we're up to?"

The chant of the dead faded. "We're listening," someone said.

Cannon fire licked the dark around Chass. She was still adrift and the TIEs were shooting from a distance, staying out of the particle cloud themselves. They'd hit her sooner or later, or the *Yadeez* would impale her on a missile.

"We're going to make another run at your freighter," Nath said. "We're going to ignore General Syndulla's order to target the nacelles and hit the biggest, easiest target: the main thrusters. Maybe we'll blow the whole ship, maybe not, but if it's dead in space and immobile the particle field won't do much good."

Chass's indicator lights flickered. She toggled switches on and off, whole rows at a time, until her reactor came online and she was thrown backward as her thrusters reignited. She might still die uselessly but now she could die fighting. That was a start.

Nath kept talking. "Of course, you fine Imperial pilots will try to intercept. You'll throw everything you've got at us—or everything you have to spare, what with the *Deliverance* bearing down on you, a Starhawk you need to prep for, and the best fighter pilots left in the New Republic picking you off. You kill the three of us bombers, congratulations—you win the whole pot. If not . . ."

"Alphabet Leader?" a woman's voice said. "This is Captain Wisp;

Squadron Three, 204th Imperial Fighter Wing. Since you've killed Captain Phesh, that leaves me senior squadron commander, and I'll say this—I can't think of a better way to put you in the ground."

"Good enough for me," Nath said.

"Good enough for me," Chass agreed.

Hail Six said something, but Chass ignored him as she burned toward clear space. She glanced behind her and saw the two Y-wings following at a distance. The *Deliverance,* meanwhile, was continuing toward the *Yadeez,* but the Star Destroyer's hull was wreathed in flames; Chass couldn't tell if the *Deliverance* was operational or a fiery hulk riding inertia. The TIEs picking at its remains stopped and also headed for the *Yadeez.* Closer to Chass was the snarl of TIEs and New Republic starfighters. Her most direct course to the *Yadeez* would take her through the melee, where she'd have a spectacular view of the last X-wings blown to bits as they strived to keep her alive.

So many of the TIEs were gone, too, though. She guessed there were no more than twenty or thirty left, between the ones tangling with Wild and Flare, the ones at the *Deliverance,* and a few flying out ahead of the *Yadeez.* Solar panels and viewport shards drifted past her; lonely ion engines sparked, the hearts of the fighters torn out and still beating after their pilots were long dead. The debris would've been gruesomely satisfying if it hadn't posed a collision hazard.

Maybe she'd add a few TIEs to the wreckage herself.

Chass turned as tight as she could, listening to her reactor wheeze. She headed for the fray and the freighter beyond it, blasting at TIEs as they converged on individual Flare and Wild fighters. The naming of the dead went on, but it was breathless and panicked, mixed with urgent cries.

"Samran Phesh."

"Vitale! Vitale!"

"*Darita?*"

Vitale's name triggered something in Chass's brain, and she suddenly understood the dead woman's earlier chatter. *Who? What? Where?* She'd been playing the old pilots' game with Shadow Wing.

Who hears the news when you die? *What* did it? *Where* did it all go down?

"Hey!" Chass shouted as the TIEs attempted to turn from Wild and Flare to spew death at the bombers. Her guns were pumping too slowly, like something mechanical was misaligned and the pulses were shearing metal. She rocked violently with each shot. "Hey!" She kept squeezing the trigger anyway—if her cannons failed, she still had torpedoes. That was all she needed for the *Yadeez*.

"*Who?*" she cried, thinking through her candidates: Chancellor Mon Mothma, who'd sent them to Jakku. General Syndulla, who was probably dead. Let'ij, the con artist. Gruyver, the cultist who'd once saved her. Yrica Quell. "Pick your favorite host of one of those pirate news broadcasts. Anyone would be lucky to get the story—"

She stopped talking as two TIEs raced her way. An X-wing attempted to cut them off but a second TIE pair intercepted it before it could close. Chass didn't change course, tapping her thrusters and turning to track the first TIEs as momentum carried her along. With sweat-soaked gloves, she rotated her airfoils and fired.

The TIEs shot back simultaneously, and she would've died if something in one of her ion cannons hadn't blown. She saw one side of her strike foil burst in light and metal, and the kick pushed her out of the way of the incoming volley. Something beneath her left arm sprayed sparks, and she screamed as she leaned away from the flames, felt her head bounce off the canopy, and kept holding down her firing trigger.

From the howl on the open comm, she was pretty sure she hit one of her targets. She wrested the B-wing back in the right direction then sprayed down the cockpit and half her arm with an extinguisher canister.

"*What?*" she asked, and her voice was shaky and hoarse. "Not you, you bastards. None of you! Maybe this garbage fighter burns when I shoot your freighter to pieces, maybe I'm caught in the torpedo blast, maybe I ram this thing up your engines and choke your flagship to death—but it's going to be spectacular, and it's going to win this whole battle."

Nath was yelling something she couldn't really hear—something about getting back into formation. The chant of the dead was being kept up by two, maybe three pilots. She looked behind her and saw Nath and Hail Six each escorted by an X-wing through a cloud of TIEs.

She might've turned around to join them but she wasn't sure the B-wing could handle it. Then she spotted the *Yadeez* up ahead and five TIEs skimming its hull on their way toward her. Probably heading back from the Starhawk.

"*Where?*" she screamed. "Right here! I'm winning the war today—*I'm* winning it, Chass na Chadic—" *Maya Hallik.* "—Theelin Queen of Starfighters and fizzy drinks! Chass na Chadic! You remember that! You remember me!"

If they didn't remember no one else would. The *Deliverance* was gone and the rest of the fleet still didn't know what was happening. It hurt her chest to think about.

To hell with it all.

She reminded herself she wasn't Nath Tensent, looking to come out ahead. She was following in the footsteps of Jyn Erso, martyr of Scarif, who'd saved who-knew-how-many planets from being blown apart by Death Stars.

The TIEs swept toward her, not yet firing—they were waiting for the perfect shot, knowing they had time to line one up. Chass loosed a volley in their direction but half her cannons were gone. She didn't come close to landing a hit, and they didn't flinch.

The *Yadeez* grew large, and its massive thrusters glowed and flickered in the fog of the particle cloud. She was coming at it from above, at a gentle angle. She pitched abruptly downward, knowing she wouldn't shake the TIEs if she curved up from below but hoping it would buy her a few seconds.

Maybe this was how Jyn Erso had felt. Maybe she'd been scared when she stared down the battle station.

Chass thought again of the false hope of the Children of the Empty Sun. She thought of where she would inevitably end up if she survived the war, useless and bound to suffer a fate so much worse than martyrdom. She remembered her confession of her nightmare at the cult's disquisition: Living on Coruscant off a New Republic stipend in a cruddy apartment. Garbage food and old furniture. No work for a professional killer, no other skills, no one she knew still alive.

I do some stupid stuff just to pass the time. Not robbery, but enough to catch the eye of local security. They go easy on me, because I'm a vet. They go easy on me the first time.

After that, I lose the apartment. Keep my gun. It all goes downhill from there.

This was the last battle. She could be Jyn Erso today, or she could let the nightmare come true.

The TIEs broke formation, mirroring her dive and orbiting the B-wing like planets around a sun. Her cockpit turned emerald in the fiery light and she veered as hard as she could into the densest section of the particle cloud—she wasn't sure if her weapons would still work there but at least she'd slow the TIEs. Her burnt arm began to pain her and she felt something moist on her temple—sweat if she was lucky, blood if she'd hit her head too hard when her ion cannon had blown.

Scintillating particle motes enveloped her, and her reactor rang like a bell. Though her console was dark one of her alarms somehow managed to shriek, warning her that something vital in the ship was broken and she couldn't do anything about it.

The TIEs kept shooting. She could barely see the *Yadeez's* thrusters through the particle fog, and cannon blasts wavered and refracted in the mist. She fumbled with manual releases, bypassing the computer to load and arm a torpedo. If the Y-wings were anywhere nearby, she couldn't see them.

The ringing engine and alarm harmonized, providing a backbeat to the chant of the dead. Chass tasted her dry lips and realized she was mumbling over the slow-tempo dirge, reciting lyrics to a warbat trance single that had spread through the galaxy's clubs a dozen years earlier. It fit the timing too well; it slipped out, and she didn't know when she'd begun.

The words were in some obscure Huttese dialect, haunting and indecipherable. She hesitated when she realized she might be heard on the open channel; but someone had joined her, a woman she didn't recognize. There was a man's voice, too, and she found herself continuing.

Wisp, "senior squadron commander" of Shadow Wing, joined in next. Chass laughed before returning to the song, adding her awful voice to the others as the chant of the dead pounded beneath what might've been (knowing the tastes of clubgoers) a love song.

She would miss this when she was dead. She missed her music chips, lost in Cerberon.

A haze of particles obscured her view; when it passed she was a hundred meters from the *Yadeez*. The freighter's thrusters would've burned away her shields if she'd had anything left; she felt their heat through her canopy. The song went on as she scrambled to aim her shot, but she saw now she was too close to escape the blast from her torpedo. If she fired, there was a good chance she'd be obliterated along with one of the freighter's thrusters.

The thought made her bones ache, and she didn't understand why. She didn't *want* to understand why.

It's okay, she told herself in Let'ij's voice. *This is it, this is what you've been waiting for, what you've been working for, the best ending you could ever have—*

When had she ever needed to persuade herself before? When had she become so terrified?

Are you better off coming home to the cult, knowing it's all a lie? Your comrades are gone. Wyl and Quell and Kairos are doomed and Nath will go next, and they wouldn't give you spit if you were dying in a desert anyway. They don't want you clinging to them after the war.

She didn't have more than a second or three before it was too late to fire on the *Yadeez*. Maybe less before a TIE incinerated her.

When did you become such a coward?

When had she started *wanting* a future, even if she couldn't imagine one?

When had she decided she wanted to live?

Had it been when she'd been embraced by the cult? When she'd shed their teachings the way Kairos had shed her shell, in the forests of that nameless world?

Was it just the music?

You're afraid, Maya Hallik. But tomorrow you'll still be alive, and alone, and you'll never get this opportunity again.

She knew it was true.

Nath was shouting something to Flare Squadron, and as Chass straightened in her seat she remembered his words before they'd taken off, after he'd told her about Let'ij—words she'd forgotten earlier: *You need someone to shoot you, you come to me after.*

She laughed loud and sudden, and thought: *I'll hold you to that,* even as tears ran down her cheeks and she fired a torpedo.

Her best chance—her only chance—was to accelerate, to fly beyond the thrusters and use the bulk freighter's hull as cover from the explosion roiling at its stern. With her wreck of a ship, her reactor ready to fail, she sped toward the closest thing to safety she could find as her torpedo hit home.

The comm died in a crackle of static and she glimpsed her cannons rupturing and trailing lightning; saw fire rise around her like floodwaters. She hoped she would make it, but alive or dead, she knew her fight was over.

III

Nath watched the B-wing speed past the detonation, buffeted by a wave of bright energy and burning gas. The cockpit cleared the *Yadeez* but the B-wing's blackened and shredded airfoil caught on the freighter's hull and shattered in an instant. The battered remains of the assault fighter tumbled into the dark, streaking fire.

Nath didn't see the cockpit break apart or the canopy splinter. He didn't see anyone eject, either. Whatever happened to Chass next, he told himself, he'd kept her alive as long as he could; but it was scanty reassurance.

The *Yadeez* was still moving. He couldn't be certain through the flames and the particle cloud but its path seemed to be curving—Chass had taken out half its thrusters but it was still capable of limping to the Starhawk. It didn't even need to *fight*, just survive long enough to spread its fog of war and let the TIEs do the dirty work.

He tried to count the pilots left. Hail Six (Genni Avremif, poor kid) in the Y-wing and five fighters between Flare and Wild. Not even a proper squadron with all of them combined. Two from Flare had gone out protecting Chass during her run; at that rate, there'd be only one survivor when Nath and Genni were finished.

"Chass na Chadic," he said, adding her to the roster of the dead while others sang. "She did good but we're not done. All fighters stay close and let's wrap this up!"

He kept his tone defiant. He could give that to the pilots remaining, though it was more obligatory than heartfelt—with Chass gone, with Wyl gone, Kairos and Quell off to Coruscant, and Syndulla out of the fight, his sense of loyalty was fading fast.

He remembered how Trenchenovu had ended. His friends had died. He'd lost Reeka. In the end, he'd fled for his life.

He kept on course for the *Yadeez* as his allies gathered and tried to fend off the TIEs. Hail Six was barely a stone's throw from Nath as they angled around the worst of the particle cloud.

He was in too deep to escape this time; all he could do was screw up his courage and put on a show. "Chass had to announce herself. You all know who I am, though, don't you?"

Wisp stopped singing. "Captain Tensent, I'm guessing? Hero of Troithe. Last leader of Alphabet Squadron."

Nath pounded the console and T5 chirruped, readying a torpedo as they came closer to the freighter. Now the TIEs stayed too close for the *Yadeez* to barrage them with missiles. "Hero of Troithe, New Republic Intelligence asset, savior of Chadawa. When we win Jakku, I might be offered General Syndulla's job. I've got you all to thank for that. But what you don't know about me—"

Faster than he would've guessed possible in the particle field, a pair of TIEs swept in and picked off a Flare fighter like a bird of prey on a weasel.

"—is what I did at Pandem Nai," he went on. "I'm the one who sneaked inside your headquarters. I'm the one who shot Colonel Nuress."

Maybe drawing Shadow Wing's ire was a mistake, but Nath figured anger was more likely to throw them off rhythm than to inspire them. The New Republic pilots roared together as they died under cannon barrages, died to protect Nath.

Fire and radiation surrounded him, and T5 did its best to keep the ship on course. Without a working targeting computer he had to hope he was in range—the *Yadeez* filled his view and he had no intention of ending up like Chass, flying too close to the blast. He loosed a torpedo, and Hail Six did the same, and Nath knew some old spacer's god was on their side when both torpedoes impacted the freighter. The last of its bright-burning thrusters went dark even as explosions tore through metal and shined like a short-lived sun.

Nath laughed and swung to port with no destination but *away*—away from the *Yadeez* and away from the Shadow Wing TIEs. The remaining New Republic fighters followed, pilots cackling. There was no more singing; no more naming the dead.

"That was fantastic—"

"They're down! They're down!"

"Stay with the captain! Protect the bombers!"

The TIEs sped after them, spitting cannon volleys and attempting to outflank the New Republic forces. Nath could see that much, though his sensors were still useless. "What do we got out there?" he asked T5. He clamped down on a vibrating panel as if he could hold his ship together bare-handed.

The droid whistled and Nath glanced to one side, past the pursuing TIEs to the burning hulk of the *Deliverance* sailing toward them. It was still bearing down on the *Yadeez,* and with the bulk freighter's thrusters gone it had a real chance of coming close.

"Hey!" he called. "You really want to be chasing us right now?"

A bolt flared past his canopy. There was no shimmer from his deflectors—those were long gone.

"I don't see why not," Wisp said.

"Sure you do. You've got to put some value on that freighter—even if you don't care if your crew lives or dies, you're just a few TIEs in a very big battle without it. The *Yadeez* is drifting toward the Starhawk and it's got the *Deliverance* on a collision course. You've got work to do, and fast, if you want to salvage anything."

More likely, the *Deliverance* would miss by a few hundred meters—steering the wrecked Star Destroyer with precision would've been a feat for any pilot. But the TIEs couldn't count on that.

Shadow Wing had the New Republic fighters surrounded. The noose was closing.

"We'll see you around, Captain Tensent," a new voice said—a man's voice, one Nath hadn't heard before. "Squadrons, defend the *Yadeez*. We've bled enough today. Broosh out."

Nath poured enough power into his thrusters to alarm T5 as the TIEs fell away. He didn't much care what they did next so long as they were off his back; he needed to reboot his systems, one by one, at a safe distance from the particle cloud.

He led his pilots away from the *Yadeez* and away from Jakku. The sky was still ablaze but the worst of the fighting remained clustered tight in orbit. A series of flashes behind him suggested the *Deliverance* was breaking apart or being carved up by the TIEs, and Nath was surprised when T5 reported a transmission coming through and he heard a woman say:

"Protect your own. Stay together—"

Yrica Quell. You really do stand by your squadron.

He hoped she was still alive, whatever was happening on Coruscant.

He switched to the encrypted New Republic channel. They were far enough from the *Yadeez* that standard comms were worth a try. "Flare! Wild! Hail! Who's still out there?"

Hail Six, Flare Two, Wild Seven, and Wild Eight reported in. His screen flashed and he saw other messages from across the battlefield—

support requests from the capital ships, calls to aid troops planetside, and a steady scroll of alerts. Just reading it exhausted him.

He slumped back as much as his harness would allow. His hands were shaking. He'd been *lucky.* He'd been so damn lucky, and it was all that had saved him from the fates of his comrades.

"Are we going back?" Wild Eight asked. "We can't let Shadow Wing regroup—"

"With five fighters, we can't do much about it," Nath said. "Fire off a message to warn that Starhawk—with the *Yadeez* adrift, our forces should be able to stay out of its particle field. We did what we were assigned to do."

His thoughts weren't on his words, though. They were on the fiery night and the hundred warships and thousand starfighters over Jakku; the times he'd played hero and nearly played martyr; how there were only so many times anyone could cheat death. He was the last of Alphabet Squadron—maybe the sole survivor, maybe just the last man fighting—and no one could say he hadn't done his part.

More than done his part. He'd finished the mission and brought pilots who'd *never* been his responsibility out safe. Done what Wyl Lark had refused to do. If he kept things up, maybe he'd get another medal.

But his medals were all he'd have if a group of strangers buried him. He'd be dead as his crew at Trenchenovu.

"Then how do we proceed?" Flare Two asked.

It was a fair question. *How do* we *proceed?* What was left of the squadrons still looked to him for leadership. "Give me damage reports," he said, buying time to think. "Ordnance stocks and fuel levels, too."

He half listened as he considered his options. His hands were still shaking. It was hard to be *rational,* to act on anything other than instinct, but he went through the motions and reflected on the choices he'd made after Trenchenovu. Sole survivor then, sole survivor now, and it was only fortune that had preserved him during missions for profit and revenge and loyalty. He didn't need another medal, but his people—he hadn't asked for it but they were *his* now—were waiting.

The last of the damage reports came through. "What about you?" Wild Eight asked.

Nath had berated Wyl for abandoning the squadrons he'd led. But the mission was over. Shadow Wing was defeated. And he couldn't be saddled with the responsibility for grown soldiers forever.

"Pulling up a systems check. It's . . . not looking good," Nath said. "Blasted torpedo launcher is jammed and I've got an active warhead in the pipe—if this ship is so much as nudged it's going to blow something fierce."

Wild Eight tried to interrupt. Nath kept talking.

"I've got to take this thing down for repairs—somewhere real gentle, maybe a low-gravity moon away from the fighting. Anyone else who needs a fix is welcome to come with me." He didn't overemphasize, didn't make a show of it, but he made sure as well as he could that they understood the offer he was making. Whether he was responsible for them or not, he'd give them a choice of their own. "Otherwise, Wild Eight—you up to take command? See what that Starhawk needs?"

Wild Eight—Lieutenant Itina—was one of the old-time rebels, from back when winning hadn't been inevitable. Nath knew what she'd say.

"Yes, Captain. We won't fail you."

"I'm sure you won't," Nath said.

A few seconds later they'd swapped goodbyes and parted ways. No one else joined Nath. *You tried,* he told himself, shrugging it off. *You carried them this far, and you barely knew their names.* He briefly wondered what he'd have done if Alphabet had survived—if Wyl had been there to judge him, if Quell or Kairos had been relying on him or Chass had been ready to jump back into the fire—then dismissed the question.

"We saved the whole fleet. We've done enough," he told T5, and plotted a course taking them far, far around the fighting to a place where they could wait the battle out.

His career with the New Republic would be over if anyone bothered to investigate and find he'd lied about the damage to his Y-wing. But while playing hero had possessed its charms it had never been a role that suited him, and the taste of freedom was sweet on his tongue.

IV

She was the last. She was almost sure she was the last. Anyone else left alive had evacuated and Hera Syndulla stood in a haze of smoke so thick and oily she could barely breathe, let alone see out the viewport. The *Deliverance*'s turbolasers pulsed anyway, illuminating the bridge in swift flashes.

Somewhere ahead of her was the *Yadeez*. She could see it when she pressed her face to the transparent metal and blinked away the smoke. Nath Tensent and the others had immobilized it yet it remained a threat; between the turbolasers and her collision course, she hoped to vanquish it once and for all. Her crew and her squadrons—Alphabet, Hail, Wild, and Flare; Meteor and Vanguard, too—had all sacrificed enough over the past year to earn finality.

A wisp of smoke slithered down her throat. She coughed to expel it, and the cough became a fit that lasted the better part of a minute and left her kneeling on the deck. *Time to go*, she told herself. *You made promises.*

She ensured the bridge controls were locked and caught a glimpse of a TIE fighter streaking past as she departed. The deck was so unsteady that she barely felt the TIE pummeling the *Deliverance* from stern to bow. Shadow Wing was doing its best to atomize the warship; there was nothing she could do about it now.

The corridor beyond the bridge was on fire. A single valiant overhead extinguisher puffed little clouds of foam into the inferno, and each cloud promptly disintegrated in the heat. Hera pulled a pair of flight goggles from her jacket, fixed them over her eyes, and ran through blazes with her limbs close to her body. She soon emerged from the worst of the fire and began navigating through the ship, ignoring the ache in her lungs and the sensation of burnt skin on her arms, legs, and cheeks. She scurried under fallen support beams and edged around sparking conduits and climbed half-melted ladders down turbolift shafts. Twice she saw bodies and checked them for life. She made sure to memorize the faces of the fallen.

After vaulting over the wreckage of a blast door, Hera found herself on an abandoned gunnery platform. The weapons readouts there were dark, but the massive viewport was clear and uncracked and she had a perfect view of Jakku and the surrounding chaos.

She shouldn't have paused. Still, she was exhausted and there was a tranquility in the spectacle of clashing warships and burning fighters and glistening bands of molten metal coalescing in the planet's orbit. She could identify the epicenters of violence by their radiance—the Imperial defense of the Super Star Destroyer shone brightest—but she couldn't tell who had the upper hand. Stopping the 204th might have prevented a terrible defeat yet it hadn't visibly changed the course of the battle.

She thought of all her friends in that conflagration, and felt—for the first time she could remember since becoming a general—truly *small*. She'd done her part, played her role, and despite feeling the weight of the galaxy she couldn't perceive how any of it mattered at all.

Stranger than the thought itself was that the thought was *comforting*.

Something shook the *Deliverance* and she heard the distant roar of explosive decompression. She hurried on, pumping her legs harder and regulating the rhythm of her breath. If she kept a good pace, she was maybe four minutes from the vehicle hangar. Plenty of time to be crushed by a collapsing corridor or disintegrated by a proton bomb; even if she made it and her escape route was waiting, there was every chance she'd be destroyed by TIEs outside or caught in some other fatal calamity.

This, too, failed to perturb her. If she faltered now—if she died having seen the Rebellion through to this moment—she would be content.

The thought of her family, of her son, squeezed her heart like a hidden hand. She'd fought so long to return to a life of peace, a life with the people she loved, that it felt almost heretical to accept the notion of dying. She wanted to survive so very much, and to see Jacen Syndulla grow into a man as kind and noble as his father. But if she *did* die, it wouldn't be for lack of desire to live; and thinking of all she'd done over the past decades, everything she'd accomplished as a freedom fighter and a general . . .

She hurtled over a gap in the deck plating and landed in the vehicle hangar just as an overhanging catwalk collapsed. She kept running as metal hit the deck behind her and smiled broadly as she saw her ride waiting twenty paces away: The VCX-100 light freighter *Ghost* was covered in debris, but her ship had been through far worse.

In a matter of seconds she was up the ramp, in the cockpit, and at the controls, igniting the reactor and bypassing the start-up checks. She'd have to blast her way through the hangar doors—they'd closed automatically when the magnetic field had failed—but the ship had been refitted and rearmed in the days before Jakku. It could get her outside.

She felt the landing gear retract and the repulsors kick in. She bit back a grin. She was flying into one of the most cataclysmic battles the galaxy had ever seen; she might have minutes to live.

But she'd done *good* in the universe, and whatever came next—the tranquility of death or the struggles of peace; reunion or tragedy—she felt satisfied with her life as a rebel.

With the *Ghost*'s guns ablaze, she left the *Deliverance* and joined the last battle of the war.

V

The last transmission Quell had received from Jakku was Chass na Chadic singing over the names of the dead. Quell almost forgot her mission then, and she wondered if Keize had forgotten his; they listened together as they flew below the Verity District, neither shooting nor attempting to outmaneuver the other. They circled the great data spheres; they spiraled into the darkness of the undercity before rising again, each vulnerable to the other as their fighters crossed paths.

Then the transmission cut out and Quell whispered "Chadic?" and the duel resumed.

Keize ran while Quell pursued. The ace of aces used his blaster cannons like a laser cutter, releasing precise volleys that sheared through towers and support pylons, sending sparks and debris tumbling into the depths. With impossible grace he adjusted momentum and angle midflight to swing around pillars and struts. He never hit anything but his targets. He did it all while denying Quell a clear shot at his fighter; her occasional blasts only left scorched, molten craters in the sides of buildings.

None of the data spheres had fallen, but one by one Keize severed the mechanisms holding them aloft. Quell wondered if they would even last long enough for him to detonate the repulsorlift generator, as he had threatened—the broad repulsor platform fed substations beneath each data sphere, too heavily armored for a TIE to destroy. But antigravity had its limits, and the massive spheres appeared doomed already.

She didn't know how to stop him. She was running out of words and she was running out of time.

"You left Broosh in command?" she asked as Keize made a second pass at a pylon serving as the spine of an endless column of residential platforms below Verity. She circled around the pylon to the right when Keize circled left and she fired wildly as she came around; none of her shots hit home, and the TIE left a black scar on the pylon's metal.

"I did," Keize said. "He'll do as well as I could have. Captain Tensent commands Alphabet?"

"Wyl Lark survived your duel in Chadawa," she said, though she hadn't heard anything from Lark in the transmissions.

"Oh? I'm pleased for his sake, though he hasn't the heart to lead a fighter wing. He would be better off on his homeworld."

"So would Rikton." She had to force the name from her lungs. She didn't know if he'd survived Netalych or been killed by Chadic or Kairos or the droids. "So would Cherroi and Wisp and all of Nenvez's cadets—"

"Rikton tried. *I* tried, Yrica, but there's no home for any of them so long as the New Republic hunts them down."

They entered an access tube between energy towers—a rusting tunnel meant for droids and maintenance workers, barely wide enough to maneuver in. Keize flew directly ahead of Quell, tauntingly easy to hit. She took the bait anyway and he skirted her volley while blasting the tunnel roof. Panels tore and fell as Keize passed; Quell tried desperately to keep her X-wing centered in the tunnel as debris battered her wings and cockpit. She emerged intact but with a crack across her canopy: a reminder not to underestimate her foe.

"What if they die?" she asked. "What if none of them makes it out of Jakku?"

"None at all?" She could hear his sad smile. "Then we have made so many mistakes I can't begin to calculate them. Even so, I don't act only for the 204th. On every inhabited planet, there's someone whose complicity in Imperial ills is recorded in that data bank. Perhaps your own brothers played informant once; or imagine a cantina owner on a forgotten world who spent six months guarding a prison camp."

She sought a counterargument as they tore through a titanic hologram of Mas Amedda—the Emperor's old vizier, face of the powerless Coruscanti government. Beads of light like rain spattered her starfighter as Keize went on: "We both know there's truth to my arguments—you've barely attempted to refute them. You're pitting yourself against me for reasons unrelated to my motivations."

She blinked away azure, spotted Keize heading beneath another data sphere. He'd cut two sections of the tripod linking it to a tower below; if he cut the third, its repulsorlifts would be the only thing keeping it aloft.

"I'm doing this because people are going to die—" she began.

"People are going to die no matter what we do!"

"They're going to die *here*, on *Coruscant*, *today*, when we drop buildings on them. That's not meaningless, Colonel. I don't believe you think it's meaningless."

He was steadying his ship, tempting her to fire—baiting her again. If she fired and she missed, she'd cut the support strut herself.

She loaded a concussion missile, hoped the prototype X-wing's launcher was functional, and sent it streaking toward the data sphere. Keize spun away as the warhead detonated against the sphere's armored casing; but the blast wave caught him, burning air and sonic impact sending the TIE tumbling. The support strut blew apart, sacrificed to save others. The sphere itself was unscathed. Quell suspected Keize had taken damage—at the least, he'd been thrown off balance.

He always had been a better pilot in space than in atmosphere.

"I don't think civilian casualties are meaningless," he said, breathless. "I *do* believe they are the cost of war. How many civilians died when the New Republic invaded Troithe? We accept the tragedy when it serves our cause.

"Innocents will always die. That's why all a soldier can do is protect her own kind—stay loyal to her comrades, safeguard the lives she can touch and see, and end the battle as swiftly as possible. We're not gods or kings—our power is over the strife before us, and all else is payment for others' choices."

The TIE flew crookedly—a result of the missile blast, Quell thought—but Keize seemed to have lost none of his deftness. He was ascending, peaking above the data spheres as he began what had to be his final pass. Before she dropped back down after him, Quell caught a glimpse of gray skies still flashing with crimson and emerald.

"I ask you—" Keize let gravity carry the TIE downward as he angled himself to shoot at support struts above—the same trick she'd used against him earlier. *His* trick, though she hadn't remembered it as such. "—do you do this because you believe in your cause? Or because of the sickness inside you?"

"I don't know what you mean," she lied.

She fired rapidly, uselessly. Keize dived between buildings and soared like a needle threading the district, each time ruining one last structure keeping the data spheres aloft. Quell could barely keep pace, barely stand the forces of acceleration on her body as she gave chase.

"You do know," Keize said. "What happened at Nacronis nearly destroyed you. The horrors there consume you. Guilt blinds you to necessity—and I don't judge that, I don't hold you to blame, but I ask you to step aside."

"I'm not doing this out of guilt," she said. She thought she said it, though she didn't hear the sound.

"I tell you this, Yrica Quell: You are *not* responsible for what happened there. Not for Operation Cinder as a whole, nor for the plan to depopulate a world. You are not responsible for the death of Nacronis."

She wanted to answer and knew she couldn't. She yearned for a message from Jakku—something to send her mind elsewhere. Nothing came.

"*I* am responsible," Keize said. "I sent the squadrons into battle. I designed the attack plan. If you had refused, nothing would have changed—the deaths would still have occurred. The responsibility is mine."

The words were a balm. More than that, they seemed to hollow her and make her buoyant. She wanted to believe, as if believing would change the past and transform her, instantly, into another person; a person far from Coruscant, unburdened by the prospect of killing her mentor or the stains on her soul.

She wanted to believe, but she'd made a pledge to herself at Cerberon. She knew what she'd done and, accepting that, she had chosen to move forward.

Keize cut a spire rising out of blackness, and the metal column creaked and toppled. Quell narrowly avoided being crushed, and she heard through her engine's roar the horrific sound as the spire struck a neighboring building and plummeted. She didn't look—she kept up her pursuit as Keize headed for the central repulsor platform. The last of his targets.

She increased her speed and shot wildly, forcing him off course and driving him skyward again. She expected he would lead her into the open and gain the advantage.

"I don't need your absolution or your forgiveness," she said. The TIE slipped through the gap between data spheres and Quell followed, knowing she was accelerating too hard but determined to smash into Keize if she couldn't bring him down. "You can't give me either."

She finished, almost gasping: "I'm through with sacrificing people. You want to stop me, you kill me."

"As you wish," Keize said, and she expected those to be the last words she ever heard. She chased him out above the district until the clouds seemed close enough to touch, and she waited for the maneuver, the twist that would eliminate her and leave him free to do what he intended.

Keize's fighter glided to one side, and she swept past him into his targeting sights.

Then a guttural voice said, "*I forgive you*," and she was saved.

VI

She had not been named Kairos when she'd been young. She had taken that name after being given life by Caern Adan, and it was no longer right but she had earned no other. She wished to remedy that one day.

She had led her foes away from the city and back, allowed them to batter her vessel until her viewport was blackened and she had devoted all her craft's energies to speed and defense. She had allowed the U-wing to pilot itself while she stepped to a loading door, steadying herself on the portal's frame as she fired her bowcaster into the sky.

Had she still truly been Kairos, she might have taken joy in the spears of light that skewered the eyes of the Empire's machines. She might have celebrated the deaths of the jailers of Coruscant, who carried out the fallen Emperor's wishes so long after his demise. She did not pity her prey, but her joy was only in the execution of a hunter's skill; the shot instead of the slaying. It was a muffled joy, too, for she knew she had another purpose.

She had come to judge Yrica Quell, the defector and killer of worlds; legacy of Adan and IT-O, who had shaped Quell and poured their lives and blood and spirits into her so that she might live on, and in doing so bound her to Kairos, whose spirit had long been mingled with that of Adan and IT-O, and who was compelled to ensure that their heir was worthy.

Kairos had her answer now.

She had returned to the cockpit in time to hear the man of Shadow Wing offer temptations. Kairos had sought shelter in the darkest clouds, eluded the baleful emerald flames of her foes, and listened. She had heard the words as more enemies had come, far too many to defeat. She had heard the pain and defiance in the voice of her sister, and she had been pleased.

Yrica Quell was worthy.

Had Kairos judged otherwise, she would have taken no joy at all in shedding the woman's blood.

(How strange it was to seek to shed so *little* blood. How unlike the Kairos she had been!)

She drew her foes through the clouds above her destination. She drew their ire, twisted in her seat and shot wild shots over her shoulder through both doorways as wind roared and attempted to hurl her from the cockpit into the sky. She could smell the scent of shields energizing air and the scorched trails of cannon blasts. She could smell the iron of the great city below.

She dived. Her enemies followed. She slipped from the clouds and a rain of energy bolts fell around her—for she had made her hunters overeager, too ready to shoot without thought. Below her, between sky and city, was the starfighter of Yrica Quell and the craft of her foe.

Kairos aimed her vessel at Soran Keize and drew the murderous rain onto both the man from Shadow Wing and her sister. She activated retro-rockets and repulsors so that her ship would slow and she said farewell to it—the vessel had served her well, the vessel her sister had called a chrysalis—knowing it would immolate and that its last burning breaths would reach Yrica Quell and Soran Keize.

This was the fire of her judgment, and she hoped that it would be the salvation of one and the death of the other.

As her U-wing broke apart and died like stars die, the woman who had been Kairos removed her harness and cast herself into the sky.

CHAPTER 24

THE CELEBRATION OF INNOCENCE

I

The world spun about Wyl Lark, blending colors like paint washed down a drain. Through the viewport of his escape pod he could see a vast darkness streaked by starships, particle bolts, and hues representing every flammable chemical used by starfaring peoples. The dusty sphere of Jakku was the only solid thing, drifting closer with every rotation of the pod.

There were sounds, too—dozens of voices crying for help and barking orders. He'd activated a comm unit but he didn't understand it and all he listened for was a familiar voice, *any* familiar voice, Nath or Chass or General Syndulla or anyone from Wild or Flare or Hail. He might've been on the wrong channel.

He was delirious, of course. He was aware enough to perceive the irony of his confidence in that fact.

He didn't remember how he'd reached the pod. He vaguely recalled fire and terrible pain (a pain that, whenever he let himself notice, returned to him). He recalled the face of Ragnell, the tattooed ground crew chief, twisted and angry as she shouted orders to unseen figures; recalled her rewiring a panel with shaking hands as the air turned gray. She'd dragged him to safety somehow, but she wasn't with him in the pod. No one was with him in the pod.

He was exhausted and if he looked down at his own body he saw a tremendous amount of blood and shards of metal where there should have been flesh. For this reason he rarely looked.

He focused on the viewport.

There was a series of flashes like fireworks; a tremendous flash at the center of a swirl of colors—a detonation bright enough that Wyl wondered briefly if he'd looked into Jakku's sun. But there was sunlight seeping from behind the planet, and after remembering this he was sure some warship had been lost—a Starhawk, maybe, or the Super Star Destroyer.

He thought of Ragnell again, and then of the face of a young Cathar whom he recalled fighting with Ragnell—screaming at the crew chief with fear in her eyes, saying something about priorities and pods remaining and General Syndulla's orders. He remembered Ragnell smiling an idyllic smile unlike anything he'd seen from the prickly woman. Then the flames again, and the odor of singed fur, and Ragnell's voice echoing through the corridor as they (*they?*) ran.

The flash from the warship's explosion hadn't yet faded, turning all the other colors pale. He heard screams that might have been celebratory.

The sounds of celebration were replaced by silence, then a soft, distant ringing.

Maybe he'd just lost his hearing.

He was alone in the escape pod. Other escape pods had been launched, though, and he was grateful to Ragnell and the Cathar. For whatever they'd done and however much they'd sacrificed.

The movements of the fleets seemed to slow down. As his eyelids became too heavy to keep open, he had a thought he couldn't explain or justify. One he was nonetheless compelled by:

The New Republic had won its war.

||

It was her shields that saved her.

Quell had once mocked deflectors as an extravagance—a safety mechanism for rebel fighter pilots too undisciplined to evade attacks. But when the TIEs descended on Verity in pursuit of Kairos's U-wing, the rain of particle bolts and the U-wing's detonation had unleashed an unexpected conflagration the X-wing's defenses had in part absorbed.

Keize's TIE fighter had been less fortunate. Whereas Quell had managed (with assistance from 4E) to steady her damaged fighter and control her descent, Keize had lost a wing when one of the other TIEs had grazed him in the chaos. Quell had struggled to track him among the rest of the Imperial craft, but then she'd recognized the scar she'd given him earlier; he was falling, maneuvering with short thruster bursts as he disappeared between the data spheres.

Two TIEs had followed her when she'd attempted to give chase—the remainder had been destroyed or scattered by the U-wing's blast—and she'd dispatched them with the three cannons left to her. Now 4E was beeping urgently and she was holding the X-wing aloft by repulsors alone, losing altitude meter by meter.

"He could've made it," she snapped. "He doesn't die that easily—he could've flown to the repulsor platform, he could still be trying to finish the mission. You understand?"

I forgive you, Kairos had said. Quell feared the woman was dead, though she strained against the thought.

The droid splashed data onto her console. Wrapped in grief and doubt, it was a moment before she recognized the sensor map of the area and saw the turbolift 4E had highlighted. She'd already dipped below the level of the repulsor platform, but the lift led from a maintenance scaffold up to the repulsor controls.

"How do we get there?"

The droid plotted a course. The X-wing continued sinking and one of its thrusters blew out loudly enough to leave Quell's head pounding.

The others spewed black smoke but they were enough to impel the craft around a tower and shove it toward their destination: an expanse of metal planking and plates barely large enough for a speeder bike, let alone a starfighter. She was nearly beneath it by the time she closed the distance, and managed to land only by tearing through the safety railings. They screamed and sparked and wrapped around her cockpit as she came to a stop, and afterward she realized how badly she was shaking.

"Stay here as long as you can," she told the droid as she raised the canopy. "If you have to leave, leave."

She was dropping to the ground when she thought of D6-L, the first New Republic droid she'd worked with. She'd grown fond of it too late; she didn't expect she'd have the chance to remedy that error with 4E, but she added a soft, "Thank you." She wasn't sure whether 4E heard.

The turbolift was inoperable, broken during the battle or shut down for security or power conservation. There was an emergency ladder, though, and the climb was long enough that Quell had to take care not to exhaust herself before she reached the top. The ascent gave her time to wonder whether Keize truly could've landed his damaged TIE or whether a toxic cocktail of panic and adrenaline was pushing her forward in place of reason. She also had time to realize she carried no weapon—not a blaster, not even a utility knife—and that she didn't know how practiced Keize was at ground combat.

Better than she was, almost certainly.

She climbed until her shoulders ached and she feared she would fall. When she reached the top she nearly dropped down the shaft trying to operate the access lever; after a few tugs it opened a hatch to the main platform. She saw instantly that her fears had not been misguided: A one-winged TIE had gouged a ten-meter-long trench in the platform surface, coming to rest less than a dozen meters from the turbolift. The TIE's cockpit viewport was cracked and missing several panels, and she saw no sign of the pilot inside or out. Nor did she spot evidence of security forces; the platform appeared to be abandoned.

In the platform's center was a solid dome housing the repulsorlift generators. These, in turn, beamed invisible energy into the district holding the data spheres aloft. Quell made for one of the crawlways set in the dome's base and paused when she encountered a trail of grime and blood. She followed it, increasing her pace.

The crawlway itself was almost comforting: The claustrophobic panels crammed with readouts reminded her of the *Yadeez* or Gavana Orbital. Emergency lights showed the blood trail continuing. As the crawlway expanded and allowed Quell to stand, she wondered if she should attempt stealth, but the flight and the climb had left her little strength. She had no intention of making more noise than necessary, but she wouldn't feign the subtlety of an assassin.

She didn't have to. She heard Keize's ragged breathing from a branch in the corridor and spied him propped against a wall in his flight suit, gloves and helmet removed. He was unspooling wire from a panel to a metal case with trembling hands, and when he saw Quell—long seconds after she saw him—he pulled a blaster pistol and aimed it her way. The barrel bobbed so rapidly she wondered if he could hit her even at such short range.

His face was soaked in sweat and his hair disheveled. She expected she looked little better. The only blood she saw ran beneath his chin and down his neck, as if he'd dribbled from a glass. But as she studied him, she realized the black flight suit was wet and torn along his leg and his side—shrapnel wounds, she assumed. If he'd crashed hard enough to impale himself he'd likely also crashed hard enough to break bones and rupture organs.

"I don't think you're going to win," she said. "I'm sorry."

"I'd prefer better odds," he admitted. He flexed his fingers around the grip of the blaster as if to still the tremors. It didn't work, and he looked exhausted by the effort. "I have enough explosives to blow the repulsorlifts, though. Proton warheads, courtesy of the 204th."

"No. You've been here how long? And you've barely started." She eyed the case and the spool in his hand. "Warheads with no detonators. You need power from the generator to trigger them?"

"Couldn't have them blow up en route from Jakku." This time he smiled, albeit bitterly.

Quell smiled, too. Then she launched herself forward, sliding down the corridor on a knee toward Keize. It was one of the only moves she remembered from her hand-to-hand training, but she hoped Keize would be taken by surprise—that he'd anticipated a longer conversation, an exchange of threats, rather than an immediate attack.

She heard the snap and sizzle of a blaster bolt; felt heat over her head but no pain. She grabbed Keize's arm with both hands, wrenching it to the side, and he let out a swift, low cry. The blaster flew from his grasp, bounced against a wall, and clattered somewhere behind Quell.

He didn't attempt to lunge past her. He didn't move from where he was. She stood, looked at his agonized expression, then slowly knelt again.

"I'm sorry," she repeated.

Keize shook his head and grimaced. "It's all right." His arm was still outstretched where she'd positioned it, as if relaxing the muscles was worse than keeping it still.

She said nothing.

Gradually, Keize guided the outstretched arm down to his side with the help of his other hand. He rested his head against the wall, but his eyes were clear and focused on Quell. "It's not too late," he said.

"Colonel—"

"Yrica. Hear me out." He swallowed, composing himself. Quell felt something wet touch her knee on the floor. "You've made your decision—you won't sacrifice more lives, and I hear you. But we can still do some good."

"I don't think so," she murmured.

He went on as if he hadn't heard. "You have the explosives. Forget the repulsorlifts. Go to my fighter and remove the ion reactor core. Wire it to the proton bombs, find a place to detonate the bundle—"

He drew deep breaths, exhausted by the effort of speech. Quell finished for him: "You want me to generate an electromagnetic pulse.

Overload the data bank instead of destroying it." He didn't disagree, and she added, "I'm not sure it would even work."

It was a while before he answered. "Aren't improvised solutions the rebel way?" His head lolled, swinging from side to side. "Maybe it *wouldn't* work. I don't know how much data we'd wipe, or what of that would be unrecoverable. But if it's the most you're willing to do—if you can wipe the records of even a few people, give a few troops a chance at real lives under the New Republic—then I'll consider my efforts worthwhile."

His whole body was shaking. He moved his good arm again, reaching for her, and she clasped his hand. She couldn't remember ever touching him before. His skin was cool and damp.

"Honor your nature as a soldier, Yrica Quell," he said. "Serve your comrades one last time."

"You like to talk about soldiers," she said softly, and ran her fingers over his wrist. She hoped he couldn't feel her own trembling. She spoke as if placating a delirious man who'd suggested something unreal; it made it easier to deny the possibility. "But it's just a word for people who fight. Nothing special."

"If that's true—" He struggled to maintain the patient tone he'd used with her through so many discussions. She caught undertones of urgency anyway. "—don't those *people* deserve to move on from this war? You know the ones who'll suffer. Your comrades, people like—"

"I know."

"—Alchor Mirro and Jeela Brebtin. Or what about Meriva Greef—"

"I know!"

Keize's fingertips dug into her skin, not hard enough to bruise. She didn't want to hear him. She didn't turn away.

"What about Rikton? Or Fra Raida? What do you suppose they would have wanted? What do we owe their memory—"

"Stop it!" She was shouting at a wounded man. She couldn't help herself. "Stop it! I cared for them, you know I cared for them, so don't act like I've forgotten who they are. I tried to save them and I couldn't. There was nothing I could do on Netalych, but they were my team."

His hand began to slip away. She held on as he spoke. "I don't doubt you. They were my colleagues, too. Rikton—" His lip curled up. "Rikton was a friend, in another lifetime."

Somehow she laughed. "I think Fra Raida was into me."

"I was aware she had strong feelings. Not those in particular."

"I was hoping she'd survived."

They were both silent awhile. The thought tugged at her mind—she *could* attempt to damage the data bank. It was a desperate plan. It might work. Maybe it was right.

Yet she didn't want to. She couldn't explain why.

"We're short on time, so forgive me," Keize said. He squeezed his eyes shut, then reopened them. She wasn't sure he could see anymore. "Rikton and Fra Raida were not unique in their circumstances. Consider what you condemn their colleagues to."

She shook her head insistently, trying to shut out his voice. There was an answer somewhere, just outside her reach, and she couldn't find it so long as he argued.

He must have seen her struggle. For whatever reason he didn't press his advantage, and she began fumbling with words, hoping to find sense in them. "Every time you say something like that—you keep describing this same future where the New Republic makes us suffer, but you never talk about the alternative."

"The alternative?"

" 'If we don't destroy the data bank they'll hunt us down.' But what if we *do it*? What's that future like?"

"It's a future in which they have choices."

"Is it? They're more like me than they're like you," she said, anxiety nearly stealing her breath. "Rikton and Raida and Broosh and the others . . . they think about what we've done and it bothers them. I know it does. They have the nightmares, just like me, and it doesn't matter what we do to the Emperor's data bank—they're going to live under a shadow for the rest of their lives.

"Leaving Shadow Wing didn't cure the *sickness* in me; it just made it easier to ignore. So maybe they're free but they're eaten away inside, damned no matter what we do because it's too late for them to choose what really matters—and the cost is a galaxy where people get away with genocide. You think *that's* going to bring peace? You think ignoring the Empire's crimes won't make it easier for the worst of us to keep committing atrocities? You talked about rioting and terrorism, well—and not to mention all of our blasted *victims,* and how they suffer—"

"Is that me? The worst of us?" Keize asked, soft and steady. "The one who isn't like the others?"

The avalanche of language came to a stop. She hadn't been making sense anyway. She faltered and shook her head. "I don't know what you are. I don't know how you live with it all."

"I can tell you—"

"Or maybe I *do.*" She laughed, the sound thick with mucus. "Hell, maybe it's easy. You said it yourself—you asked if I was doing all this because I felt guilty over Nacronis. Maybe that's not *me.*"

Now she dug her fingernails into his arm, squeezing the clammy skin. He flinched, at the pain or the argument. She rushed on. "Maybe you're the one clinging to a way to make Cinder meaningful. Maybe that's your sickness—you justify and explain everything, *everything* we've done as being about loyalty or duty or principle, about saving your fellow soldiers, when really you're just piling on excuses for the massacres in the hope that it'll all balance out. Maybe—" She'd never spoken harshly to him and she hated herself for it. She was laughing again, near hysteria. "Colonel, you're the *best* of us, but maybe you're as much of a mess as everyone else; deluding yourself because you can't live with the truth."

"The truth being . . . ?"

Her laughter faded. Keize waited, expectant and without judgment.

"We were murderous bastards," she said, "and being true to one another doesn't make it any better. It just means we don't stop when we figure out how bad it's gotten."

"Maybe," he said. "Or maybe I truly do believe in putting my people first. Maybe you've finally found something to believe in, too."

There was respect in him, but no concession. She'd hoped for another outcome and tried not to show her disappointment. "I suppose so."

"Is that it, then?" Every sentence came slowly now, as if traveling a great distance. "You find neither future we've discussed palatable, but prefer one to the other?"

"No. I don't know." She shook her head and remembered sitting with Caern Adan as he'd died. He'd meant so much less to her than Soran Keize, yet he remained in her spirit. "I don't know what any of us deserve. What I do know . . ."

She tasted the words before she spoke them, tested them for venom. She was surprised to find none. "I've accepted what I've done. I know the awful deeds I committed and I've tried to move past my guilt, because it stopped being useful long ago.

"But I haven't *forgotten* Nacronis or anything else. I live with the memory of what I'm capable of every day. I *need* the memory to do better. And wiping out the records of what we've done seems an awful lot like helping everyone else forget."

His eyes had shut again. "Then I ask you for the last time: You trust the New Republic to judge them fairly?"

The question was familiar. Somewhere in the past weeks, Quell had come to terms with her answer.

"No. I don't. But I haven't earned the right to make the call."

For a time, Quell thought he was preparing his counterargument; then she feared he'd fallen unconscious, though she could feel his pulse. Eventually the strain in his expression eased and he moved his head in something like a nod.

Soran Keize, Imperial ace of aces and the finest soldier Quell had known, was accepting defeat.

"I will miss our conversations," he murmured.

"So will I."

"I wish there were time for mijura," he said, even softer.

She didn't know the word. She didn't think he was talking to her anymore.

She stayed with her mentor until the life had gone out of him. Even after that she remained there, clasping his hand.

In the back of Quell's mind was an assumption that Imperial security would come to apprehend or kill her. This gave her no pleasure, but she wasn't afraid and she remained in the dim corridors of the generator structure as she turned over thoughts of her life and Soran Keize's life. An hour passed before she realized no one was coming after all, and that whatever state Coruscant was in its condition was dire enough that the Verity District was no one's foremost concern.

After that, she pondered whether the New Republic would come instead. If Jakku was won, word would arrive quickly and it wouldn't be long before the Imperial government surrendered. In that case, she'd need to turn herself in—General Syndulla had given her leave for a single mission, but that grace had expired.

She was considering leaving, trying to recall if Keize had ever mentioned what he wanted done with his remains, when she heard scraping along the metal floor of the crawlway. She recovered Keize's blaster and held it loosely as she stepped to the branch and peered out.

Rolling toward her was 4E, smeared with black ash but otherwise untouched by the chaos. It chimed enthusiastically when it spotted Quell, then switched to a more serious register and burbled as she approached.

"I don't understand," she said. "How did you even get up here?"

It emitted another series of incomprehensible burbles. Quell sighed and sat. She looked at herself and saw blood crusted on her clothes and her hand. She wondered what the droid thought of her, then felt absurd for wondering at all.

4E waited another moment, then buzzed and spun its cone. Its holoprojector twitched before azure light filled the corridor, particles dancing and coalescing until Quell saw the face of her mentor alive once again. Keize wore his flight suit but no helmet, and he spoke with the sobriety she expected from his speeches.

"This is Colonel Soran Keize of the 204th Imperial Fighter Wing," he said. "I am broadcasting this message in response to the New Republic attack on Jakku and my own recent failures at Coruscant.

"If you are receiving this, know that I take full responsibility for the actions of the 204th. Others will call those actions illegal or immoral, and that judgment is not mine to make; but I have gone to great lengths to ensure none within my unit had any choice but to comply with my demands. I also hid our most grievous actions from our superiors, both before and after the Battle of Endor.

"Beginning with the massacre on Tu'oon and ending with the attack on Coruscant's Verity District, this is my confession . . ."

From there, he listed a seemingly endless series of operations, specifying his role in each. Quell didn't recognize all of them. Of those she did recognize, many had been planned by Colonel Nuress, not Keize; and when he spoke of Operation Cinder (both the first and second Cinder) he made no mention of the Emperor's Messenger or the military chain of command, emphasizing his personal involvement above all else. He described ways he had enforced discipline and obedience, few of which were true.

Even in death, she thought, Keize sought to protect his people. If he couldn't save every Imperial soldier, he would try to save the 204th by sacrificing his reputation—sparing others New Republic justice and being remembered as a war criminal.

Maybe he *had* believed. And if his conviction had led him to slaughter millions, how could she hate him when her own lack of conviction had still resulted in Nacronis?

She would never know the truth of his soul, or whether her admiration for him was justified or a remnant of the Empire's conditioning.

"I wish you'd been a better man," she whispered to the hologram before it disappeared.

She wondered, in the last glimmer of the holo's light, whether she would have felt the same admiration if Syndulla had been her mentor from the start—if she would've seen any worthy qualities in Keize at all.

She supposed it didn't matter.

"Come on," she said to the droid, and they left toward the daylight spilling in through the crawlway.

III

"Don't move."

Wyl wasn't sure he could've moved if he'd wanted to. He lay very still in the escape pod and left his eyes closed to shut out the brightness seeping through the viewport.

He was still delirious, he thought, but his hearing had returned. He should've been worried about his friends, but none of their faces would stay fixed in his mind.

"I'm seeing a lot of blood, but we can't leave you here." There was the sound of something heavy shifting—the pod door, maybe? "Where'd you come from? The *Ravager*? The *Eviscerator*?"

He didn't recognize those ships. Something seemed wrong with the question. "The *Deliverance*," he said.

There was a long pause. Wyl finally opened his eyes and saw a black helmet looking down at him. Oxygen tubes ran from the helmet to a chest piece.

"What's your name?" the TIE pilot asked.

"Wyl," he said. "Wyl Lark."

The pilot cocked his head and looked down at him a long while before laughing. The sound was muffled by the helmet, but it sounded fresh and joyous.

"Hell of a thing—I've heard a lot about you, Wyl Lark. Let's get you home safe."

He felt gloved hands on his body, touching him gently at first to see where he flinched from the pain, then working to bring him upright. Wyl had a thousand questions but no voice; amazement swallowed all his words.

IV

Nath flew low above the desert, kicking up enough dust to muddy the Y-wing's sensors and make T5 grumble. "I know, I know," Nath growled, "but much higher and the bioscanners won't do any good. Not to mention we'll be that much clearer a target for any ground troops—looks like nobody told them the battle's over."

He increased his altitude anyway and angled toward the rocky hills at the desert's edge, too stumpy and eroded to be called mountains. T5 sent a metallurgical report to his console (plenty of scraps, a few massive wrecks, nothing that looked like a whole fighter or escape pod within five kilometers), and he waited for life readings. *Probably better if nothing shows,* he thought. *It'll only mean trouble.*

He knew he was lying to himself. If anyone from his squadron was alive, he meant to find them no matter the danger.

After knocking out the bulk freighter he'd spent the rest of the battle "repairing his ship," keeping his distance from the fighting, and sniping at any TIEs that got close. He hadn't fled the system. He'd even recorded escape pod trajectories from afar. His alibi wouldn't hold up to close examination, and he wouldn't come out looking like much of a hero compared with Lieutenant Itina and the others who'd returned to the fray; but he'd stayed alive when many—maybe most—of the crew and pilots of the *Deliverance* hadn't.

He'd made the best choice he could. The only choice, if he was to be true to himself. The New Republic, galactic peace, all that garbage— Wyl and Chass had believed. Quell and Kairos, too. Nath Tensent, though? He'd fooled a lot of people and nearly fooled himself, but he'd never truly bought into the dream of a better world. He'd just surrounded himself with zealots, and that made good camouflage.

(Besides, he'd neutralized an enemy that might've cost the New Republic the battle. He'd be damned if he felt guilty for not doing more than *that.*)

T5 pinged loudly and sent over a new report. Nath frowned and tapped the screen.

"Homing beacon, huh? You sure it's from the *Deliverance*?"

T5 chimed once.

"All right. We'll take a look."

He adjusted his course to take him deeper into the hills. They'd spotted plenty of escape pods already, including a few from the *Deliverance* that hadn't survived landing, and he had to suppress the hope rising in him. If Wyl *had* somehow made it out—

He ignored the thought. The great piles of dun rocks blurred and he cut his speed, allowing his sensors to recalibrate. In the distance he spotted a glint—something metallic matching the beacon's coordinates, half buried in a landslide.

He switched to bioscanners. No life signs at the pod's location, but there were two signatures in motion less than a kilometer away. Instinct told him to open his throttle and hurtle toward the site, but he cut speed again until he was moving slow enough to see whatever was on the ground. (Slow enough to guarantee he'd be blown out of the sky if he turned out to be chasing a stormtrooper with a surface-to-air rocket.)

Come on, brother. Be out there.

He passed over a hilltop and T5 squealed so fiercely that Nath was sure, for an instant, they were under attack—that he'd made the fatal mistake he'd been dreading all day, and that he was going to die not in battle but on a rescue mission. He grinned at the irony, ready to face his final moments, then understood the droid's reaction: In a narrow valley ahead two figures trekked among the scree. One wore the black suit of a TIE pilot; the other was lean and dressed in what looked like shredded civilian clothes, supporting himself with an arm around the pilot's shoulders.

"You sure?" Nath asked. "You sure it's him?"

He pushed the Y-wing as low as he could without choking the survivors with grit. T5 was beeping in the affirmative and as they came closer Nath got a better look: Wyl Lark was hobbling through the sand and gravel, leaning into his companion and laughing. The TIE pilot's helmet was off and the expression Nath saw was similarly joyous—they looked like two siblings reunited after years as they waved frantically at the Y-wing.

Nath felt a grudging sense of admiration and amusement. Maybe all Wyl's outreach to the enemy hadn't been wrongheaded. He'd just been playing the long game.

"You call it in to the New Republic, all right?" he told the droid. "Convince them it's a priority pickup. Don't mention Wyl's name, in case he's tagged as a deserter—just tell them it's a wounded man from the *Deliverance,* and patch me through if they don't take it serious."

He circled around to reassure the pair they'd been spotted, but he didn't look for a place to land. He didn't have room in the Y-wing for a passenger or any supplies to offer. More to the point, he didn't have anything to *say* to Wyl Lark after everything they'd been through. If Nath had been wrong about Wyl's choice to leave the squadron, well— Wyl had vindication without an admission from Nath. And the kid would be better off not knowing Nath had disappointed him in the end, leaving the battle before the last of the work was done.

Their paths were separating. Nath was glad Wyl was alive.

T5 made a disappointed noise. "Not this time," Nath said. "Come on—Chass's odds are worse, but we're not writing her off until we've picked through more wreckage than this. If she brought that B-wing down, it should be within a few hundred kilometers of where the *Deliverance* dropped its pods . . ."

He trailed off as Wyl and the TIE pilot came back into sight. Both were looking skyward, away from the Y-wing, pointing to something in the clouds in the obscuring light of the western sun.

Chass na Chadic wasn't sure if she'd made a mistake.

She was alive. That was a shock by itself, really; her cockpit had stayed intact after the loss of her airfoil, doubling as an escape pod as it tumbled and tangled with wreckage, finally falling to Jakku in the torn-open belly of a Star Destroyer. She could see sky and mountains and even a swath of desert from the remains of her bomber high in the warship's hull, and she thought it wasn't the worst view to die with.

Because she *was* dying. She'd chosen life, only to be crushed between her seat and her console. Her legs were numb, her arm was burnt, she was bleeding out very slowly, and she was thirsty. She'd chosen life and what she had to look forward to was a lingering death over hours or days.

Maybe she'd have been better off with the blaze of glory.

She alternated between states of boredom (when she counted the specks of ships crossing the sky; or tried to guess how long she'd been trapped; or attempted to catalog every song from her lost collection) and blossoming panic (when she wondered if there was a way to hasten her death; or grew terrified by the thought of being rescued and never recovering, suffering the same nightmare future as usual—only this time without legs).

Sometimes she prayed the way her cults had prayed, only with a simple message to one man: *Nath Tensent, find me. You said you'd shoot me if I needed you to shoot me. Find me!*

Jakku was hot, and her oxygen recirculators had failed. Sometimes she licked the sweat salt off her lips and chin.

Some hours into her ordeal she saw a flying speck that didn't move like a ship. It descended in canted circles and slowed and sped at odd moments, and when it came closer she thought she saw outspread wings. Other specks followed, and she wondered if they were carrion birds come to scavenge the dead. That didn't seem right for a desert world like Jakku—would carrion birds be so *big*?—but people said strange things lived in the Western Reaches.

Each bird, upon descending to a certain altitude, ceased spiraling downward and headed out over its own strip of desert. She made out enormous iridescent wings, stubby heads, and outstretched claws. She wondered if she was hallucinating when she saw that on the back of each creature sat a humanoid rider, limbs wrapped tight around their mount while craning their neck to see below.

Chass didn't understand. She felt lucid and awake. She stared as several birds and their riders dropped out of her sight, then returned to the sky minutes later bearing burdens that might have been bodies.

She recalled stories her mother had told her (before the cults, when Chass had been no older than three or four) of spirits from the sky who carried the souls of the dying to another world. Then she recalled a different story—Wyl Lark's story, of the Hundred and Twenty of Polyneus, who had learned to fly the great beasts of their homeworld.

She remembered Wyl slipping away during the journey to Jakku before announcing his resignation. She began to laugh as she realized that, deserter or not—alive or not—he'd done his part one last time.

One hundred and nineteen Wyl Larks were out there, all searching for survivors.

Chass lay back, closed her eyes, and waited.

VI

Outside the crawlway on the repulsorlift platform, Yrica Quell found Kairos among the living.

The woman stood straight-backed in her stained and torn garments, despite the new cracks in the chitinous plates covering her face and the thick fluid like blood or pus welling at those plates' edges. She looked like she'd survived catastrophe—more than a fifty-meter fall, more than a battle on an occupied world at the center of the galaxy—yet remained brave and unbowed.

"You brought it up the turbolift shaft?" Quell asked, indicating the astromech behind her with a tilt of her head.

"Yes," Kairos said.

"Thank you," Quell said. Then, faster: "And for what you did up there. I would've died if I'd been alone."

"Yes," Kairos said, apparently without humor.

Quell smiled anyway. She swallowed it and searched Kairos for any indication of weakness. She found what might have been *weariness* instead—a slight sag in the woman's shoulders, a sway in her arms, but nothing specific to injury. "Are you okay? Physically, I mean?"

"Yes," Kairos said a third time. There was quiet delight in the word. "Are you?"

"I'm bruised. I'm sure I broke something—I always do." She glanced at her flight suit and shrugged. "The blood isn't mine."

"I know." Kairos cocked her head, and Quell saw that one of the plates had begun to detach from whatever was underneath—like a peeling scab, or an eggshell separating from its membrane. "They won. The New Republic won at Jakku. There are broadcasts playing in the undercity."

"Good."

It was an inane thing to say, but Quell had been resigned to a New Republic victory since shortly after the Battle of Endor; hearing the news now felt like a statement of the obvious.

Even as she thought this, however, she began to tremble. The galaxy had changed, and it would be the New Republic that would define the way she lived—the way *everyone* lived—forevermore. It *was* a profound change, even if her instinct was to reject it. She thought she was glad.

"Anything from the squadron?" Quell asked.

"No. The transmitter was destroyed." She paused, and Quell expected her to say: *I hope they are well,* or *I'm sure they survived,* or even *They might be dead.* But that wasn't Kairos's way, and Quell pushed aside her own worry as Kairos added: "I think it will be dangerous here soon. Find a place in the city where no one will look until the New Republic comes."

Quell nodded, though she wasn't sure *how* she would find safety— she didn't know Coruscant, and on foot the vastness of the city, the way the sky hid behind the tallest buildings even near the upper levels, was intimidating the way the confines of the generator crawlway had been comforting. She was bred for claustrophobia, for artificial lights and hard vacuum outside her windows.

The droid behind her buzzed quietly, as if offering its assistance. It was only then that Kairos's phrasing struck her. "What about you?" Quell asked.

"You are my sister, and the heir to those dear to me. But I have made my judgment, and you no longer need me."

"That's not an answer." She understood more than she would've expected, but she was too tired, too overwhelmed by all the day's events, to fully comprehend. "Are you coming with me?"

"I am pleased for Adan and IT-O," Kairos said, with something like the interrogation droid's amused tolerance. "I am pleased you've become what you are. I am changing, too, and I am ready to move beyond my bond to this war."

"Are you dying?" Quell's voice was suddenly small.

"I am *changing*." Kairos stroked the loose chitin. Only a thin film held the plate to her face now, and other plates had begun sliding free as well. "The ship is gone. My chrysalis is broken. The war is ended, and only you remain of those whose blood and spirit mixed with mine. Now *you* have changed, and I am becoming—"

Kairos mouthed something and shuddered, as if struggling with the limits of language.

"I cannot return to my people," Kairos said, and turned away from Quell to face the city. "I will not be a *shaman* or a warrior anymore. I am *new*, Yrica Quell, and the first thing to touch my skin will not be linked to pain or destruction."

The first chitin plate dropped to the platform with a wet smack. Another piece hung from her chin.

Quell wanted to step forward. She stayed where she was. "Can I look at you?"

"No," Kairos said, and there was ecstasy in her voice. "What I become next will not be what I was. I am leaving, and I will find a place where I do not need a shell—where my spirit and blood resonate with the air and life around me."

"What does that mean? Where are you going?"

Kairos placed her hands over her face and turned, just enough to look back at Quell—just enough for Quell to see one of the woman's dark eyes, and a glimpse of something below the peeling chitin like newborn flesh.

"Somewhere beautiful. I will find it. Be very well, my sister."

With that, Kairos turned again and stepped to the edge of the platform. When she jumped—a small motion, a quick bending of the knees and a spring—Quell caught her breath and rushed to the edge, stepping over a trail of ichor. She looked down and saw a narrow catwalk ten meters below the platform, and Kairos—or whoever she was now—striding briskly and comfortably, *lightly* along it, toward some destination Quell couldn't fathom.

Quell began laughing and knelt on the metal. *Be very well, my sister,* she echoed, as if the woman could read her thoughts; and she felt tears on her cheeks, and the longer she knelt the more came. She wept not only for Kairos, and for the loss of Kairos, but for all the pain and joy she'd experienced yet never allowed to surface.

She looked out at the city, tears falling onto the levels below like rain, and with the droid behind her she smiled and wondered what the future would bring for all of them.

PART FOUR

VICTORY'S PRICE

CHAPTER 25

ENDURING SCARS OF FLESH AND SPIRIT

I

"So . . . what are we going to do about Lieutenant Quell?"

Hera Syndulla stood across from Mon Mothma, chancellor of the New Republic and leader of the known galaxy, as the human poured two glasses of water from a ceramic ewer sculpted to resemble a Skakoan squid. After she'd spoken, Mothma crossed the vast office and returned to Hera's side, passing her one of the glasses as they settled into cream-colored armchairs.

The synthleather seemed to envelop Hera as she leaned back. In that moment she was certain it was the most comfortable chair she'd ever sat in. She'd barely slept in the weeks since Jakku, and this meeting on Nakadia had been her most pleasurable task in a while; the war was over, but the challenges never stopped.

"Have you talked to her personally?" Hera asked.

She recognized the crease of Mothma's brow, the line added to her already lined face—the indication that she'd delegated a task she felt responsible for to someone she didn't altogether trust. "I saw transcripts of her interviews, but I haven't had the time. For what it's worth, Intelligence has confirmed her story—the security footage from Coruscant shows her and Keize exactly as she reported."

"I told you she would cooperate."

"You did, and I believed you." Mothma's lips quirked into a smile. Hera read the meaning: *I believed you, but it's my job to make sure.* "She is comfortable, by the way—I had one of my people arrange it. House arrest, but an apartment is more comfortable than a cell."

"I wish you could talk to her," Hera said, then added, "Thank you."

Mothma sipped her water. "Intelligence has sent upward of fifty agents, plus security, to study the data bank Keize attempted to destroy. It's encrypted, but we've already unlocked sections and Cracken is confident we'll have the rest in time. He says we'd have stumbled on to it sooner or later but that Quell's information gave us a tremendous head start—like you, he's requested an expedited hearing to determine her status."

Hera frowned. "Meaning . . . Intelligence wants her freedom contingent on her continued assistance?"

"Meaning he wants to know what's happening one way or the other. I don't blame him for that."

It was a rebuke so gentle and subtle Hera almost didn't catch it. She nodded to indicate she understood. New Republic Intelligence was picking up where the military had left off, following up on thousands of leads daily and trying to assess a galaxy's worth of threats; General Cracken needed to know what assets he had to work with. Hera felt fortunate not to be in his position.

"The hearing won't amount to much, of course," Mothma went on. "We're not equipped for it yet, so *expediting* means I pull strings until our overworked advocates sign off on whatever I decide." She sighed. "Tell me what you think of her? I'm not asking you to shoulder the burden—but give me your opinion, as someone who was there."

Hera had been awaiting the question for days. She still wasn't sure how to answer. "I think," she said, attempting to read Mothma's expression and failing, "that Quell's actions after Cerberon, regardless of authorization, were laudable. She infiltrated an enemy unit without assistance or a means to coordinate with our forces, and she led us to the 204th despite those obstacles. That saved countless lives on Chadawa; and if we'd never found Shadow Wing at Chadawa, we wouldn't have been prepared to deal with them at Jakku. How much she contributed to Keize's work is arguable, but she ultimately reported on Keize's plans for Coruscant and personally stopped who-knows-how-many deaths during that attack."

"She didn't exactly come back willingly," Mothma said. "Two of your pilots had to retrieve her."

"Chass na Chadic and Kairos defied orders." Hera shook her head. "I'm confident neither of them was diplomatic about it, but I'm not going to assume Quell *wouldn't* have returned on her own. She didn't have the chance."

"All right. Granted." Mothma lifted her glass while her eyes remained on Hera. "Now say the rest."

They knew each other too well—liked each other too much—to play games. *Let's get to the truth, then.*

"Quell's record with the 204th is . . . concerning, even before Endor," Hera said. "And when I chose her to lead a squadron, I didn't realize the extent of her actions after the Emperor's death. None of us did. She was a willing participant in Operation Cinder and she was actively involved in the destruction of Nacronis—and she lied about it.

"I like Quell. I believe she's changed. But her victims can't speak up because their civilization died with their planet, and I can't ignore that."

It hurt to say the words. If Hera had trusted Mothma any less, she would've kept them to herself.

"It would be easier," Mothma said quietly, "if we weren't setting precedent. If the decision could be sealed, like it would be in the Empire—never subjected to public view, with no consequences; no one to answer to but our own peculiar consciences."

Hera laughed dubiously. "Is that an option?"

"Maybe if Keize's attack and postmortem proclamation hadn't been so public. Maybe if fewer people knew, but—no. Justice works best in daylight anyway, and practically speaking we were going to encounter a case like hers sooner rather than later."

"Meaning?"

"I'm not looking to make an example of her," Mothma said, too swiftly for someone who hadn't considered the possibility. "But this is the start of a very long process. The Emperor's data bank cataloging his people's atrocities isn't public knowledge, and the Senate hasn't yet determined the full process for trying Imperials outside the topmost levels of government. Each of those items impacts the other, all of which is to say . . . Soran Keize wasn't entirely *wrong* to believe the data bank is a potential threat to a lasting peace."

Hera arched her brow. "You read those transcripts pretty closely."

"I did." She shrugged. "I believe in justice. I also believe that for the galaxy to survive, reconciliation must occur. The New Republic will not hold together if we spend the next ten or twenty or fifty years divided into rebel and Imperial, yet true reconciliation requires honesty. It requires we stare at what we've done as a civilization and come to terms with it. The data bank can help, but only if the Senate—and the galaxy as a whole—has the appetite for self-examination over revenge."

"Especially since the data bank gives us an endless list of crimes to seek justice—or revenge—for," Hera agreed. "You can't blame people for wanting restitution from ex-Imperials."

"No, and I don't object on principle. Pity those ex-Imperials make up a dangerously large portion of our population. Quell has the poor luck of being at the start of the line. I won't make her an example, but she will send a message whether we intend it or not."

Hera stood and stepped to a small window looking onto the surrounding settlement. Nakadia was an agriworld, uncosmopolitan and formerly ignored by most of the galaxy; symbolically perfect for the latest seat of the New Republic government. Its buildings were squat and simple, and Hera could see where they disappeared into fields of grain just before the horizon.

But Nakadia had seen its share of fighting—battles few people besides the Nakadians remembered. Even Hera only vaguely recalled the
reports, yet she was sure the Emperor's data bank named soldiers
who'd inflicted suffering on the locals. How many nightmares, she
wondered, did Nakadians endure every night because no one acknowledged their pain?

And yet, she thought. *And yet* . . .

"One last thought," Hera said. "If I may?"

"Always," Mothma said.

Hera turned from the window and looked at the chancellor. She
wasn't the orator Mothma was. She didn't have to be so long as she was
clear and direct and true.

"The Rebellion got dirty sometimes, but the dream was pure. The
ideal was pure. If we were still rebels, we would've forgiven her, and
you know it. I don't like the thought that winning's made us harder."

"Nor do I," Mothma conceded. "But there are luxuries we no longer
have. We were a storm, shifting and chaotic, battering the walls of a
fortress of evil. Now we're rebuilding where that fortress stood, and
we—I—have to consider whether each stone in our foundation can
carry the weight of the future."

They were silent awhile. Eventually, Hera decided she'd been dismissed and began to walk toward the door.

Mothma stopped her with a gesture. "Still, if we lock Yrica Quell
away for her crimes, after everything she's done to redeem herself . . . ?"
She sighed and smiled sadly before finishing: "What hope do any of
them have?"

Hera had seen pictures of Quell before she'd ever met her, from Caern
Adan's dossiers. Quell's images had been taken during New Republic
processing after her surrender on Nacronis, when she'd been covered
in cuts and bruises, one arm in a sling. She'd had a glasslike sharpness,
then—as if she'd been equally likely to shatter or to injure.

There was no brittleness to her now, as she sat on a low table in the
apartment she'd been assigned. She was thin, and her hair had grown

out so that wisps often fell in front of her eyes. But she looked unafraid and certain of herself. When Hera had entered, she'd noticed the deliberate way Quell had relaxed her shoulders and turned and taken her seat—the movements of a civilian hosting a visitor, not an officer seeing a superior.

Hera squatted across from Quell and said, "You're going free."

Quell furrowed her brow. "What?"

"Chancellor Mothma says you're going to go free. There's even a medal in it—I'm not sure which one—for exceptional bravery and service on Coruscant." She smiled as she said it. Quell's expression remained flat.

"I don't understand," Quell said. She wrapped the fingers of her right hand around her left wrist, stroking her arm. "I don't understand."

Hera softened her tone. "There were several requests for an expedited decision about your status. Mothma looked at your case just yesterday, and it's all finalized as of this afternoon."

Quell said nothing, so Hera went on. "It's not a full pardon. The Senate's debating putting restrictions on ex-Imperial troops with certain records—limited voting rights, weapons prohibitions, that sort of thing. There're a few bills under consideration. Mothma thinks it'll end up varying planet-to-planet, but—" She laughed softly. "—I'm rambling. You're free, Yrica. Congratulations."

Quell stood from the table, took several paces and turned back. Hera stood as well. This time she waited.

"No consequences at all," Quell said. "That's what it ends in?"

"You faced your share of consequences."

"I certainly don't deserve a *medal*," Quell said. She laughed scornfully. "You know that."

"What you deserve," Hera said calmly, "is a question for philosophers. If you're looking for unfailing judgment from a one-year-old government, you're going to the wrong place."

Quell closed her eyes and nodded. "I take your point."

There was a self-awareness in the words that made Hera flinch.

You've never had good experiences looking to government for moral guidance, have you?

She stepped toward Quell, slowly enough that she could halt and back away if the woman showed discomfort. But Quell stayed put, and Hera put a hand on her shoulder.

"If you don't like the medal," Hera said, "think of it as a political decision. There are a lot of people with opinions on what should happen with you and people like you—but the chancellor thinks this is best for the New Republic. A way to signal to ex-Imperials that even if their leaders can't go free, there's a path to normalcy for them.

"Mothma also thinks—*I* think—that if it's not perfect justice, it's still close to fair. Can you live with that?"

She felt Quell's shoulder rise and fall as the woman took slow breaths. Quell looked quietly bereft, as if recalling a death grieved long ago.

"Yes," Quell said. "I have to."

"Come on," Hera said, and squeezed her shoulder. "Let's get something to eat."

They didn't go far from Quell's apartment. They found an outdoor table at a sparsely occupied café where locals played dejarik and grumbled about offworlders driving up prices. Hera paid for the meal—local fare, a groundnut stew for herself and thin seafood porridge for Quell—and carried the conversation. She talked about her father and her homeworld, and her desire to visit Ryloth again. She said little about the more difficult decisions she had to make, about her military commission or about her son.

Quell needed normalcy, not stress. Hera had other friends she could lean on.

After they finished, Hera walked Quell back to her apartment and said, "Think of what you've been given as an opportunity. It's not a reward—it's not vindication for what you've done or haven't done. It's a chance to do something fresh with your life."

"I don't know what that would be," Quell said.

"When you find it, you will."

With that, Hera bid Yrica Quell farewell.

II

The Rim's Edge cantina was mostly stairs—broad platforms holding tables and chairs, narrow staircases leading up and down the dark stone walls, mazes of stairs that led nowhere—and Nath Tensent felt every one in his knees. He was getting old. He wasn't old *yet,* but he was getting there.

He'd been to the Rim's Edge once before, the better part of a decade ago. Back then it had been a dank pit in an abandoned monastery on a nameless planet bordering the Unknown Regions, sparsely occupied by outcasts drinking nervously in the cavernous space. It was still a dank pit but now, four months after the Battle of Jakku, the planet was named Freerock and the cantina was packed with everyone from pirates to Jakku refugees to explorers and fortune-seekers and ex-Imperials in hiding.

Nath pushed his way through a cluster of Rodian prospectors and spotted his man in a corner alcove. It wasn't a smart place to sit—it was high enough to afford a good view of the cantina, but it left nowhere to run. Nath hauled himself up the last few steps, approaching the table.

"You look light on cash, brother," Nath said. "Buy you a drink?"

He dropped into a chair before the man could object. Nath's tablemate was short and lean, with slick black hair that crept down his scalp like a mass of untended vines. "Not looking for company," the man said.

"Sure you are, Bansu Ro," Nath said. "You're just not looking for *me.*" He leaned back in the flimsy wooden chair and spread his arms as wide as he could to show he wasn't holding a weapon.

Make yourself a nice, big target, Nath told himself. *Put him at ease.*

"You know my name," Bansu said.

"I know a lot of things about you. Been doing some reading. I know you were born on Lothal, though you split from your family when they sided with the rebels. That taint stuck with you at the Imperial Academy, and you almost ended up with a career making shuttle runs, only—"

"Captain Tensent," Bansu said.

Nath grinned as he watched the man's hand go to his right hip. "You sold your blaster this morning, remember? I was going to say, *Only the 204th Imperial Fighter Wing liked your aptitude tests, and took you in.*"

Bansu scowled. He scanned the room rapidly before returning his attention to Nath. "You hunting us down for Syndulla? Yrica Quell tell you all about me?"

"Yes to the second—though I also pulled a lot from your Intelligence files—but no to the first. I'm not working for the New Republic anymore."

"The 'Hero of Troithe' gave up his loyalties?" Bansu's hand went to his left hip, now, where Nath glimpsed the hilt of a vibroknife. "I don't think so."

"You clearly haven't seen *my* file." Nath shrugged. It wasn't the first time he'd heard that particular sentiment, and he tried not to let it rankle him; either the reputation would fade or he'd find a way to capitalize on it. "Look, you're in dire straits so you may as well hear my pitch. I'm offering you a way to resolve all your current troubles."

"And purchase new ones?"

Nath grinned. "Exactly. You see, I'm putting a crew together."

Bansu Ro said nothing.

"I'm not a patriot or a true believer—just looking to earn a profit and do some good. I was thinking about my next move, and said to myself: *There's some fine out-of-work pilots out there. Maybe see what you can do for them. Be charitable, Nath.*

"See, I've already won over your friends Creet and Nord Kandende—that kid was in a *real* bad spot, let me tell you—and I've got a list of other candidates for recruitment. There're plenty of credits out there for a team of freelancers with the right guidance."

"Nord Kandende is an idiot," Bansu Ro said.

Got you, Nath thought.

"Sure is," he agreed. "But you *do* like Creet, don't you? And it's not like you got a lot of other options—"

He was interrupted by a series of squeals and pings behind him. He held up a hand to Bansu in the universal wait-just-a-minute signal and turned to T5. "What? What took you?" Nath asked. "You couldn't handle the stairs?"

The droid emitted a staccato set of buzzes. Nath felt his muscles tense. "All right," he said, then turned back to Bansu and slapped his palm on the table. "Got some business to see to. You think about what I said. Swing by Roderick's in a few hours if you want to talk more."

Bansu Ro looked bewildered as Nath rose from the table and followed T5 out of the cantina. "Check if there's a bounty on him," Nath muttered to the droid. "Just in case you blew my only shot."

Five minutes later they were in a decaying cloister on the opposite side of the outpost. Nath's Y-wing sat on the scorched and cracked paving stones, and standing before the vessel was a thin, olive-skinned youth wearing a simple tunic and pants. The youth ran fingertips over a section of the ship's nose that had been freshly painted and repaired. Only a few traces of the old squadron insignia remained.

"Got to say," Nath called, "I'm real curious about how you found me."

Wyl Lark turned and smiled, and Nath forced himself not to react at the sight of the boy's reconstructed face. The medical droids had done good, patching in artificial bone around his nose, right cheek, and eye socket, but there were visible seams and webs of scarring where organic flesh met synthskin.

"It's not important," Wyl said, and crossed the cloister until he stood with Nath and T5. "It's good to see you."

"You, too," Nath said, which was the truth—though he suspected neither of them would leave without ill feelings. "You didn't just get out of—"

"No. No." Wyl's smile flickered. "After the medcenter, I was recuperating on Polyneus awhile. I've been traveling two weeks now."

"Good. No, ah—trouble with Syndulla, then?"

"No one mentioned the word *deserter,* if that's what you're asking. I know there are people who blame me, but—well, I think my people helped sway opinions behind the scenes."

"Hell, you earned the right to do whatever you want. Everything you did with Alphabet? You deserve a medal more than me."

"Maybe. But you wear it better."

Nath snorted and glanced about the cloister. Something moved in the shadows—one of the ghost monks, as the locals called them. "Look, I'd love to catch up but it's kind of a delicate moment. Can we meet back tomorrow morning? I can buy you a good meal—decent meal, anyway, good as they come around here—and maybe we can find some trouble with the—"

"What are you *doing* here, Nath?" Wyl sounded tired, as if an exhaustion in his bones had metastasized into his voice.

"Taking care of some business. Nothing worth talking about."

"Isn't it?" The tone was pointed. Then Wyl briskly shook his head. "I'm sorry. It's been a long trip, and I'm glad you're all right, and here I am giving you a hard time—"

Nath gestured dismissively as he curled his lips into a smile. They'd reached the moment faster than he'd expected. *Probably for the best,* he thought. "Go ahead and say what you want to say. Figure we can be frank with each other."

Wyl looked about—maybe he'd spotted a ghost monk, too—then back to Nath. "I know a little about where you've been. I know you were at Ankhural awhile, and that you transferred a lot of credits to one of the weaponeers there. I know you spent about a week at an outpost on the edge of the Sovereign Latitudes—"

Nath laughed and Wyl, startled, paused. Nath explained, "They just call them the pirate territories these days."

"The pirate territories, then. I followed up at Gangxi Station, too. The point is, that's all enough to make a person worried."

You don't know half of it, brother. Nothing about Netalych, or the other places Nath had made contact with Shadow Wing. Or Wyl was holding back, but Nath didn't think that was likely.

"Nasha Gravas send you?" Nath asked.

"She didn't send me," Wyl said, which struck Nath as careful phrasing. "I don't know what you're doing, and it's not my place to tell you how to live. But you were—you *are* my friend, and it scares me to think you're going back to the sort of business you were in before the rebels."

If he hadn't known Wyl better, he would've felt patronized—he could see Wyl choosing his approach delicately, trying to frame it all for Nath's benefit. But he also trusted Wyl's sincerity, and the effort wasn't manipulative, just misguided. "I appreciate the concern. You know as well as I do I take pretty good care of myself—"

"I do, of course I do."

"—and that the New Republic was never going to be a good fit for me long term. The Rebellion was fine—plenty of breathing room there, and the cell leaders needed all the help they could get—but I've never been a law-and-order type. All those rules were starting to chafe."

"More than they did in the Empire?" Wyl cocked his head. "I can't believe that."

"Empire had rules, but it didn't have so many *expectations*—not where I was stationed, anyway. Made the whole business a lot more palatable."

It was all true, yet it was also the pitch he'd planned to give Bansu Ro. Nath knew Wyl; Wyl also knew Nath, and the kid would sniff out an incomplete story.

"The New Republic," Nath said, slower and sober, "needed me to be something I'm not. Simple as that, and I'm not willing to be in that position."

"You were exactly what the New Republic needed," Wyl said. "You were what we needed, every day. You did tremendous things. You helped people. The other pilots thought the world of you."

"Sure they did," Nath said, "and I enjoyed it while it lasted. But the longer I stuck around—the longer I stayed with *Alphabet*—the closer I got to being killed. The closer we *all* got to being killed, because we were playing at being heroes as much as fighting a war. Wyl—"

He paused, considered what to say and how to say it and what he might regret later.

"Wyl, none of us should've survived those last days. The fact all five of us from poor Adan's *working group* are still alive? That makes us the luckiest sons of sows to ever jump in a cockpit. I've gambled enough to know you don't keep doubling down after a streak like that, and even if the next year, or two, or five are a little less risky—" He stopped again, sighed, and reoriented his thoughts. "I can live with risk. Risk's not the problem. But when I say I'm not willing to be what the New Republic needs? I mean General Syndulla would've died without resentment if she'd gone down at Jakku. I can't say the same."

"I understand," Wyl said. Nath eyed him dubiously, but Wyl shrugged and said, "I do. Looking at it that way, I'm not what the New Republic needs, either—for different reasons, but neither of us are the right people to be . . ." He fumbled for words, then laughed sadly. "I don't know. Whatever comes next."

"Glad you see it that way."

They stood in awkward silence. T5 buzzed softly and Nath rapped his knuckles on the droid's top. Wyl stroked a fingertip along the seam between his synthskin and organic flesh, as if brushing away something that had lodged there. "Can I ask you something?" he said, and Nath nodded.

"Sure."

"Why did you stay with us as long as you did?"

He frowned in surprise. "You mean with the squadron?"

"With Alphabet Squadron, after Pandem Nai. Yes."

"Man's got to earn a living somehow, and—hell, you might as well know, if no one told you. Even before I started working for Nasha Gravas, I was on Adan's private payroll, just in case he needed—"

"No, that wasn't—" Wyl shook his head again. "I didn't know that, but I'm really not shocked. That wasn't it in the end, though—you'd earned your money and you were *scared*. What you're saying now about dying, you'd been thinking it for a while and you kept going out there. At Chadawa, at Jakku, I *saw* you keep fighting. So why did you stay?"

The words roused irritation inside Nath. He tried to tamp it down. "Why do you think?" he asked. T5 buzzed again; Nath glared at the droid, then nodded. "Fine. You needed me. Not only you, but the whole squadron—I probably saved all your butts at one point or another. When all of you were gone, I bailed."

"And now you're going back to piracy?"

"Something like that."

Wyl might or might not have known the specifics, but Nath certainly wasn't in the mood to share.

"You're not a good man," Wyl said.

It should've angered him. It deserved a rough response, at least. But Wyl said it with such gentle conviction that Nath laughed uproariously before saying, "Most of us aren't. Just a few who know it, though."

Wyl smirked and paced a few steps to his left. Then he turned back around, all humor gone. "The thing is—you *can* be. When you decide to stand with someone, you're one of the most loyal people I've met. You're a natural leader—you *did* save all of us, more than once, and you made sure we were fit for duty.

"If you could surround yourself with the right crew, you could do *so* much for the galaxy. You don't have to sacrifice yourself or risk death all the time—you just need people you can trust to pick the right battles."

Nath released a long breath. He watched Wyl's soft-shoed toe dig at the paving stones. For the second time that day, he felt he was getting old.

"Come with me," Nath said.

Now it was Wyl's turn to look surprised. "What?"

"Come with me. Be part of my new crew. You'll love it when you meet the rest of the team—"

"I can't." Wyl smiled sadly. "I'm never shooting a gun again, Nath. I can't."

Nath waved the offer away. "I know," he said, and he felt no disapproval—only a keen disappointment, as if some sentimental object was drifting from him in zero-gravity, close yet unreachable.

Neither man spoke awhile. In time, Wyl said, "Thank you, though," and brushed nonexistent dust from his hands and stepped backward. "I'm really glad you're all right."

"You, too, brother," Nath said. "You see any of the others, you wish them well for me."

They said a few more polite words before Wyl left through an archway leading out of the cloister. Nath watched him go and when Wyl was finally out of sight he clapped his hands, the sound resonating through the too-quiet space.

Could've gone worse, he thought. *Could've gone better, but it could've gone worse.*

T5 made a low droning sound. Nath kicked the astromech with the side of his boot. "What're you making noises at me for? Go after the kid!"

The droid chimed and beeped, and Nath shook his head. "I can figure out how to fly the ship. You go after him. Take care of him—he needs you, buddy."

The droid was silent. Then its rockets ignited and it made it halfway out of the cloister in a single hop. It was rolling onward even as its dome spun and its photoreceptor focused on Nath, watching him as it moved away.

Nath laughed and gave a wave. He waited till T5, too, was gone before walking over to his Y-wing and standing in the shadow of its landing struts, staring at its scratched and carbon-scored underbelly.

Guess I've got to add a droid to my recruiting list, he thought. Briefly, he considered selling the Y-wing, but he'd been through enough changes; he wanted something familiar around.

Wyl would be fine. T5 would be, too. So would Nath Tensent. He needed to check in on the team he'd gathered so far and keep them out of trouble before paying Bansu Ro another visit.

He remained under the bomber in the cloister for a long while anyway.

Night came.

When he left, he was thinking about Nasha Gravas.

Why was New Republic Intelligence keeping an eye on him, he wondered, and what were the odds they needed a team of deniable freelancers?

Caern Adan? Maybe your dream will come true after all.

III

It wasn't the nightmare, but it wasn't great, either. Chass na Chadic's mustering-out pension had been reduced to one year thanks to her disciplinary record. Eleven months after Jakku, that left her not much cash and only a month to find more. Therapy had been more frustrating than helpful, and when she'd missed an appointment (not her fault—the tram had broken down) and been told the bearded snake-woman she liked at the clinic couldn't reschedule for another month ("But a droid is available right now!" the cheery desk clerk had offered), she'd given up on therapy altogether. She'd stuck around Corulag anyway, because it was where her medcenter was and she didn't have anywhere better to go.

She'd tried getting in touch with Nath once. He'd spoken with her on the medical frigate over Jakku, and he'd told her to reach out if she needed work. But he hadn't responded by the time her messaging account was suspended, and there was no guarantee he'd received the transmission anyway.

So she'd bummed around Curamelle for a while, left that city for Crullov when she'd seen the difference in rental prices, and ended up in an apartment the size of a closet in a complex occupied by death stick addicts and scrappers. She'd kind of enjoyed it—tight quarters meant all the neighbors knew one another—though she never got a full night's sleep. Then she'd come home intoxicated after a really good evening watching the bands at the Little Orto street fair and found security forces raiding the building. That had ended that chapter of her life as a New Republic veteran.

It hadn't gotten better from there. The dark thoughts crawled back into her head and stopped ever crawling out, even on half-decent days. Sometimes she hid her blaster just to make toying with it harder.

The last push came when she spotted two Children of the Empty Sun showing holos of Let'ij outside a free clinic. She'd seen a lot of new cults sprout since Jakku, but it was the first time she'd heard anything about the Children operating outside Cerberon. She'd felt a severe homesickness and an even worse nausea, and the next day she'd started pulling together credits for a shuttle offworld. She hadn't been sure where she was going; but she'd known she had to act.

All this had brought Chass to where she was now, standing at the door of a small-time cargo operator on Spirana. City lights created a luminous fog to the east, but the fields around her were desolate. No one came this far into the sticks unless they had to.

Chass had to.

She hit the door buzzer. A minute later the heavy metal barrier slid open, revealing a sparse waiting room with windows looking onto a private office and a landing pad. Emerging from the office was a woman in a mechanic's jumpsuit, whose stride hitched only an instant when she saw Chass.

"This is a surprise," Yrica Quell said.

She didn't sound surprised, though that was true to the woman Chass remembered.

Not much else was. Quell held herself differently; there was a casual slouch in her usual rigid walk, and her hair looked like she'd been trying to keep it in a military style while trimming it herself. Her nose was still crooked.

Chass thought about turning around, but it was too late. Leaving would've been more humiliating than staying.

"You owe me," Chass said. "For all the garbage you put me through? You owe me big. We agree?"

"Yes," Quell said.

"Okay." Chass nodded, and jutted her cane at the woman's chest. "So here's the thing: I need a job, and I don't have a lot of options."

"Come on in, and we'll talk," Quell said, and if a hint of a smile touched her lips it came and went so fast that Chass couldn't be sure what she saw.

IV

Wyl Lark lived in the village of Ridge, where he'd spent most of his youth and grown to manhood. He used his days to befriend and care for the sur-avkas who'd grown old or been injured or become sick or were otherwise dependent on the village to survive.

He rarely flew.

He lived among the many siblings and cousins he'd loved for as long as he could remember, and spent his nights drifting among the communal homes. Yet he found himself reluctant to share stories from his years away, and too many ordinary things had changed in Ridge for him to feel like he'd never left. Ridge was still beautiful, and the people still kind; but Ern had died, and Yanda now sent children to carry cider to the houses instead of carrying it herself, and a species of bright-orange flower had displaced the wild sunberries. They were small changes, yet together they informed the character of a place. Wyl struggled to reconcile what Ridge was now with what it had been in his mind.

He had nightmares. He'd never had nightmares as a pilot, but he had them now.

Others among the Hundred and Twenty had similar troubles, he knew. He met with them now and then, and they spoke quietly and hiked through the forests and confessed fears and the joys war had brought them—joys that shamed them now. They exchanged frustrations about their prosthetics. They all agreed that the people of Home looked at them differently, and some were bitter but most were not.

These meetings were too few, because the Hundred and Twenty came from across the planet and arranging a gathering always proved challenging. Still, Wyl found the meetings reassuring.

His life wasn't a bad one, as he often reminded himself. Yet neither did it feel complete, over a year since he'd returned from his last journey offworld—his journey to see Nath Tensent, taken in part because he'd been restless weeks after arriving.

Homecoming was more difficult than he'd ever imagined. But his love for his world was undiminished.

One day, having journeyed to Cliff to consult with a Sun-Lama about treating a sur-avka's mangled claw, Wyl spent the afternoon with one of Cliff's elders. He'd called Conna Dew his friend since he'd been fourteen years old and she had scolded him for spying on a stranger's wedding feast. "Either you're interested, and you go introduce yourself and ask to learn; or you're not, and you give those poor people their privacy," she'd told him, and they'd been close ever since.

"My old caretaker," Conna was saying as they yanked the desiccated husks of dead creeper vines off her house, "has decided at the age of ninety-nine to become a Sun-Lama. Which would be perfectly fine if he didn't insist on sharing every detail of the secret lessons with me! *I* don't care about the 'esoteric teachings,' but I told him I wouldn't lie if someone asks me what he's revealed."

"Maybe the Sun-Lamas will exile you both," Wyl said with a smile. He felt a vine disintegrate in his palms as he tugged.

"Oh, I'd be delighted to see them try. But I think they'd only ask me politely to leave, and I'd say no, and the punishment would be me getting the side-eye for the rest of my life."

"May it be a long one," Wyl said, and Conna snorted.

They worked in comfortable silence before she said: "You're looking healthier than last time."

She'd rarely asked directly about his struggles reacclimating. Twice he'd confessed everything anyway; she'd always been good at giving him space to speak.

"It's getting better," he said. "It's still hard."

She nodded brusquely. "Well, I'll mention this at the entirely wrong time, then, since who knows when I'll see you next: The Hik'e-Matriarch is talking a lot about the galaxy these days, and what it means to be part of the New Republic. She's worried we're too *isolationist.*"

"Isn't isolationism one of our founding principles?" Wyl asked.

Conna laughed. "That's what *I* said! But apparently she thinks it's better if we have *some* influence on what the New Republic is up to, unless we want to split off altogether. Me, I think she feels we've got political clout after that business rescuing everyone at Jakku, and she's loath to see it forgotten before we get anything for it."

" 'Use the voucher before it expires,' " Wyl said. "That's what they'd say in the purse worlds."

"I know what a voucher is, Wyl Lark. I *do* read." She shook her head, then winced as her tug at another vine sent a cloud of dirt billowing from the cliffside. "Anyway, she's sent out a call—same as she did for the Hundred and Twenty—only this time she's looking for ambassadors and diplomats. One of them's going to get to be *senator*."

Wyl laughed, and collected debris in his arms to drop in the pile they'd gathered. When he was done, Conna stood with her back to the wall of the house, arms folded across her chest. She waggled her eyebrows.

"You're not serious," he said.

"You'd be good at it! You're a hero—you'd go in with credibility," she said.

"I'm a deserter. That doesn't help."

"Yes, but Home loves you, and that means you never need to worry about reelection."

"I don't know anything about politics."

"You know everything about building relationships. Let your aides and the Hik'e-Matriarch write the bills and advise on policy, at least until you figure it out. You'd be there to represent us, because you understand Polyneus. And you understand the galaxy, Wyl."

He watched her a long while, trying to understand what she saw in him.

"I'll think about it," he said.

V

Six years after the war they were together again. Most of them, anyway.

"—this guy keeps telling us, 'You pay for that shipment or I'm going to come back with my men and *make* you pay.' He's at fault, though, and he's a freaking flower salesman. We figure it's bluster—"

"I'm sure this story ends well."

"It ends *great*. So one day, we hear the door buzz and there's these three Chevin brothers with hands big enough to smash your head into jelly—"

Yrica Quell looked across the living room table and listened to Chass and Wyl. Chass leaned over the lavender-smelling dessert plate that had briefly borne store-bought icecake, almost knocking over her wineglass as she gestured. Wyl was less animated but he sat straight-backed as he listened, smiling gently as recirculated air blew his hair across his scars.

Yrica sipped her brandy and closed her eyes.

"—sees the mandala hanging on the office door and says in this deep, ridiculous voice, 'You are follower of the Church of Nine Ways?' I'm not an idiot, so I lie and say 'Yes'—"

It had been two years since they'd last seen Wyl, but they'd both been on Spirana while Wyl was visiting Perithal, so Yrica and Chass had thrown something together and he'd arrived at the house that evening. Yrica suspected he'd gone to some trouble to arrange it; she also suspected it was more for Chass than for her, but she didn't mind. He was good company.

"—and suddenly it's me and Quell and the three Chevin staring down this guy, who gets real apologetic real fast—"

"How did we get to this topic?" Yrica asked.

"I asked how business was," Wyl said.

Yrica opened her eyes again. "We're doing all right. The long-term contract with the medcenter keeps us afloat. It's getting harder to make money on in-system runs but we're not really equipped for interstellar hauling."

"And she doesn't want to do it," Chass added, falling back into her chair with a shrug.

"And I don't want to do it," Yrica agreed. "Do you need more wine?"

Chass agreed, and Wyl—out of politeness, Yrica thought—agreed as well, and Chass and Yrica asked about Wyl's work, and the ventures he was passionate about, and whether he was still involved with the man they'd briefly met two years earlier. Wyl didn't linger on the Senate (he knew his audience—Yrica didn't talk about politics, and Chass cared only about the broad strokes), admitted he'd broken up with Tareesh some months back ("Screw it, you're young," Chass offered by way of consolation), but circled back to the second question, talking about the Reconciliation Project and the ongoing effort to find volunteers. "I know I ask this every time," Wyl said, "but if you're ever willing to come and be a part—"

"I really can't," Yrica said.

"That's all right. If you're ever ready."

She nodded. The silence was broken only by Chass's collection of amulets and charms, clinking like wind chimes in front of an air vent; and by the burbling of T5 and 4E, both of whom were recharging by the front door.

"Hey," Chass said. "You hear anything from Nath?"

Wyl pursed his lips and shifted uncomfortably before finally offering: "No."

"You want to explain that long pause?" Chass asked.

Wyl smiled wryly. "No."

Yrica nodded. Better to leave the subject alone, she knew, and was surprised to hear herself ask: "How much trouble?"

"I don't know," he said. "That's the hard thing. I don't have contacts on the intelligence committee anymore, and Gravas and I—" Wyl sighed. "He's alive, I know that. I worry about him sometimes, but what is there to do?"

"He made his choices," Yrica said. "No one can change his path but him."

Her voice was harder than she'd intended. Wyl nodded carefully. He seemed to take no offense.

"Speaking of the old days," Wyl said, "did you ever look for her?"

Chass appeared puzzled before enlightenment dawned on her face. The wine was slowing her down; Yrica had understood instantly.

Last time they'd all met, Yrica had been considering searching for Kairos. She'd been haunted by dreams about a woman without a face. "I didn't," she said. "I was going through some things back then, but after talking it over—" She indicated Chass with her head. "—I realized that if any of us will do fine on her own, it's her. She can find me if she wants me."

"I wish I'd gotten to know her," Wyl said. "I think about that time, after she was out of the suit, when I was so wrapped up in myself—"

Chass snorted. "Yeah, I don't think it would've made a difference if you'd been hanging out with her."

"Maybe not," Wyl admitted.

Yrica rotated her glass and tasted her brandy again. "I'm glad she got her fresh start."

Talk of Nath and Kairos led to talk of General Syndulla and others, and they began down the meandering, inevitable path Yrica had known they would take by evening's end. There were side treks—recollections of Troithe and the special forces crew of the *Lodestar*, Chass's tipsy tribute to the B-wing, "the greatest fighter ever flown"—but soon they spoke of the dead. They lingered on each name for a while, giving due tribute to Sergeant Ragnell (whom Yrica had known best) and Sata Neek (whom she'd never met). They spoke at length about Caern Adan and IT-O, and about Vitale and Denish Wraive, and soon they were going around the table reciting the victims of war: Sonogari. Fadime. Ubellikos. Neihero. Snivel. For every survivor, there were a hundred dead to remember.

Yrica had to stop herself from offering the wrong memories: Rikton. Xion. Nosteen. Raida. The dead of the 204th, whom she carried as Wyl and Chass carried the dead of Riot and Hound squadrons. She knew it wasn't the time, so she spoke of the fallen from the *Lodestar* and the *Deliverance* instead. There were enough to go around.

Eventually the ritual came to a close. Chass was drunk by then, and became fixated on heading into the city together and infiltrating the port security office. ("They're bastards!" she yelled, "human supremacist bastards!" and from what Yrica had seen at customs Chass had a point.) Wyl insisted, calm but firm, that his senatorial credentials wouldn't get them inside. Yrica promised she'd send him specifics the next time they ran into trouble. Grudgingly, Chass agreed to go to bed.

The three of them stood. Chass embraced Wyl, then shoved him away. Then she went to Yrica and, surprisingly delicately, kissed her on the lips before stumbling to the bedroom. She left her cane behind.

Wyl helped clear the table and said nothing until closing the bottle of brandy on the counter. "From your father?" he asked.

Yrica shook her head, surprised. "My brother Thren. He lives in Santrapei, three hundred kilometers east. How'd you know it was family?"

"You mentioned it once," Wyl said. He gestured to the bedroom. "When did *that* happen, by the way?"

She shrugged, feeling the stiffness in her shoulders. She remembered Wyl was a friend and slowly relaxed. "A while back."

"It looks good on you. You needed each other."

Yrica nodded and slid the dishes onto the shelves, which hummed as they began their cleaning routine. When she turned back around, Wyl was still watching.

"She forgives you, you know," he said. "She did a long time ago."

She pushed her back against the counter so she wouldn't sag, and nodded slightly. "Maybe," she said.

She asked Wyl if he needed a place to spend the night, but he told her no, he had a ship waiting; so she took him by speeder to the port and they said their goodbyes and promised not to wait so long before they met again. The wind blustered and snapped at Wyl's garments as he lingered outside the passenger door, T5 beside him on the dark and empty road.

Yrica was about to depart when he leaned in through the open speeder window and said, "There's one other thing. There's someone I'd like you to meet, if you're willing."

She shifted uncomfortably. She wasn't fond of ambushes. "Here?"

"I wouldn't do that to you," Wyl said. "Someone who reached out to the Reconciliation Project. They got in touch with me, I wanted to talk to you—"

"Who?"

"A survivor."

Yrica gripped the speeder's control yoke, staring past Wyl's left shoulder and steadying herself on the lights of a control tower.

"She was offworld when it happened," he said. "She lost family on Nacronis, and she—"

"What about the recordings?" Yrica asked. She bit down the tremor in her voice. "We spent enough hours making them."

"She's seen your statements and interviews. But she wants to meet one-on-one with some of the pilots who didn't cooperate. She says it's for closure, the project director thinks she wants to change their minds . . . I just think it would go better if she met you before she heads to the prison. Nothing official, just a conversation."

"Okay," she said.

"I know it's not easy—"

"I said 'okay.' "

Wyl looked like he wanted to reach out to her, but the door was in the way. He stroked T5 instead and thanked her, and she managed a smile and said goodbye again and sped away before he could say more. She breathed a sigh of relief when she was on the road.

She didn't hold the request against him. It was part of the work.

Back at the house behind the cargo office she checked on Chass, feeling sad and tired and glad they'd all had the evening. She sat by the bed awhile, toying with Chass's cane (she'd brought it in from the living room without thinking) and when Chass woke Yrica apologized for disturbing her.

Chass only grunted and asked, "Wyl want anything? He always wants *something*."

"Nothing important," Yrica said. "Go to sleep."

Chass rolled onto her side and dragged a pillow against her face. Her muffled voice asked, "You coming?"

"In a while."

When she was sure Chass was sleeping soundly she left the house again and climbed into the cargo shuttle—a Helotek Loadhauler she'd bought from a junkyard and spent the better part of six months refitting and persuading to fly. The design was an unauthorized knockoff of the Empire's old *Zeta*-class vessels, but the parts were cheaper and it lacked the Zeta's armament.

Yrica liked that about the Loadhauler. It was noisy and wobbled and got hot as a star on atmospheric entry, but she hadn't flown a starfighter or anything else with weapons since Coruscant. Since she'd condemned what was left of the Empire to face what they'd all done.

She'd followed the hearings and trials when her heart allowed it; stepped away and focused on her work when it didn't. She'd never put in to get her record expunged. She still couldn't vote or take government contracts, and she wasn't in any hurry. It was the same reason she'd turned Wyl down more than once, when he'd asked her to join the Reconciliation Project full-time: She'd forfeited her right to speak and to judge.

She started the shuttle and it lifted off the tarmac. She felt herself smile as air rushed beneath her and wind pushed at her wings, and she plotted a parabolic course that would take her up into orbit, then down at the best speed the ship could muster.

She loved to fly. Whatever happened next, she didn't want to give up flight.

As acceleration pushed her into her seat, she thought about the dead she hadn't spoken of with Chass and Wyl. She thought about Grandmother and Gablerone, Tonas and Barath. She thought about her mentor, and everything that had shaped Soran Keize into what he'd been—a murderer and a soldier and a fierce protector of his people, who'd left an indelible stain on her soul and freed her from the Empire.

She thought about Nacronis, and all those who had died there.

She would never stop thinking about Nacronis. But Yrica Quell soared, and it was joyful.

ACKNOWLEDGMENTS

What's left to say, really? This book owes so much to so many people, most of whom I've mentioned before and who I'm glad to call out again: My editor, Elizabeth Schaefer, for bringing me aboard and encouraging my mad ideas and helping me through logistical snarls and half-baked drafts with unflagging good spirit. Jennifer Heddle, for advocating for me and offering a much-valued second set of eyes. The rest of the Lucasfilm crew, too—Matt Martin, Pablo Hidalgo, and Kelsey Sharpe, among others—for assistance and incisive comments large and small. Shelly Shapiro and Frank Parisi for guiding me into the world of *Star Wars* novels in the first place.

Thanks as well to Jo Berry and Mitch Dyer for being such game partners—no pun intended—in integrating the universes of Alphabet Squadron and Vanguard Squadron. Likewise, thanks to Jody Houser for sharing the toys from her *TIE Fighter* comic, particularly in this last book. And, as always, thanks to my unofficial *Star Wars* military adviser, Charles Boyd.

Last, this trilogy builds on decades of *Star Wars* work from hundreds of creators (and likely owes a debt to all of them, to one degree or another). Consider this a particular note of appreciation for Michael A. Stackpole and Aaron Allston, whose original *X-Wing* novels electrified the fandom and proved starfighter novels could succeed both artistically and commercially. Alphabet Squadron wouldn't exist without them, and I am truly grateful.

ABOUT THE AUTHOR

ALEXANDER FREED is the author of *Star Wars: Alphabet Squadron*, *Star Wars: Battlefront: Twilight Company*, *Star Wars: The Old Republic: The Lost Suns*, and *Star Wars: Rogue One* and has written many short stories, comic books, and videogames. Born near Philadelphia, he endeavors to bring the city's dour charm with him to his current home of Austin, Texas.

alexanderfreed.com
Twitter: @AlexanderMFreed

ABOUT THE TYPE

This book was set in Minion, a 1990 Adobe Originals typeface by Robert Slimbach (b. 1956). Minion is inspired by classical, old-style typefaces of the late Renaissance, a period of elegant, beautiful, and highly readable type designs. Created primarily for text setting, Minion combines the aesthetic and functional qualities that make text type highly readable with the versatility of digital technology.